SOLD

SOULFIRE

SOULFIRE

Amanda Hemingway

LITTLE, BROWN AND COMPANY

A *Little, Brown* Book

First published in Great Britain by
Little, Brown and Company in 1994

Copyright © Amanda Hemingway 1994

A CIP catalogue record for this book is
available from the British Library.

ISBN 0 316 91051 1

Typeset by M Rules
Printed and bound in Great Britain by
Clays Ltd, St Ives plc

Little, Brown and Company (UK) Limited
Brettenham House
Lancaster Place
London WC2E 7EN

PART I

THE PURSUIT OF TRUTH

1

The hardest thing about being a journalist is learning not to care. Leo Sands, editor of the *Ely Watchman* and my earliest mentor, used to tell me: 'Micky, you're being sentimental again. Emotional. Slushy.' He would prod the papers in front of me with a choppy finger, and his brown distressed-leather face would bunch itself into a caricature of disapproval. 'Concentrate on the *facts*. Facts – facts – facts.' Prod – prod – prod. 'Individual vision distorts reality. Your mind is like a misshapen lens – convex, tinted, biased. Distrust your mind; learn to minimise distortion. Truth is its own argument. Let it shine through clear glass: no colouring, no angles.' I did my best. I was eighteen, working my year between sixth form and university. My heart bled for every old lady robbed of the nest-egg in her teapot, every tenant ejected by an unscrupulous landlord, every single-parent baby, every underdog, scapegoat, maverick, dreamer. My heart bled so much that but for Leo's advice it might well have bled itself dry. But my ambition to be a good journalist was in the end more compelling than the impulses of my heart.

Long afterwards, when I was leaving the *Sunday Times* to join the television research team for *Quest*, another editor wrote of me: 'Murphy has a passion for truth which transcends all pity.' I didn't tell anyone, but I was proud of that. I saw myself as an agent of Pallas, clear-eyed, tearless, unflinching. I had learned to discipline the facile sympathy and reckless commitment of the teenager; my heart, in general a dependable organ, no longer quailed or quickened so easily. I was, I believe, not selfish but self-centred: self-contained, self-assured, self-reliant, all self. In my career I would dissect the lives of others like a scientist picking a tumour out of a laboratory rat, but my personal space was filled only with me. I lived in vestal solitude, my job become a cause, dedicated to the pursuit of truth. Truth at any price.

I met Shirley Prosser in Sainsbury's early in 1990, next to the delicatessen counter. As far as I was concerned the Prosser affair had been over months ago. Following the TV investigation there had been extensive newspaper coverage, questions in the House. Eventually a dubious CID superintendent had been discreetly retired and Guy Prosser and two of his colleagues were now on remand, charged with laundering drug money. No doubt his four-bedroomed house in St John's Wood, his motor launch in Brighton Marina, his Porsche, his wife's BMW and his son's Scalextric were all up for sale. I wasn't going to weep for him.

Shirley didn't look as good as on the last occasion I'd seen her. She wore the same sugar-pink lipstick and day-old mascara, but the shadows round her eyes were natural and her synthetic blonde hair was showing dark at the roots. I have a bad memory for faces and I didn't recognise her until she started shouting at me. People turned and stared, caught between embarrassment and curiosity. She poured out a stream of insult and cliché, and I stood like the proverbial statue, longing to bolt, furious at myself for my inhibitions, my cold statue's face, my instinctive upsurge of guilt. Somehow, I sensed that deep inside she was even more shocked by her own behaviour than I was. But she could not stop. This was what fate had done to her, this was what I had done to her: she had become the sort of person who made scenes in supermarkets, who lost control and ranted and screamed. No longer a pretty middle-class wifette but a bruised, coarsened creature with the vocabulary of a guttersnipe.

She could not stop.

'Doing your shopping, are you? What do you eat – smoked salmon and caviare? Oh – asparagus soup – *gourmet* soup. Fucking gourmet soup for a fucking gourmet bitch. My whole life paid for that soup – my fucked-up life for a fucking tin of soup! What did we do to you? Tell me that. Why did you hate us? Or do you just do it for the fucking gourmet soup?' Fucking – fucking – fucking. She wasn't used to the word. She didn't know where it belonged. She just lashed out with it like an unfamiliar weapon. 'Fucking heartless bitch.'

Heartless. Yes, she said that. I remember she said that. So much for me and my dependable heart.

I didn't hate you. I did my job . . .

I couldn't say it.

'You don't care, do you? You and your fucking nosy TV show, pretending to be so moral and superior – ruining people's lives just for a good story. You don't care who gets hurt – you just don't care. What about *him*? What did *he* do to you? Is he worth more than a tin of gourmet soup?' She thrust her son forward. I suppose he was about nine. He cringed away as though trying to hide – from me, from his mother, from the prying pitying stares of the whole world. His face was red and congested with embarrassment. There is no shame so terrible as the shame children feel when their adults let them down. 'Do you know what they did, the other kids at his school? They said he had to be branded because his father was in prison, so they took his clothes off and they painted all over him. They painted jailbird, criminal, fuck, shit, prick. Kids of *ten*. They couldn't spell jailbird or criminal but they could spell fuck, shit, prick. And he just stood there – he didn't try to fight or run away – he just stood there, because he thought he'd done wrong and he was being punished. *He thought he deserved it*. Even when the teacher came to stop them she said he just stood there, shivering. How do you feel about that, Miz justice-loving Murphy? Does that make you fucking happy? Will you put that in your soup and eat it?'

'I'm sorry.' I knew whatever I said would sound inadequate and idiotic. It did. I *was* sorry, bitterly, painfully sorry, but it was hardly likely to comfort either Shirley Prosser or her son. She didn't want comfort. She had lost all the normal restraints of civilised society: fear of exposure, of injury, of public mortification. She wanted only an outlet for her rancour. Even Mark's humiliation at school had become a weapon to be used, regardless of his feelings. Unwisely, I tried to say so.

'You've got to stop this. You're not hurting me: you're hurting yourself, and your children. You've got to—'

'You *bitch*!' The venom in her voice almost made me step back. She was very close to me now – blind, numb, senseless with rage. 'HOW DARE YOU PREACH AT ME! So I don't hurt you, Mark doesn't hurt you, nothing hurts you! Miz Godalmighty Murphy! Take that, and see if it hurts. And that. And that!' She began hurling the contents of her trolley at me. This time I moved, but too late. A tin struck me on the shoulder and something which might have been pâté, fortunately in a plastic bag, slapped against my cheek. 'Why don't you eat *that*, Miz Murphy? This is pain – my pain, Mark's pain! Eat it!'

That was the moment when the manager arrived. Tactful assistants surrounded us, impeded us, came between us. I found myself picking up Shirley Prosser's shopping and replacing it in her trolley. A young man in a Sainsbury's overall had hold of her arm: his grip looked firm but not unkind. She was starting to cry. I explained the situation to the manager in an undervoice and offered to leave, uncomfortably conscious that my self-restraint, my polite magnanimity, everything I did must be gall and worm-wood to Shirley. But she wasn't noticing any more. An elderly lady with an evil twinkle in her eye said brightly: 'Pinched her old man, did you?' I went.

Out in the car park, I sat for ten minutes waiting for my pulse to slow down and the sensation of nausea to diminish. And all the way home I kept seeing Mark Prosser's face, imagining I had glimpsed under the dishevelled fringe a paint smear like old blood. I drove much too fast.

Back at my flat, the Doubts were there waiting for me. I had known they would be. I shut the door, sat down, began to pull off my boots, and they tapped on my shoulder. For a few minutes – a half-hour, an hour – I was lost. One boot off, hunched on the edge of the sofa, frozen at a thought. I had had Doubts before, of course, but not for some months. This time, I knew instinc-tively I was in for a long, lonely session. There was nothing to be done. I could not drag them into the open, confront them, chal-lenge them – how can you challenge something as nebulous as a Doubt, something which only ums and ahs, hints, evades, nig-gling at the back of your mind unwilling either to advance or retreat? They would not be hurried. When they were ready, they would come forward. They would begin to grow heads, acquire recognisable features, reiterate well-worn arguments. And in the small hours, when I was exhausted and sleepless and I could feel the darkness of an endless universe pressing itself against my flimsy windows, then at last they would become vocal and accusatory, and sharpen their teeth to tear at my soul. It was familiar territory, but that did not make it any easier.

In due course, I remembered to remove my other boot. My foot had gone numb, and I welcomed the slow anguish of returning circulation. When I could stand, I changed into leggings and a loose sweater and made coffee. If I had been a man I would have got drunk. Or if I had been a woman. But it was a long time since I had felt like a woman: I was Micky Murphy, a unisex name, a unisex spirit – a spirit as cold as frost in April and as insecure as the ozone layer. I made the coffee black and bitter although I prefer it milky. At six o'clock, I switched on the BBC news. They were pulling down the Berlin Wall, and for a little while the sight of those happy crazy faces, all shiny with tears and laughter, blotted out the image of Mark Prosser. For a little while.

Everyone tells me I am lucky in my flat. 'You should do it up, Micky,' friends say, meaning well. 'It could be *really nice*.' I don't want to do it up. I can't afford the money, I can't afford the time; if I am honest, I can't be bothered. It is in a mews near Kensington High Street, a cluster of three small rooms and one big one above a garage which I share with a neighbour. The three small rooms are kitchen, bathroom, bedroom; the big one is a living room which doubles as a study. My work desk occupies one end; uneven bookshelves climb from floor to ceiling; a palisade of files keeps the world at a distance. In the remaining wall space assorted pictures provide glimpses of a courtyard dappled with Italian sunshine, a bare landscape washed with pale mauve twilight, a pyramid of Dead Sea fruit and a spaghetti forest flecked with tiny pink fish. There are bottles of wine on the bookshelves – my favourite Pouilly Fuissé, and Vinho Verde for unwanted guests – and books everywhere: by the loo, by the bed, by the cooker, wherever I may feel like reading. The bathroom tiles are chipped. The wardrobe door won't shut. I like it that way. The chaos has evolved along Darwinian lines, responding to my particular needs as to environmental or climatic changes: I can locate any note or reference within minutes. Order in disorder, method in my madness. I would never be able to work or relax in a sleek designer apartment, with all my files put away in cupboards and the kind of bedroom where you have to dress up in Janet Reger lace merely to go to sleep.

But that evening, comfort eluded me. The Doubts waited, patiently: through the news at six, and seven, and nine, through coffee and more coffee, uneaten supper, unwanted bed. Eventually they began to solidify, creatures of ectoplasm gradually assuming a coherent form and the echo of a voice. One of them, inevitably, became my mother – my adored, adorable mother, whose butterfly charm ensnared everyone she met – my father, my step-father, my two step-brothers, the vicar, the daily help, the gardener, the fishmonger – everyone except me. With me, the charm failed: a spell gone wrong, a musical instrument whose sweet silvery note was suddenly out of tune. She would succumb to the weaknesses of motherhood; carp, criticise, nit-pick, becoming by turns wistful, hopeful, pathetic, pessimistic. 'A journalist?' she had said, when I was in my teens. 'Oh dear. All that drinking whisky in seedy bars, and having to pester nice people, and worm things out of nasty ones. Anyway, I hate the news: it's always so depressing. No, darling, you'll have to think of something else.' She has never been able to change my mind or influence my behaviour but her lightly uttered words slid into the recesses of my subconscious and stayed there, returning when I least wanted them. One particular accusation, reiterated often throughout the years: 'Darling, you're becoming so *hard*. It must be the company of all those dreadful hacks. Such an appropriate name, don't you think? They hack away at their poor victims until there's nothing left. I only wish . . .' But what she only wished was always left unsaid, a hint, a might-have-been. An only wish. This night was no different. She perched on the edge of my thoughts, a fragile faery creature with a Joan Greenwood drawl and silver hair lifted from her forehead in a secret breeze that seemed to blow especially for her. 'So *hard* . . . Michelle darling . . . so *hard* . . .' She never calls me Micky.

I told myself I could deal with my mother. I had done so often enough. My step-father, two years dead, hovered in the background, a senior civil servant with an OBE and an inherited income, his manner invariably formal, his personality as delicately grey as his Savile Row suit. He had been, not a weak character, but reserved, supportive rather than assertive, quintessentially remote. He was always in the background; it was his spiritual home. Sometimes, I felt my mother still expected him to be there, still turned to him automatically for a word of affirmation, reacting with faint surprise when there was no longer any response. When I was at school, there had been murmurings: 'A secretarial course . . . such a bright girl . . . I have a friend at the Ministry.' I had thanked him – I always thanked him – and gone my own way. The murmurings came back now, in the background as usual, a quiet grey presence radiating quiet grey disapproval. I tried to ignore it.

My real father was more difficult. There were long periods when I could not remember his face at all, except for the scars. The only photographs I have were taken before the war, when he was young, classically handsome, upright, fearless; after the war, he had avoided being photographed. But I could feel his eyes, though I could not see them, eyes as clear and steady as English rain, sad, trustworthy eyes still fearless even after all the fear he had known, gazing at me out of the shadows of memory, out of my mind and into my heart. Under that rain-bright, rain-steady look I was pierced with an inexplicable pain – not because I had lost him, or because I had forgotten his image, or because I fell short of the standards he had set for me, but something of all those, and something more, something deeper, a stirring, a feeling, like a dream which vanishes on waking, leaving only the afterglimmer of a vision too beautiful to bear. With my father, memory and imagination had become confused: his eyes grew deeper and clearer over the years, and the things he had said or might have said would come to me with all the certainty of recollection. I was eleven when he died, too young, surely, to have absorbed all his philosophy. Yet I knew, I was sure I knew, what his attitude would have been. 'Live by what you believe, Mila, just don't forget to make room for the beliefs of others. Always listen. See the other point of view. Open your mind. Above all, try not to hurt people. In the end, that is the most important thing, and the most difficult. To get by without hurting people . . .' He had flown his Lancaster over Germany and dropped bombs and killed civilians and written poetry about it, and he knew, better than anyone, that the most important thing in life is not to hurt.

I looked at my asparagus soup, congealing in its bowl, thick green skin forming on thick green liquid. 'This is my pain – Mark's pain!' Shirley Prosser had said. 'Eat it!' *Eat it.* And there they all were, my father, my step-father, my mother, Shirley, Mark, friends, strangers, a bowl of soup on the table. All accusing me. Outside, beyond the traffic noise, the night waited, huge and silent. The clamouring voices seemed to float away and be swallowed up in the looming darkness. The silence that followed was more dreadful than any accusation.

I knew that, too. The night outside and the night within. The abyss that opens when you turn your gaze inward and inward in search of your own soul. I had been there before, half asleep or half awake, lost in a vision which might have been daydream or nightmare. It was always the same.

I was alone in the dark, stripped of name, identity, personality, all the packaging which makes up a human being. I was searching for something. And suddenly I saw a minute gleam of light, a solitary spark against all that endless, lightless nothing. As I drew nearer, I saw that it was a tiny flame, like a candle flame without a candle, a single flickering dancing mote of brightness. And somehow I knew that this was my self, my soul, the object of my search. But it seemed so frail and small, and the dark so vast. I cupped my hands around it to protect it, and the light shone through my fingers, turning them to flesh and blood, golden and rose. And for an instant, a fraction of eternity, the flame burned up, tall and thin as a blade. But soon, I knew, a great wind would come from the depths of the void, and blow upon my candle flame, and extinguish it forever.

2

The next day was a Friday. I didn't go into work: I had already arranged to take the day off in order to spend a long weekend with my mother. After a night pestered by assorted phantoms any desire to see one of them in the flesh had vanished, but I had promised: filial duty or dutiful affection held me to it. I went.

I drove out of London around midday. On the way, I stopped at a couple of shops in a familiar routine: flowers for my mother, champagne truffles ditto, wine to drink with dinner. At least I was going home. For all the comfortable disorder of my flat, I still tend to think of Grey Gables as home. It had been my father's house; when he died, it had passed to my mother. On her remarriage, my step-father had simply moved in, relegating his elegant Chelsea residence to the status of an outpost. My step-brothers, Nigel and Jeremy, came to stay during the university vacation, when not hitch-hiking round Europe, smoking pot or sleeping with their girlfriends. After they had outgrown these things and settled down to become solid citizens, they brought their wives and children. The children swung on my swing and fell out of my tree, scraping their knees and tearing their clothes in time-honoured fashion. The wives called my mother Dear Veronica, or even Vee, and resigned themselves, in her company, to taking second place with their menfolk. My step-father filled a vacancy in my father's chair. I once heard an absent-minded neighbour commiserating with him on the tragic death of Squadron Leader Annesley – 'Such a fine man, so talented – as if my father had been a beloved relation rather than his predecessor. When she remembered, my mother did her best: she put away the photograph of my father in full uniform taken before he was shot down, and called herself Mrs Annesley Cloud, and insisted that I also added Jolyon Cloud's surname on to my own. But my mother's concentration was too fickle, or perhaps the house itself was too deeply imbued with my father's presence. Anyway, he remained. It was strange that only since Jolyon's death had I begun to feel my father slipping away from me, as though the living man had reinforced the ubiquity of the dead, filling his armchair, his seat at table, his space, his role, as unobtrusive and essential as a stand-in. Now the man has gone the ghost, too, has receded: the atmosphere is dominated by my mother. Yet Grey Gables is still a house and not merely a bolthole, full of life and change, tranquillity and sanctuary, memories and people. A home.

It lies a few miles outside Cambridge, in the village of Askham. There are trees to ward off the skyline, large areas of patchy lawn, haphazard flowerbeds and vagrant shrubs. In the middle, the house itself, designed by an admirer of Lutyens, with a long sweep of tiled roof and gables to match its name. If it has ever been grey you cannot actually tell; the weathering of the seasons has reduced it to an indeterminate non-colour somewhere between grey and brown and the walls are overgrown with a variety of climbing plants, all of which have long been out of control. Some windows are unopenable for Virginia creeper, while a lattice left carelessly ajar in the summer months will be impossible to close: eager little tendrils will have curled around the latch and shinned over the sill. There is a vegetable garden at the back full of vegetables which no one ever eats; raspberries grow feckless as briars; moss pads the steps like a cushion. At that period my mother employed a part-time gardener of incredible decrepitude whom she could not bring herself to coax into retirement and a schoolboy who came at weekends to mow the lawn. It didn't matter. People who visit me there laugh when I say I hate untidiness, but Grey Gables isn't untidy, just natural, friendly, wild. As in my flat, I know where everything is: every scent, every memory, every summer shadow. Inside, my mother moves the ornaments now and then, changes the curtains and the upholstery. She has taken to reading *Country Living*, leaving a still life of spilled fruit on the kitchen table, or an earthenware jar of pussy-willow in a place where I am certain to trip over it. But these are details. Arriving that Friday just before three, too late for her to complain because I would not eat any lunch, I anticipated a weekend of idleness and repose, a temporary cure for insomnia. It was something I both longed for and distrusted. After all, I was a journalist, pledged to expose reality in all its ugliness; Grey Gables was a privileged retreat. But I needed to relax.

My luck was out. My mother emerged from the front door while I was parking the car, looking much as she had looked the previous night. The zephyr breeze played with her hair, and her most enchanting smile lilted its way across her face. Faint lines only served to emphasise the lilt; faint hollows defined her large eyes and small bones. I noticed with circumspection that she was wearing earrings and face-powder, and the smile was tinted pink. Visitors.

'Darling, I'm so glad you got here in time! I was afraid – not that it matters if you're late, of course. You know you can come when you like. But I did so want you to meet him!'

I picked up my bag and followed her into the hall. Him. My mother's worst failing, a failing common to most mothers of single daughters. It had first appeared about four years after my divorce, when I showed no sign of marrying again. I was thirty-two now, and it still surfaced at regular intervals. The matchmaking syndrome. Thus afflicted my mother became, in my eyes, banal, embarrassing, almost vulgar.

So there was a him.

I said without any particular inflection: 'I'm not late because I didn't say when I expected to arrive.'

'No darling, of course not.' She wasn't attending. 'Do listen. He's a collector of some kind – antiques, paintings, that sort of thing. He's frightfully artistic and intelligent and amusing and I'm *quite sure* he's not a pansy. I'm half in love with him myself. If you don't want him, I'll have him – he might prefer older women.'

She always said that, as if it would fire me with the spirit of competition. It didn't. She was already entering the dining room, laughingly indiscreet, her words surely audible to anyone inside.

I went in after her, braced, unbending, coolly polite, depositing my bag on a chair and surveying the remnants of a buffet clearly intended for three still spread on top of the sideboard.

'Darling, if you're hungry—'

'I'm not hungry.'

She was right about the man, of course. She usually was. Her judgement was unerring, infuriating, unforgivable. He was obviously artistic and intelligent and amusing – and probably heterosexual. I can't even remember his name. He said the same things they always said. 'You look so like your mother' – I stood half a head taller even though I was wearing flat shoes and she had courts with two-inch heels. 'Why did you cut your hair?' – in front of an old snapshot in which my hair hung down almost to my waist. And 'I understand you're a writer.' My mother invariably said I was a writer. She thought it sounded better. I'm a journalist, I explained ruthlessly. A TV journalist. Exposés. Crass sensationalism. Really? How interesting. 'I'm sure you exaggerate. You don't look at all like a crass sensationalist.'

In desperation I went out to the car and retrieved the wine, the chocolates and the flowers. My mother accepted them with an air of delighted surprise. I always brought her wine, chocolates, flowers; she would have been deeply hurt if I had omitted to do so. Her charm wrapped us round like a cobweb, elusive, fluttering, clinging, impossible to brush off. The unfortunate man was entrapped and bewitched; I was merely entrapped. He stayed for tea; an invitation to dinner seemed impending. Something had to be done.

'I'm terribly sorry,' I said, 'but I'm tired out. I simply must go to bed.'

That did it. When he had gone, I found I was shaking – from ill temper, accumulated tension, hours of polite self-control. I ran myself a bath and slid thankfully into the scalding water. My mother came in, ostensibly to gossip; I knew she was fighting the urge to reproach me and I almost hoped she was losing.

'He was awfully sweet,' she said in an edged voice, 'don't you think?'

'Awfully.' I considered the matter. 'Yes. Sweet. Sweetly awful. Intelligent and artistic – oh, and amusing. I hate amusing men: they make me feel so dull in comparison. I hate intelligent men:

they make me feel stupid. And I hate artistic men on principle. Next time, I want a football-playing moron with no sense of humour. Also gay.'

My mother surrendered to her feelings.

Later, in my bedroom, I sat in front of the mirror rubbing cream into my skin and studying my reflection with an attempt at detachment. It is odd how difficult it is to see yourself clearly, even in the most accurate mirror. Do I really resemble my mother? I do not have her cobweb charm, her lilting smile, her enormous violet-shadowed eyes, her high-pitched voice with that husky crack in it as though she is permanently on the verge of laryngitis. My voice is ordinary, my eyes deep-set, rain-grey like my father's: it has always been a point of honour for me to take after my father. I cannot smile naturally for a mirror and I have never tried to cultivate any charm. My body is narrow but too tall, out of proportion, all legs like the Cranach Venus. The bones of my face seem to be in the right places but I do not have the elfin delicacy of my mother's bone structure. My hair, flaxen in childhood, now mousy, is streaked a fairer shade of blonde and worn in a boyish crop with a few long strands spraying over my forehead. I have it cut each month, my principal sop to vanity. I once read in a magazine that if the hair looks good then everything else will pass, and I have adhered faithfully to this maxim, probably through indolence. My mother is always trying to pressure me into buying clothes – real Clothes, thoroughbred Clothes with a pedigree and labels everywhere to prove it, out of Harrods by Donna Karan, out of Brown's by Gianfranco Ferré. Mostly, I have resisted the pressure – another point of honour. I like my jeans tight and my sweaters loose, and the pride of my wardrobe is still my father's old flying jacket and RAF cap, both a little too big for me but more distinctive, more personal, than any *haute couture*. I had my last official photo done in the cap, worn at an angle with the peak over one eye. My father's name is inside the rim: Squadron Leader Michael Annesley. Almost my name. Before I changed it.

I do not want to take after my mother. There is a story she told me once about my father, whom she loved, in her fashion, very dearly. Almost all her loves are dear, dear but not deep, emotions light as whipped cream, melting in an instant into sweetness

and air. Yet for all her lightness and shallowness she has an infallible instinct for the quality of others, detecting integrity, or the
lack of it, often at first sight. She is drawn to strength and goodness as night creatures are drawn to light, valuing that which she
does not possess. So she married my father, he, no doubt,
bewitched by her like so many men, loving and in the end,
maybe, pitying her. I always visualise him pitying her. 'You see,'
she confessed to me, 'I couldn't bear his scars. I loved him, I
truly loved him, but I couldn't bear even to look at them. The
thought of kissing, touching that side of his face made me sick.
I couldn't help it: that's how I am. I hate ugliness – especially
ugly people. He understood. Michael always understood. He was
the most wonderful, the most understanding man in the world.
Do you know what he did? He promised me we would only be
together in the dark. He said he would never even kiss me in
daylight. And he never broke that promise, not in all our years of
marriage. At night he told me to imagine that his face was whole
and perfect, and I used to imagine it, and then we were happy. Do
you see, darling, how special he was?'

'You shouldn't have told me that,' I said. 'It isn't the kind of
thing you should tell *anyone*.'

'But Michelle' – she was honestly bewildered – 'sweetheart, I
only wanted you to appreciate what a wonderful man he—'

'I loved his scars,' I said. 'When you really love someone, you
love all of him, every part, both the ugliness and the beauty.
Eventually, if you love him enough, that which is ugly becomes
beautiful to you, and precious, so you would not have it changed.
I kissed his scars. Even when I was very little, four or five years
old, I remember sensing that they were – intrinsic to him, necessary, unique. I wanted to kiss them. They were as dear to me
as lips or eyes.'

'If you love enough,' my mother repeated slowly. 'I suppose I
am not capable of loving enough. I love someone for a little, and
then he is gone, and it fades, and I love someone else. But you
see, darling, your father understood. He didn't mind. He was
always understanding, and forgiving, and special. I wanted you to
know that. Perhaps . . . you're like him. One day, you'll love
someone enough, maybe too much. They say great love is marvellous, but as far as I can see it brings nothing but pain. You

should try to be more like me, Michelle darling. Love little and often, but never too much. It isn't a comfortable thing, to love someone too much.'

I did not say anything more. I was afraid to find myself like her, not in feature but in nature – afraid to find in my own character something of her cold airy spirit, her will-o'-the-wisp affections. The secret of her charm, I realised, is simply that she does not – cannot – care; she is too ethereal a creature for mortal love. And sometimes, when I looked round my solitary flat, when I considered my self-centred, career-dominated lifestyle, my unfluttered pulse, my unbroken heart, I feared that all my vaunted ideals and dedication were merely another manifestation of the same inadequate humanity. Solitude for its own sake: a persona pared clean of all emotion. My mother, at nearly sixty, is still a species of *belle dame sans merci*; as for me, my only passion for a long while had been for truth, a passion that 'transcends all pity'. The comparison was an uncomfortable one. I wanted to be my father's daughter, to find in myself his courage and strength, his capacity for love; but I knew I would never have his tolerance. That particular Friday, I was having one of my imaginary conversations with him. His voice was indistinct but the words were clear enough. He was smoking his pipe: since his face began to grow dim, I have often used the symbol of his pipe to restore him to me. I pictured him tamping down the tobacco, and the flexing of his lips as he inhaled, and the thin trail of smoke drifting upwards and spreading into a haze across his face. Only his eyes shone through, holding mine. I wanted to ask him, not how he could have forgiven her, but how I could forgive, or excuse, or forget. 'You have no right to forgive her,' he said. 'Don't you see? That kind of forgiveness is a form of arrogance: looking down on lesser beings from a lofty moral height and judging them. Who the hell are we to sit in judgement on each other?' He used the word 'hell' gently, not violently, which somehow made it more emphatic. But I *mind*, I thought. I mind so much that whenever I think of it I can taste the bitterness. He didn't say anything but suddenly his scars seemed to come into focus, a vivid detail of puckered red flesh. He had crash-landed the Lancaster on a raid in 1944, and woken up in a German hospital with half his face burned away. 'What is the use of bitterness?' he said, and the half of his mouth that still could smiled as he said it. 'Bitterness doesn't heal: it only burns the scars in deeper. This is war, Mila. The mark of Cain. Nothing will rub it out. What your mother gave me was all she had to give. Love in the dark. How could I – how could anyone – be bitter about that? Don't resent her for my sake. Love her for my sake, if you can't manage it for your own.' And he added, even as the fantasy faded into pipe smoke and emptiness. 'She loves you.'

She loves you. The words insinuated themselves occasionally, when I was off guard. Maybe it was true; maybe she did love me. Not the spun-sugar, whipped-cream love she felt for her menfolk but an emotion almost deep, almost real. Motherhood was her one lapse into humanity, the fatal weakness which had diminished her to the crudest level of being. She must have loathed her swollen distorted body, the dragging heaviness of her belly. She must have feared the pain of giving birth, and the ugliness more than the pain. And then, with the baby at her breast, a tiny, naked, wriggling thing, wholly dependent on her, perhaps the overwhelming tenderness that new mothers are supposed to feel swept through her, transformed her, leaving its imprint on her forever. Whatever the truth, as a woman she was untouchable, invincible; her siren song enslaved any male in the vicinity. As a mother, she was gauche, fallible, ill at ease, and her lullabies were always out of tune. I love her because she is my mother, not for my father's sake or my own: I am by turns dutiful and hostile, impatient and unfair. Understanding the situation does not improve it.

Friday night was little better than Thursday. I slept fitfully, and the Doubts invaded my dreams. I woke exhausted with dreaming, unable to remember more than a kaleidoscope of blurred images, all of them unpleasant. The dawn chorus was tuning up in the garden: a godawful row. I often wonder how the countryside got its reputation for peace and quiet; the murmur of London traffic is a far gentler sound. After the birds had shut up the light began to leak through the curtains, and I had just made up my mind that further rest was impossible and I might as well get up when I fell suddenly and unexpectedly asleep.

This time, I slept till past noon.

I came downstairs to find coffee in the kitchen and the vicar in the drawing room. My mother disposed of him with her customary finesse, but not before he had asked me how things were in the glamorous world of television. I thought of my cramped office, furnished in beige and filing cabinets, and of my producer, Alun Craig, who looks like a cross between a terrier and a weasel, with a dash of sewer rat thrown in. My own appearance at that moment was hardly stylish: some of my hair had been flattened in sleep while other bits stood on end, and the nightwear I kept at Grey Gables consisted of a thermal one-piece reminiscent of antique combinations and a red furry dressing-gown with a scorch mark on one sleeve.

I said the glamorous world of television was fine, thank you.

After the vicar had gone I drank several cups of coffee, skimmed a newspaper, and decided I was better. The Doubts were in retreat; I was myself again, or the person I thought of as Myself, the supercool investigative journalist who kept her more muddled emotions tidied away in beige filing cabinets and got on with the job. No more qualms. Not for a while, anyway. My mother produced smoked salmon and toast for lunch but did not press me to eat: so I ate. Smoked salmon was probably in the same category as fucking gourmet soup but I couldn't starve for good. Mark Prosser was in the filing cabinet and I liked smoked salmon.

Later, I gave my mother an abridged account of my confrontation with Shirley. I knew I was being perverse: she would certainly be shocked, perhaps distressed, and discussion of the encounter was no longer necessary. Still, I wanted to talk about it.

'I wish you wouldn't get mixed up with all these dreadful people,' my mother bemoaned. 'Hacks, and criminals, and tarts. It's so frightfully *sordid*.' She obviously visualised Shirley Prosser as a kind of gangster's moll.

'They're not "dreadful people",' I said. 'If Mrs Prosser lived round here you'd probably meet her socially. At local functions, you know. She's a yuppie, of course, and not quite our class, but we aren't supposed to live in a class society any more so you'd be extra nice to her in order to show you hadn't noticed. Her husband would play golf with your friend the collector of antiques –

when not in jail – and her kids would be in the school play. All of them respectable members of the community.'

'Oh dear,' said my mother, inadequately. 'Darling, why did you do it? I mean, if you *must* be a journalist you could interview film stars, or be a theatre critic, or work on one of those arty programmes very late at night where everyone takes themselves so seriously. It would be so much *nicer*. Catching criminals is up to the police: that's what they're for.'

'In this case,' I said, 'the police officer concerned was being paid off. It happens. The police aren't incorruptible: nobody is. If *Quest* hadn't investigated, Guy Prosser and his pals would have got away with it.'

'Oh dear,' said my mother again. And: 'What exactly did they do?'

'They laundered money.'

'I wish they wouldn't call it that,' my mother remarked. 'I always picture them in a sort of huge launderette, loading banknotes into washing machines Anyway, what does it actually mean?'

'Financial juggling. Moving large sums around so no one will know where they come from. Inventing companies and assets to cover up your real source of income.'

'It doesn't sound so very bad.'

'On one end,' I said, 'is Guy Prosser, a casebook yuppie with a nice wife and nice children and a nice handicap at golf. On the other end are drug-dealers and murderers and a lot of bloody miserable victims who are either desperate or dead. That's what the world out there is like, Mummy. Life is real; life is nasty. I have to do what I can. Sometimes people get hurt, innocent people, even children. Sometimes it's my fault. But I can't opt out just because of that. The only way to be sure not to hurt people is to do nothing, and if all those who believe in right and justice do nothing then nothing will get done. The drug-dealers and the murderers and the corrupt businessmen and the corrupt police will have a clear field.'

Try not to hurt people, my father had said, in a dream, in a thought. I do my best. I cannot do nothing.

'A couple of weeks ago,' my mother commented, 'the vicar gave a sermon on punishment and revenge. You know:

Vengeance is mine, saith the Lord. Charles said it was better for
the guilty to go unpunished than for the innocent to suffer.'

'Someone always suffers,' I said. Suddenly, I felt very tired of
it all. 'Whatever you do, or don't do. There's too much suffering.
He's right and I'm right and Shirley Prosser's right and we all disagree. Result: suffering. Inaction doesn't help. We just have to
keep trying.' I had no intention of allowing the Doubts to take
hold again. I had argued my way back to a reasonable degree of
sanity and that was that.

I wondered if my mother understood.

'Darling,' she said after a pause, 'this conversation really has
become far too *earnest*. It's the weekend, after all: you're supposed to be relaxing. I know life is frightfully grim and
unpleasant but *not*, thank heaven, in Askham. What would you
like to do this afternoon?'

Outside, it was raining. The garden was still threadbare in the
aftermath of winter: twiglet shrubs, leafless trees, shaggy tufts of
grass. 'Nothing,' I said. 'Just for once.'

After dinner that evening we sat in the drawing room. My
mother listened to her favourite piano concerto, I flicked through
a book. There was a fire in the grate and a reading lamp at my
elbow but no other light. The windows glittered darkly with
rain. I knew when my mother fell asleep because her head
slipped sideways and her mouth dropped open. She would never
have allowed herself to fall asleep with anyone but me; no lorelei,
even one nearing sixty, snoozes in a chair with her mouth open.
In that moment, I loved her very much. The book in my lap was
my father's third collection of verse, published after his death.
Before the war he had been a solicitor; afterwards, he had gone
back to the law, but only for a short period. When my grandfather died leaving a substantial legacy he gave up office life to
write: many of his poems had already been printed in newspapers
and magazines and he gathered them together in an anthology,
along with what was then a very famous essay on the emotional
after-effects of war. He went on to produce other essays and
commentaries, some literary criticism, an analysis of Elizabethan
verse, a biography of John Donne. He gave a series of lectures
and was interviewed now and then on the radio; but he didn't

really like that kind of exposure. His early poetry, according to the cognoscenti, is about the survival of the spiritual man in the brutalising arena of modern warfare. It was very popular in its day: he was one of the Few, a battle-scarred hero obviously writing from profound personal experience. His later work, which I prefer, concentrates on simple things, country scenes, domestic moments, echoes of war diffused in images of peace. Both the public and the critics lost interest but he never minded, barely noticed; the status of a hero had always embarrassed him. He retained the respect of people who could not remember what he had done to earn it, and when he died of cancer in 1969 – he had given up cigarettes but he couldn't do without the pipe – several papers published long obituaries, and much was made of his 'compassion and sensitivity', his 'reclusive habits', his 'secretive talent'. Meandering through a book most of which I knew by heart, I realised how lucky I was to have that – my father was long gone but I still had his words to feed imagination and embellish memory. I regretted only a little not having a later photograph. Words are better than photographs. A photograph shows only the face, but words come from the soul.

The fire had died down: a few leftover embers flickered redly around a crumbling log. I switched off the light. The room was laced with shadow, softened with the afterglow of the fire. Outside, the Night was waiting. I could no longer hear the rain. I went to the back door and opened it. And there was the Night, above me, around me – not the night of the city, a flat blackness tinged with the sallow glare of streetlamp and neon, but a country night, alive and magical, full of stirring trees, breathless wind, the hush of rain. The bank of cloud was moving away now and a threequarter moon sailed into the clearing sky, turning the retreating edge of cumulus to silver. And beyond was not the void of my inmost fears but an infinity of stars, endless, numberless stars, a million unknown worlds glittering away under the canopy of a single universe. I breathed deeply, and it seemed to me that the wet cold air and the remote starfire flowed into my lungs together, and I was filled with a Night that was illumined forever.

I drove back to London late Sunday afternoon. Before I left my mother gave the antiques collector her last shot. 'I could invite

him for a drink.' She was almost pleading. 'Just for a drink.
Next time you come down . . .'

'If you do,' I said, not too seriously, 'I won't come down at all.'

'But darling,' she persisted, 'you're nearly thirty—'

'I'm thirty-two.'

'It's been such a long time since—'

'Ten years.'

'*Ten years*! Well, there you are. You can't pine away for ten
years: it's like something out of a Victorian novel. I thought
your generation prided yourselves on being frightfully modern.
Here we are in the nineties – or is it still the eighties? I'm never
sure – and you're all supposed to rush around being liberated and
having lots of affairs and—'

'Catch AIDS? I don't think so, thank you.'

'Of course not!' my mother snapped. It didn't suit her to snap,
but with me she tended to forget what suited her. 'I didn't mean
you should be *promiscuous*: you know perfectly well I didn't. But
you have these condoms and things, and . . . oh, darling, I just
want you to have one or two *little* affairs, till you find the right
one. If you don't let yourself get close to anybody, how will you
ever fall in love again? You're so pretty, so *wasted*, and being in
love is so nice. You ought to be in love – you ought to be *loved*.
Michelle, can't you try to be more . . . more frivolous and romantic? Just occasionally? You know I only want you to be happy.'

'I *am* romantic,' I said lightly. 'That's just the trouble. Not
frivolous, but romantic. I can't fall in love by wanting to, or
because you have arranged it for me. One day I'll look across a
crowded room, and see him – Him, with a capital H – and that
will be that. Pow. Zap. Love. Until then, you can have the
antiques collector.'

'And if you don't?'

'Then I don't. I've got my job. That matters a damned sight
more to me, right now, than love affairs. I'm not pining away,
either: not for Patrick or anyone else. It's just – you can't force
it. Mummy—'

'I know.' She hugged me, and I didn't say it. *I'm sorry I'm not
different, I'm sorry I'm not more like you*. It wasn't true, and I
didn't say it. It would only have been a sop to the tenderness
which was unnatural to her and uncomfortable for me.

She said: 'I only wish . . .'

Back in London, back in my flat with my open-plan filing system and my designer-free fixtures and fittings, I told myself I was glad there was no one to welcome me, no one to fuss over me, no one to bother me at all. I went to bed with a book – you don't need a condom with a book – and fell asleep in the second chapter. For the first time in ages, I dreamed of Patrick. My ex-husband. He had turned into an antiques expert who was trying to date my tin of asparagus soup. We were on the *Antiques Road Show* and he was examining it in great detail, peering at it through a magnifying glass. 'It's absolutely genuine!' he pronounced in triumph. 'You see the hallmark? Sainsbury's . . .'

I woke up feeling like Queen Victoria. I was Not Amused. My Doubts had never before included Patrick, nor any other lover. I didn't want him – especially not in my dreams.

I read another chapter and went back to sleep, this time, without guilt or ghosts.

3

I missed having a lover. My body missed it, teasing me at regular intervals with bouts of insomnia, or overreacting mischievously to the biceps and thighceps of screen actors whom I knew, in real life, would merely bore me. And every month I was seized with a pre-menstrual fever which included hot and cold flushes and fantasies that would have outraged Buñuel. Masturbation provided ineffectual relief. It was like scratching a mosquito bite: for a minute or two the itch disappears and then it comes back worse than ever. But I did not intend to be ruled by my libido. Work burned up energy, preoccupied my mind and crammed my daily routine. I worked hard.

I had had relationships since my marriage, of course; but none of them really meant anything. There were old friends who had become, for a short period, a little more than just friendly; instantaneous attractions which had fizzled out over lunch or in bed; a two-year sexual marathon which had generated no corresponding mental rapport. I had felt affection, fondness, brief desire, companionship – but no love. Never love. As I told my mother, you can't force it. After the two-year sex-only stint, I had grown tired of looking for it in the wrong bedrooms. It was six months since my last encounter, a weekend affair which had proved so unsatisfactory, both mentally and physically, that I had begun to fear I was destined for a future of nun-like purity. I would be filled with a raging hunger which, I was sure, would sweep away reserve, temperance, common sense, yet as soon as I found myself in bed with a man all passion would vanish. My body became cold and unresponsive, my mind detached. Sometimes I wondered if it had always been like that, under the veneer of teenage enthusiasm or the trauma of my first experiments after marriage. Even when lust was sated, I felt no post-coital euphoria, no inner peace, only a vacuum where warmth and feeling should have been. I did not miss Patrick, but I missed what I had felt with him. I missed making love.

We met in my third term at Sussex University. I was nineteen, Patrick twenty-one. He was doing one of those complicated courses involving several different subjects, philosophy and psychology, or sociology, or anthropology: I forget the details. He changed more than once, dabbling in Oriental studies in passing, quickly interested, quickly bored, ending up with an honours degree in philosophy. He did little work in any subject: it wasn't necessary. He had the kind of lightning intelligence that could absorb an idea or a set of facts, comprehend it, play with it, use it, discard it, all with the minimum of mental exertion. He could argue about anything, demolishing the opposition with glittering salvos of eloquence, yet I think the less articulate often sensed an essential defect in his argument, a missing element – depth or sincerity – which they in their slowness could not indicate or expose. For myself, I was dazzled by his superficial brilliance, his ardour, his flashes of cynicism. He had little spare time for study since he was passionately involved in the business of being a student: sitting in, campaigning, writing leaflets, making speeches. Later, he became president of the Students' Union. His background was Irish working class: hence, or so I assumed, his left-wing ideology and flair for rebellion. He switched from anarchist to socialist to communist according to his mood, ready to man the barricades for any cause or none, to down pens and defy authority. Catholicism had given him an antipathy to all religions. Poverty had given him a contempt for all wealth. I fell for him on sight, one evening in the bar where, as usual, he monopolised the conversation. Opponents hesitated, stammered, and were swept aside; non-combatants listened in admiration. I joined them.

He was attractive in a style typical of the natural rebel. He had something of Cassius's lean and hungry look, with a lop-sided smile that could turn his expression all to mischief – the

mocking, know-it-all, faintly cruel smile of the agent provoca-
teur. His body was thin and spare and muscular, his face sparse
flesh on thin bones. There were cinnamon-coloured freckles
across the bridge of his nose and on his shoulders and forearms.
I remember noticing them, during sex, when I was biting his
shoulder, and afterwards when his arm lay limply across my
breasts. I loved those freckles. His eyes were hazel, narrow and
very bright, all sparkle; one eyebrow quirked upwards; his hair
was too long on the nape of his neck. He had a slight brogue
which grew stronger when he was drunk or aroused, a blurring
of the voice as soft as Irish mist. I loved all of him, every inch,
every freckle, every cell of his body. I loved doing things with
him which I had not enjoyed with other men, taking his penis in
my mouth, tasting him, toying, tantalising, exploring with my
tongue to find all the most sensitive places, learning his responses
until they were as instinctive as my own. Afterwards I would pillow my head on his belly, and hear his stomach rumble, and
laugh at him, and he would pull me up until I was right on top of
him and complain he was hungry – he was always hungry – and
a long time later we would eat. There is nothing like being in
love, loving and being loved, a wonderful sensual romp with
cocktail breaks and dinner breaks and sex and sleep and more
sex. But it works only with the right person, in the right circumstances. A touch of falsity, the hint of a sham, and the weakness
spreads like a hairline crack, until the whole beautiful fragile
structure disintegrates. Sometimes the cracks have been there,
invisible or unobserved, from the beginning.

We were married in a registry office one summer's day in
1979. The bride wore jeans; so did the groom. We both laughed
a lot. For Patrick it was, I imagine, an impulse, a gesture, a different kind of experience. For me, despite the jeans and the
laughter, it was serious and forever.

Forever lasted little more than a year.

It was partly my fault: I was young and idealistic, and I
assumed he shared my every principle. I never looked beneath
the high gloss of his convictions to see if there was anything
there. The truth was, he could believe in any creed, fight any
crusade, advocate any viewpoint – until it palled. He was not
insincere: it was merely that his ardours were too shallow for

him to understand sincerity. It was all a game to him, an exciting, challenging game which he would play to the best of his
multiple abilities. And when he had played a while, and won a
little, it was time to move on to something new. What I had
seen as shining integrity was simply the tinsel glitter of charm –
my mother's charm, the charm of the people from the hollow
hills, who mingle with earthier mortals for mere amusement,
and cannot really feel or deeply care. But he did not have my
mother's instinct for quality, or any awareness of his own failings. He loved me – if love it was – for my privileged
background, my long curtains of hair, the image of himself that
he glimpsed reflected in my mind. He was good in bed because
he was good at all forms of sport: football, cricket, tennis, sex.
Once I had seen through him – once I had seen the charm, and
the shallows, and the emptiness of his heart – my feelings
changed irrevocably. But falling out of love is a slow and painful
process. There was a period when I hated myself for my
betrayal of him, for the inconstancy which I had discovered in
my own character. After all, he had not intended to deceive me:
I had deceived myself. I knew I should have been able to love
him in all his weakness, but I could not. My grand passion
shrank to a semi-adolescent infatuation, and I felt cheapened by
a delusion both so total and so commonplace. It took me a long
time to get over my disillusionment with Patrick, but it took me
longer still to recover from my bitterness against myself.

'The trouble with Patrick,' his sister Ailean told me, on one of
our rare visits to his home, 'is that since the day he was born he's
been spoiled rotten. He's had five older sisters and a besotted
mother to fuss over him and make much of him – and I was as
bad as any of them, believe me. As for Father, he'd prayed and
prayed for a son and when God provided he couldn't get over the
miracle. Family, friends, neighbours – everyone treated Pat as if
he was something the angels had brought for Christmas. We
were poor enough, but he never went without. If we couldn't
give him cake for tea someone else would. He's not soft, mind
you, but if he's tough it's because he's made that way: nothing
ever happened to toughen him up. He's always been the same:
too bright and too sure of himself and so full of charm he could
break your heart with a smile. When he's dead, he'll outsmart the

Devil and talk his way through the Pearly Gates, though his
sins be as black as a witch's hat. I know him.'

She paused as if for comment but I said nothing. I believe I
thought she was jealous. She didn't look it, or sound it, but I
could think of no other explanation for her attitude.

'Listen,' she went on. 'I'll tell you something about Pat. Then
you'll understand. When he was nine he climbed over the wall
into old Mrs Tranter's garden to pinch her apples. She had a big
tree and the loveliest apples since Eden – too many to eat on her
own, but she wouldn't give any away. She was rich and bad-
tempered and as tight as Scrooge himself. Anyway, she caught
Pat and the other kids ran off, thinking she would call the gardener to beat him black and blue. So he put on a face that would
have melted the Spanish Inquisition and told her he wanted them
for his mother, who was sick and dying. Well, she made him say
where he lived and she marched him off home, and there was
Mother, all twelve stone of her, blooming with health and her
cheeks as red as any apple. Did Mrs Tranter lose her temper?
With anyone else she would have had his hide. But not Pat.
No – she laughed fit to crack her face and asked him to tea the
next week. After that, he used to have tea with her every month.
She lent him books, encouraged him to go to university, said he
was too clever to be stuck in a place like Kilkenny. She even left
him some money in her will. All through stealing apples and
telling lies! You see, everything's always come easy to Pat. Some
people are like that. It's in their stars.'

I said – because I had to say something – 'He's very special.'

'So long as you know it,' said Ailean.

In retrospect, I am not sure if she was trying to warn or
admonish me. *Everything's always come easy to Pat.* Make
excuses, make allowances, ignore his faults – as he does. He's
special.

By the time I knew what she meant, it was too late.

Patrick had recently graduated and was starting his doctorate; I
was working freelance for various newspapers. We were still
attached to the university but most of our friends had left and
Patrick had relinquished his NUS activities. We shared a house
with three undergraduates: two were immersed in study, the

third in rugger. It was 1980, Thatcherism had arrived, political agitation was going out of fashion. Patrick appeared twitchy and frustrated. He said he felt displaced, as if the world had moved on and he had been left behind, trapped in a backwater by a turn of the tide. He dismissed his thesis as pointless and irrelevant, an exercise in academic self-indulgence. I concluded he was missing his friends and suggested a weekend in London with his former boon companion James Lombard. James had been Patrick's opposite in every way; wealthy parentage, conservative outlook, chronically drunk, ideologically bored. They had argued continuously: James invariably lost and never bore a grudge. I wasn't especially keen on him but I liked their mutual tolerance, seeing in it evidence that for all his revolutionary fervour Patrick could still be broad-minded. Now, James had a flat in SW6 and a position in his father's merchant bank. We spent two days with him and on the Monday I went to do an interview for a magazine. Patrick said he would see me back in Brighton in the evening.

He returned later than I'd expected, sparkling with anticipation the way he used to before a demo or a showdown. 'I've got a job!' he announced.

'What?'

'I've got a job.' He gave me a quick hug, a kiss on the cheek. He was excited, alert, pleased with himself. He knew I would be pleased too. Patrick never had any Doubts. 'I'm going to chuck the thesis: it's a waste of time, anyway. We'll go to London, get somewhere decent to live – no more sharing, no lodgers, just the two of us and a garage for the company car. Think of it! Me – and a company car!' His grin was half rueful, half smug. 'We're going up in the world, my darling. It's about time. I've had enough of scholastic penury. I hate this house and so do you. Come to think of it, I hate Brighton. All English seaside resorts are the same: full of people who are too boring to go anywhere else. I can't stand the place. We're heading for the big city: new home, new job, old friends. Well, what do you think? Like the idea?'

I asked: 'What's the job?' But I knew the answer.

'The bank, of course. James fixed it up as soon as he knew we were coming. I had the interview today – only a formality, really: his dad made me an offer straight off. The thing is, in the old days James was always pressing me to give the bank a try, but naturally I wouldn't hear of it. Anyway, that's all changed now. He said he could tell how pissed off I was the moment he set eyes on me. Let's face it, I wasn't made for the peaceful atmosphere of academe.'

'It never used to be peaceful,' I pointed out.

'That was when we were undergraduates. Now we've quit the scene and everyone's turned respectable. We're just watching from the wings while the play goes on without us – and a bloody dreary show it is too. If I stay here any longer I'll turn into the sort of trendy young don who lectures in skin-tight jeans and screws all the prettiest students. You don't want that, do you? Here – I bought some champagne. Let's celebrate.'

I don't think he ever understood what was wrong. I tried to explain, I really tried, but he didn't seem to take it in. With his flashfire intelligence I thought surely he ought to see my point of view; but although Patrick might change his own opinions as often as his socks he couldn't appreciate anyone else's. I felt sick, the sort of churning gut-sickness that comes with fear. This was the man I loved and for the first time I was seeing him clearly – and I knew that what I saw had always been there. Jigsaw pieces fell into place: Ailean in Kilkenny, and James – James who had obviously estimated his dazzling arguments at their true worth. This was the real Patrick, the spoiled child of fate to whom everything was a game. When I looked at him, his attractive invincible façade seemed to shrivel inwards, and there stood a tawdry, bony creature with a cheap smile and glittering eyes, mouthing blarney. The man I loved. I lay beside him that night without touching him. I couldn't sleep, couldn't make love. The thought of leaving him terrified me. But by the morning, I knew I would have to go.

There was no choice, no question of a dilemma. I didn't try to change him because you can't change people. He was himself and I was myself and that was the end of it. I had to leave. It was just a matter of summoning up the courage. I sensed, at heart, that further discussion was futile, yet I still found myself attempting to explain, to clarify my position. But it was difficult to clarify anything when the surface of my mind was all doubt and muddle. Patrick could out-argue me in minutes, without even hearing what I had to say. He was too clever for me, too clever for himself. I sometimes picture him, after I left, looking round the empty bedroom, still not sure what had happened to make me go.

We were divorced by post a couple of years later. Afterwards, he married the daughter of the board of directors. The daughter of one of them, anyway; I don't suppose it mattered which. My mother hadn't liked Patrick and claimed she wasn't surprised. 'The only thing is,' she said, 'I don't think you should have taken it all so . . . *coolly*. Too much composure simply isn't feminine. You should have broken down occasionally.' I didn't tell her I was ashamed to weep for him, ashamed of having married him. I cried only once, alone in my room at Grey Gables, when there was no one by to see me. 'I don't understand your generation,' my mother had said capriciously. 'Is it so easy to leave your husband?' Yes, it's easy. Like pulling your own arm out. The arm is infected, gangrenous, and you know it has to go, but it hurts, it hurts. And after, you still feel yourself clenching the fingers of a hand that isn't there any more.

A few months ago a friend of mine met him at a dinner party.

'I haven't seen him since we split,' I said. 'How did he look?'

'All right. Bit baggy under the eyes, bit saggy under the jaw. All right, really.'

'Not fat or bald or anything?'

'Oh no. He works out every week: he talked about it. He's the kind who works out every week and talks about it. He's probably got co-ordinated tracksuit and running shorts and the latest thing in trainers. That kind. Was he very attractive?'

'I think so.'

'I wondered. He's got that little-boy appeal which is devastating at twenty but on a man his age just looks immature. As if he was dressed up in teenage clothes. Still, some women go for it. My hostess obviously thought he was a catch for her party.'

'Is he . . .' I hesitated. 'I mean, he used to be very amusing. Good company . . .'

'To tell you the truth,' my friend said ruthlessly, 'I thought he was a drag. He's a wine freak who evidently knows a great deal about the subject and insists on imparting his knowledge whether you want to hear it or not. We got a lecture with every bottle. I

was bored to sleep. His wife said he was "passionately interested" in wine but she looked passionately fed up, and I didn't
blame her. She must have to put up with his passionate interests
every day of the week. Was he any good in bed?'

'Passionate,' I said, with a grin that felt crooked.

'He's gone off,' she said wisely. 'You can always tell.
Something in his wife's face. He's bored and she's bored and
they stay together for the kids or in order to placate Daddy. It's
Daddy who has the money, I understand. And the pull at the
bank. Anyway, Micky, you're well out of it.'

'I know,' I said.

Patrick with his glittering talents and his lightning mind had
become a dinner-party bore with an empty marriage and a heavyweight father-in-law controlling his destiny. I minded more about
that, somehow, than the old, old ache of divorce and disillusionment. It seemed to me that he had achieved nothing, amounted to
nothing. The love of my life. I wondered if things would have
been different if I had stayed, and knew they wouldn't, but I still
felt that his failure was partly mine, my responsibility, and the
aftertaste lingered like that of an evil medicine.

4

I was back in the office on Monday. 'Good weekend?' said Jeff Salter, the assistant producer.

I smiled, which he could, if he wished, take as an affirmative.

He was a nice man – the sort of nice man who is invariably deserted by his wife, two-timed by his girlfriends, and who always picks up the cheque. He had good looks without sex appeal, humour without mischief. I liked him and felt sorry for him and had once or twice – late at night, over the last drink in an empty bar – turned him down. So did other nice girls.

It was like him to inquire, if only in passing, about my weekend. It was like Alun Craig not to.

'By the way,' I said, 'I ran into Shirley Prosser in Sainsbury's last week.'

'Shirley Prosser?' Alun frowned briefly. Wives, in his view, were irrelevant unless they were prepared to talk. Families were irrelevant unless they were in the Mafia. Anyway, the Prosser investigation was already a closed file in his mind.

But I had to tell him. 'Guy Prosser's wife,' I said. 'Jeff's giving evidence when the case comes up. Remember?'

It was Jeff who asked: 'What happened? Nasty scene?'

'A bit. She screamed a good deal. The management removed her.' I saw no point in mentioning Mark.

'Did she actually attack you?' Alun said sharply.

'You could say so. She assaulted me with a lethal weapon – a portion of Sainsbury's pâté, I think it was. And one or two similar items. She threw them at me.'

'Were you hurt?' He wasn't anxious for my welfare, I knew, or even particularly interested in it. He only wanted to find out if this was something we could use, at a future date, if there were any spin-offs from the Prosser case.

'The smell of garlic will never wash off,' I said.

'Pity.' Absent-mindedly. 'Did you get a tape?'

'No,' I responded with careful gentleness. 'I don't usually walk around Sainsbury's with my tape recorder to hand.'

'You should,' Alun snapped. He wasn't joking.

The traditional image of the investigative journalist is that of a hard-boiled, hard-drinking maverick, dedicated and devious, incorruptible and unprincipled, a slippery modern Robin Hood defending the poor and wronged against rich Mr Bigs and the might of the establishment. The truth is more prosaic. Few of us are genuinely dedicated, fewer still incorruptible, and a good many cannot hold their drink. The penslingers, Leo Sands used to call us, solitary wordsmiths riding in to clean up the town, liars and cheats and shit-stirrers far seedier than the villains we seek to dislodge. It was a comparison uniquely apposite for *Quest*. The programme specialised in targeting individuals rather than the big impersonal institutions. 'Bad guys make good TV,' Alun Craig always said: he was partial to flippant one-liners. He liked to find one or two central figures and build the story around them, in the case of certain prominent personalities – such as Derek Hatton or Ernest Saunders – using their own charisma against them. The title had been intended to give the impression of a campaign from more chivalrous days: white knight against black, the woodcutter's son against the dragon, or maybe a modern Don Quixote, tilting at windmills. But once in our offices chivalry went into the wastepaper bin. We went after our dragons, not with magic swords, but with concealed microphones and videotape. And neither Jeff nor Alun fitted well with the fashionable concept of the journalist as anti-hero, let alone as white knight.

Jeff Salter was the stooge: thorough, dogged, painstaking, uninspired. He never overlooked a detail, no matter how trivial. He would spend long hours poring over the electoral register in search of an elusive name, or rifling the contents of a dustbin for discarded mail, or leafing through files twenty years old for a morsel of dirt. Drink and divorce made him bellicose but as a rule he was patient and even-tempered. He had the kind of non-descript appearance that can merge into the background anywhere; medium height, medium colouring, medium features. People might meet him several times without a glimmer of recognition, and he could tail someone unobserved for long periods. He always got the most boring jobs, often covering for Alun, who relied on him more than was usually appreciated. They made an effective partnership, but it was Jeff who did the leg-work; Alun supplied leadership, insight, genius. On the other hand Jeff, though unassertive, was considered by all but his ex-wife a likeable human being. Alun Craig was neither likeable nor human.

Half Scottish, half Welsh, he always reminded me of some lines from a song by Flanders and Swann. 'A Song of Patriotic Prejudice', I think it was called. The Scotsman, they claimed 'is mean, as we're all well aware, and bony, and blotchy, and covered with hair', while the Welshman is 'little and dark, more like monkey than man'. Put these two descriptions together and you had Alun Craig. He was five foot six, with an uneven pallor and hair cropped short at the sides and standing up in spikes on top of his head – not the artwork of a punk hairdresser, I was sure, more like the raised hackles of some animal sniffing the spoor of a dangerous quarry. His jaw was patched with bristles where he had skimped shaving and he had a moustache which never quite grew to maturity, merely hovering in a shadowy fashion above his upper lip. His eyebrows sprouted in tufts on either side of his nose and spread upwards towards his temples, so he always looked as if he were in the early stages of lycanthropy. His bones were small and knobbly, his eyes had the beady gleam of ani-mated boot buttons, his infrequent smile was hungry, impish and mirthless. As a journalist he was brilliant, unscrupulous, universally loathed and almost equally admired. His were the flashes of inspiration, the hunches that always led somewhere, the wild guesses that turned out to be ninety-nine per cent accu-rate. He had the ability to piece together a complete picture from a few isolated clues, and once the picture was clear in his mind he would do anything to obtain the necessary evidence. All jour-nalists have a moral blind spot when it comes to getting a good story, but in Alun Craig this defect was the dominant trait in his personality. He would use blackmail and bribery, the stick and the carrot, the hard sell and the soft: the end justified the means and no means were too underhand. On one occasion, when I was trying to get a crucial piece of information from a particularly reticent witness, he had suggested quite seriously that I should sleep with the man in order to help him loosen up. I didn't lose my temper because there was no point. Alun would never have understood that he had asked me to do something both degrading and immoral; he had no concept of either degradation or immorality. He was constantly in trouble with his superiors but he knew – and they knew – that he was too good to fire, no matter what the provocation. The legal department had nightmares about him.

It was because of Alun that *Quest* had acquired its reputation for both reckless speculation and deadly accuracy. A couple of complaints had been pushed through, with much string-pulling and legal wheeler-dealing: polite apologies had been offered which no one but the apologee would ever remember. We had lost one notorious libel case, fortunately with minimal damages, suggesting that the judge, at least, had been unconvinced. (In that we had been lucky; most judges have an automatic prejudice against the investigative journalist.) It had been good publicity. In general *Quest* was feared by anyone on the receiving end and respected, if reluctantly, by colleagues and rivals. I had been there since the beginning, initially as the token female, expected, in my mother's words, to 'worm things' out of susceptible men or to employ the woman-to-woman approach with wives, girlfriends and secretaries. Later, the jobs I was given were less selective. By now, Alun Craig had virtually forgotten my sex, which from him was a compliment, and used me because he trusted my ability, though he had a problem with my principles. Alun always had a problem with other people's principles.

At first, I loathed him. I had joined the team because it was both a change and a challenge, but in the early days I found his whole character so repulsive I could not imagine continuing to work with him. However, I had gradually learned to admire his talent, and there were unguarded moments when I could almost have liked him, if only for his disregard of authority and his sheer bloody cheek. Touch pitch, my mother would have said in an I-told-you-so voice, and you will be defiled. I touched pitch. Sometimes, I caught myself laughing at his horrible jokes, sharing his gloating satisfaction when the victim was well and truly on the hook, squirming, unable to escape. Alun was no less loathsome, but I had come to accept his loathsomeness. It was born in him, an intrinsic part of his nature, or so I believed. You cannot blame the toad for being ugly, or the rat for stealing garbage. These are the native characteristics of toads and rats. Alun was himself, single-minded, heartless, amoral – and an outstanding journalist. I was Micky Murphy, number three on the programme, the pitiless investigator with a passion for truth. We worked well together.

On that particular Monday we had a couple of new cases to look into. Most of our material came through the post, anonymously or otherwise; Alun would sort out anything he thought might be of interest and we would make a preliminary investigation. A story had to fulfil three conditions: first, it must be good television; second, it must be true; third – and most important – we must be able to prove this to the satisfaction of our lawyers. Alun's instincts were unerring on one and two but for all his ruthless tactics a good many hopeful projects came to grief on point three, often after weeks of work. Failure was part of the routine. Sometimes Alun went fishing on his own, using a network of informers that even Jeff knew nothing about, in search of the real dirt on one of his particular bugbears. There were certain well-known individuals against whom he conducted a species of private vendetta, always convinced that one day their murky past would be uncovered and his malice vindicated. The few heroes that contemporary society provided he hated with an inflexible hatred – Richard Branson, Bob Geldof, people with intelligence, charisma, public integrity, worldly success. I often wondered if the mole in his nature was a secret jealousy, unrecognised by everyone including himself. He had brains and his own brand of power but he would never be a real star, never be attractive or popular. And so he maintained that popularity was a cheat and charm a weapon of manipulation: the favourites of the masses were frauds putting up a hypocritical façade to disguise a deformed ego and a career riddled with every conceivable kind of infamy. For Alun, there were no heroes: only idols with feet not of clay but of shit.

I wasn't surprised when I saw the file on Vincent Scarpia Savage. I had never heard the name but here, obviously, was yet another dynamic businessman whose meteoric rise had exacerbated Alun's inner daemon. Inside the file there were a few letters, a ream of typescript from some minor environmental group and a bundle of cuttings. I began to sift through them.

Alun was already launched on a summary.

'. . . not too much background yet but it's all there. He was a golden boy just down from Cambridge who got mixed up in a mortgage fraud and did time for it. Made his money in California – real estate. Now he wants to grab what he can over here. Father's British: an MP. Dead, I think. Mother's an Italian prima donna. He's the kind of creep who's born with a silver spoon in his mouth and thinks he can use it to help himself from everybody else's dinner plate.'

'Did you say his mother was a prima donna?' I interjected.

'Yes.' Brusquely. Alun wasn't interested in opera.

'Not *Jolanda* Scarpia?'

'That's the one. Got him a passport to LA high society, I suppose. He's knocked off half the actresses in Hollywood, according to the *National Enquirer*. Mr Macho: fast cars and fast sex. Should arouse your feminist instincts, Micky. That's why I'm giving it to you. You're going to hate this man.'

Perhaps because it was always personal for him, Alun liked to elicit the same response from his colleagues. But I remembered Leo Sands on impartiality. 'Absolutely,' I murmured.

'Read that stuff from the environmental gang. It's a local operation: the secretary wrote to us. They've folded now, for obvious reasons. Get past the waffle and the story's a beauty. Seems Savage is part of a cabal planning to put up a new shopping centre near Ashford in Kent. You know: supermarkets, office space, new rail link and Chunnel connection; jobs created, all the usual spiel. As always, the site is bang on a beauty spot next to some village. The villagers got together with demonstrations and petitions and made a lot of noise. The leading spirit was the wife of the planning committee chairman, one of these angry, unmade-up women in her early forties. Two kids and nothing to do till she found a cause. She marshalled the local Greens and drummed up support from the big organisations, Friends of the Earth and the wildlife people. Apparently, there's a river in the area and this rare warbler was supposed to be nesting on the banks or something. The river was very photogenic and everyone got nicely worked up about it. The planning committee withdrew permission – then suddenly they turned round and changed their minds. No official reason given. Just "a flexible policy with regard to altered social conditions and the deteriorating employment situation". A load of blah. *But,* according to the secretary, Savage had dealt with the woman. Got her into bed somehow – I expect she was sexually frustrated as well – and then used it to blackmail both her and the husband. She was afraid of looking a fool, he was afraid of looking a cuckold. Even if she'd brazened it out the scandal would have destroyed her credibility and hubby's respectable public image would have gone straight down the drain. Still, she might be ready to talk now. The complex isn't built yet, her marriage is cracking under the strain, and she's angrier than ever. Suggest to her this is Savage's standard modus operandi. It might well be – he looks that sort of smooth dago con artist. He's going to repay attention: I can feel it.' Alun invariably said that at the start of a case, filled with a vicious enthusiasm for every new target.

'I pumped Dempster about him. He's a big star on the international scene – one of the jet set – on the A list in Beverly Hills. You know a few high-class socialites, don't you? Give them a try: they may have some gossip which might provide a few pointers. And get hold of a picture of him with Princess Di: there's bound to be one.' He paused, doodling furiously on the pad which our secretary provided specifically for that purpose. 'I have a feeling about this one,' he reiterated. 'This small-town scandal – blackmail and sex – it's just the beginning. Check his background, his private life, any detail, no matter how small. Talk to everyone. This guy is . . . virgin territory.' He savoured the idea like a vampire licking his lips in anticipation of fresh blood. 'Nobody's touched him yet. The Americans have just sniffed around his love-life. He's been operating out of the country since he was released from jail and now he wants to come home. Well, we'll be waiting for him.'

Virgin territory. So that was the attraction. Alun loved to find a victim the others had missed, stealing a march on his rivals, sinking his canines first into the jugular; his excitement was almost erotic. That time, I remember thinking he was being over-optimistic, and doubting if there was really much of a story to unearth. Sex and blackmail were all very well, but we would need more than a little cheap chicanery to justify the attentions of prime-time television. The mortgage fraud was a long way in the past, and Savage had paid for it. I would do my best, and when nothing further materialised Alun would lose interest with face-saving rapidity.

'Perhaps I ought to fly to LA,' I suggested sweetly. Our budget did not extend to glamorous foreign travel until progress had been made and dazzling results were imminent.

Alun ignored my sarcasm. 'Get on with it, Micky,' he said. 'I want to get this guy. He's lived safe for too long.'

Typical Alun Craig talk. He turned to Jeff with the other case and I picked up the Savage file and went back to my desk to look through it at leisure.

It didn't take me long to decide that the letters (all anonymous) and the typescript had been orchestrated, if not actually written, by the same person. Possibly the secretary of the grandly named Walmsley Village Action Group for Environmental Conservation, who had composed the typescript herself and whose accompanying note bore an illegible signature. Reading her account, I detected more than a trace of the Pankhurst spirit, and a painful disillusionment with the heroine who had betrayed her cause. Savage she seemed to regard with the special vindictiveness that such women reserve for the most masculine kind of men. I suppose Alun imagined I would feel the same. When he remembered my gender, which was not often, he automatically assumed I was an ardent feminist. I let him. I don't like labels, but it would have been a waste of effort telling him so. Running through the press cuttings, I remained determinedly unbiased. Savage obviously had both money and contacts: his name appeared in conjunction with other names, celebrated, influential, even illustrious names. He was mentioned dining, dating, partying, occasionally doing business. Photographs showed him on the deck of a yacht or gracing some society event in black tie with attendant bimbo. The pictures were none of them very clear but he seemed to be dark and good-looking, with a sombre line of eyebrow and a thinly Roman nose. He never smiled for the camera. The paparazzi had only been able to catch him in profile, looking down, looking away: evasive, inscrutable, uninterested – I could not be sure which. Such snapshots are rarely informative. The object is to take the victim off guard, to expose and embarrass, but such exposure can only be superficial and in any case, Vincent Scarpia Savage did not seem to be in the habit of dropping his guard. That in itself was intriguing. After a few minutes' reflection I got out my address book (I refuse to have a Filofax) and settled down with the telephone.

By the end of the morning I had arranged meetings with Miss Arbuckle of the Walmsley Village Action Group and the angry Jan Horrocks, wife of the planning committee chairman. Her husband had evaded my questions and refused to see me. A City friend had told me a great deal about the probity of Vincent's father, Sir John Savage, who had died in a car accident a few years ago. There was something about that which teased at my memory, something I ought to know, a faint tarnish on the upper-class, upright, upmarket lustre of the honourable businessman and incorruptible back-bencher. I asked the wrong question and my friend became cagey. A moment of weakness, he insisted, in a man of old-fashioned principles. It was all very tragic. 'What was all very tragic?' I enquired of no one in particular when I had rung off.

'Of course!' said Jeff. 'Savage! I wasn't thinking. Alun must have been out of the country or he'd have remembered. Tabloid stuff really; not your scene, Micky. MP bonks local party secretary. She had an invalid husband, multiple sclerosis I think, so it didn't look very nice. She was rumoured to be pregnant and the husband was incapable. Accusing fingers pointed at Sir John. He stiffened his upper lip and said nothing. Fatal. Someone talked to the press and that was that.'

'And then,' I said, 'he died . . .'

The story had come back to me now.

Jeff grunted. 'Send Fizzy to check it out,' he suggested. Fizzy, otherwise Felicity, was our PA. 'There must be a file on it somewhere. At the time, no one talked of anything else for at least ten minutes. I think the inquest decided it wasn't deliberate. More likely too much on his mind – loss of concentration. Of course, there was a lot of sympathy for him locally. Wherever locally was.'

'Had he been drinking?'

'Can't recall. Doubt it. Anyway, he was killed, the baby didn't materialise, the mistress refused to sell her story to the *News of the World* for a hundred thousand quid, and nobody sued for libel. It all faded out and another scandal came along to take its place.'

'I don't suppose it's relevant,' I mused. 'All the same . . .'

'I want everything,' said Alun, walking in opportunely from a regular passage of arms with the lawyers. 'Everything!'

I went back to the phone. I listened to my stepfather's stock-broker lamenting the trade deficit and a contact in the property business giving me a long and unnecessary saga about Nick Van Hoogstraten. Neither of them knew much about Vincent Scarpia Savage. He was straight from Hollywood, mean, moody, and malevolent, but there were few specific details available. Apparently he had once turned up at a meeting in an Armani suit, a breach of etiquette which delayed negotiations for a month, caused the share index to fall several points, and induced the chairman of a rival consortium to drop dead from a heart attack. Another source, however, declared that this story must have been exaggerated. Nobody, he assured me, no matter how long he had spent in America, would arrive for an important meeting in Armani.

I spent my lunch hour trying to track down a number for Jolanda Scarpia somewhere in the world and in the early afternoon I rang New York. My old schoolfriend Phyllida Khorman, née Benz, knew more about jet-setting US businessmen than any City contact. She had married most of them.

'Darling!' she shrieked. 'You don't really mean *Vincent*? Gorgeous Vincent? Is *he* the new man in your life? How *fabulous*! I can't believe it – his usual type is some glamorous beauty straight off the cover of *Mirabella*. Not that you couldn't be a knock-out, Micky, if only you would get some decent clothes.'

Phyl, like my mother, is always trying to interest me in Clothes.

'Idiot,' I said. 'My curiosity is professional, not personal. How well do you know him?'

There was a short silence, more noticeable in Phyl's conversation than a scream. 'Not well,' she said at length. 'Come to think of it, who does? Even in LA, people just know about his girls and his cars and his fast-lane lifestyle. He doesn't have intimate friends. I've seen him at parties a few times, mostly in California. We've been introduced, shaken hands, swapped comments on the weather. He's polite in a minimalist way: no small talk, no compliments, says just enough for courtesy and that's it. He doesn't look interested, he doesn't look bored. You never know what he's thinking. I like to believe there are banked-up Italian fires behind the mask but frankly, darling, you just can't tell. Did you ever meet his *mother*?'

'No.'

'Nor did I, but I've heard about her. They say you could fry an egg on her temperament. He might have reacted against that, sort of frozen up inside. My analyst says people do react against their mothers sometimes.'

'I know,' I said. 'Never mind your analyst. You called him Gorgeous Vincent. *Is* he so gorgeous? I'd been visualising a smoothie with a kind of oily Latin charm, but . . .'

'He hasn't any charm at all,' Phyl said baldly. 'He doesn't need it. The implacable façade is much more fascinating. I once saw him pick up a girl at a party – not just any girl either, quite a well-known actress – and he only spoke *three words* to her. Honestly, Micky, three words! I could swear to it.'

'Did you envy her?' I asked with a grin.

'No way. Apparently, they spent a couple of nights together and then six weeks later at a charity gala he failed to recognise her. What's more, I'm not sure it was affectation. He fucks a lot but I think it's just sexercise: I don't believe he's ever been involved. Pooh Ashley says he's really gay – but Pooh says that about any man he fancies. You know Pooh.'

'No I don't,' I said firmly. Only Phyl could get away with calling a friend Pooh. His real name, by my recollection, was Winthrop. 'Get to the point. What about Savage's business affairs? Has Farzad come across him?' Farzad was Mr Khorman.

'I don't think they've done any deals but they played tennis once,' Phyl offered. 'Farzad says Vincent doesn't like the game much but obviously had to win: he slammed the ball across the court like a bullet. It's a sure sign of the killer instinct. Farzad says he operates like a crocodile, coasting along very patiently and as quiet as a log until he's ready, and then suddenly he lashes out and before you know where you are you've lost an arm and a leg.' It sounded like a fair description of Farzad's own method of operating, as far as I could tell, but I didn't say so.

'Is he a crook?'

'I don't know,' Phyl admitted. 'It isn't the kind of thing Farzad ever *defines*, if you know what I mean. I'll pump him, but I have to be careful. He likes you, darling, but he does rather *disapprove* of you.'

'I'll bet,' I murmured inaudibly.

'He says you should give up that job and spend more time being a woman.' She sighed soulfully. 'He's so macho about things like that. I know he's utterly wrong but I do adore it.'

'I'll get back to you,' I said, and hung up.

The next day I went down to Walmsley. It was a commuter village of the kind that litters the southern counties, expensive houses hiding behind pruned hedges and Dulux dogs romping on sprinkler-green lawns. The plebs lived in a row of rather ugly cottages stretching from the church to the post office on one side and from Ye Olde Tea Shoppe to the Hart and Hounds on the other. Miss Arbuckle had a small house behind the church with a view over the fields to the photogenic river. I dutifully admired but declined to take pictures. There were willows growing aslant the brook which, no doubt, showed their hoar leaves in the glassy stream in due season, but I did not feel they would have an inspirational effect on Alun Craig and the public had seen more than enough of them. I accepted a cup of tea and launched straight into the object of my visit. It took me only a short while to conclude that Miss Arbuckle was not, after all, the prime mover in the case, but she was reticent on the subject of her fellow campaigners, though on no other points. 'We decided,' she said, and 'We thought it was best.'

'Who's "we"?' I asked bluntly.

'Well – you know, us. All of us. Except Jan, that is. I was so distressed about Jan, Miss Murphy. Shocked and distressed. You see, I really *respected* her . . .'

And so on.

The more I listened, the more convinced I became that there was little here to justify the involvement of *Quest*. A minor local scandal, that was all, sex and spice and not quite nice but nothing provably illegal, certainly nothing in the big league. These be country matters, I reflected, still influenced by the willow-hung river. What the hell was Alun doing sending me here? And in the background, I thought cynically, there was probably some village bigwig who had a grudge against the developers for not buying up his own spare watermeadow, rare warblers and all. At lunch time, I escaped to the pub, where I listened in vain for gossip. Finally, I resorted to the direct approach, but the response was vague. The river was a good thing, the development was a bad thing, the developers were all wicked profiteers with no concern for the environment, but 'we need the jobs'.

'Anyway,' the barmaid confided to me in an aside, 'there's lots of environment left, isn't there?'

'If you ask me,' grunted the token rustic, swivelling his evil eye in my direction, 'the trouble is all these journalists. Too many bloody journalists. The papers is full of 'em.'

I was unable to deny this.

My interview with Jan Horrocks was more interesting, but useless, since she refused to go on the record. She was handsome in a forceful way with an untidy cloud of hair and an expression of restless discontent which might have been a recent innovation. She seemed both angry and bitter but her resentment appeared to be aimed more at her husband than anybody else, perhaps because he was still around.

'What about Savage?' I said, adding candidly: 'He used you, lied to you—'

'Oh no.' Unexpectedly she smiled. 'He never lied to me. He didn't need lies. He was a good opponent. We were in an all-out fight – no holds barred – and Vincent was worth fighting. I believed in what I was doing, I hated everything he stood for, but it was fun. Oh, it was fun. And now . . . I'm left with David. He doesn't want a divorce because of the children. Or the hassle. Or maybe because he loves me: it doesn't matter. I used to think he was so sweet and shy, but lately he just seems ineffectual. It isn't that people change when they get older, you know: they merely become more the same. Reliable becomes stuffy, diffident becomes paranoid, safe becomes boring. I wasn't in love with Vincent, you understand. He just showed me that I wasn't in love with anyone else. He went through my life like the great storm, leaving everything in ruins. And I don't care. I really don't care.'

I took a few notes during my interview: she didn't mind that. I also made a tape – I had a sneaky little recorder in my handbag with a microphone poking unobtrusively from under the flap – but I didn't tell her. I didn't intend to use it, only keep it for reference. 'Don't quote me,' she said. 'I don't want to be involved. I want to help, but I don't want to be involved. Or perhaps I simply wanted an excuse to talk about Vincent. Anyway, it's your fight now. Good luck. I don't suppose he's ever been beaten.'

My fight? That was the Alun Craig approach. I was the ice-cool seeker after truth, unaffected by the smell of battle. I didn't want anything as personal as a fight.

Back in the office, Fizzy had deposited a further stack of cuttings on my desk. More details on Savage's mortgage fraud, comprehending an impressive number of noughts and several reputable building societies. Picture of a youthful Vincent arriving for trial with long seventies hair and his face tightened into the mask which had later become habitual to him. Contrasting picture as a Cambridge graduate wearing the only smile in the collection and accompanied, even at twenty-two, by the inevitable ravishingly pretty model girlfriend. Additional picture of the girlfriend, just for the hell of it. Various items on Sir John, his impeccable reputation, his blameless life, the disaster which had tainted one and ended the other. Long obituary by Piers Percival, described as 'the well-known art collector and a close friend of the deceased'.

'Getting there yet, Micky?' Alun inquired, craning over my shoulder. I imagined his nose twitching hopefully like a hound on the trail.

'Lots of scandal but not much else,' I said frankly. 'I simply don't think this is our style. The mortgage fraud is his only actual crime in this country to my knowledge, and he did six months in the Scrubs for that. He doesn't seem to have repeated the mistake. The real dirt on his business deals will be in the States. I'll try Phyl Khorman again but Farzad won't talk on principle: he and Savage are birds of a feather – probably vultures. In any case, the great British viewing public won't go for dastardly deeds in America unless they have a reference point at home. You're always stressing the importance of the British connection. It isn't strong enough.'

'What about his family?' Alun rifled moodily through the litter of papers on my desk. 'There's all this stuff on Sir John. How does that tie in?'

I could sense his hunger and frustration. He hated to let go before his teeth had even got a grip.

'They were estranged,' I said. 'I finally got the gist of it from my City friend. Vincent's pater dropped him when he fell foul of the law. End of the relationship. Attempted reconciliations failed – he was even cut out of the will. Colourful but not criminal, as far as I can see.'

Alun was looking more and more dissatisfied. 'His mother?' he snapped. 'The diva?'

'She ran off when he was four,' I said. 'I've been trying to reach her as a matter of routine, but it's probably a waste of time.'

Alun crushed a handful of clippings in a psychotic fist. 'Why isn't there anything on her in all this rubbish?' he said.

'The rubbish on Jolanda Scarpia,' I explained, 'would wallpaper this entire building. Twice. I want to be able to get to my desk.'

Alun made a noise between a sniff and a snort and prowled away, not a tigerish prowl but a rat-like progress, the motion of a rodent in search of something, or someone, on whom to sharpen his incisors. In his hand he still clutched a photo of Vincent Scarpia Savage, handsome and guarded, tight-lipped against a vista of Californian wealth. I knew he would study it and brood, the dark secret jealousy fermenting away in his spirit, embittering his whole existence. I was afraid it might be difficult getting him to give up on this one.

I went back to the phone with a sigh. I seemed to be spending half my life on the phone.

I wasted a good deal of effort locating one of Savage's college contemporaries who admitted, under interrogation, that he hadn't really known him and added as an afterthought that nor had anyone else. Then back to the City, to a contact of my contact, who opined that it was the revelation of his son's business methods which had shocked Sir John into his early grave. Vincent's standard procedure, as practised in his west coast territory, was to find out by underhand means when property values in a particular area were going to skyrocket for some reason. Then he would buy up the local slums, knock them down, throw old people and children on to the streets, and put up a tower block which was then resold or leased for an extortionate price. After which he would drive off to a charity ball in Beverly Hills with the latest thing in rising starlets on his arm, and make a poker-faced donation to Third World poverty. 'If he's going to try to bring those kind of methods over here,' said my contact's contact, obviously flourishing his old school tie in defiance, 'he's got to be stopped.' He added, not quite so loftily: 'We've got too many bastards operating like that already.'

'The question is,' I said, 'what *has* he done over here? I need a local angle.'

But other than the Walmesley Village affair there was no information. And in Walmesley, I reflected, Savage had victimised not a desperate underclass but a committee of complacent nimbies and a local heroine carried away by her greener passions.

I called Phyl again, feeling unhopeful.

'Darling, it's impossible. I asked Farzad a couple of questions, very subtly, but he became suspicious at once. When I said it was for you he practically went through the ceiling. He says I'm not to talk to you about anything but clothes, cooking, and babies.'

'What?'

'I know, I know. I don't intend to stick to it but I have to let him think he's the boss. I'll do whatever I can for you, darling: you know that. Just don't be too optimistic.'

'Unlikely,' I said with a dryness that was lost on Phyl.

On Friday morning I shelved further researches and went to talk to Alun. Savage was definitely a bad guy, I told him, but I just didn't think he was our kind of bad guy. Not yet, anyway. I

suggested diplomatically that we should put him on file for future
reference and see what he got up to next. Alun was poring over
some material from Jeff Salter while I spoke – notes on a
London-based armaments engineer selling some of his nastier
designs via Cardoen in Chile to Saddam Hussein in Iraq. I could
almost feel his body tingling with expectancy. Alun was always a
little in advance of the fashion.

'Yes, yes,' he said impatiently. 'Vincent who?'

Back at my desk, I put the file inside another file and wedged
both in the back of the cabinet under S. There were dozens of
similar cases cluttering the drawers, the gnawed-off ends of old
plots which never came to fruition. I remembered Jan Horrocks –
'It's your fight now' – but I was not going to be pressurised into
pointless regret. I was no huntress torn reluctantly from the
chase; Athene was my role model, sitting in judgement, passion-
less and detached. I thrust a pang of unworthy emotion into the
cabinet with the files and left it there. And I really thought that
was the end of it.

5

Several weeks went by devoted to other matters. I forgot Vincent Savage and I almost forgot Shirley Prosser, although I had acquired a distaste for asparagus soup which I have retained ever since. Summer arrived, not gently as in days of yore but abruptly, almost crudely, moving in overnight to unveil an electric-blue sky and blistering sunshine. Everyone talked of 'the greenhouse effect' and tried hard to look as if they thought this was a bad thing. The Water Board, with a race memory of interminable rain to counteract, panicked and prophesied yet another drought. In the office, our air-conditioning failed. Alun Craig sat at his desk in a state of feverish concentration, damp patches of sweat on his shirt, shiny patches of same on his face. His hair stood up in greasy spikes on the crown of his head like the quills upon the fretful porpentine. His tie looked as if it had been recently used in a hanging. 'Micky!' he called.

I unstuck myself from my chair and went over.

'Vincent Scarpia Savage.' He rolled the names around his tongue before spitting them out, like a masochist savouring something unpleasant. 'How's that progressing? Give me a run-down.'

'If you remember,' I said carefully, 'we agreed to sit on it for a while. There isn't enough on him in this country, his activities have been mostly in California. It's a job for the Americans.'

'If we leave it to the Americans,' Alun said caustically, 'he'll be running for president.' *Quest* might be serious journalism, but its producer was as insular as any tabloid editor. 'Micky, I'm disappointed in you. I give you a prize bastard – upper-class, public school, posh university and prison – the kind of shit who uses anyone or anything to get what he wants, including women, and what do you tell me? "It's a job for the Americans!" Sit on it, shelve it, forget it, it isn't our baby. A job for the Americans! Is that the best you can do?'

The scorn in his voice was obviously intended to lacerate, but I refused to indulge him by flinching. He must have come up with something new, I thought. That would explain this sudden revival of enthusiasm.

'Take a look at him,' Alun said, jerking me across the desk to enable me to do so. A new and glossy photo of Savage had been taped on to the side of the nearest filing cabinet, a position formerly occupied by Derek Hatton, Gerald Ronson and Guy Prosser. 'Take a good look. It's all there – there in the photograph. Look at his eyes. Under the handsome face and the tailored suit he has the soul of a hyena. His cuff-links probably cost the equivalent of a year of your salary. People have gone homeless and hungry, lives have been ruined for those cuff-links. And what happens when you compute the cost of the hand-made silk shirt, the Rolex watch, the gold signet, the cars, the cocktails, the houses, the whores? Are we going to let him get away with it? Are *you* going to let him get away with it?'

I sighed. I was still studying Savage's eyes – the eyes of a man glancing disdainfully at a paparazzo rather than those of a dangerous animal. Of course, a hyena might well glance disdainfully at a paparazzo, were the two of them ever to come face to face. 'All right, Alun,' I said. 'You can cut the pep talk. Do I assume something new has materialised on this one?'

'I've had a tip-off,' Alun admitted. 'I told you to check out his family. You missed half the story. If not more.'

'I've got a number for Jolanda in Italy, but I still don't think—'

'Not Jolanda. The names I've been given are here.' He handed me a piece of paper. 'Elizabeth Savage – she's Sir John's sister, Vincent's aunt. Brought him up. Married but reverted to her maiden name. There's an address for her there. Richard Garoghan – that's her son. No address.'

'And Crystal Winter?' I read, bemused.

'Some model. Ex-girlfriend of Vincent, married Richard. Now divorced. Talk to all three of them. Get them on tape, on video:

promise them anything as long as they'll go on the record. According to my sources, there's a story here that makes *Dallas* look like *Rupert Bear*.'

'Who *are* your sources?' I enquired, without much expectation of an answer. Alun was even more reticent than most of us on the subject of informers.

'The horse's mouth,' he said shortly, managing to sound both omniscient and noncommittal

As long as the results don't come from the other end of the horse, I thought.

I went to see Elizabeth Savage two days later. On the phone she sounded receptive, although whether she would be equally amenable in front of a camera I didn't know and at that stage was not going to ask. The first thing was to find out what, if anything, she could tell me. I still wasn't convinced there was enough substance here for a programme. But Alun's appetite had evidently been whetted anew and the sight of Savage glued to his filing cabinet in the 'place of dishonour', where Alun could stare into his disdainful eyes every minute of the day and see imaginary hyenas, meant an obsession had taken root. Like Robert the Bruce, I would have to try and try again.

My own feelings were contradictory. When I had been given the case my research had been methodical, my checking as thorough as time permitted, my enthusiasm tepid. I had met Alun's attempts to titillate me into a lust for battle with suitably cool amusement. But underneath – against my will, against my judgement – I was intrigued. 'Distrust your mind,' Leo Sands had said, but my problem was not of the mind but of the gut, a tug of primitive emotion I had rarely felt and always resisted. Not Alun's vampirism nor the feminist ardour automatically attributed to me but something dangerously close, the urge to take up a challenge, to charge into combat, slingshot in hand, David against Goliath. Too many of our targets seemed to me essentially weak, greedy children, morally underdeveloped, snatching clumsily at toys that did not belong to them. But Savage, I sensed, might just be in another category: a hungry, deadly, wary creature, indifferent to whomever he might hurt, in business or pleasure. Not a hyena but a panther, with designer pelt and keep-fit muscles, picking his way delicately through the jungle, ignoring any law but his own. Perhaps he was intelligent enough to have made a conscious choice, at some significant turning point in his life, rejecting all human kindness for a Nietzschean creed, survival of the fittest in an ugly world. Whatever the truth the challenge was there, tempting me from the path of unbiased reporting. Jan Horrocks' words came back to me: 'Vincent was worth fighting.' Alun Craig had been right – as was all too frequently the case. To hell with self-discipline, self-control, self-restraint. I wanted this fight. I could almost have stuck Savage's photograph on my own filing cabinet, taunting myself daily with his cold gaze. Leo would not have been proud of me – I wasn't proud of myself – but I could not lecture my passion out of existence. I wanted to take on Vincent Scarpia Savage and win. Just like in all the best thrillers. I wondered what my father would have made of it – my father who had taught me my principles, and how to doubt them. I pictured him in my mind and found to my surprise that he was laughing. The image must have come from my earliest childhood, when I was struggling to surmount one of the huge everyday obstacles that confront the toddler, and my father laughed at the spectacle of my baffled determination. 'I'm an adult now,' I told the memory, tartly. 'The obstacles have changed.' But somehow I was reassured.

I caught the plane to Newcastle and picked up a hire car at the airport. Elizabeth Savage lived in a place called Ridpath, where Sir John's family home had been situated and where Vincent had grown up. 'The house is sold now,' she had explained. 'I have a cottage in the village.' Her directions were precise and although I expected to get lost, I didn't.

The cottage proved to be two buildings knocked into one, with a lot of whitewashed plaster and natural finishes. Thick walls kept out the summer heat, and a draughty fireplace and open doors provided for the circulation of air. I felt chilly, but Elizabeth Savage was evidently impervious to temperature fluctuations. She was a large woman, not flabby but solid, with broad shoulders and gardening muscles in her arms. Her complexion was weathered oak, her hair greying, uncut and uncoloured. Her clothes had lost almost all their original shape and hue and adapted themselves to her needs like a well-worn habit on an elderly monk. I had seen pictures of Sir John and I noted the resemblance, but his strong bones were too big for a woman and her jaw was too heavy, her forehead too high. She had a quality I recognised at once, unique to tramps and aristocrats: she was totally oblivious to her appearance and to the opinions of others. She made me tea and sat me down in the living room with a view of the garden which had developed those muscles. Beyond, a field, a windbreak of conifers, a house or two. And then the land rose up into a ridge against the sky, with here and there outcrops of bare rock thrusting through the balding soil. I was reminded of the legend of the ice-giant Ymir, whose body the Norse gods used for the substance of middle earth. It seemed to me that in this wild, bleak landscape I could see the very contours of the dead giant, meagre flesh falling away from jutting bones. Even in the bright sunlight the country looked desolate and unfriendly.

At one point the ridge dipped and I could see beyond a conical hillock, like a tumulus. It appeared deliberate, man-made rather than the work of the gods, with an air of forgotten purpose: a defence, a sacrificial mound, a barrow. On its summit there was a cluster of trees, darkly leaved, huddled together as though hiding a secret.

'What is that?' I asked Elizabeth Savage.

'That?' Her gaze followed mine, thoughtfully. 'We call it Allweathers.'

'It looks like something out of a fairy tale,' I said lightly. 'If you sleep in the shadow of those trees on Midsummer's Eve you will dream you are in fairyland, and when you wake a hundred years will have slipped away in a single night.'

She laughed. 'I used to think so,' she said. 'When we were little we would run round the trees widdershins, my best friend and I. Seven times seven was the magic number which would unlock the door into the hill. Unfortunately, we were never sure which way widdershins was, and our knowledge of the seven times table wasn't very good either, which was perhaps why we failed.' She paused for a moment, then added: 'I used to go there alone sometimes, too. I told myself it was safe as long as I didn't go into the trees. It was in the trees that something would happen. I went up there one evening in 1944, when I was thirteen. That was where I found him. In the trees.'

I looked a question.

'I remember seeing his face emerge from the shadows . . . just his face, hanging there, disembodied. His skin looked bluish in the moonlight and there was a darkness in his eyes – an inner darkness, not the darkness of the night. I thought he was a ghost. I ran home, shaking all over. The next morning, when I went back to find him, he'd gone. But I knew someone had been there – a man, not a spirit. There was an empty cigarette packet on the ground. I took it with me, as if it was a kind of talisman. I searched for him all day.' She seemed to contemplate her younger self with a curious mixture of nostalgia and tolerance, an older, wiser woman recalling the antics of an impressionable adolescent. I tried to visualise her at thirteen, skinny – surely skinny – with protruding knees and elbows, straight hair scraped back from that great solemn forehead, intense eyes, determined mouth. 'I found him in the barn at Allweather Farm, hiding among the hay bales. He was a deserter, of course. He'd been in the RAF, a fighter pilot. He'd been there practically since the beginning. And then there was an incident – a friend was killed, one friend too many – and his nerve went. Suddenly, you know. I expect the psychiatrists have a name for it nowadays. Anyway, I understood.'

'My father was in the RAF,' I said. I was using him, creating a bond, but what did it matter? It was the truth. 'He was in bombers. He crashed in Germany towards the end of the war. Half his face burned away.'

She glanced at his RAF cap, which I had discarded on the table. Maybe it was my imagination that she looked slightly sceptical. 'He sounds like that poet,' she said slowly. 'You wouldn't know him – before your time. He was quite popular in the late forties. I read all his stuff. It went out of fashion very quickly.'

'Michael Annesley,' I said. 'My father. Murphy was my married name.'

'I see.' This time, she surveyed me with muted approval, as if to say: you have the right background, the right relations. You are One of Us.

I felt cynical.

'What happened to the deserter?' I prompted. It might be irrelevant, but I knew it was important to let her tell me things in her
own way, at her own pace. And Elizabeth Savage was not the sort
of person to dole out information at random, without a purpose.

'I helped him to hide, took him food. He'd been on the run for
a fortnight: he was very tired. He told me he was trying to get to
Scotland, to some cousins on the west coast who would shelter
him. He wrote his mother's address in Newcastle on the cigarette
packet, so I could send her a letter to say he was all right. I can
still see how his hand trembled holding the pencil. I knew he was
ill but he wouldn't let me fetch a doctor. After three days they
came for him and took him to prison. It probably saved his life.'

She took a mouthful of tea; so did I. She didn't appear to be
disturbed by her own story; her attitude remained distant, faintly
amused. When she continued it was in the same light matter-of-
fact tone, without anger or regret. 'The Savages were an Army
family,' she said. 'There was a Savage at Waterloo, another at
Mafeking. One of my ancestors was massacred with Gordon at
Khartoum. My father was a colonel, retired; in 'forty-four John
was serving and Richard – my second brother – had just been
killed at Arnhem. Neil – the youngest – was terrified the war
would be over before he was old enough to join up. Desertion, in
my father's view, was the most terrible crime in the book, far
worse than mere rape or murder. Cowardice in the face of the
enemy. He took a leather strap and beat me till my shoulders
bled. I cried so much I thought I would die of it – not the beating, but that awful emptiness after crying, when you have no
tears left. But I never doubted I'd done the right thing.'

I said: 'It was barbaric.'

She smiled. 'You're very modern. My father . . . wasn't. Here:
this is a picture of him.' She passed me an old photo from the top
of the dresser: a man in uniform, with an Edwardian moustache
and a profile as inflexible as the Rock of Gibraltar. A second
photo showed the three brothers, the two eldest also in uniform.
All of them were clean-cut, clean-shaven, cleanly handsome.

'Is Neil still alive?' I asked.

'Oh no. He joined in 'forty-five and was killed almost immediately, somewhere in Germany. It was an accident, actually:
one of those things. He was standing in the wrong place and a

tank reversed over him. Poor Neil: he was always rather scatterbrained. It destroyed my father, I think, because it was so pointless. You wouldn't have thought him barbaric if you'd seen him then.

'Anyway,' she went on, 'after the war John came home. He'd decided to resign his commission and go into business. He used to talk to me about it: how we were going to build a better world, where no one would be poor or hungry again. He went into insurance, pension schemes, that sort of thing. I daresay you know about that. It was all part of the spirit of the time: there was a hideous mess to clear up but afterwards everything would be different. A shining future. John really believed in it. Mind you, he may have been an idealist but he was shrewd, too. What the Scots call canny. My great-grandfather married a mill-owner's daughter: that's where the family fortune came from. So you see, John had good mercantile genes as well as military ones. He made a lot of money and he helped a lot of people. The two aren't necessarily incompatible.'

'And you?'

'I did what all nice young girls were supposed to do. I "came out", went to suitable parties, danced with suitable young men. When I was eighteen I packed a bag and went to Newcastle. I still had the cigarette packet with the address on it. His mother's address . I'd treasured it the way some women treasure a pressed flower.' A faded smile etched lines of age and self-mockery in her weather-hardened cheek. 'I didn't know if he'd be there but I went anyway. And there he was. Waiting for me. He'd been living at home since he got out of prison at the end of the war. Until I arrived on the doorstep and announced I was going to marry him.'

I could see her clearly now, at eighteen still over-thin, with a gawky schoolgirlish figure, no permanent, little make-up. She had been reckless, wholehearted, painfully sincere and in those days, I was sure, unenlivened by any sense of humour.

I said: 'You never mentioned his name.'

'Michael, like your father. Everyone called him Mike. Mike Garoghan.' The smile again, both softening and ageing her. 'Poor Mike. I'd been in love with him since I was thirteen. From the first moment I saw him, in the circle of trees on Allweathers, I knew he belonged to me. It didn't occur to me that he might not feel the same. I told him everything that had happened, from the beating to the suitable young men. A week later we got married. I'd hidden him, looked after him, been faithful to him: I suppose he felt under an obligation. Or maybe it was just the weak character yielding to the strong. He'd had a girlfriend, Doreen or Maureen, but she didn't count any more. My father disowned me, of course, though John kept in touch. Mike's family were very ordinary – he was just a garage mechanic – but I didn't mind. I'd never done a job in my life but I went out to work, first in a shop, then in a factory. I'd have done anything for him, anything at all.'

The unthinking snobbery in her words annoyed me. Poor Mike, I thought, poor ordinary Mike, compelled to live with so much noble self-sacrifice. As a punishment for desertion, it must have felt like a life sentence.

'Richard was born in 1951. My father was dead by then; my mother died not long afterwards. John had married Jolanda and her baby arrived in November 1950, just six months before mine. He should have been christened Richard, really, and my son would have been Neil, but Jolanda didn't like the old family names; she wanted something more exotic. Vincente, she used to call him, pronouncing it in the Italian style. I didn't go to his christening but John came to Richard's. Mike was getting very difficult by then. He used to skip work and drink too much, or just sit around and brood. Sometimes he wouldn't speak to me for days. We never had scenes – I've always hated scenes – and I didn't complain, but I minded when he didn't seem to care about the child. One night a couple of years later he went out drinking and didn't come back. I found him with the girl – Doreen, Maureen. It's odd that I can't remember. That was when I realised he'd been seeing her all along. I went home and in the morning I packed my bag – the same bag I'd brought with me – and took Richard, and got a bus to Ridpath. And that was that.'

I wondered if I was supposed to comment, but I refrained. She was a strong, decisive woman who had always taken strong, decisive actions. A woman of few doubts. She did not expect my sympathy but I sensed she expected my respect. Well, I respected her. I saw some of the inflexibility of the long-dead colonel in the daughter he had beaten but had been unable to intimidate. It struck me that when she was younger she must have resembled one of the more uncompromising mediaeval saints.

'You went back to your maiden name?' I prompted.

'It wasn't a conscious decision,' she explained. 'The villagers all knew me as Elizabeth Savage. When I came home with a baby they began calling me Mrs – a courtesy title, I suppose. But I was always a Savage. So was Richard. He kept his father's name – I felt that was right – but he was my son. My blood.'

'And Vincent?'

'Vincent was . . . different. Too dark, too daring, too chancy, too quiet. He took after Jolanda, at least in looks, and I think John was afraid he might take after her in character as well. Mind you, I didn't dislike her. But she wasn't – it's an old-fashioned thing to say now, I know – but she wasn't quite a lady. She used to pretend her family were very aristocratic but actually I believe they were just peasant farmers from Tuscany. She was like a child who had never grown up, all appetites, want, want, want. And early success hadn't helped. She could be very sweet, for days sometimes, as if she was making a big effort, and then suddenly she would turn into a termagant. People like that don't have a proper moral sense. After she ran off with that producer John was determined she shouldn't be allowed to see Vincent. He thought that if the boy was completely separated from her influence he could mould him as he wished, eradicate those tendencies in his character – but heredity was too strong for him. Or maybe it was simply too late. Vincent was always the cuckoo in the nest. He was far more *contained* than Jolanda, of course; she had a very open personality – unsophisticated – all her moods were totally transparent. Vincent, even when he was little, appeared unnaturally reserved, as if all that temperament and hunger were bottled up inside him, turning sour, and might break out at any time without warning. He was clever, too. Jolanda was talented but very ignorant, really.'

'Did you love him?'

I hoped the question might catch her off guard, but although she seemed surprised she was not disconcerted. 'No . . . no, I didn't. I tried, but he was not a lovable boy.' Elizabeth Savage didn't have enough love in her, I thought. She had loved Mike

Garoghan, and had transferred that love to her son, but she only had room for one passion at a time, and little to spare for mere affections. 'Richard loved him,' she added, and the smile on her face – the smile for Richard – made her briefly younger instead of ageing her. 'Richard was always perverse. He would have loved almost anybody, if only because they were difficult, or lonely, or unpopular. He had a generous heart. It's a dangerous gift, dangerous for the giver. For John's sake, I tried to be glad that the two boys were so close, but nonetheless, it used to trouble me. Women are pragmatists: we're not sentimental. I couldn't love Vincent merely because he was my brother's son, and I didn't want Richard to love him too . . . too rashly, either. I always thought Vincent was unreliable. Unsafe.'

'But they remained friends,' I said, 'even though you didn't approve?'

'It wasn't a question of approval. I was worried, that was all. After Jolanda absconded Richard and I moved into Weatherfray. John begged for my help. I recall he said something to the effect that he would be a father to Richard if I would be a mother to Vincent. John believed passionately in the importance of the family unit. I think he saw our parallel single-parent status as an act of fate: we were destined to fulfil each other's needs. Together, we would be able to provide the balanced home environment our children required. I agreed with him in principle, but I am not a fatalist. Anyway, I did my best. I was always fair. At that stage Vincent was very young and I suppose, like John, I thought he would be manageable, away from Jolanda.'

'What about Mike Garoghan?' I asked. 'Did you allow him to see Richard?' I phrased the question with care and kept my thoughts to myself.

'He was never very interested. He took Richard out now and then, that was all. After our divorce came through he married that girl and they emigrated to Australia.' She added reluctantly, as though making a concession: 'I believe Richard writes to him occasionally.'

'Is he like his father?' I persisted.

'No. He's a Savage.' She paused, folded and unfolded her lips, let them relax into a rueful grimace. 'He's mechanically minded. That must come from Mike. None of the Savages . . .' None of the Savages ever changed a wheel for Donald Campbell, or tickled a carburettor for Henry Rolls, I thought sardonically, filling in the gap. 'He was mad about engines, even as a little boy. Especially aeroplanes. He used to leave bits of his models all over the house. John paid for his flying lessons when he was twenty. Richard wanted to pay him back, he hated what he saw as avuncular charity, but I persuaded him against it. John would have been so hurt. Richard was much more his kind of son than Vincent; that's why he left Weatherfray to him. It was only a gesture: he knew Richard couldn't afford to maintain it. Anyway, Richard sold the house and used the money to set up his own company. He was doing research into aircraft design – aerodynamics, that sort of thing. I don't know much about it but I gather he had an international reputation. He was going to do well.'

'And?'

'He went bankrupt.' She got up abruptly and went to the back door. I took the opportunity to change the tape. The machine was in plain sight, I had asked if I might use it, but I wanted her to forget it was there. She stood looking out into the garden. Against a haze of sunlight her silhouette loomed large and dark, motionless and somehow permanent, like a rock or a tree. Even her hands did not betray tension. She returned to her chair and sat down again with an air of steady purpose. 'You're a good listener,' she said. 'I'm not used to talking so much, particularly about myself. I expected it to be a bit like a visit to the dentist. Probes, drilling, grilling – the words are more or less the same. But you've made it almost painless. So far. You're a very good listener.'

'It's part of my job.' She was obviously working up to something.

'You know, I expected someone quite different. Someone more . . . hard-boiled.'

'I am hard-boiled,' I said. 'Like an egg.'

She didn't believe me. 'You've listened very patiently. A lot of what I've told you must have seemed beside the point. But you have to understand something. You're interested in Vincent. I'm not. I'm interested in Richard. I wanted you to know the whole story, how I came to be part of it. I wanted you to *see* us – John, Richard, even Mike. I wanted you to care what happens to us. You look like a person who cares.'

'Eggs don't care.' I had encountered her attitude before. It always sounded alarm bells.

'Maybe not. Mothers care, however. Don't the psychologists say they care especially for sons? I've tried so hard not to be over-protective, over-possessive. But Richard is all I have and I want him back. I think you can help me.'

'Is that why you're dabbling in the muddy waters of investigative television?' I enquired gently.

'Muddy waters . . . yes, I suppose so. I'm so relieved you're the kind of person you are. It makes it much easier.' You're One of Us, I thought with renewed cynicism. She had almost put it into words. 'I didn't like the idea of doing this, but it's necessary to move with the times. As I said, I don't believe in fate. But when you called, it seemed like an indication, a sign pointing the way I have to go. I know programmes like yours *can* do good. So . . .'

'So you're talking to me,' I summed up. 'Because of Richard.'

She nodded. 'Because of Richard.' The veneer of humour and tolerance had been stripped away. Her face looked wooden, ruthless, bleakly resolute.

The moment had come for direct questions. 'Exactly what happened?'

'I don't know the details – Richard wouldn't tell me – but Vincent was involved. He'd come back not long before John's death. There was a big scene in John's study at Weatherfray. Village gossip said Vincent wanted a reconciliation and John refused, but I can't believe that. John would never have rejected an olive branch, least of all from his own son. Anyway, a couple of weeks later the story about Hester's pregnancy was in the newspapers. I imagine you've read it. It must have been a coincidence – Vincent might have guessed about the affair, but he couldn't have known anything specific – still, I thought it was a little too pat. Maybe Vincent just brought bad luck. The journalists had been sniffing around for a while, after all. John and Hester – it was one of those secrets everybody knows but nobody tells. They were very discreet, so discreet I doubt if they knew they had fallen in love with each other until long after it happened. As it was, if it hadn't been for the publicity they would probably have gone on quite comfortably. It was really very sad.

I liked Hester Bradley. She was a sensible woman.' She hesitated, frowned a little, smiled a little. 'I seem to have gone off the point again. Vincent . . .

'I remember him at John's funeral, in the village church. Making the right moves, saying nothing, with this look on his face, not grief, not regret, just a sort of blank hardness. I watched him all through the service and his expression never changed. Richard said I was prejudiced. I think he believed in Vincent's stiff upper lip. I didn't.'

'Do you mean' – I was cautious – 'you thought Vincent had something to do with Sir John's death? Or just with the revelations in the tabloids?'

'No. Neither. I simply don't know. But he had something to do with Richard's bankruptcy. It was after the funeral, you see, that Richard began seeing Vincent again. He was in this country quite often and there was a financial arrangement of some kind. Richard was determined to trust him. But when the company went bust, Richard thought it was all his own fault. That's why he went away. I didn't even have the chance to talk to him. He felt he had let everybody down, so he went away.'

There was pain in her face but, as with her maternal emotions, the effect was rejuvenating: for an instant I caught a glimpse of the girl she had been, proud, vulnerable, slightly insensitive, single-minded in her ardour. 'I thought, if you could discover the truth – if you could expose Vincent . . .' She was stumbling but she pulled herself together, began to select her words. 'He was at the bottom of it. I haven't any proof but I know he was. Richard had been like a brother to him, more than a brother – they went through Gordonstoun together – right up to college, and Vincent ruined him. The humiliation of it wrecked his life. When Crystal walked out she took the children. He had nothing left. Nothing at all. Vincent had destroyed everything.'

'Why?' I asked.

'Why?' She started, but brushed the query aside. 'Who knows? Lifelong envy, wanton malice, years of silent brooding. John preferred Richard, although he did his best to conceal it. Still, I daresay Vincent knew; children always know. Jealousy can germinate slowly over a long period of time. Vincent would have taken care not to let it fade.'

'What about Crystal?' I enquired artlessly. 'Wasn't she Vincent's girlfriend before she married Richard?'

'Yes, but it didn't matter. Vincent had dozens of girlfriends. If anything, he was probably gratified to see Richard picking up his leavings.'

Elizabeth Savage didn't like her former daughter-in-law, I concluded without surprise.

She might have heard my thought. 'The trouble is,' she confessed, 'I never felt Crystal was good enough for Richard. I expect all mothers say that about their sons' wives, don't they? I seem to be growing increasingly banal. But she left him just when he needed her most. Anyhow, I don't think Vincent would have rated her high enough to care what she did, or with whom she did it. To him, women are merely something else to use. I rather imagine he throws them away when he's finished with them like empty paper bags. He's never loved anyone. There's no love in him, no warmth; just black festering passions.' She leaned forward on the table, thrusting thick fingers through her thin hair. 'If Vincent was exposed,' she resumed, 'if he was publicly disgraced, Richard would be exonerated. People would see they could have confidence in him. He could make a fresh start. He could come home.' She stared at the tape recorder, then at me. 'You must help us.'

'Look,' I said frankly, 'you've given me a lot of opinions but no facts. I need real data. I respect your judgement, but we can't denounce Vincent just by telling everyone, on your say-so, that he was a nasty little boy.'

There was a short silence, a silence pregnant with hesitations. 'I'll have to talk to Richard. You said he went away. Where did he go?'

'I don't know.' She was a bad liar. The inconsistency of her attitude annoyed me, but I did not think it was due to apprehension. Possibly she felt she must consult her son before committing him to a course of action she had chosen.

'I'll have to see him,' I reiterated.

'I'm sorry.' Her voice was final. I foresaw some boring research ahead.

'So,' I said, 'you want me to help you, but you can't give me any factual evidence and you won't put me in touch with the one witness who can. All I have is what the courts call hearsay and supposition. With so little to work on I'm not sure my producer will wish to proceed with this. However—'

'But you must go on with it!' she said, shaken.

'Maybe.' I switched off the tape. 'It depends what else we can come up with.' I didn't say: it's up to you. Elizabeth Savage was sufficiently perceptive. She had taken the point already.

In the late afternoon we walked up through the village to Weatherfray. This was the ancestral home of the Savages, the property Sir John had left to Richard Garoghan 'as a gesture' and which Richard had promptly sold to assist in financing his own company. The place where Vincent had grown up.

'Where does the name come from?' I asked.

'Oh, it's old – much older than the house. That was built by my great-grandfather after he married his heiress, about a hundred and fifty years ago. It's a monstrosity. You'll see. But the name Weatherfray, that was the name of the house which stood on the site originally. My great-grandfather knocked it down – what there was left of it. It may have had a ghost or two but there was no roof and only a few walls. There used to be an etching of it somewhere – it must have been sold – an artistic ruin with the moon just emerging from behind a cloud and the black shadows of twisted trees. I remember it fascinated me as a child. The trees were cut down, too. My great-grandfather planted his own.'

Another single-minded, strong-willed, heavy-handed Savage, I thought. There was obviously a long line of them, stretching right back to the first primaeval ape who had refused to climb into the safety of the trees with his mates. He stood up on his hind legs and strode off across the plains in pig-headed pursuit of evolution. Those weaker primates conscripted into following him were eaten by giant bears and sabre-toothed tigers but he would not turn back, he was determined to go his own way and make his own life. From ape to Savage. But the aeons had fled by while he remained unchanged, obstinate and inflexible, fighting the treacherous currents of civilisation. He despised weakness, abhorred cowardice, clung rigidly to an outdated moral code. His head, which he invariably kept when all about him were losing theirs, was bloody but unbowed. I both liked and loathed him. And I wondered how much of the primaeval ape lived on in Richard Garoghan and Vincent Scarpia, Savages of the modern world.

We had left the village behind now and were walking alongside a low wall. In a few minutes we came to iron gates, standing open and rusted into position. The gravel driveway was patched green with weeds. On the wall a new stone plaque, artfully weather-worn, bore the legend 'Fray Castle'.

'The latest owners changed the name,' Elizabeth explained. 'They said there was a castle here once, in Norman times. That's nonsense, of course. The house has changed hands twice since we sold it. They keep doing up the interior, installing central heating and glamorous bathrooms and so on, but nothing gets done about the grounds. A place like this has to be properly maintained. These city people, they think the countryside looks after itself.'

She did not seem to have any doubts about her rights of trespass. After all, I reflected, her family had built the place and lived in it for four generations. Like the weed-grown driveway and the rusted gates, she belonged.

We came through a thicket of shrubs obviously in need of the maintenance Elizabeth had mentioned out on to a wide lawn. Beyond, there were formal flowerbeds, cypress trees, the spout of a dry fountain poised over an empty stone basin. In the hot sun the cypresses had the quivering, flame-like quality of trees in a Van Gogh painting. The drive bisected lawn and gardens and swept up in front of the house, a massive architectural aberration that appeared to have been designed by an exponent of Victorian Gothic as a set for Hammer House of Horror. There were towers bristling with finials, elaborate crenellations fringing the slate roof, a plethora of lancet windows, a heavy oak door more suited to an abbey overhung by an arch of corrugated stone. It was built, Elizabeth told me, partly in ashlar removed from Hadrian's Wall, a common building material in that area. In the brilliant light the stone looked dust-pale and every ridge and knuckle of carving cast an underlining shadow. Behind, there was a sombre line of trees, and then the ragged crest of the scarp, rearing upwards. Still farther off I could see other heights, steeper and wilder, shimmering in the heat haze that lay along the rim of the sky.

I turned to Elizabeth and saw that she was watching me with a satirical eye, evidently waiting for my reaction.

'It's impressive,' I responded, properly awed. 'A monstrosity, as you said. What's it like inside?'

'Worse. Or at least,' she amended, 'it used to be. Draughty, gloomy, antiquated plumbing. I remember when I was little lying awake for hours listening to the pipes gurgling. My mother had read us a story from the *Arabian Nights*, about a djinn in a bottle, and I was convinced there was one trapped in the cistern, bubbling with fury because he couldn't get out. The *Arabian Nights* really is most unsuitable for small children.

'Anyway, it's all changed now. The two young men who bought it from us wanted to turn it into a sort of hotel-restaurant: authentic surroundings, very good food in minute quantities, all frightfully expensive and recherché. One of them was a chef and the other a wine waiter, I think. They used to invite me to tea and pretend they wanted my advice – did I like this colour scheme, how about these curtains, could I bear to revisit the place and see what they'd done? Actually, they made it look rather gorgeous. Good taste – and they knew a lot more about art history than I did. Or any of my family, for that matter.' The ageing smile flickered across her face. 'John always consulted Piers when he wanted to buy a painting.'

'Piers Percival?'

'That's right. He was a close friend of John's – of us all.'

'How did they meet?' I enquired.

'In the Army. I know it seems unlikely – Piers was such a refined, sensitive sort of person – but in fact I believe he was rather brave. Very cool and disdainful under fire. He's got a wound he doesn't talk about, something internal; he still suffers from it. I used to meet him at parties occasionally, the year I came out. He was always very kind to me.'

We were right in front of the house now. Gazing up at the façade, I almost missed Elizabeth's next words.

'He's Richard's godfather.'

'Oh?' I was surprised. Somehow, I had formed the impression this honour must have been accorded to her brother.

'It was John's idea,' she explained. 'They came to the christening together. John said it would be good for Piers to have something other than antiques to care about. Richard didn't see much of him, though. They hadn't a lot in common. I sometimes wonder if it would have made any difference when things went wrong, if Piers had been more involved.'

I added and subtracted Piers Percival from a mental list of possibles to interview, all within the space of a minute. 'About Weatherfray,' I resumed. 'Why didn't the restaurant work out?'

'One of the young men ran off with a local boy,' she said. 'A gipsy type, very good-looking. All terribly E.M. Forster. I suppose the other one didn't have the heart to go on. The house was sold to some Arab businessman. As far as I'm aware, he never came here at all. He went bust, and the house was sold again. The present owners are an American film director – a woman – and her husband. They're the ones who changed the name. I expect they thought calling it a castle was more romantic.'

'I like Weatherfray,' I said.

'The villagers have started saying the place is unlucky,' Elizabeth continued. 'Broken marriages, broken relationships, people going broke. They say there's a jinx. Possibly the new owners changed the name in order to try to change the luck.'

'Did it work?' I asked idly.

'I told you,' said Elizabeth Savage with what sounded almost like a sigh, 'I don't believe in luck.'

6

'Well?' Alun Craig said when I arrived back in the office on the following day. It was not an eager, demanding, anticipatory 'Well'; it was brisk and preoccupied.

I summarised the relevant portions of Elizabeth's story. 'It's all based on suspicion,' I said, 'rather than fact. I'm still not enthusiastic about it.'

I was lying through my teeth and Alun probably guessed it, but he wasn't sure.

'We-ell . . .' This time he dragged the word out for as long as possible. 'Maybe you've got a point. We need more than suspicion. Maybe this bastard just isn't ready for us yet.'

Alun was lying through his teeth too.

'Maybe.' He was trying new tactics to provoke me into defending my case, but I didn't feel like playing his games. I rarely did. I waited; he waited: it was a stand-off.

Then he grinned – a humourless diabolical grin full of those uneven teeth through which he lied so readily. 'Come off it, Micky. What about Richard Garoghan? What about Crystal Witch-Hunt? Drop that cool disinterest for once and let the natural journalist show through. It's too hot to stand around looking like a glass of iced boredom. Work up some sweat on this one, will you?'

'She can't,' Jeff said. 'The hotter it gets, the cooler she gets. That's our Micky.'

'Bullshit.' Alun glared at me moodily for a minute, then snapped the grin back into place. 'You know, if you weren't so bright you'd be an upper-class prig.'

I grinned too, I couldn't help it. Sometimes Alun had the irresistible malignity of one of Steven Spielberg's gremlins. 'All right, Craig,' I said. 'It's Crystal Winter, not Crystal Witch-Hunt, as you know quite well, and I'm seeing her on Friday afternoon. You supply enthusiasm; I'll supply efficiency. OK? Richard Garoghan's going to be more difficult. He seems to have ridden off into the sunset and as yet I don't know precisely which sunset. Still, he's a pilot; that's a starting point. Since you're so keen, what are you going to do?'

'I'm concentrating on the business end,' he said tersely. 'In California.' I looked mildly enquiring and after a moment he elaborated. 'Savage is in partnership with a man called Carson, seventy-odd and semi-retired. Judas Carson.'

'These American names,' I remarked. 'Is it appropriate?'

'Probably. But he won't tell tales on Savage. According to my sources, he's an alley cat who's been in every dustbin and has now staked out a nice hearthside where he can grow old.' In his screenwriting, Alun employed neither metaphor nor rhetoric, but in everyday discussion he would flourish both. 'He won't want to stir things up; he's too comfortable. But they had another associate who's supposed to be disgruntled. He quit or got fired, I don't know which. Anyway, he might be prepared to talk to us.'

'Name?'

Reluctance made Alun increasingly brusque. 'LeSueur.'

'If he's so disgruntled,' I mused, 'why hasn't he talked to the Americans?'

Alun shrugged. 'Maybe no one asked. Who cares? If he's ready to spill the beans I'll go and listen.'

'Aha,' said Jeff. 'I detect a research trip in the offing. Ten days on expenses in the City of Angels.'

'This is bloody important – possibly the most important angle we'll get. As the producer, I'm the person to handle it.'

'Creep,' I said. 'If you do go, I shall expect to be sent in search of Richard Garoghan. Wherever he is.'

Alun didn't comment.

On my desk, Fizzy had left a file on Crystal Winter which consisted mostly of photographs. The majority were face-only shots advertising Récamier make-up, misty close-ups reduced by artistic effect to little more than painted features on an acre of impossibly perfect skin. Her eye colour varied from cerulean blue to silver, but in many of the pictures, so did her complexion. 'She was the Récamier Face for years,' explained my friend Annabel Purdey, fashion editor on one of the leading glossies. 'They fired her when she was twenty-six for an eighteen-year-old, and then some in-depth survey concluded it was a bad move and they brought her back again. There was a whole skincare range named after her: Crystal Clear astringent, Crystal Pure cleanser, that sort of thing. Eyeshadow was Crystalline Blue, foundation Winter Beige. She must have done very well out of it. Models like her get paid the earth to live in the country inhaling unpolluted air and eating yoghurt, and then the credit goes to liposomes and collagen.'

'She's very pretty,' I said, alighting on a full-length photograph in which she sported sixties eyeliner and a spangled green fishtail. Long tresses were spread coyly over bare breasts. 'Why on earth have they dressed her as a mermaid?'

The phone at my ear responded promptly. 'The Mermaid Collection. Bath foam, body lotion, etcetera. That was the campaign that really made her name. For heaven's sake, Micky, it was an advertising classic! Cecil Beaton designed the tail. Don't you read magazines?'

'I read *The Economist*,' I offered.

'I don't know how you expect to keep in touch,' said Annabel severely. We had met as newcomers on Fleet Street; she brought the same investigative fervour to the fashion pages that I reserved for hard news, but she had only a limited awareness of a wider world. If you asked her about a leading politician she would probably be able to tell you where he bought his tie, but would have little knowledge of his politics. She called it concentrating on essentials, and I often wondered if she might be right, at least when it came to politicians.

'I can't find any fashion shots,' I remarked, reverting to the subject of my call. 'Doesn't Crystal do clothes?'

'No, of course not. She's too short for the catwalk. You have to be at least five foot eight, and she's only five five. Her main assets are face and hair.'

'Personality?' I hazarded.

'Are you asking if she has one? Don't be silly: she's a model.'

All ordinarily attractive women – myself included – are quite prepared to concede superior beauty to a rival, provided we feel we have the edge in charm and intelligence.

'Character, then,' I said. 'Is she a spoiled bitch with a brain the size of a pea and an ego as big as Greater London? Or don't you know?'

This was deliberate provocation. Annabel had an informer in every salon: if Claudia Schiffer put on an ounce of weight, she would have seen the scales. 'Of course I know,' she said indignantly. 'It's merely that I didn't want to be over-nasty. If you're seriously interested in Crystal Winter, I'll give you a serious judgement.'

'Go on.'

'Well, she's not the usual type. You know: quick success, a few years in the limelight, provident marriage, graceful fade-out. She's survived a long while, and for that you need something extra, not only exceptional good looks but luck, stamina, the X-factor – whatever that may be. She's not a star like Jerry Hall or Marie Helvin, but she wants to be. She's trying to get into acting now, shed a husband and picked up an agent. Don't know if she's making any progress. The thing is, I can't see it. Marie's got vivacity and charm. Jerry's got legs and Mick Jagger. Crystal has possibly one of the prettiest faces around, but so what? A pretty face can get you on a magazine cover but I never heard it could get you off it. She's not spoiled and she's not stupid and everyone who's worked with her says she's terribly sweet – too, too modest and unassuming – but those are negative qualities. She was lucky with the Récamier contract. She's going to need more than luck now.'

'And you don't think she's got it?' I conducted.

'You're going to see her, aren't you?' said Annabel. 'Judge for yourself.'

I went to see her, in a terraced house in Knightsbridge a long way from the unpolluted country air once stipulated by Récamier. Crystal Winter, however, showed no visible signs of deterioration. Even without the aid of soft focus she was indecently pretty, with a small triangular face like a Siamese cat, slanting blue eyes set above slanting cheekbones, mouth sculpted into a perfect pout. Her complexion was pale fawn (Winter Beige, perhaps?) and her long, long hair was the colour of black chocolate and as smooth as ironed silk. I knew she was in her late thirties but she looked no particular age and any faint indications of wear and tear seemed only to accentuate the piquancy of her features.

I disliked her on sight.

'Do you mind waiting while I change?' she said. 'I've only just got in from my dance class.'

She was wearing a plain black skirt over a black leotard and she looked and moved like an off-duty ballerina, with a sort of precision elegance. Her figure was impossibly slender yet subtly curved, like an art deco nymph. I haven't been self-conscious since my teens but she made me feel overgrown, awkward and leggy. I reflected unreasonably that it was typical of her not only to attend a dance class but to mention that she did so, implying as it did a combination of self-discipline, physical fitness and artistic flair. I do yoga from a videotape and work out now and then at a local gym. Like most people I regularly intend to exercise more and discover with equal regularity that I have neither the time nor the energy.

I said politely that I didn't mind waiting.

Crystal dispatched the foreign help to make tea and showed me to the sitting room. When she had gone I checked out the bookshelves: there were Penguin classics of Jane Austen and the Brontës, a full complement of Shakespeare, Stanislavsky on the Method and Olivier on Olivier. Evidently Crystal took her thespian ambitions very seriously. Also the inevitable Jackie Collins and Jilly Cooper, and several biographies of female celebrities: Callas, Gelsey Kirkland, Imelda Marcos. Beside the bookshelves there was a desk with framed photographs on the top which I studied with my usual interest. I adore looking at photographs, not exotic landscapes and Roman ruins but photos of people, sepia prints of Victorian ancestors, holiday snaps of drunken friends, wedding pictures of bored bridesmaids and starry-eyed couples who later split. Moments of history, glimpses of character, clues. But there was little here for my imagination to work on. Crystal with elderly parents; Crystal with offspring, one of each sex. Studio portrait of Crystal and daughter, probably from her last job for Récamier, where the co-ordinating complexions of mother and child had been used to demonstrate the efficacy of their latest anti-ageing cream. She had been about thirty-three then and had subsequently relapsed into wife-and-motherhood until her husband went bankrupt and rode off into the sunset. Did he ride or was he pushed? I wondered. There were no pictures of Richard Garoghan. Nor had Elizabeth Savage displayed any. It was almost as if, after his departure into exile, there had been an unwitting conspiracy to expunge his very image, to abandon him to an enforced oblivion. Elizabeth, no doubt, gazed on his picture in secret, while Crystal had almost certainly snipped him out of all family shots and consigned him to the rubbish bin. For the first time, I began to feel angry on his behalf.

So much for detachment.

The foreign help came in with the tea and Crystal followed, wearing loose trousers and a looser tunic with her hair in a high ponytail. She resembled a species of designer coolie. We went through the routine plaint about the heat and how wonderful it would be if one didn't have to stay in London. Then I started the tape.

'Tell me a bit about yourself,' I invited, 'before we get on to other matters.'

If she was flattered she didn't show it. Beauty can be a mask concealing not merely defects of character, but character itself. I remembered Annabel's carelessly catty words: 'Too, too modest and unassuming.' I should have paid more attention. And among the photos there were none of Crystal in her heyday, rubbing shoulders with the famous. It might be calculation, it might be a genuine simplicity. But Crystal did not look simple.

'Is Crystal Winter your real name?' I enquired, knowing it wasn't.

'Hardly. I was born Christine Farrow.' The phrase distanced her from the event. 'Winter was my mother's maiden name; Crystal just seemed to go with it. And it's nearly the same as Christine: friends can still call me Crys if they want to.' She smiled a beautiful triangular smile which matched her beautiful triangular face. 'I wouldn't have got far as Christine Farrow, don't you agree? Labels are all-important.'

It was fair comment. After all, in my very different job I had always found it useful to adhere to the more plebian Micky Murphy rather than the upper-class Michelle Annesley Cloud.

'Do you use your married name at all?'

'No.'

I had provided an opening for her to talk about her marriage and she ignored it. I had the impression she didn't even see it.

I tried again. 'You were married very young, weren't you?'

'I was twenty-one.'

'And before that,' I persisted, 'you'd been dating Vincent?'

'Oh – Vincent.' This was what I had come to discuss, and her tone acknowledged it. She altered her position slightly and it was as if she was rearranging herself – her expression, her attitude, the disposal of her hands – to face an ordeal or act out a part. A dancer assuming the correct pose to begin her solo. 'I don't know if I can make you understand. I was nineteen when I met him and very . . . susceptible. My career had really taken off, everyone was making a fuss of me, and I thought life was going to pan out like a romantic novel. Vincent was handsome and aristocratic and rich – the Marquis of Vidal with a dash of Heathcliff. Do you read Georgette Heyer?'

I smiled reluctantly. 'Occasionally.'

'Then you know the type. He had a bad reputation with women and didn't seem to care about anyone. That can be terribly attractive to a teenager.' Also to an adult, I thought derisively. 'I sensed he was morally . . . unbalanced, but I believed he was in love with me and I would be able to change him. I suppose I was very silly, really.' There was none of Elizabeth Savage's amused tolerance here, only an aloof self-contemplation. 'He was just a glamorous delinquent. He still is. Most guys grow out of delinquency – boys become men, they grow up; but Vincent never did. He's always been sort of dark and twisted inside. Always.'

For a moment there was truth in her voice, showing through the performance. And something else. Anger, maybe; vehemence, enmity. I wasn't sure. I saw one carefully disposed hand tighten on the arm of the sofa.

'Did you know he was involved in something criminal?' I asked.

'No. How should I? He talked about business but I didn't

really take it in. I thought he was just being clever. So did he. Even when he was arrested I assumed it was all his American partner. It wasn't until later that I began to see things differently.'

'How' – I picked my words – 'how close were you?'

'Do you mean, were we actually engaged?' She paused, also picking her words. But instinct told me nearly all her words were hand-picked anyway. I hid my surprise. 'Who told you about that? It wasn't in any of the papers.'

'I heard,' I lied.

'Yes, I see. It wasn't true, of course. I wanted to make a gesture, when Vincent was arrested, to show I intended to stand by him. I suppose it was a kind of bravado. Richard was against it. He said the tabloids would be on to me like hawks. Then Vincent was released on bail, and he . . . he didn't like it either. Once he realised the way things were going, he cut himself off from everyone. He wouldn't even let me visit him in jail.' There was another pause, almost as if she faltered, but neither lip nor voice trembled. 'He was determined to play the lone wolf.'

'And . . . did he ask Richard to take care of you?'

The angled eyes looked straight at me, registering sarcasm. 'No,' she said quietly. If I hadn't been hardened, I would have felt cheap. 'He didn't care. After the arrest, I don't believe he thought about me at all. I imagine he was pretty shocked at what was happening to him. He seemed to think Sir John would be able to get him off the hook, but . . .'

'But?'

'It didn't happen.'

'So you began seeing Richard.' I let it hang for a few seconds before elucidating. 'It must have been inevitable. You were thrown together by circumstances, both close to Vincent, both anxious for him. Had Richard always been attracted to you, do you think?'

I wondered if she would succumb to temptation and seek to convey to me the idea of herself as a helpless siren unconsciously enchanting every male in her vicinity. But Crystal showed clearly that she was above vulgar self-advertisement. Possibly she knew she was so pretty that she didn't need it.

'I don't know. He was always charming and friendly, but then, he always is. If we went out in a group, he talked mainly to Vincent. He was polite to me, that's all.' Intuition told me she was adhering to the letter of the truth like superglue, but I didn't interrupt. 'It was only after the arrest that he . . . well, he was wonderful. I was dreadfully upset and bewildered and he looked after me, advised me, protected me from the press. It was awkward because I didn't have any status with Vincent's family; I was just another girlfriend. Vincent hadn't told his father that we were . . . going steady. But Richard showed them I was in a different category; I wasn't a little slag they could just shrug off.'

The sudden crudeness startled me and I sensed it startled her, as if an old grievance had taken her off guard. 'He took me to Weatherfray for the weekend. I'd never been before. Elizabeth didn't like me much, but that was because of Richard. I suppose she saw it coming before I did. She must have been jealous of me from the start. Some mothers find it hard to let go of their sons, don't they?'

'And Sir John?'

'He was a bit stiff at first but when Richard had explained things he unbent a lot. I think he was sorry for not understanding my position right away. After that he was very kind, really.' She fell silent for a moment, and her blue cat-like stare was fixed on some remote emptiness on the far side of the room. 'I was very lonely then. My whole world had collapsed and I felt I had no one to turn to.' I speculated briefly on the role of her own parents, her other friends. Presumably they didn't count. 'There was only Richard. He was there whenever I needed him. He told me to phone him in the middle of the night if I couldn't sleep and at work during the day if some reporter was pestering me. And he was fun. Vincent was glamorous but he wasn't fun. There was one day when Richard borrowed a motorbike and we went slumming, out into the country to a pub by a river. We drank beer and ate pub food. I'd never drunk beer before. Richard said I wasn't to worry about anything that day, not even my figure.' She added, as if it was original: 'He made me laugh.'

I tried hard to imagine a much younger Crystal, perhaps without make-up, her face shaded only with the watercolour tints of first youth, laughing in a carefree fashion over a ploughman's and a pint of bitter. It was impossible. If Richard Garoghan had actually been able to accomplish this transformation, he must be something of a magician.

'He used to talk about himself and Vincent, half joking, half serious. "Vincent's the heir," he used to say. "Looks, money – he's even got brains. Plenty of O-levels and A-levels and a degree at Cambridge. Me, I'm the penniless nephew with a dad whom even my mum thought wasn't quite quite; I don't have a classic profile and my classical education passed me by. I've never been good at anything except engines. But I'm terribly, terribly charming. Don't you agree?"' She should have smiled at the recollection she had conjured, but she didn't. 'He was, too,' she concluded. 'Very charming.'

'Was he really fond of Vincent?' I asked, remembering Elizabeth Savage on the subject.

'Yes, he was. That was what made it so difficult, when we . . .' She hesitated, apparently without embarrassment, then changed tack. 'They were at school together, you know. Richard told me about it. Vincent fought this bigger boy who tried to bully him – Richard, I mean – and practically beat him to pulp. He was always rebellious and in trouble. But Richard said he was fearless too, and loyal. Loyal.' She reran the word, her expression even more incalculable than usual. '"Vincent's got this black streak," Richard said. "It drives him to do crazy things, sometimes bad things. It's as if he's got his eyes so firmly fixed on the goal that he doesn't notice whom he flattens in the process of reaching it. That's how he got into this mess" – he meant the mortgage fraud. "He was so busy trying to impress my uncle that it just didn't occur to him to consider the ethical implications. Sometimes . . . he can't see clearly through the darkness of his own nature." I think that was the phrase Richard used. He did care about Vincent, you see. They were best friends as well as cousins. But he didn't have any illusions about him. That's why it was so *stupid*—'

She stopped abruptly, uncurled herself from the sofa, walked to the bookcase and back. When she sat down again I saw she had taken a cigarette from a silver box on the desk. I said: 'I thought models weren't supposed to smoke. Isn't it bad for the skin?'

'I've quit working for Récamier.' It was almost a snap. 'I can smoke if I like.'

She held the cigarette like a fourteen-year-old who wants to appear sophisticated. It was the one moment when I warmed to her.

'What did Richard do that was so stupid?' I probed gently. Like a dentist, as Elizabeth had said.

Crystal smoked carefully. 'It was when he was setting up his own company. Sir John had left him a legacy, so we had some capital of our own, but it wasn't enough. We were moving as well. Richard's old firm was in Coventry but he wanted to relocate nearer London. This place is about the same size as our house in Sherbourne, but obviously it was a lot more expensive. Anyway, Richard was going to the banks for extra backing when Vincent began making overtures. I don't know the terms of the proposal but it gave Vincent a lot of power. Richard said it was a wonderful offer and he had to trust him. He kept saying that – he *had* to trust him. He knew Vincent had never forgiven him for – for us, but he let himself be fooled. He just *gave* Vincent the opportunity to break him. "Of course Vincent hated me," he said afterwards, "but he also loved me. It was a toss-up which side won." He said it so – flippantly, as if it didn't matter. But it was our whole life, and he'd thrown it away, because he had some futile idea of giving Vincent a second chance.'

Her bitterness towards Richard was evident. He had been charming and supportive to her when she needed it, but she clearly did not like it when his charity extended to anyone else. However, I was still not sure what she really felt about Vincent.

'*You* didn't trust him, then?' I suggested.

'I don't know. I was stupid, too.' She spoke coolly again, at one remove from her narrative, her betraying emotion switched off. The cigarette lay in a pristine ashtray burning away by itself. 'For a while, yes, I wanted to believe Vincent had changed. I too.'

She closed her beautiful mouth without any particular emphasis, but a pause lengthened which I realised I would have to break.

'I gather Richard's left the country,' I said. 'Do you keep in touch?'

'Only through our lawyers.'

'I need to get hold of him. Surely you must have some idea—'

'I can't help you.' Her tone was flat. 'He sends me money, the children write to him. It's all managed by the lawyers. That's how he wanted it.'

'Why?'

'He's a man.' Briefly, she sounded like other women, uniting us, or trying to, in a common disparagement of the opposite sex. 'He can't live with failure. His ego can't take it. Besides, he knows it's all his own fault.'

'How does he know?' I surmised. 'Because you told him?'

'If he came home,' she said, 'he would have to face that. His failure, and his fault.'

Double guilt.

'Couldn't you have done something?' I said. 'You must have money of your own. All those years with Récamier—'

It was none of my business and her expression showed she knew it. Fortunately, that was when we were interrupted. The door opened and a girl of about ten came in wielding a cordless phone.

'Excuse me,' she said with scrupulous politeness. 'Mummy, it's Brendan. He wants to talk to you privately. He says it's important.'

To talk about me, I guessed, catching a hint of *gêne* in Crystal's swift sideways glance.

'My agent,' she said, appropriating the phone. 'Would you mind if I . . .? This is my daughter. Snow, look after Miss Murphy.'

She went out, phone to her ear, closing the door firmly behind her. I was left with the girl. Snow. Evidently Crystal had adopted the American habit of giving her child a noun not a name. Moon, Star, Heaven: this was the nomenclature in vogue among the Beautiful People. Crystal undoubtedly considered herself one of them. Snow, I thought, was an unsuitable choice, with too many of the wrong connotations, but presumably Crystal had decided to ignore all that. I wondered how her daughter felt about it.

She sat on the sofa with her shoulders hunched, bare toes plucking at the carpet. She had none of Crystal's studied grace nor the natural poise of some children: her posture was effortlessly clumsy, her good manners faintly farouche. Twig-thin legs bulging only at the knee and ankle protruded from beneath the long T-shirt which was all she appeared to be wearing. She had inherited her mother's slanting bones and features to match, but in her the ensemble had been slightly disarranged, a millimetre here, a millimetre there, and instead of being beautiful she was merely odd-looking, almost plain. With her elongated neck and crooked eyes she recalled a Modigliani portrait. Her hair lacked Crystal's black chocolate richness; it was a plebeian dark brown, cut fairly short and scraped into a washing-up brush ponytail on the crown of her head, inadequate strands spraying from a thick twist of elastic. Her eyes were not blue but a very pale grey, nearly silver, like the eyes of alien children in science fiction stories. Her gaze kept flickering towards me and then skidding away whenever it encountered mine. Children are often described as candid and unselfconscious, usually by besotted adults who have forgotten what it is like to be too small in a very large world and not yet sure of the rules. Snow, like any other little girl left by a thoughtless parent in the company of a stranger, looked both furtive and embarrassed.

'My name's Michelle,' I offered, by way of an ice-breaker. 'My friends call me Micky.'

I held out my hand and presently she shook it, rather doubtfully.

'How old are you?' A routine question, but it would do for a start.

'Eleven and a half.' She was still at the age when halves and quarters counted.

'You look older,' I lied promptly, knowing how to please.

She considered the compliment, possibly with satisfaction. 'Laura Williams doesn't think so,' she volunteered. 'She's eleven and threequarters and a boy once thought she was thirteen. She *says*.'

'Is Laura Williams your friend?' I asked.

'No.'

We appeared to have come to a full stop. This time, however, it was Snow who reopened the conversation.

'Would you like some more tea?'

'Yes please.' I didn't want it, but I thought acceptance would be more encouraging.

She handled the teapot cautiously, as if it might suddenly decide to misbehave, coughing and spluttering of its own accord.

When I had taken the cup and duly sipped she said unexpectedly: 'Micky's a boy's name. Do you mind having a boy's name?'

'Well, you see, I was called after my father, Michael. I loved my father very much, so . . . I like having his name. But he always called me Mila – everyone else calls me Micky.'

She relapsed into the tortuous thought processes of childhood. Her expression, I noticed, had something of Crystal's inscrutability.

'My daddy calls me Penny,' she said at length. 'So does Jo, and all my schoolfriends. Only Mummy calls me Snow.'

Bloody Mummy.

'Who's Jo?'

'He's my brother. Jo short for Jonas. That's like in the Bible.'

'Why does your mummy call you Snow?'

'It's my name. I have lots of names. Penelope Snow Crystal Garoghan. I was born in a snowstorm, Daddy told me. And Mummy says if I grow up to be a model I can call myself Snow Crystal. She says that's a good name for a model.'

'Do you want to be a model?'

'No.' Penny – I couldn't think of her as Snow any more – picked up a biscuit, took a bite, put it down again. 'I want to be an engineer, like Daddy. Jo says girls can't be engineers but he's wrong, isn't he?'

'Of course he is. You can be whatever you like. Does Jo want to be an engineer too?'

'Oh no. He wants to be in the SAS and jump out of an aeroplane with a parachute, but that's just because of some film he saw on TV. He's only nine. You don't want *real* things when you're nine. When I was nine I wanted to be an explorer and go up the Amazon. Now I'm older I know that's silly. An engineer is a *real* job.'

'I think you have to be good at maths,' I said. 'Are you?'

She grimaced. 'Not very.'

'Never mind. Winston Churchill was bad at maths, and he won the Second World War.' A drastic précis of history, but Penny seemed to appreciate it. 'Your daddy's away at the moment, isn't he? You must miss him.'

'Yes.' Her small face was tight and pale.

'Do you know where he is?'

I felt like a traitor, insinuating myself into the confidence of an unsuspecting innocent, wheedling information from her. I told myself her situation was quite different from Mark Prosser's; after all, I was trying to find evidence which would exonerate Richard Garoghan, not incriminate him. But that was incidental. I was a journalist doing my job with customary opportunism. It didn't make me feel wonderful.

Penny had brightened at the question.

'Of course I do. He writes to me – really long letters. He writes to Jo, too, but not so long. And he sends pictures: palm trees and things. He's in Barbados.' She added, helpfully: 'Barbados is an island in the Caribbean. I looked it up in the atlas. Daddy says it's awfully hot and sticky. And there are lizards in his *bedroom*.' She obviously found this unbelievably exotic.

'Do you know the address?'

'No: we have to send the letters to the lawyers.' She brooded for a minute. 'I hate lawyers.'

'Very sensible. Tell me more about Barbados.'

'It sounds very beautiful. It's a coral island: that means it's all made of coral, the rocks and the beaches and everything. I thought coral was pink but Daddy says the beaches are white crumbly sand, like sugar. And there are sharks and humming-birds and frogs as big as bread-and-butter plates.' Penny, it was clear, visualised her father living in a welter of flora and fauna. 'Did you know that's where the Spanish Main used to be?'

'Yes, I think I did. It's not logical, is it? I always thought the Spanish Main should be somewhere near Spain.'

Penny, while agreeing with me, launched into an elaborate explanation, no doubt culled from Daddy, of how the Spanish Main had acquired its tropical location. 'There were lots of pirates,' she said, 'only they called themselves privateers because they were British and fighting the Spaniards so it was all quite legal really. The islands are still full of pirates and smugglers, Daddy says, drug-smugglers mostly, but they aren't romantic any more, just wicked and greedy. I'm never going to take drugs. Daddy says they make you stupid.'

'He's right,' I said. 'The point of drugs is to make you feel life is marvellous when it isn't, so you wander round in a fantasy all the time, and don't try to change anything. That's stupid.'

'Life isn't marvellous,' said Penny abruptly, 'is it?'

She had tucked her feet under her on the sofa and she looked so small and fragile, sitting there with her legs folded up like a grasshopper and her crooked features fixed in an expression of peculiar intensity. Small and fragile. Fragile and strong. I thought of all the things lying ahead of her like great mountains waiting to be climbed, puberty and adolescence and the rugged lifelong process of growing up. She would have to be strong. I am not maternal or sentimental about children, I never gush over dribbling babies or force unwanted kisses on disgusted toddlers, but in that moment I loved her, a fierce irrational movement of emotion that took me painfully unawares.

I said: 'You want your daddy back, don't you?' Stating the obvious.

'Mmm.'

'Well, don't tell Mummy or Jo, but I'm going to find him. I'll try to bring him back to you.' And I added, recklessly, idiotically: 'I promise.'

Never, never make promises. Above all, never make promises to children, who will remember them and feed on them and fall asleep with them night after night for weeks, even months to come. There was no excuse for me. Penny was not battered or starving, she didn't gaze at me out of large soulful eyes. Her unhappiness was nothing exceptional, a mundane unhappiness far less than the sufferings many children have to endure. No excuse.

She stared at me out of slanting alien eyes and I did not know whether she believed me or not.

Crystal returned to find us sitting in silence. 'I hope you've been entertaining Miss Murphy, Snow,' she murmured automatically.

'Yes, thank you,' I said, answering for her.

Penny got up to go, threw me a last, long look, and left the room.

'I'm sorry to keep you,' Crystal said. 'I'm afraid I'm a bit disorganised these days.' She appeared totally organised, even to the negligent spread of her fingertips across a convenient cushion. 'My agent wants me to do a screen test. I don't know if it'll work out. Acting for the camera is very different from modelling.'

'I heard you were going into acting,' I said.

'There's a family precedent,' Crystal explained. 'My mother was an actress: Mona Winter. To tell the truth, she wasn't particularly successful. She had one line in an early film for Ealing: that was her moment of glory. After that, she married my father and gave it up.'

'I'm sure you'll do better.' I meant to be polite; I sounded bored.

'You don't understand.' There was a new edge to Crystal's voice. 'I can't spend the rest of my life just sitting at home like a vegetable all day, dragging round the supermarket looking for reductions, going to dull parties with dull couples. I must do *something*.' It was a familiar protest. I am a liberated woman, not a mere housewife. I want a career. I want to be a wannabee. But there was something behind the clichés, a note of hunger or desperation which was real. 'I envy you,' she declared, to my astonishment. 'You have a job which provides – excitement. Stimulation. I envy you that.'

If it was a ploy to gain sympathy it failed. You chose to go for the storybook ending, I thought. You swapped Vincent for Richard, got married, and lived happily ever after for the next fifteen years. Living happily ever after is very tedious. Crystal was in the classic position of so many women in the richer countries. Economic prosperity was taken for granted; domestic bliss had begun to pall. She wanted Fulfilment. Whatever Fulfilment might be.

'You shouldn't waste time envying me,' I said. 'Journalism isn't very exciting. A lot of dreary leg-work.' I switched off the tape to show the interview was over. 'I hope the screen test goes well.'

'Thank you.'

'Think of it as good practice. We'll be wanting to film you later on, naturally.' I was sure that would please her.

She rose to see me out. 'If there's anything else . . .?'

'Oh – yes. One more thing.' There was a question which had been nagging at the back of my mind since the subject was mentioned, a minor question, possibly irrelevant, which I had forgotten to ask. 'About the mortgage fraud. You said Vincent had a partner.'

'That's right. An American. He debunked to the States with all the money and left Vincent to carry the can. They couldn't charge him, anyway. Vincent was the one on all the documents.'

'This American,' I asked, 'can you remember his name?'

'Yes, of course. It was very appropriate.'

'Oh?'

'Judas Carson,' Crystal said. 'You see. Very appropriate.'

Instinctively, I concealed surprise.

'I see.'

'Judas Carson!' Alun Craig pounced on the name like a wolf spider on a mouse. '*Now* you tell me. Why the hell didn't I hear this before? I know, I know – Savage did time for the fraud so it's history. He's paid for it; let's not hold it against him. Let's be terribly British and play fair with a bastard who's never played fair in his life. We're journalists, not officers and bloody gentlemen. Micky, why didn't you check this before?'

'Because I checked it just now,' I said. 'You've got the information, and you've got it in plenty of time. What do you make of it?'

Alun threw me a regulation glare before subsiding into cogitation. He would take a tangle of data and pull it this way and that like a snarl of coloured wool, plucking out a strand of yellow, then one of green, unravelling indigo from purple, crimson from magenta. 'Judas Carson in England,' he muttered. 'Doing the dirty on Savage. Grabbing the profits and leaving his partner to take the rap. It was probably his idea all along. He was older, experienced, a crook from birth. You bet it was his idea. He used Savage – the novice just out of college and trying out his baby teeth on a prey too big for him. Carson used him and ditched him. And then what? Suddenly they're pals again. Making a packet and sharing it. Partners for life. Out in LA. Carson's become Savage's mentor – yes, his mentor . . . Do they trust each other? Does the hyena trust the jackal? No – they just converge on the same carcase and split the pickings.'

'"I'll go with thee,"' I quoted, '"cheek by jowl."'

Alun, who thought most literature superfluous, ignored me.

'Are you quite sure it's the same man?' Derek Binns suggested brightly. He was the most junior member of our team, brimming with youthful optimism and newly acquired worldly wisdom. According to Alun, he had wet rot behind the ears and was insulated from almost everything by the exceptional thickness of his skull.

'Of course it's the same man,' I said. 'There couldn't be two men with a name like that, even in America. How are you getting on?'

He had been delegated to search the telephone directory for anything to do with pilots, engineering, Barbados, or any combination. I was putting my money on some sort of localised air taxi service.

'Um . . .' Derek looked ineffectual, which, Alun claimed, was what he did best.

'I'll give you a hand,' I said, leaving Alun to pick nits out of his own Gordian knot.

By the end of the week I had located Richard Garoghan, working for a company called Windhover Air Taxis based in Bridgetown. 'I've left a message for him twice,' I told Alun. 'He hasn't phoned back. The third time I called I'm pretty sure he was there but refused to speak to me. We aren't going to get anywhere by phone; the situation's too delicate. This one needs the personal touch.'

'The question is,' Alun ruminated, jabbing at his notepad with a spluttering biro, 'will it be worth it? You haven't got much out of any of the others.'

His unfairness was routine and I disregarded it. 'You want Savage,' I said. 'We need Garoghan. He isn't going to be whistled home; he'll have to be lured.'

And I added decisively, conclusively: 'I'm going to Barbados.'

The week ended in a major row. Despite my determination, Alun, as always, had other ideas. He declared that to pay for two sets of air fares was putting an unnecessary strain on our budget; he could fly back from Los Angeles via the Caribbean and conduct all the interviews himself. I pointed out that he had left it to me to investigate Vincent's personal life, Richard Garoghan was my pigeon and I intended to be the one who put him in the pie. In addition, the saving on air tickets would be minimal – a straightforward return is always cheaper than elaborate round trips – and I wanted to go to Barbados. Alun had a regrettable habit of appropriating all the most glamorous foreign travel, invariably for the best possible reasons. On this occasion, I wasn't going to let him get away with it. What with the heat, the frequent explosions of fury and the bottled-up passions in between, the atmosphere in the office became so thick you could have cut it into cubes and packaged it.

Saturday found me sunbathing in the garden at Grey Gables.

'I wish you would remember your bikini,' my mother complained. 'Supposing Barraclough were to turn up? He's very old; it might affect his heart.'

Barraclough was my mother's decrepit gardener.

'It's Saturday,' I said. 'He doesn't come at weekends.'

'Well . . . Charles might come to tea.'

The vicar.

'If he does,' I said, 'I'll tell him I'm returning to my roots. Eden before the Fall. Only in a state of nature can I expect to rediscover Man's first innocence. Or Woman's, in this case.'

'For heaven's sake, darling, that isn't funny. Charles would probably feel obliged to take you seriously; he's so afraid of being behind the times. There was a programme on Channel Four the other day about the relevance of the Church in modern society, and now, poor sweet, he's worried about being upstaged by the evangelists. Apparently, they make God more marketable. Charles' religion is the stuffy, old-fashioned variety which you couldn't market at a bring-and-buy without a pot of marmalade thrown in.'

'Good for Charles,' I said, feeling inconsistent.

The phone rang inside the house and my mother drifted away to answer it, unhurried, knowing patient friends would wait at least twenty rings for her to pick up the receiver. Cordless phones had not yet invaded Grey Gables. My mother said she would not have a telephone that could follow her around, 'even into the loo, darling: just think of it. One must have *some* privacy.'

Two minutes later she called me in.

'If Charles is coming,' I warned her, 'I'm damned if I'll get dressed.'

'It's for you,' she said reproachfully. 'Phyllida, from America.'

I took the receiver.

'Phyl!'

'Micky, how are you?' The familiar shriek. 'I'm lying beside a pool on Long Island drinking iced tea and it's hell. Honestly, sheer hell. The humidity here is so awful I feel like a dead haddock. All limp and clammy. I can't talk for more than a minute or two; I simply have to get back in the water.'

We proceeded to talk trivia for several minutes. Then: 'Listen: are you still interested in Gorgeous Vincent?'

'Yes . . .'

'How would you like to meet him?'

'What d'you mean, meet him? Unless he's another Van Hoogstraten with a Napoleonic ego and the soul of a lead pencil he's hardly going to chat freely to me. He won't want to take the gloss off his public image. He'll just reach for his lawyer and say "No comment" all the time. And he certainly won't go anywhere near the camera.'

'No, no – you don't understand. I meant an informal meeting. Sort of – undercover.' Her voice dropped half an octave and I pictured her dipping her sunglasses.

'Phyl—'

'*Listen*. I'm going down to the island next week with Pooh. The Ashleys have a place there and it's the Langelaans' party. And it suddenly struck me: Vincent will be there.'

'At the house? On the island? Which island? The oceans are full of them.'

'At the party. I wish you would pay attention, Micky; I'm trying to help you. Vincent and Pete Langelaan are business associates of some kind; they're both in real estate only Pete's east coast and Vincent's west. Anyway, the Langelaans always have a party on the island at this time of year – don't ask me why – and Vincent always goes. Let's face it, anyone goes who can get an invitation. Pete's a schmuck and I loathe Deirdre but the party will be fabulous. You can come and stay with me at the Ashleys' and Pooh and I will take you. Undercover. You see? Isn't it a brilliant plan? You needn't say you're a journalist; you needn't say anything. You'll just be an old friend of mine. You can do a Mata Hari act with Vincent: he'll tell you all his secrets over a glass of champagne among the hibiscus bushes.'

'I doubt it.'

'*And*' – this was obviously the clincher – 'you get to see *me*. It'll be wonderful: we haven't seen each other for ages. We can talk and talk and talk. Well? What do you say?'

'Phyl, I'd love to, but . . .'

'But what?'

'Who are the Langelaans to start with? And *which island*?'

'Dominique,' said Phyl, answering the second question first. 'It's one of the Grenadines: the smallest, I think. Not the Dominican Republic: that's somewhere quite different. The sea captain who discovered Dominique named it after his mistress, or so they say. It's frightfully expensive and there are no hotels or tourists *at all*, just private houses and luxury yachts and villages for the natives. Everyone's rich, even the natives, because they get paid the earth to look after the houses and yachts while the owners are away.'

'Paradise for the privileged,' I said. 'Like Mustique only more so. I've heard of it. What about the Langelaans? I infer they are among the super-privileged. Do they have a yacht, a house, or both?'

'Both,' said Phyl instantly. 'Several. You should have heard of them, too. They're old, *old* money. A Langelaan once bought half New York State off the Indians for a string of wampum and a packet of tulip bulbs. They've been doing business that way ever since. Pete's incredibly mean but Deirdre fancies herself as a society hostess so he has to fork out every so often. He consoles himself by boasting about how much he paid for the Krug and the caviare; you can hear him counting every cent. My manicurist knows a waiter at Raoul's and they say he's a lousy tipper.'

'I don't object to people being rich,' I remarked, 'I only object if they're mean.'

'I'm rich, but—'

'You're not mean.'

'Of course not. Anyhow, I'm not as rich as the Langelaans,' Phyl concluded with an air of virtue.

'Won't they mind if you turn up with an unknown friend?'

'They wouldn't mind if I brought half a dozen. Deirdre thinks I'm a social asset. I married all the right people.'

'Which reminds me—'

'Farzad will be in Hong Kong,' Phyl explained with immediate comprehension. 'That's why I thought of this. He would never have agreed to it. I love him madly but he really is *very* trying about you. Still, he's not going to run my life – or spoil my friendships. Darling, you will come, won't you?'

'It depends,' I said.

'On what?' Phyl was impatient of quibbles.

'If the Grenadines are near enough to Barbados,' I said, 'I'll know the Devil is on my side. Then I'll come.'

I hung up and, like Penny Garoghan before me, consulted the atlas. The Caribbean was bordered with a scattering of island specks, some of them so tiny they were scarcely green. I found Barbados easily enough, but Dominique was apparently too small, or too exclusive, to get a mention. Perhaps the combined influence of its millionaire inhabitants had gained for it a species of cartographical ex-directory listing. However, the other members of the group were there: Grenada, Bequia, Mustique, Carriacou, Canouan. Magical romantic names conjuring visions of tasselled palm trees, spotless white beaches, an emerald sea shading to deeps of sapphire. I took a minute to picture myself wandering along such beach in my favourite bikini, an affair of minuscule triangles whose original colour had long since bleached to a sort of papyrus. The Grenadines, I decided, were definitely near enough to Barbados.

'What on earth are you doing?' asked my mother.

'Going to the Caribbean,' I said, 'to meet a man.'

'Darling!'

'It's work, Mummy, only work. *Quest* – although Alun doesn't know it yet – are going to be sending me to the tropics after all.'

'But I thought you said your producer wouldn't pay your fare?'

'He will now. I'm going to a party. Even Alun Craig can hardly tart himself up in high heels and lipstick to attend a society binge. It'll probably be a wasted effort, but we can't afford to let the chance go by. Anyway, I'm going to make damned sure that's how Alun sees it.'

'You're going to the party to meet the man,' said my mother, in exactly the same tone in which she might have quoted: *She swallowed the spider to catch the fly.*

'That's it.'

'What sort of man? Not another crook?'

'Another crook. A crook of the *beau monde* wallowing in ill-gotten wealth. Dark, brooding good looks masking dark, brooding personality. He makes his money throwing sweet old ladies out of their homes and putting up tower blocks full of yuppie executives in their place.'

'Oh dear,' said my mother. 'Why can't you have a job where you get to meet *nice* people?'

'There aren't any nice people,' I said idly, my mind elsewhere. 'Only a handful of slightly less nasty ones.'

I arrived at the office on Monday to find Alun in a meeting with the legal department.

'Someone's going to sue,' said Jeff. 'Isn't it exciting?' He looked about as excited as a bowl of cold rice pudding.

'If Alun isn't careful,' I retorted, 'it might just be me.'

'I can't think why you want to go to the Caribbean. It's too bloody hot here.'

'That's just it. I want to cool off. On a beach, in a bikini, with waves swishing across the sand towards me.' I sat down in Alun's chair, preparing for battle, just as Fizzy placed a stack of mail on his desk. Alun's personal mail was sacred and she looked faintly shocked when I leafed through it, even though I would never have dreamed of opening anything.

'No summonses yet,' I remarked. 'What's this?'

'This' was a brown envelope – not the shade of pale diarrhoea favoured (appropriately enough) by government departments but a delicate café-au-lait, the paper thick and luxurious, the address printed in italicised lettering, mocha to co-ordinate with the coffee. Alun's correspondent clearly had not only rather foppish tastes but a word processor programmed to indulge them. Mildly intrigued, I was still staring at the letter when Alun came back.

He snatched it away immediately. At the time, I thought nothing of it. The inviolability of his personal post was one of many objectives for his paranoia.

'Get out of my chair, Micky,' he snapped.

'Send me to Barbados,' I said, 'and I might.'

I told him about the party. Jeff weighed in with judicious

moral support; Derek opened his mouth and then shut it again at a glare from me, and Fizzy lubricated the situation with coffee. Alun gave way by inches, as though he feared he was setting a precedent. Having made my point, I didn't push too hard: it wasn't necessary. There was only a slim chance that anything useful would come of the party but Alun had always fancied slim chances, long odds, dark horses. I knew he would be unable to pass this one by.

'Run a tape,' Alun said, 'all the time. Perhaps you should have a wire?'

'Not feasible. I'll be in an evening dress with too many gaps.'

'Can you manage a camera?'

'Don't be ridiculous. A tape will do it. Leave it to me.'

'I know this is going to be a waste of money,' Alun said, gazing antagonistically at his doodle pad.

'Maybe.'

'You'd better make the most of it, Micky. This is not the moment for maidenly scruples. Whatever you have to do, make bloody sure you do it.'

'Whatever you have to do, Micky,' Jeff echoed with a grin.

'Bastard,' I said to Alun.

I said it without rancour.

PART II

ACHILLES AND PATROCLUS

1

Vincent Scarpia Savage was born at the family home on the morning of 12 November 1950. Jolanda had wanted to retire to a private clinic in a welter of flowers and good wishes, but John Savage wanted his son – he was convinced it would be a son – to come into the world at Weatherfray, the place where he would grow up and which he would eventually inherit, just as his father, grandfather, and an assortment of other ancestors had been born and grown up there. John promised his wife he would import doctors, nurses, and additional minions to provide all the cosseting she could wish for, and at length she gave in. They were very much in love; giving in still had its charms for her. Afterwards, she would describe the scene as if it were part of an opera, with the prospective father striding up and down in the wings uttering staccato commands to which no one paid any attention, and herself at centre stage, supported by two doctors, tenor and baritone, and a chorus of nurses, midwives, and other extras. The child was born at sunrise, whereupon she launched into a triumphant aria: '*All'alba vincerò*'. Rumour had it this was why she chose the name Vincent. Jolanda told this story so often it passed into legend and more mundane details were duly forgotten by all concerned.

The baby was a standard specimen, neither too big nor too small, totally bald, and bawling loudly enough to drown out a dozen arias. His eyes were scrunched into cracks above round hard cheeks and the round hole of his mouth, from which emanated a volume of noise out of all proportion to his diminutive vocal cords. He was red as a tomato with fury at being wrenched from the comfort of the uterus into this vast alien world, where air was thumped forcibly into his lungs and goggling entities leered over him making ridiculous cooing sounds. All the lovely squishy mucus was washed away and he was left unnaturally bare and clean, swaddled in a shawl so he could no longer kick out at his tormentors, and served up to his parents like the main dish at a banquet. A large paternal digit descended into his palm and he wrapped his tiny fingers around it with boneless strength. John Savage, his normal stoicism already weakened by the emotional impact of fatherhood, felt his heart squeezed in that infantine grip.

'A strong, healthy voice,' said the older and fatter of the two doctors – the baritone, in Jolanda's version. 'He takes after his mother. The genes of an opera star.'

'Nonsense,' John snorted. Torn between elation and the desire to preserve his stolidity, he alternately glowed and glowered, but the other persons present were too preoccupied with the baby to notice.

Peace supervened only when Jolanda, determined to breastfeed, applied the new son and heir to an exposed bosom. This was long before her famous diet, and the breast in question was a large, creamy gold affair, with a dusky nipple as big as a plum. Once Vincent had grasped the basic principle he tucked in, to the accompaniment of vigorous sucking noises. Jolanda crooned, the doctors beamed, the chorus chirped and twittered. The redundant father, still embarrassed by his own sentiment, retreated into the next room and poured himself a large whisky.

In those early days Vincent was immediately and obviously Jolanda's child. He had a voice that could wake the whole house even when the nursery was moved to the top of the West Tower; his skin, when not flushed with rage, gluttony or indigestion, acquired a warm golden hue; and the first feathers of hair to sprout from his bald pate were as black as jet. He romped all over his mother's opulent body as if it was a mound of cushions, while John, feeling it behoved him to assert masculine authority, would bark orders that were never obeyed and then lapse into play, relegating discipline to a more sober future. It delighted him to see Jolanda's character so clearly reprinted in her infant son: from the start Vincent was candid, greedy and audacious, going on long crawls of exploration, climbing those objects that stood in his way, cramming into his mouth anything that might be edible. On one occasion he demonstrated his initiative by pulling down the fold-up steps on the kitchen stool, scrambling laboriously on to the draining board, and throwing an entire set of Spode dinner plates on to the flagged stone floor, which did them no good at all. John later wondered why he should feel a twinge of secret pride at this idiotic and destructive exploit.

Yet it was because of Vincent that he started to find fault with his marriage. He loved Jolanda for those very qualities which he felt he ought to deplore: she was unrestrained, un-English, earth-child, peasant girl, overreacting to the fall of a rose petal yet indifferent to major cataclysm, tumbling from light mood to dark with no consideration for her own dignity or the comfort of those around her. He had always seen her as essentially immature, adorably irresponsible, in need of masculine guidance and protection. With Vincent, she possessed not simply a baby but a playmate, an ally in her every mood, a fellow conspirator with whom to disrupt the household. He graduated from crawling to toddling, his blue eyes deepened to green, his black hair grew into a thick swatch which his mother would allow nobody to cut. Jolanda petted him, played with him, spoiled him, pandered to every childish whim. A nanny who dared to smack him was dismissed on the spot; another, attempting to impose a daily routine, left on the verge of a breakdown. Jolanda would descend impulsively on the nursery and snatch her son from breakfast or supper or afternoon nap, spiriting him away for games of their own. Once she even plucked him out of the bath and carried him downstairs, naked and dripping, to enliven a dull cocktail party. She took him on expeditions to London, shopping in Harrods and lunching with producers, while the prospect of her return to the stage was discussed at length and in detail. 'Vincente must always be in the theatre when I am singing,' she declared. 'He will have a box entirely to himself. He is my inspiration.' Star-hardened producers blenched and back in Northumberland John, scenting problems from afar, felt his sense of duty catching up with him.

'When you married me you promised you would give up your career,' he reminded his wife. 'You said that was what you wanted.' And, rather more sharply: 'My son was not born in a trunk.'

Sometimes he suspected her of acting not merely on impulse but in mischief, deliberately undermining their domestic régime.

Each new nanny was an enemy, and mother and child would plot her downfall together. John lectured Jolanda, and she was instantly contrite, demolishing his severe façade by melting into tears. At other times her molten eyes would flash with maternal ire as she accused her husband of trying to destroy her son's natural affections, transforming him from a warm and loving Italian *bambino* into a cold, repressed English boy with perfect manners and no heart. As for Vincent, John spanked him, with more resolution than vigour, whereupon the child, humiliated and furious, would scream for as much as an hour afterwards with all the force of his operatic lungs. By the end of 1953, when Elizabeth Savage returned to Ridpath with her own very different son, the marriage which the newspapers had originally labelled a romantic idyll had become more like a scrum.

The two children were expected to play together as a matter of course. From the adult point of view they were cousins, the same sex, nearly the same age and size, therefore they would automatically be friends. Neither Vincent nor Richard saw things quite this way. They were both unused to the company of their contemporaries: Vincent, six months older and on his own territory, was jealous of his seniority, possessive of toys he rarely touched, instinctively aggressive and potentially bossy; Richard, normally sunny-tempered, was slightly daunted by the strange environment and the hostility of his new cousin. They circled one another warily, miniature gladiators abandoned by those who claimed to love them in the deadly arena of the nursery. Then Richard, growing bored of the suspense, made a grab for a toy car. Vincent snatched it away; Richard promptly headed for another. Small blows were exchanged, unnoticed by the nanny, who was tidying a cupboard at the far end of the room. Richard had never been in a fight in his life but he retaliated without hesitation; Vincent, who had done a good deal of punching, had never been punched in return. Paternal spankings were not in the same category. He opened his mouth to yell, since spineless adults were easily afflicted by excessive decibels, and then, seeing Richard, shut it hard. His rival had not yelled. They glared at each other for a minute or two and then pounced. The horrified nanny tried in vain to pluck them apart, agitated mothers surged up the stairs, recriminations flowed thick and fast.

'Richard is a good, well-behaved boy. He has *never* struck another child!'

'Vincente! *Poverino!* Did this wicked *cattivaccio* hurt you?'

John, arriving last, was dismissive. 'Boys always fight,' he said. 'It's healthy. Let them get on with it.'

But the mothers, clutching their respective offspring to throbbing bosoms, were not inclined to take the risk. Elizabeth staged a dignified retreat. Vincent, forcibly separated from his late opponent and left in possession of the field, was conscious not of triumph but of disappointment. It occurred to him suddenly that Richard was much more entertaining than any of his toys. This was the moment to yell, and he yelled, loudly and imperiously, stopping the various parents in their tracks. Then he wriggled from Jolanda's slackened grasp and ran towards Elizabeth. 'Want him back,' he stated. 'Play with me. *Giochiamo. Giochiamo.*' It was a favourite suggestion of his mother's.

Elizabeth looked unconvinced.

'I told you,' John said with satisfaction. 'Let them get on with it.'

Reluctantly, Elizabeth deposited Richard on the floor. Vincent took his wrist and tugged him away from all these tiresome adults to a corner where they could sort out the pecking order by themselves. 'Don't let them do each other any real damage,' John told the nanny. 'Otherwise leave them alone.'

Although all three parents had encouraged the ensuing intimacy, only John viewed it with unqualified approval. Elizabeth tried hard to be pleased about it but claimed, with some justification, that Vincent led his cousin into mischief; Jolanda inevitably countered by putting all the blame on Richard. In fact, though Vincent was initially the leading spirit, Richard was not slow to follow him; Weatherfray, with its jungle of carved oak and stags' heads, its magical pictures, numberless hiding places and breakable ornaments, offered far greater possibilities for adventure than the terraced house in Newcastle which he had left. And outside there was the garden, where the boys could get green stains on their clothes and catch worms, beetles, and each other's germs. Elizabeth rented accommodation in the village but Richard spent most of the day in the charge of Vincent's nanny, leaving his mother free to sew cushions and curtains, which she did very badly, in order to supplement the allowance she received from her brother. 'I refuse to be totally dependent on John,' she said with valiant pride, and kindly county neighbours sent her their needlework, passing it to their housekeepers afterwards to be done all over again.

'She is silly,' Jolanda commented in a fit of petulance. 'Your family are supposed to support you; that is what families are for. She just likes making a martyr of herself.' In general, however, the two women endeavoured to co-exist in reasonable amity. Elizabeth hid her serious-minded disapprobation, Jolanda her light-hearted contempt, and both kept a watchful eye on their sons.

At that time, Jolanda was more suspicious of Elizabeth than her child. 'He's an ugly little boy,' she asserted, often when Richard was within earshot, 'but he has a sweet smile.' Richard was not actually ugly, but set against Vincent's beauty he appeared rather ordinary, the urchin beside the princeling, his squab nose and small blunt features betraying proletarian ancestry. His eyebrows would crinkle together in concentration and then go winging upwards in a swift change of expression, his eyes suddenly round and sparkling with childish devilry, the smile which even Jolanda found winning transforming his face. It was a smile which would stand him in good stead for the rest of his life.

The cutting of their children's hair being a sensitive issue with mothers, Elizabeth, like Jolanda, was obsessive about it, though with very different results. She performed the task herself, presumably as a labour of love, but as she had no more talent for cutting hair than setting stitches, Richard was left with an uneven crop and a fringe that was always longer over one eye than the other. Jolanda, noticing the discrepancy one afternoon, took a pair of scissors and trimmed it into line herself, a careless gesture which almost led to a showdown. But although, in any confrontation, Jolanda's bosom could effortlessly out-heave that of her sister-in-law, on this occasion she gave ground. She had acquired a certain respect for Elizabeth's obstinacy, and, as one mother to another, she recognised that she had transgressed an unwritten law. Graceful apologies were offered and accepted, and in a few weeks Richard's fringe had returned to its former lop-sided state.

But Jolanda's tolerance of the mother and warmth towards the son could not endure. Possibly she missed the emotional dramatics of *Tosca* and *Aida*, roles which had provided a natural outlet for her turbulence. Whatever the cause, she felt an increasing need to invest her everyday life not only with the laughter of her lighter humours but also with the storms and jealousies of her darker ones. The dreadful pressure of a normal routine and a happy marriage was becoming too much for her: she had to break out. John made the mistake of indicating, once too often, that she had every reason to be content; Jolanda, to whom the idea of contentment was anathema, screamed in the blackness of her frustration and smashed more expensive china than her son had ever accounted for. Vincent, taking his tone from her, was becoming more and more unmanageable. And when John, in an attempt to encourage some sort of discipline, cited Richard as an example of infant good manners, Jolanda had found a grievance. It was she who first accused John of preferring his nephew, an accusation to which she would revert whenever rational argument outmanoeuvred her. Jolanda had no inclination for rational argument. She had decided to enact the beleaguered lioness protecting her cub, and she became so entangled in her own fantasies that she began to believe every chance-spoken word. In the theatre, it made her an outstanding performer; in the home, a disastrous parent. Elizabeth, an unflinching witness to too many major scenes, kept silent. Privately, she could not credit that a sensible and intelligent man like her brother could fail to have a sneaking preference for Richard. At that stage, she did not dislike Vincent; she merely thought him spoiled to the point of ruination. John, driven behind an undemonstrative façade by his wife's histrionics, never thought to mention that he loved his son. And Vincent absorbed the myth which Jolanda had initiated so that years later, when adult son opposed ageing father, the niggling doubt would always remain.

Jolanda met Frank Cavalcanti at a Christmas party in London in 1954. The following spring she left home, husband and son for good. The Italian-American impresario whose aim was to turn grand opera into classic film had already had a *succès d'estime* with *Così Fan Tutte* and *The Magic Flute*; now, he wanted to try his hand at tragedy. He needed a prima donna of exceptional talent, someone with not only a voice but acting ability, glamour, screen presence. In Jolanda he saw the raw material that he required. Her tantrums would be refined into temperament, her voluptuous good looks whittled down to the acceptable norm of beauty. The camera made much of her huge midnight green eyes, the cheekbones to rival Loren, the arrogant bow of her mouth. Cavalcanti told her she was trammelled by the bonds of matrimony: she must follow her star regardless of bourgeois morality and conventional love. Although the sixties had not yet arrived he spoke lyrically of the artist's obligation to reject and be rejected by society, to pursue his (or her) art in a state of absolute freedom, unconstrained by custom or principle. Jolanda, only half understanding, drank it all in like a witch's brew and was immediately spellbound. Cavalcanti became not simply her producer but her guru, her Svengali, inevitably, her lover. Determined to wean her from any distractions he transported her to Beverly Hills, where she could reject society in style. He gave her a chihuahua and a team of expensive lawyers, the one to pre-occupy her affections, the other to convince her, after prolonged legal machinations, that she would be unable to win custody of her son. She wrote Vincent letters which John would not allow him to receive, not chatty accounts of her day-to-day activities but love letters full of naked longing and passionate endearments which shocked John to his English core. 'Vincente, *carissimo*, I miss you so terribly. Soon we will be together, I promise – these wicked *avvocati* with all their talk of influences and injunctions, they cannot keep us apart. Your father would never be so cruel, so *sadico*, as to take you from me forever. It is nine months – no, ten – since I saw you and you must have grown so much. I try to picture you, my darling, darling boy, to imagine holding you in my arms. The other night I dreamed that *stupida* Elizabeth had cut off all your beautiful hair and I woke up crying and crying. Franco could not understand what was the matter . . .'

But Franco understood only too well. The chihuahua having proved a failure, he saw to it that a punishing work schedule and the Hollywood social whirl gave her little leisure for dreams. Unable to stick to a diet she finally resorted to swallowing a tape-worm, which consumed her body from within just as her own precarious ego consumed the life-force that drove her. She became improbably slim, a creature both defenceless and dangerous, with enormous eyes that could transmit every emotion in the book and a voice that shook the world. On screen, she glittered like a shoot-ing star, her course set to self-destruct. Cinemagoers who had never heard of Puccini fell in love with her, newspapers designated her angel or monster according to editorial idiosyncrasy. She returned to Italy to make her début at La Scala, and spent the preceding night sleepless and violently sick. In the morning she went to the Duomo, and knelt in the shadows of the eternal arches to pray to a God with whom she had so often lost touch. That evening when the pro-Callas claque began throwing rotten tomatoes Jolanda reached inside a conveniently situated receptacle and began throwing tomatoes back at them. The audience of hypercritical connoisseurs took her instantly to their collective heart. The show proceeded in triumph and Jolanda emerged immortal. Frank Cavalcanti had cause to feel satisfied with his creation before he discarded it.

Before she left Weatherfray there had been a degree of rapprochement with the latest nanny. Her official title was Nanny Dixon but the boys called her Dixy and in the end so did everyone else. She stayed. She was young and plain and unsure of herself, the kind of person who communicates better with children than with adults. Nobody had warned her that her new mistress was a dragon in human form and Jolanda, torn between elopement and stability, was too distracted to terrorise or scheme against her. The untutored Dixy admired her exotic loveliness and was bewitched by absent-minded flashes of warmth. The night she went, Jolanda came to the nursery. If she had ever showered the new nanny with injustice and vituperation it would have been forgotten in the urgency of the moment; fortunately, she hadn't.

'I am going away,' she confided. 'It is a great secret: you must not tell anyone. I cannot even say goodbye to Vincente. That is why I have to trust you. When I am gone, you will explain to him. You will say that I love him and I will come for him. I do not know when, but very soon. I have to go because it is my art that calls and I cannot sing trapped here like a bird in a cage. I must get out, I must sing again, but I love him more than anything in the world – tell him that – and we will be together very shortly. *Fra poco*, tell him. I am depending on you, you understand. *Mia cognata* Elizabeth, she has made a martyr of herself and now she will try to make a martyr of my poor John. She will be very moral and very boring and she will tell him I am a wicked woman and maybe they will both tell Vincente also. But you will tell him the truth. You will explain that I love him and I will come for him soon. You must not fail me. Do you understand? You must not fail me!'

The hapless Dixy, confronted by such a desperate plea – and such a disastrous responsibility – was both horrified and distressed. How could she not respond to Jolanda's entreaty – particularly when her skinny arm was clutched in Jolanda's fevered grip and the bosom in front of her was heaving like an earthquake? Yet she owed a loyalty to John Savage as well.

'I – I'll try,' she stammered, knowing it sounded inadequate.

Jolanda knew it too. 'To try is not enough,' she insisted. 'I am trusting you. For my sake – for Vincente – you *cannot* betray my confidence. You will swear to me – yes, on the Bible – swear to me that you will take care of my son, that you will tell him every day how I love him, that you won't let them turn him against me. Swear it!'

The nursery was provided with a Bible, an abridged version considered suitable for children but still a Bible. Dixy, a Methodist, took her religion seriously. But the book was thrust between her resisting hands and the tidal wave of Jolanda's agitation swept her away. She found herself repeating the meaningless oath in a shaken whisper. Beyond the windows evening was drawing in; a single lamp threw a light which did not reach the corners of the room. Jolanda's air of tragedy and the climate of impending crisis was unlike anything she had encountered in the whole of her sheltered life. She felt as if she had been suddenly deposited in the middle of a play where she was unfamiliar with the plot and the lines allotted to her were not what she would have said at all.

The next day Jolanda was gone. It should not have been a complete surprise but nonetheless John was unprepared for such emotional devastation. He locked himself in his study for twelve hours with the scribbled note which was all the explanation she had left for him and his own thoughts, reappearing around dinner time with an expression of unshakable self-control and no appetite. Elizabeth took his hand, a rare gesture for her, and they sat in silence while cold chicken came in, grew a little colder, and went out again and John's obligatory glass of wine stood inviolate beside his plate. Jolanda, at meal times, would eat and talk at once, remembering her table manners for half a minute and then forgetting them again, picking up the bones in her fingers in the continental fashion. If she was depressed or unhappy she would eat nothing, and John would have to coax her back into a frame of mind where she would accept sustenance after all. But now her chair was empty and the traditional equilibrium of the dinner hour undisturbed. Elizabeth thought of saying 'I know how you feel', 'It will pass', and other banal consolations, but she didn't. She loved her brother very much.

In the morning John issued his edict to the household. As far as possible, Jolanda was never to be mentioned, particularly in front of the children. She had gone, of her own free will, leaving the husband she had vowed before God to love and honour and the son it was her duty to cherish. Instead, she had preferred the artificial glitter of the theatre (John had not heard about Cavalcanti's films) and the charms of a lewd foreign roué. John could not expunge her from his memory, nor, perhaps, from his heart, but he could see to it that her contaminating influence was not permitted to interfere any more with the upbringing of his heir. In the years to come he would feel a pang of cold horror at the recollection that it had once enchanted him to see Jolanda's qualities recurring in her child. Her openness, her rashness, her greedy appetite for life – all these apparently harmless traits metamorphosed into fatal weaknesses which, if not suppressed, would lead inevitably to some unspecified catastrophe. Even when Jolanda's treacherous ghost was no longer visible behind the stony façade of her adult son John would be watching for her, for the flicker of her expression, the echo of her voice.

In the house her personality was too vivid to be easily erased and for a long time the sombre atmosphere of Weatherfray seemed to retain the aftertaste of her presence, like lemon zest in a heavy cake. For Dixy, torn between the terrible oath and her obligation to her employer, Jolanda haunted every empty room, every unforgiving minute. Her reproachful eyes stared out of the darkness when Dixy lay down to sleep, sometimes a wronged Fury, sometimes a weeping, desperate creature whose voice reached into her dreams. 'Tell Vincente I love him – I will come for him soon – tell Vincente – soon, soon . . .' The words faded into hopelessness and there was only her God, the authority who had witnessed her promise, standing in the background like a solicitor waving the children's Bible on which she had been forced to swear. There were moments when it appeared to poor Dixy that she had placed not merely her hand but her signature in blood on the ominous Book.

Eventually she went to see John. After she had handed in her resignation, burst into tears, and protested repeatedly how happy she was at Weatherfray and how fond of the two boys, he managed to draw the whole story out of her. Taking upon himself the role of God – a role in which, from Dixy's viewpoint, he was to continue more or less permanently – he absolved her of her oath, cleared her conscience for her and disposed summarily of any lingering qualms. Jolanda had taken advantage of her, she had sworn under duress, she was never to think of the matter again. As for her resignation, that was out of the question. Elizabeth and Richard would be moving in shortly but his sister could not possibly cope alone. Although Dixy had only been with them a few weeks the children were already much attached to her, and they needed her, they *all* needed her, now more than ever. There was to be no more talk of leaving; she must dry her eyes and go and speak to Cook about supper for the boys. Cook was in a bad mood so she would have to be tactful.

Having got through confession and absolution in the style of a Catholic rather than a Methodist, Dixy went off happily with her penance. Jolanda's reproaches might break her sleep occasionally even long afterwards, but she was content to trust in John. Once or twice Jolanda wrote her hysterical letters, accusing her of treachery in one sentence, beseeching her help in the next, which John, recognising his wife's handwriting, was able to intercept. The issue of the unfulfilled oath put the seal on his determination that she should not be allowed access to her son: he thought she had behaved disgracefully, making Dixy an innocent victim in her own mismanaged affairs. His lawyers found her letters very useful in demonstrating her instability and the importance of separating her completely from an impressionable child. As for Jolanda, when she was an old woman she would still cite the oath, and call down hellfire on Dixy's soul for her dereliction of trust.

Dixy stayed until the boys went to Gordonstoun at thirteen years old. Her gentle affection for Vincent partially supplanted the dimming memory of his mother, at least in his conscious mind. But a couple of months before she left he overheard his father and aunt discussing Dixy – they were writing references for her future employment – and the subject of the oath came up. John praised

Dixy for her conscientious attitude; Elizabeth was more interested in apportioning blame to Jolanda. Neither of them noticed Vincent, shrunken into the shadows with which Weatherfray abounded. He listened in silence, and in silence went away. He had not understood all the ramifications of the situation, but he knew Dixy had made a promise to his mother, a very solemn and serious promise which she had not kept. The mote of warmth which she had reanimated inside him went suddenly cold.

2

Vincent was four and a half when his mother went away. Still malleable, his father declared optimistically; too young, surely, to retain any clear recollection of her. Long afterwards, Vincent would claim that although he could not remember her face as a composite picture he could remember details: a smile that lit up the room; a rainstorm of tears; the many notes of her laughter, from a contralto chuckle to a soprano shriek; the smell of her perfume, something pungent and spicy with traces of sandalwood and ambergris. When, as a grown man, he went to see her at last, the first thing he failed to recognise was the perfume she wore. Above all, he recalled the sensation of her presence, diffusing a glow compounded of vitality and personality, affection and charm. Once that glow had vanished it could not be replaced. John, grown sterner overnight, no longer played with his son and had never been prone to glow. Elizabeth was authoritative, scrupulously fair, sometimes kindly but not a radiant figure, and Dixy's little light was too soft to penetrate the shadow on his spirit. When he understood that Jolanda had really gone he did not scream any more. For several days he scarcely ate and would not speak at all, rising in the night to pad from room to room on bare feet, staring dry-eyed at the places where she should have been. The local doctor made appropriate medical noises and Elizabeth strove repeatedly to reassure her brother: 'It's not your fault. There's nothing you can do. Give him time.' Richard, too young for comprehension, operated on instinct. He would follow his cousin on his fruitless search, always a little behind him, plucking at his sleeve when Vincent seemed inexplicably remote. He punched and kicked him into friendly tussles, stole his favourite toys to nudge him into possessive wrath. His antics had a quality of stubbornness, a spoiled child's refusal to accept dismissal or be lightly thrust aside. But Richard was not spoiled. It was his persistence which gradually brought Vincent back to reality, and in the years that followed it was Richard alone whom he would love and trust without reservation.

John found it difficult to be sure how much his mother's absence affected Vincent and how much was due to the natural changes of growing up. His tantrums disappeared with infancy; he could still become angry, often violent, but his temper acquired an edge which had little to do with self-indulgence. Faced with Elizabeth's disapproval and John's incipient paranoia, he learned quickly to clench his jaw and say nothing. In the past, like Jolanda, he had given way to every emotion; now, emotion was put under wraps, bottled up, repressed out of existence. The discipline began at home; public school reinforced the process. His thoughts and his words were kept separate: thoughts were secret, mutinous impulses which he could not control and would not share. No one knew if he thought about Jolanda.

At school, he found a physical outlet in sport. Gordonstoun proved an ideal environment, offering a wide range of invigorating activities. While beating up another boy in the classroom on some slender excuse did not go down well at all Vincent discovered that on the rugger pitch he could beat up his compeers on no excuse whatsoever, and provided he emerged with the ball at the end of it everyone would be pleased with him. He had no team spirit so they made him captain, and as long as his team-mates did as they were told they usually won. He liked winning because that was the object of the game; he did not believe in sportsmanship. But if he felt any victory euphoria that, like everything else, was concealed behind a cultivated taciturnity. On one occasion when his father was among the spectators he went so far as to run to him after the match with a gleam that might have been triumph in his eyes. John, however, felt obliged to comment on Vincent's tactics, which, he said, savoured more of a gang-fight in the slums than a sport for gentlemen. The gleam vanished, and Vincent went off with Richard without a word. 'Uncle John didn't mean it,' his cousin said easily. 'He doesn't like to praise one, that's all. You know what that generation are like.' He deepened his voice and uttered in Blimpish accents: 'These young people, they aren't what we were when we were boys. They simply don't know how to Play the Game.'

Richard's light-hearted mockery didn't even raise a smile. 'I don't give a shit about playing the game,' Vincent said.

John, meanwhile, was talking to Piers Percival, who had accompanied him for a rare glimpse of his godson. 'Maybe I was too hard on the boy,' he admitted. 'But I won't have him turning into a species of hooligan. The whole point of sport in schools is to teach the principles of honourable competition – to encourage a sense of fellowship and *esprit de corps*. Vincent seems to have no concept of anything beyond putting the entire opposition in intensive care. The games master ought to insist on more self-restraint. I'm always afraid . . .'

'You're afraid Vincent takes after his mother.' Piers set out the unspoken sentence with a sort of elegant deliberation. 'That may not be the problem, you know. The trouble is he takes after you both. There are certain chemicals – I cannot immediately recall which – that are relatively innocuous by themselves, but when mixed together they combine to form a high explosive.' He added, with apparent irrelevance: 'You're a bloody fool, John. You always were. I should never have introduced you to Jolanda.'

'I was a fool about her, certainly. Perhaps if I'd been firmer . . . Anyway, I don't intend to make the same mistakes with my son.'

'So you'll make different ones,' Piers retorted with the licence of an old friend.

John ignored this. 'He's a human being, not a chemical concoction.'

'Every human being is a chemical concoction,' Piers pointed out. 'That is a precise statement of fact.'

There was a pause while John refrained from further comment and Piers contemplated it.

'He's a beautiful boy,' he remarked at last.

'I suppose so.'

'Richard is not handsome, but they look well together. Achilles and Patroclus. They seem very intimate. Brought up in the same house, sent to the same school – I daresay it was inevitable.'

Involuntarily, John changed colour. 'My God, you don't think . . .?'

Piers took pity on him. 'No I don't,' he said with the authority of experience.

'If I believed for one moment—'

'I said *no*,' Piers reiterated decisively. 'They'll fall out fast enough when the right woman comes along. Or the wrong one. Get back to finishing your sentences, there's a good chap. I'm growing tired of conversing in hiccups.'

Overlooking this sally, John resumed in more temperate tones: 'I've always been very glad the boys get on so well. Vincent doesn't have many close friends – if any. I like to think Richard's a good influence.'

'Richard,' said Piers in his most finicking manner, 'is what they call a nice lad. No doubt he will get nicer. He has the sense of fellowship and *esprit de corps* which you so much admire. I understand he is academically competent but does not waste his time on the arts. He has been caught mimicking his masters and indulging in – er – schoolboy pranks. I am sure he is popular with the boys and will later on be popular with the girls. I fear he is not my type. I mean that in the purely spiritual sense, of course. I can't imagine we will ever have much to say to one another.'

'He's your godson,' John reminded him.

'That's why I'm here. It's a responsibility I assumed to please you – and to please your sister. I have always had a weakness for Elizabeth. She should have been the Queen. She has a sense of duty far in excess of the duties she has to bear. As a girl that gave her a certain rather endearing pathos. However, my affection for you both doesn't inspire me to be sentimental about young Richard. As for Vincent, if you want my opinion—'

'I don't,' John interjected.

'You can have it, anyway. Vincent, in my view, is far too well controlled for someone so obviously volatile – too silent when he should be bellowing with rage, too solitary and aloof even in the company of his Patroclus. He is going to give you – and a great many other people – endless trouble. He'll sulk in his tent one minute and slaughter a decent chap like Hector the next. And Richard's undeniably good influence will wash off him like water off the proverbial duck's back.'

'Tell me there's nothing I can do,' said John.

Piers obliged promptly. 'There's nothing you can do.'

But Vincent was not sulking in his tent just yet. At Gordonstoun, he wasn't permitted the leisure. When not massacring the opposition at rugger he went in for athletics, tennis, cricket, rock-climbing, orienteering. Even tennis, which he considered a game for girls, and cricket, which he claimed sent him to sleep, he played with a vicious energy which gave him an unreturnable serve in one and made him a lethal bowler in the other. In between he devoted the minimum of time to his studies, gaining good grades with little effort and thereby disturbing his father still more. End-of-term reports related both his brilliance and his lack of concentration, and John frowned over them, too easily troubled for his changeling son. None of the Savages had ever been brilliant at school; a respectable competence or a limited area of ability, such as that evinced by Richard, was far more appropriate. Since Jolanda's intelligence had not been outstanding, Vincent's academic achievements escaped the stigma of heredity and entered the realm of mutation, something John did not find reassuring. He himself had been a good scholar, above average but not exceptional, working hard for every exam. He had played rugger for Oxford according to strict sporting principles. He was not envious of his son's careless talents – indeed, he wished rather to be proud of him, to stand tall among other, less fortunate parents, accepting their compliments with becoming embarrassment. But whenever he tried to praise Vincent an undercurrent of unease would always intrude, and his embarrassment at any compliment was uncomfortably genuine.

Richard, meanwhile, was a far from uncritical Patroclus. He followed Vincent in his sporting pursuits and other, less orthodox, exploits, initiated a few exploits of his own, rarely lost his temper and never lost his head. His sense of humour made him more popular than his cousin, at least with his classmates; a spate of practical jokes in his early teens did less for his popularity with the staff. He was the only person from whom Vincent would listen to criticism, for Vincent knew instinctively that behind his back Richard would always defend him, even if he thought he was in the wrong.

In their first term at Gordonstoun there was an incident with the class bully: a rumour was spread around that Richard's fatherless state meant he was illegitimate, and several boys got together to torment him. Their leader was an unattractive Flashman with a permanent sneer already affixed to his immature features and a

reputation for toughness based mainly on his own cryptic utter-
ances. He had the sandy eyelashes so much abhorred by novelists,
large fists and a small mind. Wary of Vincent, who looked tall and
forbidding, he saw in his shorter, less threatening cousin a potential
victim. Richard was outnumbered and overweighted; by the time
Vincent arrived on the scene he was already being subjected to a
juvenile form of torture. The ensuing scrimmage put Flashman in
the infirmary and left Vincent with a black eye, a split lip, and six
of the best. Once Richard was released he had done his fair share of
the fighting; nobody would attempt to victimise him again. But
Vincent himself was not averse to a little casual bullying when the
fit took him, and as they grew older Richard's propensity to stand
up for the underdog often brought them into conflict. Occasionally
they actually came to blows – single combats very different from
the puppy-fights of childhood. Vincent fought dirty, Richard with
staunch determination. The other boys would watch, breathless,
waiting for cataclysm; but the end was always the same. Vincent's
fist would drop, Richard's incorrigible smile would twist across his
swollen face, and the two of them would go off together to nurse
their bruises and invent a suitable tale for their housemaster.

'You're a bastard,' Richard told his cousin, more than once.
'Everyone says so and I know so.'

'*Va fan culo.*' His bilingual infancy was long forgotten but
Vincent had taught himself to swear in Italian and was rather proud
of it.

'Uncle John thinks I'm good for you; I heard him telling mother.
He said I'm a nice boy. You've got the looks and the brains but I'm
a nice boy. Pretty bloody, isn't it?'

Vincent grinned. Away from the tensions of Weatherfray,
Richard could tease his jealous insecurity into little more than a
joke.

'He hasn't a clue,' Vincent said.

At eighteen, the cousins went their separate ways. Richard, always
set on aeronautical engineering, went to Imperial College in
London. Vincent opted for Cambridge because his father suggested
Oxford. He was not much interested in furthering his studies but
university life offered many other opportunities and he knew a
degree might be useful. He chose history because it was easy, or so

he said, but when he forgot to be blasé he would discuss at length the power games of Cesare Borgia or Napoleon's progress from Corsican corporal to downfallen idol. ('From an island to an island,' Vincent quipped, 'with an empire in between.') He read Macchiavelli's *The Prince* on holiday one summer and was to claim, ten years later, that it changed his life. Richard, more discerning, said it pointed him in the direction in which he had always been going. Asked what he wanted to do, he invariably answered: 'Make money.' John, the successful entrepreneur, was unsympathetic. He tried to imbue Vincent with his own creed, a nation with freedom and economic security for all, created and upheld by big business with a conscience. But Vincent dismissed his idealism as hypocrisy and focused on essentials: 'You're rich and powerful. That's what really counts.' Long arguments eroded the nerves of everyone in the vicinity. John was by turns exasperated and angry, his principles unflinching, his jaw set, his backbone ramrod-straight. Vincent was rebellious, caustic, and obdurate. Looking at him John saw, not the mirror of his own stubbornness, but Jolanda's erratic genes returning to plague him. Vincent regarded the huge insurance company which John had built up so carefully as a means to an end; for John, it was the company itself which mattered. 'I came through the war,' he told his son. 'My brothers didn't. War teaches you the important things in life: trust, honour, a sense of community. Enough to eat and a decent place to sleep for every man. My personal wealth is incidental. The war made me a responsible adult. You're a child still – you see the world as a nursery full of attractive toys, which you can play with or smash according to caprice. You have no understanding of anything except your own greed. No self-respecting businessman would associate with you.'

'He thinks I need a war!' Vincent fumed later. Richard, as usual, was his audience. 'Perhaps you would like to start one? I need to be shot at and blown up in order to attain manhood! His thick head is stuffed with crap about rites of passage and comrades under fire. He and his pals fought for us and made a better world – this septic isle set in the slimy sea – and now, if you please, we're not allowed to live in it. We're supposed to stay in our playpens and be good. Our whole generation is condemned to perpetual immaturity by the fact that Britain is at peace with her neighbours. Inspired, isn't it? He can't even argue rationally; he only knows how to hold forth.'

'You're shouting at me,' said Richard. 'Did you shout at him?'

'No.' Vincent was suddenly cold. 'I can't; you know that. If I shouted at him he'd know he was winning. He hates it when I stay cool and reasonable. I can feel him . . . hating it.'

'Reasonable?'

'I reason,' Vincent snapped. 'That's reasonable.'

The interior of Weatherfray offered an appropriate backdrop for such altercations. Electric lighting skulked behind fringed lamp-shades or in curtained alcoves; wiring and switches were concealed in chinks in the linenfold panelling. The furniture was mainly of the solid Victorian variety, mahogany sideboards and armchairs upholstered in balding velvet or moth-eaten brocade. Both John and Vincent had four-poster beds. Carpets had faded or darkened according to daylight exposure and all the silverware looked tarnished. Successive housekeepers had done their best with dusting and polishing, but maids were in increasingly short supply and they received little encouragement from above, neither Jolanda nor Elizabeth having much interest in domestic management. Sound-effects included the thudding of ponderous doors, the creaking of empty stairs, and the tittupping feet of spiders scurrying down darkened passages. The antique loos flushed with the clanging of heavy chains and a thunder as of great waterfalls in the distance. Even in the quietest hour of the night there would be little groanings and squeakings as though the whole house fidgeted in its sleep. In many of the rooms, family portraits frowned down on their descendants with varying degrees of disapproval from above mutton-chop whiskers or through a chilling monocle. Several were in uniform; one on a horse. Their womenfolk posed in the crinoline and the bustle, in bare shoulders and fichus, all of them apparently attempting to uphold the standard set by their Queen, since they were plainly unamused. Great-great-aunt Caroline, reputedly a beauty, had been given a sort of pre-Raphaelite grace by the winsome brush of Val Prinsep, loose tendrils of hair frothing around her temples and her mouth as full and red as a squashed peony; but even he could do nothing with her uncompromising stare. That expression was repeated not only in John's rigid censure and Vincent's defiant scorn, but even in Elizabeth's restrained disappointment and Richard's quiet obstinacy. The eye colour was different but the look was always the same. Elizabeth tried not to show her regret that

Richard had not outgrown his childish obsession with engines but the force of her own nature was too much for her. Richard avoided argument with teasing and flippancy but every so often he would be jolted off guard: the eyes of mother and son would be locked into that hereditary glare. John, preoccupied with Vincent, had little time to sympathise with his sister. 'Nothing wrong with engineering,' he said. 'Practical subject. Aeronautics, isn't it? Tell you what – the boy had better learn to fly while he's at it. We'll sort something out in due course. Twenty-first birthday present, maybe. No sense in fussing over him, Liz; he's a man now.'

Only Vincent, Richard reflected, could interpret such casual interest as a preference, and use it to nourish his private demons.

At Imperial College, Richard played hard and worked harder. The time allotted for play usually took him to Cambridge, where Vincent, bored by his studies, scarcely worked at all. Away from Gordonstoun there was no need to compromise with a disciplined regime: he considered himself a man of the world, too sophisticated for enthusiasm, too blasé for effort. He still played ruthless rugger and unsporting cricket, but much of his energy was channelled into a new, far more absorbing form of physical exercise: girls. At school, they had not featured in the curriculum; during the holidays, the cousins had been restricted by the lurking presence of parents to tussles in damp grass with the more amenable local maidens. Frequently, they had shared the same one, comparing notes afterwards with a candour rare among men. Richard was naturally generous in everything, including sex; Vincent was naturally experimental. They had discovered the female orgasm together with a village girl called Catriona, a plump sixteen-year-old with an impressive bosom who was known as the Fat Cat and had a reputation she was doing her best to uphold. After a bottle of Romanée-Conti which Vincent had pinched from his father's cellar and which none of them, least of all Catriona, really appreciated, they inveigled her into the trees on Allweathers, nestling into the hollow where Mike Garoghan had hidden some twenty years earlier. Catriona giggled and panted; the boys just panted. They had never had the same girl at the same time before (Vincent had staked a tenner on her compliance) and since she seemed slightly reluctant they lingered over the preliminaries, kissing a breast each and fumbling simultaneously in her knickers. Presently Catriona gasped and came, tugging painfully at their hair and racked with tremors of a seismic violence.

'I didn't know girls could come like that,' Vincent remarked, fascinated and aroused.

'Nor did I,' said Richard. 'Wow!'

Back at home, Vincent picked up his copy of *Lady Chatterley*, formerly their sexual handbook. It fell open at one of several marked pages. '"She was ocean rolling in the dark, dumb masses,"' he read with new scepticism. 'Bullshit. It's that wobbly bit in the middle – what do they call it? The clitoris. As far as I can see, Connie Chatterley hasn't even got one. This book is useless.'

'It's the clit,' Richard concurred.

Armed with this radical discovery, the cousins launched into the halcyon days of their studenthood, days of wine and roses, freedom and opportunity. No more parental complications, no more wrestling in the grass long after the outdoor season had ended. It was the era of sexual liberation; AIDS had not yet come crawling out of the woodwork and everyone was on the Pill. Vincent concentrated on quantity; Richard, who was having an affair with a female lecturer, on quality. He buried his incorrigible smile in a beard in an attempt to look older and grew his ragged curls down to his shoulders. The beard vanished with the lecturer but the length of his hair continued to distress his mother, who felt that fashion had conspired to provoke her. When other differences failed she would revert to the subject, against her better judgement, brandishing the garden secateurs like the scissors with which she had once shorn his crooked fringe. Richard would laugh, plant a filial peck on her cheek, and shake his uncut locks tauntingly in her face. Elizabeth, who had learned humour from her son, could only laugh with him. Without being actually handsome, Richard had that unique brand of charm which operated not only on friends and strangers but also on his nearest and dearest. Charm is a quality which tends to fail in the home, withering under the banal irritants of everyday contact. But Richard's mother could not resist him for long, his uncle made allowances for him which he would never have made for Vincent, and Vincent himself loved him too well to allow any rivalry or envy to come between them. But there were two sides to the coin: if

Richard had the gift of winning love easily, he also had the capacity to love in return, not lightly but unstintingly, without hesitation or doubt. It was a gift which only Elizabeth foresaw might lead him into trouble.

Vincent – according to his aunt – had no capacity for love. Even John sometimes questioned whether his son was capable of any softer emotion, seeing in him coldness, rebellion, bitterness, cynicism but not an atom of visible affection for anyone or anything. Once or twice, Richard tried to defend his cousin, but he found it hard to put into words something he understood only by intuition and his elders, crediting him with chivalry rather than perception, dismissed his opinions indulgently. In fact, Vincent distrusted the weaknesses of his own heart: with Richard he had no fear of betrayal or disillusionment but his mother had deserted him and his feeling for his father had become warped with a lifetime of misunderstandings, pushing him too often to the edge of humiliation and pain. As for his girlfriends, they were invariably transient, objects of lust not love, picked for their looks, for a challenge, for variety, for anything except a relationship. Vincent had no problem attracting girls and unless drink or temper had made him indifferent he always pleased them in bed, excited by the sense of power thus induced. 'You can pull them,' Richard told him one day, 'but can you keep them? I'll bet you wouldn't know how.'

'The trouble is,' Vincent said idly, 'by the following morning the conversation always runs out.'

'That's your fault,' Richard insisted. 'Not theirs.'

'Are you telling me I'm boring?'

'Yes, I suppose I am. But don't worry; I'm sure it's only girls who think so. I find you quite good company now and then.'

Vincent laughed, his momentary anger dispelled by the gleam in Richard's eye. 'Your problem is you're always in love,' he said sapiently. 'Therefore you want me to be in love too. It gets people like that, I've noticed. Love is one of those diseases where the sufferers are only happy if everyone else is sick as well. That way they don't feel quite so stupid, breaking their silly hearts because some girl didn't call when she said she would, or went to the cinema with another guy. But I'm damned if I'm going to make a fool of myself just so we can go starry-eyed and soft in the head together.'

'You're dodging the issue,' Richard said. 'I'm not in love all the time; I just take girls seriously. You should try it. After all, girls are people too.'

'Girls are people too!' Vincent echoed scornfully. 'You ought to get a T-shirt printed.'

'If you promise to wear it,' Richard said, 'I probably will.'

It was not long after this conversation, at a party in London, that Vincent met Crystal Winter. It was a party typical of its time: that is, every aspect of the entertainment was liable to cause permanent damage to the health of the guests. They were herded into a room closely resembling the Black Hole of Calcutta with the temperature of a sauna and the kind of strobe lighting which stimulates epileptic fits. Live music from a rock band with too many amplifiers for the confined space pummelled their eardrums; they were offered a punch made from cheap wine supposedly spiked with turpentine (one of the hosts was an artist); and the various illegal substances in circulation included cannabis resin that appeared to have been processed by dung beetles and a range of multicoloured pills whose original purpose in life no one seemed to remember. Carcinogenic tobacco fumes hung heavily on what little air there was. It was not surprising that a well-known neurologist, writing a decade later, would claim that a generation who had survived such parties was capable of anything.

Crystal was not a regular partygoer; it was bad for her looks. Unlike many models, who make the most of their brief spell in the limelight with little thought for the future, she took the long view. Even at nineteen she prided herself on both prudence and temperance. She was not going to burn herself out in a few years; Crystal was determined to endure. Her complexion was the most perishable facet of her beauty, therefore she cherished it, petted it, fed it with skin food and woke it up with astringent and put it to bed with night cream. She drank alcohol infrequently and never smoked. Nor did she seek the bubble reputation, even in Dempster's column: the flashlight glimpse of glory as the one-date-stand of a celebrity was not the kind of fame she wanted. Only a couple of weeks earlier she had turned down a long week-end with a short rock star, sensing it would lead nowhere. She did not intend to be used, abused or hurt. At the party, her escort for the evening was just an escort, nothing more. He got drunk in the first hour and retreated to the loo to throw up, and Crystal wandered through the crowd in search of someone she knew, trying to decide whether to wait for him or go home immediately. In the flickering darkness she passed Vincent without noticing him. He, too, paid her little attention, until an acquaintance commented that she was 'that model' and added as a footnote that she was the prettiest girl in the room. 'Is she?' Vincent glanced in the direction of her receding figure. She was wearing her off-duty clothes, jeans and a Biba T-shirt. Her loosened hair wrapped her shoulders like a cloak.

'Lovely hair,' Vincent said. 'Which model?'

'*That* model,' his informant said simply. 'Saw her face on a magazine cover last month.'

Due to the noise level, conversation had to be conducted in a shout, with the speaker's mouth placed close to his auditor's ear. Richard, who had been attending with difficulty, told his cousin: 'She looks like a nice girl. Not your type.'

If he sounded mischievous it was lost in the general cacophony. Vincent took the challenge at face value. The next time Crystal drifted past he tucked a hand under her arm, gave her a brief smile and steered her outside. 'We can't talk in there,' he said. 'Not without yelling, anyway. What a bloody awful party.'

'Do I – do I know you?'

'Not yet.'

They were standing by the open door; the light from the hall slanted along his cheekbones and cast dramatic shadows in every hollow of his face. She had tilted her head to look up at him; she thought he must be at least six foot, perhaps more. His dark beauty made her instantly wary.

She said: 'I'm here with a friend.'

'Where is he?'

'Sick.'

'Why don't you go and mop his brow? Or aren't you on those terms?'

'Not really,' she admitted.

'Let's go, then.'

'Go? But I don't even know you!'

'If we leave together,' Vincent pointed out, 'then you'll get to know me. The only reasons for staying are to get stoned, to get pissed, or to have sex on the floor. You don't look to me like the kind of girl who would go for any of those, but of course—'

'No, I wouldn't,' Crystal interrupted. 'But I'm not a pick-up, either.'

'I haven't picked you up,' Vincent said. 'I've kidnapped you.'

They went to a club which stayed open till two, had a drink in a corner and danced close together on a very small dance floor. Crystal could feel the hard rugger muscles under his shirt; he wore no aftershave and his body smelled warm and sexy. She had never before been conscious of the smell of maleness. The men she met in the course of her work were usually camp photographers, homosexual models, advertising executives in steel-blue suits with steel-sharp smiles, the occasional celebrity at a publicity event who appeared to regard her as a potential accessory. Vincent, with his long black hair and the unmistakable glitter in his eyes, seemed as wild and exotic as an Indian brave, indecently virile, impossibly unsafe. The motion of the dance and the lack of room to manoeuvre pinioned them together. He trembled; she trembled; the ridge of his stiffened penis was pressed against her abdomen. She was almost a virgin, inexperienced and unawake; she had never had an orgasm with a man. But her thighs clung to his independent of her own volition and the heat from his loins seemed to permeate her anatomy, filling her with an unfamiliar languor. When they left, she was thankful for the night chill which cooled her limbs and cleared her head.

'I'm a career girl,' she declared in the taxi. 'I really don't want to get involved.'

It was a line which she had often found effective, disarming on her lack of intentions while at the same time throwing down the gauntlet to the male ego. Besides, she reassured herself, it was basically true.

At her parents' house, she did not offer him coffee or ask when she would see him again, though her self-restraint needed an effort of will which alarmed her. Neither will nor restraint had been seriously tested before. He enquired about her phone number but did not make a note of it or promise to use it and the cab drove away after a deliberately careless goodnight kiss. Crystal was left at her door, clutching her common sense. Vincent sat in the back of the taxi, repeating her number over and over since he had no paper on which to write it down.

'Well?' Richard asked when his cousin returned. 'Did you get anywhere?'

'Somewhere, not anywhere,' Vincent said, stretching out on top of his sleeping bag. Richard's room did not possess a spare bed.

'I told you she was a nice girl.'

'Don't be so old-fashioned. "Nice girls" went out with the fifties. She just requires . . . perseverance.'

'And will you?' queried Richard.

Vincent had closed his eyes, intending to demonstrate boredom. 'Will I what?'

'Persevere.'

'Maybe.' Without actually seeing it, he sensed Richard's grin. 'Don't get ideas. This isn't love: it's just a different kind of lust.'

'I hope she breaks your heart,' Richard said. 'What's her name?'

'Crystal Winter. She made it up. It's really Christine Something.'

'A name to freeze your balls off,' Richard remarked with glee.

'Oh, go to sleep.'

Subsequent weekends found Crystal on the train to Cambridge or Vincent on the train to London. Both of them were unsure of the situation, ill at ease with their new-found emotions. Vincent was negligent, sometimes cruel, resisting the snare of commitment, torn between infatuation and self-contempt. Crystal thought she was in love and drew on all her resources not to show it. The very qualities which made Vincent desirable also made him dangerous; she knew that once he was certain of her feelings he would either exploit them or simply lose interest. Yet she also believed that deep down inside he loved her and with patience that love could be coaxed to the surface. She saw no contradiction in this: she was nineteen, a little romantic, neither as prudent nor as wise as she imagined, her mental processes distorted with wishful thinking, her vision blurred with dreams. Her best weapon was the strange composure which she had possessed even in childhood, when the impassivity of her small face had intrigued her contemporaries and fascinated adults. 'What does she think about?' they would speculate. 'A penny for your thoughts!' Less attractive children could think away unregarded; little Christine was invariably the focus of curiosity. 'Where's the penny?' she would ask, and they would laugh and praise her infantine wit, leaving her baffled and empty-handed.

Vincent never tried to bargain for her self-communings but she was almost sure he wondered about them, tantalised by the stillness of expression which had led her father to dub her 'the little sphinx'. Artifice came naturally to her; both her sorrows and her pleasures were always hidden. Even the smile which illuminated her face gave nothing away: it was decoration, not revelation.

Crystal knew she was not spoiled: her parents had been too stretched paying the rent and the gas bill to have much left over for pocket money or presents. At one time, egged on by her friends, she would go into the local branch of Woolworth's to pinch lipstick and chewing-gum; the assistants were leery of light-fingered school-children but when Crystal put on her most inscrutable expression, which at twelve passed for innocence, and asked with exquisite politeness for something at the back of the shop, few ventured to suspect her. When she was older, she would refer to such activities as a normal part of growing up, a phase which everyone went through. But although she enjoyed few luxuries she was always the most important member of the family, adored by her father and brother and groomed by Mona from infancy for the stardom she herself had never achieved. She won a Best in Breed in every baby contest, peeped from under a floral hat as a demure Miss Pears, posed as a bridesmaid in a mail-order catalogue and a flower fairy in a detergent commercial, and gained enormous prestige among her classmates by appearing in *Jackie*, sporting fashions for the stylish thirteen-year-old. She was always the one who led her ballet class in exhibition dances at the church fête or was chosen to present the bouquet to a visiting dignitary. By the time she had realised that she would never make the height requirement for the catwalk, Nympheline had hired her to advertise shampoo; the Récamier contract followed. Now, she was Crystal Winter, a cover girl at the top of her profession, the immaculate product of her own ambition. But success had not spoiled her, either: everybody said so. She was never late, never irritable, never unreasonable. She did not have hangovers or throw tantrums. Vincent had disturbed her flawless equilibrium but she was determined not to let herself down; other girls pestered their boyfriends on the telephone, wept and stormed and were eventually discarded, but not Crystal. Never Crystal. Romance was not going to be easy, but an easy romance would scarcely be worth having. And Vincent, with his brooding good looks and aura of careless privilege, was unquestionably what she wanted, a suitable hero for the success story of her life. Resolution and calculation had always obtained for her whatever she desired; she had no intention of losing her head now Cupid had entered the game.

On several occasions she tried to draw Vincent into talking about his home and family, believing that in such confidences lay the key to unlock his affections. She was a good listener, or so she had been told: she didn't interrupt and her absorption in any recital appeared complete. But Vincent was not a good talker. All his life, he had revealed his thoughts – some of them – only to Richard. He had never known how to pour out his heart.

'You're very close to your cousin, aren't you?' Crystal said, prompting cautiously.

'Very. We were brought up together. He's my first cousin, but he's always been more like a brother. No – if we'd been brothers we might have resembled each other, in which case we'd have been at each other's throats from birth. Fortunately, we're totally different. I suppose he's my . . . my best friend. My better self. Don't you have a best friend, Crystal? Someone with whom you share the secrets of your bosom? I thought all girls had a best friend.'

'No,' Crystal said. 'I never share my secrets.'

'You know, you are unique among women.' Vincent's tone was light, almost dismissive, but his eyes were fixed intently on her face. 'I used to imagine Helen of Troy looking the way you look now. I pictured her standing on the city walls gazing out over the battle, never batting an eyelash, never shedding a tear. Down below Menelaus fought Paris for her sake, and Achilles slew Hector and dragged his body in the dust, but her expression didn't change. She stayed ice-cool, untouchable, remote. *Like a long-legged fly upon a stream, her mind moved upon silence.*' He was only twenty-one after all, he was at Cambridge, and despite his philandering he had had more education than experience.

Crystal remembered the story of Helen only vaguely and hadn't read Yeats, although she guessed the line was some sort of quotation. She said nothing, doing her best to live up to the metaphor. Vincent, unaffected by a lull in the conversation, said nothing either.

When she felt her mind had finished moving on silence and

could come back down to earth Crystal resumed: 'I wish you would tell me more about your parents. I know you don't get on with your father, but you're fond of him, aren't you?'

'Am I? He doesn't seem to be fond of me. He's always had a soft spot for Richard, though – and who can blame him? I'm a very unsatisfactory son.'

'Is that all you can say?'

'There's no more to be said. I despise him for a hypocrite; he disapproves of me because I'm honest about all the wrong things. A recipe for confrontation. He's the sort of person who tells you what he did when he was a boy and then wants to know why you're not doing it too. When you point out that the world has changed radically since then he just says: "Not for the better." Why so many questions, anyway? Relatives are a dead bore. You can't possibly be interested in any of mine.'

'I'm interested in you,' Crystal said.

'*I* see. You want all my little complexes to come crawling out of their holes so you can examine them. Hard luck. I won't play.'

'Why?' Crystal enquired. 'What are you afraid of?'

'For God's sake! Not that one, *please*.'

Crystal opened her mouth to apologise, then shut it again. An apology would be fatal, an admission of weakness. Instead, she persisted. 'What about your mother, then? You never talk about her at all.'

'I told you, she ran off when I was four. That doesn't leave much to talk about.'

'Aren't you curious about her?'

'Why should I be?'

'Because she's your mother.' Crystal was determined not to be shocked. 'I mean, she was such a big star, and so beautiful. Mummy says she was always in the news. Don't you remember her at all?'

'Hardly.' Vincent was curt. 'All I ever knew of her was what I read in the papers.'

'Do you care?' she asked softly.

'Care?' The idea was obviously alien to him. 'No. I feel . . . like a Martian reading about events back home, twenty years after emigrating to Uranus. Last Saturday's *FT* said she's supposed to be making a comeback. The critic didn't sound optimistic. He spoke of "the tragic ruin of a magnificent voice". For me, it had all the

personal relevance of a weather report. If you've finished the inquisition, shall we go out? I could do with a drink – the story of my
childhood is bloody tedious. I had to live through it; I don't need to
talk about it as well.'

'Maybe you do,' Crystal said.

'You poor cow, you've been reading Freud. I wouldn't have
thought it of you.'

'Don't talk to me like that.'

'Then stop trying to analyse me.' The hardness was still in
his face but his tone had altered, becoming both rougher and gentler. 'I'm not a puzzle you have to solve for us to be together. The
past doesn't matter; nor the future. Live in the present. Take
pleasure . . . in the present.' He had drawn her close to him and
suddenly she could see the pulse in his throat, feel his body
at fever-heat under his shirt. 'You don't need to know me. I don't
need to know you. I love you – because you are as cold and
unreachable as the moon. I want to touch the moon – I want to
hold the moon without tearing it from the sky. I break things. I'll
break you, if you let me. You know that. Don't let me. I want to
possess you, to be inside you, not to – not to—' He was speaking
into her hair, into the hollow of her temple, into the parting of her
lips. She heard only the word *love*, the magic word – all the rest
was the ramblings of his delirium. The languor was pervading her
limbs, weakening her, turning her bones to water and her blood to
fire. This time, she did not fight it.

In the end, it was a long while before they went out.

A fortnight later, Vincent went to the Newmarket Races with a
college friend. He didn't take Crystal: much as he wanted her in
bed, he had no intention of being saddled with her at every event
in his social calendar. They were invited by his friend's father, who
had a horse running in the Guineas; the party also included an
assortment of businessmen, a couple of wives, and a good deal of
champagne, but no other young people. Vincent, who considered it
sophisticated to be bored everywhere except on the sports field,
realised at the outset that on this occasion he was not going to find
it difficult. Besuited company directors stared with lifted brows at
his jeans and tasselled leather jacket. His friend, who, in common
with the rest of his generation, was regularly at loggerheads with his

parents, proceeded to get very drunk. Vincent, riled by the silent disdain of his seniors, placed a staggering bet on a horse which could not possibly win and then turned his back on the race.

'Savage,' said a balding legal eagle, polishing pristine spectacles. 'You wouldn't be the son of old John Savage, by any chance? Silver Shield Insurance?'

'Wouldn't I?' said Vincent. His horse, Winter's Chill, which he had picked for its name, had just come in sixth.

'Good chap, John Savage,' ruminated the lawyer, oblivious to Vincent's hostility. 'At Oxford with my uncle. Fine reputation. A man of integrity. No flies on him, either. Pays all your debts, does he?'

'Ask him.' Vincent, rigid with fury, kept his temper only because he knew his interlocutor expected him not to.

The lawyer, with two decades of courtroom brangling behind him, merely smiled and turned his attention elsewhere. 'Good answer,' said an American at Vincent's elbow. 'None of his darned business. At your age, you want to gamble a bit. I sure as hell did. Still do, if it comes to that.' When Vincent offered no response, he continued easily: 'Big man, your father?'

Vincent shrugged.

'OK; it's none of my darned business either. Well done, kid. There aren't many boys your age who know how to keep their mouths shut. How long you got left at college?'

'I'm in my final year.'

'Give me a call some time, if you're in London.' A business card was flipped casually in his direction. 'I'm going to be in the UK for quite a while. I'll buy you lunch. I like a man who doesn't talk much; he listens the more.'

Vincent, whose father often accused him of not listening at all, stuffed the card in his pocket without even bothering to look at it. He didn't say thank you since he felt under no obligation to thank the man for a favour he had not requested.

'You call me,' the American reiterated, undeterred. 'I'll remember you.'

'Carson,' said Vincent's friend later, only partially sobered. 'Pally with Dad. Familiar with father: paterfamiliar. Comes over here, runs into Dad somewhere, Dad says: Let me introduce you to a few chums who will cut your throat. Thanks buddy, says Carson, but let me cut your throat first. *That* kind of familiar. They buy each other expensive lunches and swap crocodile grins.'

'He didn't look dangerous,' Vincent commented.

'They're the worst kind. Don't you remember *Alice*? "He welcomes little fishes in with gently smiling jaws."'

'I'm not a fish,' Vincent said. 'Didn't you know? I'm going to be a crocodile when I grow up. Where in America is he from?'

'Not New York.'

'That's helpful.'

'Could be Texas. Or Chicago. Or – no. California. That's it: California. The Golden State. Hence his yellow suntan and the perfection of his crocodile teeth. He's very big in . . . in . . .'

'In?'

'Very big in something. Bound to be. Dad doesn't bother with anyone who isn't big in something.'

'You're pissed,' Vincent said, extracting the business card, now rather creased. '*Judas* Carson. Bloody hell. Still, if he's big in something he must have improved on the original thirty pieces of silver.'

'Thirty pieces of silver was a lot of money in those days,' his companion remarked. 'You have to allow for inflation. What are you going to do about that bet of yours? You must be overdrawn up to your eyeballs. Will your father cover you? Mine wouldn't; yours might – if you offer him your guts in recompense.'

'I shan't ask him,' Vincent said.

'What will you do?'

'I'll think of something.' He smoothed the card unsuccessfully between his fingers. 'Something . . . big.'

3

Judas Carson had arrived in America as Yehude Karzhinski, off-loading at Ellis Island, where a weary immigration official wrote him down as Judas Karzin. He anglicised the surname to Carson after his father's death. He had come from a small village in the Balkans consisting mostly of consonants: it was claimed variously by Serbs, Croats and Bosnians, according to who had the most guns at any given time. When they tired of shooting each other, the locals would get together and have a pogrom against the Jewish community. His mother, dying of influenza the winter after their arrival in New York, confessed to him that he was probably not Karzhinski's son: she had been raped in one such pogrom approximately nine months before his birth. His younger sister had died during the voyage and at ten years old he was left alone in an alien city with the man who was (probably) not his father. It was 1929. The nation was drunk on bootleg liquor: bad gin and big crime were a way of life. Judas played truant from school to run errands for the gangsters, who were unable to resist employing an urchin so aptly named. Jacob Karzin, a tailor, stitched industriously, spent what little he earned on his misbegotten son, and followed his wife out of this harsh world some four years later. Judas, as he had always done, looked after himself. He learned little in school but a great deal outside it, becoming by turns pickpocket, petty thief, huckster, blackmailer, bagman – seizing any opportunity to broaden his professional experience.

When the war came he was conscripted into the Army and sent to Europe, where he found further scope for his entrepreneurial activities. Using a contact in a PX, he provided war-weary Italians and newly liberated French with the necessities they had missed: tinned ham, cigarettes and Scotch. He arranged for Gallic beauties who had long lost their national chic to trade sexual favours for nylon stockings, and at a *manoir* in the Rhône valley he swapped a brace of steaks for a small painting he fancied signed by someone called Corot. It would eventually hang in his house in Bel-Air among other works of corresponding value but assorted taste, and dinner guests would be bored by the story of its acquisition. When he reached Berlin he was able to liaise with a Russian who supplied him with caviare for the officers' mess; 'Caviare to the generals,' quipped an erudite master-sergeant. Judas had never read Shakespeare but he duly learned the source of the quotation in order to resurrect it later on, like the painting, to demonstrate his knowledge of culture.

After the war he followed the pioneer trail west to seek his fortune, joining a former comrade-in-arms who was based in Los Angeles. No longer content with pickings, he wanted to make big money – to make it, steal it, embezzle it or print it himself, it did not matter. He had the hunger of the immigrant, stateless, uprooted, with the memory of an empty belly too close for comfort, eager to claw his way to the top of the heap. He dealt in real estate in a country where the natives squabbled over every square metre not with guns but with dollars, and land bought for a song could be sold for a grand opera. Judas grew fat on the difference. By the early seventies, when he was dipping a finger in foreign pies, he had a Tudor mansion all of fifty years old, its half-timbering overhung with palm and jacaranda, its swimming pool inlaid with extracts from the Bayeux Tapestry in glittering mosaic. His waistline had thickened to fill the space behind the wheel of his Porsche, his suntan had advanced as his hairline retreated, expensive teeth gleamed in an ingenuous smile. He had an affection for the British, or so he said, ensconcing himself at the Dorchester; Europe was so civilised, he liked to get back to his roots. Listeners who assumed those roots were Irish were not corrected. He was setting up a London-based property company and he needed a front man, someone with a reputation and a name that would inspire confidence in both business associates and building societies. After some checking he found that John Savage had the reputation, Vincent the name.

In due course Vincent called, adopting a don't-give-a-damn approach which Judas recognised instantly from his own attitude in his first deals. He affected to have forgotten his luncheon invitation; Vincent, biting back anxiety and temper, became monosyllabic and prepared to ring off. The lunch date materialised without further manoeuvring. During the meal, Judas confided with beautiful frankness that he needed an English associate to give his new company credibility in the UK market. He was a great believer in the value of half-truths; they were so much less effort than lies. 'You've no experience, but that's not important; I'm experienced enough for the both of us. You've got your father's name: that's handy. I know – you're young and ambitious and you want to make it on your own. Get wise, kid: don't junk your assets. That isn't smart, and I think you're smart. We'll pull off a few quick deals and you'll be able to kiss goodbye to family hand-outs, if that's what you want. For my money, you're crazy, but that *is* what you want, isn't it? You got too much pride. My old man died when I was fourteen, left three dollars and eighteen cents and a jacket with no sleeves which he hadn't finished stitching. He was a tailor: worked half the night for peanuts. If he'd had any dough I'd have taken it but all he left me was a lesson. Never be a sucker. You remember that, kid. Don't work your guts out for peanuts and never turn your back on money. It's all the same stuff, wherever it comes from. You've never starved or you'd know that. I learned early but you've lived soft; you've got to start learning now. Fast. You wait till you're desperate. You can't eat pride.'

It was a remark that Vincent was to recall much later. At the time, he only said with all the coolness he could summon: 'I don't intend to ask my father for anything. Ever. So if you're trying to bleed him through me, forget it.'

'Hell, no.' Between mouthfuls of underdone steak, Judas made Italianate gestures acquired long ago from mobster friends. Having located Vincent's weak point he did not mean to aim too obviously or hit too hard. 'I like you, kid. I even like your pride. That's genuine British aristocracy: the upper lip so stiff you can't swallow. I like that: it's straight out of a book. You're straight out of a book, Vincent. I'm just giving you a little advice. Something to think about for the future. Get out in the real world.'

No arrogant, would-be tough twenty-one-year-old likes to be told he's living in fairyland.

'Thanks for the lecture,' Vincent said coldly. 'If I ever want advice, I'll try to remember it.'

Judas laughed silently, like the crocodile to which he had been compared. 'You won't want advice,' he said. 'You wouldn't ask for help if you were on your way to the firing squad. You know what, kid? No matter how this deal works out, I really like you. Just keep that in mind. Whatever happens.' He meant it, too. Judas liked people easily and found it equally easy to stab them in the back. He would produce the truism about not letting sentiment interfere with business as if it was an original thought.

'So what's the deal?' Vincent asked.

Afterwards he was to claim, for the benefit of the lawyers, that he had never really understood. But Vincent was no fool. Beneath the veneer of shady legality and slick commercial cliché he was quick to appreciate not only the arithmetic of the scheme but the dubious ethics on which it was founded. The one detail which escaped him was that he could be held responsible. His name was in the company title, his signature on every contract. He would never have admitted it but it made him feel important, necessary, a part of that business world which his father had said would never recognise or accept him. He was determined to show John that not only could he make money, he could do it at the expense of the smug, self-righteous corporations whose hypocrisy he had always denounced. 'Building societies help no one,' he would declaim. 'They are just greedy Shylocks getting fat on usury, encouraging people to borrow and borrow and then bleeding them white for the interest. Even the name is a mockery: they build nothing – they are parasites battening on the labours of others. They have created a society full of home-owners who don't actually own their homes, a credit-based community top heavy with debt. They deserve to be suckered.' It did not occur to him that the long-suffering home-owners whose situation he deplored might end up paying for Carson's scam. He visualised every bank, building society and insurance company to be run by paunchy executives in a selection of old school ties, getting rich on the crackle of a contract. 'Besides,' he told Crystal, 'a valuation is only an opinion. If they want to lend huge sums on such a basis, that's their mistake. One man can say a place is worth thirty thousand, another can say seventy thousand. We're just making a profit on a difference of opinion.'

The plan was a simple one. A surveyor already on Carson's illicit payroll would grossly overvalue various properties, building societies would put down the money, Carson's company – Vincent Savage Enterprises – bought them 'for development', and Judas and his associates pocketed the excess cash. A few instalments of the mortgage might be paid for the purpose of credibility, but, as Judas pointed out, the investors would get the property in the end, so they really had little cause for complaint. They had paid over the odds, but, inflation being what it was, in a few years' time the buildings would doubtless catch up with their original valuation. Nearly thirty transactions had taken place before questions were asked and Judas decided it was time to retire. He went back to Los Angeles, taking with him his surveyor, his solicitor and the profits. He left Vincent a brief note.

'I really liked you, kid, but that doesn't change the rules. You wanted to learn about business; I taught you. Don't make the same mistake twice.'

Vincent, reading it in an empty office, forgot to crush the sheet of paper into a ball and hurl it contemptuously into the wastepaper bin. He could only stare and stare at it until the words ran together and the sentences became meaningless. He heard footsteps in the corridor, a slow, heavy tread, but it was not the police. Not yet. Only the porter wanting to know if there was anything he had left behind, and whether he wished to give a forwarding address. No, Vincent said, no address. No point. Anyone who wanted him would find him soon enough.

Outside in the street, he told himself it would be useless to panic. On the other hand, it was equally useless to stay calm. He thought of going home – since he had come down from Cambridge he had been sharing a house in Chelsea with Richard and another friend – but he knew his cousin would instantly perceive the trouble in his face and he did not want either criticism or sympathy. Not then or ever. He needed a drink but the pubs weren't open yet so he went into a cheap coffee bar, the kind he normally never patronised, and sat down on a plastic stool at a plastic counter to drink his way through two cups of a thin black liquid with a lot of sugar. The carbohydrates probably helped: when he had finished his brain still felt numb but at least he knew what to do. The only constructive thing he could do. He went to find himself a lawyer.

*

It was a long while before Vincent understood he might really go to jail. After his arrest, he thought that the ruthless disrespect of the police and the subsequent publicity was the worst that could happen. He could fight his interrogators, seeing them as the enemy, outnumbering and trying to browbeat him: opponents to be defied and defeated. But the conflagration of flashbulbs outside the magistrates' court, the out-thrust microphones, the braying voices, the view-halloo of the pursuit as he plunged into the waiting car – all this was the stuff of nightmares. He knew he must not flinch and he scorned to hide his face, striding through the mob like a zombie; but inwardly he was stunned. He felt like the bull in the bullfight, the boxer against the ropes, listening to the shrieking of a crowd who wanted blood for blood's sake, without cause or purpose. The press had sensed they were on to a good thing. His background and private life were dissected with lofty disdain by the quality papers, with sensationalist relish by the tabloids. The court case was naturally sub judice but the reporters were free to animadvert on his high living – 'astronomical bets on horses' – his family and his friends. Crystal, at first tempted by the image of the faithful girlfriend, later retreated behind large hats, dark glasses and discretion. Her rash declaration of an engagement was an irritant which Vincent rapidly dismissed from his memory. In the solitary horror of his predicament he did not want public gestures, clinging loyalties, paraded emotions. Richard's understated support was the one thing he trusted. When he was released on bail John arrived, stiff-necked with shock, tortured by the sense of his own failure, half prepared to rant, half prepared to forgive. But Vincent asked no forgiveness. He would not defend himself, would not speak. His silence provoked his father to a tirade of fury, which provoked Vincent to further silence. Their quarrels had become a battle royal which neither would lose, neither could win. 'He can help you,' said Vincent's lawyer. 'You're his only son. Ask him. If he paid back the money, or some of the money—'

'No,' Vincent said flatly. 'I'd rather go to jail.'

'You may have to.'

And gradually he realised the truth. Without his father's assistance, he would go to prison. He, Vincent Scarpia Savage, ex-Cambridge and Gordonstoun, would be shut up in a cell like a common thief. Unthinkable, impossible – yet as the trial approached that prison wall seemed to grow in his mind, blotting out the future. His lawyer, who had started with optimism in order to boost Vincent's confidence, converted to pessimism to erode his obstinacy. 'What's the use of pride?' he would say, unwittingly echoing Judas Carson. 'It won't impress the jury. You'll have to try for a little humility. For openers, you could practise on your father.' But Vincent's pride was integral to his nature: he could not relinquish it so lightly. He remembered other words of Judas not so long before, a back-handed compliment which, no doubt as intended, had gratified his vanity. 'You wouldn't ask for help if you were on your way to the firing squad.' But vanity, like pride, could not be eaten. It would not impress the jury. Yet a part of his object had been to demonstrate his independence: he could not bear to cast himself on the paternal bosom, a reluctant prodigal son, humble, remorseful, transformed out of his own being into the filial pattern card his father presumably desired. Weeks passed, judgement drew nearer; his thoughts grew bars to enclose him, with no way out. In the end, it was his cousin who convinced him. 'You'll go to jail for stubbornness,' Richard said. 'That's what it boils down to. You and Uncle John are both so pig-headed that you won't ask his help even in extremis and he won't help unless you ask. I never heard of two adults being so bloody ridiculous. If you go inside he'll break his heart but he's too old and too stupid to come down off his high horse. Give him a chance. Ask him. What will it cost you?'

'Everything,' said Vincent.

'Nothing,' said Richard.

Vincent went to Weatherfray the next day. John had almost given up expecting him. The long suspense of the wait made him more unyielding than ever; his manner was gruff, his welcome sombre; he hid his profound relief even from himself. Their attempted reconciliation went wrong from the beginning. Vincent, present not simply against his will but against his character, hardened immediately; his essay in humility became a stony admission of wrongdoing, monosyllabic and begrudged. When John demanded some indication of repentance he withdrew even that, claiming he had only followed in the paternal footsteps: his sin was not dishonesty but failure. John, as ready to blame himself as his son, was appalled. Haunted by the memory of an undisciplined child and a doting, feckless, wanton mother, in the shock of that moment he saw Vincent's whole upbringing as one long history of over-indulgence. 'I spoiled the boy,' he told Elizabeth later. 'I should have been stricter. The fault is as much mine as his.' Less articulate than his son, his distress found expression in the raising of his voice, the pounding of his fist, the utterance of trenchant phrases which Vincent dismissed as platitudes. 'What's wrong with platitudes?' John stormed. 'A platitude is a saying which has been used so often because it's true. You're typical of your generation: anything that's good and enduring you have to denigrate with a cheap label. Honour, faith, principle, all those things are just platitudes. Platitudes! Well, I'm a simple man: I believe in platitudes. I've lived my life by old-fashioned values and I'm going to see you do too until they damned well come back into fashion! Right and wrong don't change no matter which way you twist them. Throw away the clever spurious tags and stealing is still stealing. I've fathered a thief and I'm not going to try and buy anyone off to save face: I'll take the consequences and by God, so will you! Maybe in prison you'll learn the morals I couldn't teach you.'

Vincent opened his mouth then shut it again, very tightly. There was a shaken silence. John was flushed; his son livid. In the sepia gloom of John's study, surrounded by the soaring spines of unread books, dusty shadows hanging from curtain and cornice, it might have been a showdown from another age: Victorian patriarch disinheriting rakehell heir. The inadequate daylight ignored John and concentrated on Vincent, the pallor of his concave cheek, the disorder of his long black locks. Possibly the atmosphere of Weatherfray, redolent of antique melodrama, had affected them both: their quarrel was modern but their attitudes were ancient, time-hardened, as immovable as the furniture.

At length Vincent spoke. 'You don't learn morals in prison, Dad.'

His voice sounded both very harsh and very young, and for an instant John wavered. Vincent hardly ever called him Dad.

But Vincent sensed the softening though he could not see it, knew he had courted it, using the appellation he never used, and he clenched his trembling hand, set his mouth, stared at his father with all the insolence he could muster. He could not weaken, not by so much as a nuance, whatever it cost him. Savage glare met Savage glare, and the instant was lost.

Back in London, Vincent told his cousin: 'No go.' He said it as lightly as he could, as if it was a trivial affair whose outcome meant little, but inside he felt sick. Richard put a hand on his shoulder which he did not try to shake off. He had always prided himself on being a loner, aloof from his fellow men, needing no one; now, for the first time that he could remember, he felt genuinely alone, consciously lonely, cut off from all human contact by walls of glass through which he could not reach or communicate. As though he was already in a prison of his own making. Crystal was almost forgotten, relegated to the ranks of other girlfriends who had come and gone in his life, leaving no lasting imprint. Even Richard's gesture felt somehow remote, as if the hand that lay on his shoulder was in another dimension, a different time. After the court case only a little way ahead his life seemed to come to a full stop. He realised presently that this was fear, this cold emptiness inside him. He knew it was weak and childish to be afraid but although he fought the sensation he could not quell it. He was a man, he thought he was strong, and yet he was frightened like a child because he was going to prison. It was all he could do to keep from shivering.

At the last minute, John changed his mind. It was too late, of course – too late to pay off the irate building societies, too late to stop the slow inexorable machinery of the law. His solicitor ummed and ahhed but the court was convened, the jury selected, the judge bewigged and gowned: justice could no longer be muzzled or halted in its tracks. John paced the floor and fumed. The floor in question was Piers Percival's Surrey mansionette, whence he had repaired after a final session at the solicitor's office. Piers was not encouraging. 'Too late is worse than never,' he said. 'You had your chance and you spurned it. There's nothing more you can do now. Leave well alone.'

'I have to go into court tomorrow.'

'The press will eat you for breakfast and Vincent – if he's in a state to notice you – will probably assume you've come to gloat.'

'I'm still going. Will you come?'

'No, I will not. He's your son, not mine. He isn't even my godson. Richard, happily, is far less bother. I have no intention of being a martyr in Vincent's cause when he himself would certainly be the last person to thank me for it.'

'I thought you liked him,' John remarked.

'I never said that.' Piers was finickingly precise. 'I find him an interesting study – rather like a Goya painting. He intrigues, fascinates, revolts. I would not want to hang him in a room I use every day.'

'Don't talk about hanging,' John said. 'Things are bad enough.'

'Don't overreact,' retorted Piers.

In court, as Piers had predicted, the press mobbed John on arrival and departure, his son ignored him in between. Vincent went through the trial like an automaton, standing up and sitting down to order, answering both his own counsel and the prosecutor in the same brief monotone, gazing blindly ahead of him while other witnesses gave their evidence. The jury thought his brevity curtness, his monotone indifference, his unseeing gaze laden with dark purpose. The judge, who had sent his own son to Gordonstoun some fifty years earlier, thought Vincent had betrayed the Spartan ideal and would certainly have commanded a flogging had the law allowed it. Like most judges he believed that with the velvet and ermine he put on the mantle of Solomon: it was not enough to do his job and pronounce sentence, he felt obliged to pontificate as well. Vincent, he declared, had not needed to swindle large sums of money, he was rich and privileged, even clever, every door was open to him, golden opportunities were scattered at his feet. He could not plead the feeble excuse of necessity or hardship to justify his crime; he had acted solely out of greed, without morality or scruple. In so doing he had broken faith with his school, his college, and above all his parents, upright citizens of unblemished reputation who had deserved better of their child. (The judge, who regularly fell asleep at the opera, was unaware that Vincent's mother was Jolanda Scarpia.) Let us hope that in prison he would use the time to reflect on the error of his ways.

John writhed at the sympathy thus offered and the grandiloquent echo of his own uncompromising statement. Richard, struggling to reach his cousin before they took him away, saw him over the intervening heads: their eyes met and held but there was no time for words and they were too far apart for a handclasp. Afterwards, it was Richard's turn to feel sick, sick and angry, though he knew the whole business was Vincent's own fault and there was nobody else to be angry with. As for Vincent himself, he hardly registered the judge's pompous jeremiad. From the beginning of the case he had found the entire scenario theatrical and arcane, the judge a Dickensian caricature, the jury a collection of dolts who thought and heard only what His Honour dictated. When the verdict was announced he half expected someone to shout 'Off with his head!' while the court officials turned into a pack of cards. He wanted to laugh aloud – to laugh and laugh – to show his contempt for them all. But his lips were clamped together and his vocal cords paralysed. Unreality had become real, the theatre was a courtroom, the playing-card people had condemned him. He could not laugh and he must not cry. All he had left was dignity. A short way off he glimpsed his father, breasting the crowd towards him; but the guards hustled him from the room without waiting. When they asked him if he wished to say goodbye to his family he said no. They put him in the van; the doors slammed shut. By the time John asked for him, he had already been driven away.

Crystal heard the news on the radio, where she sat at home with the phone off the hook and her long hair, escaped from the towel, sprawling down her back like waterweed. She had allowed herself to be dissuaded from going to court; by this stage she had run through both her wardrobe of large hats and her taste for tabloid exposure. Instead, she stayed in and washed her hair. Why not? she said to her mother. Life goes on. It had been one way of filling in the snail-slow hours until the result which could only confirm her fears. Richard had warned her what to expect, months before, but the baldly worded news item still shocked her. Guilty. Eighteen months in prison. It was the end of her romance, the end of her careful dreams. If she had a romance to end. Fate had been shredding the petals for some time, pulling the rose apart, until all that remained was an empty calyx and a few grains of anguish. She told herself that she would have waited for him – waited eighteen months or eighteen years – if he had only asked her; but he had not asked. In claiming a non-existent engagement she had made her *beau geste*, and he had brushed it aside. The implication was uncomfortably obvious. She tried to imagine being there to meet him when he came out, but even by the standards of fantasy the image was unlikely. Crystal Winter, top model, with her perfect face and her perfect behaviour, was not going to hang around outside a prison for a futureless ex-convict who might not rush into her arms, might not even see that she was there. On the radio the news had finished; the familiar round of pop music resumed, tap-tapping at her ears. She leaned her forehead on her hand in a pose that was studied by instinct. Her lower lip shook.

'Here: have a cup of tea.' Mona Winter, determined to anticipate disaster, had made a fresh pot with every news break since lunch. 'You know, I can't help feeling . . . well, at least you didn't *marry* him.'

Crystal did not comment.

'Will you write to him? I really don't think—'

'I'll decide.' Crystal lifted her head, showing dry eyes. 'Right now, I don't know. I just don't know. I doubt if he's thought about me much lately. As the trial got nearer he got – more distant. It's funny, really' – she didn't look amused – 'his family seemed to accept me and Richard's been wonderful, but Vincent and I – we've just grown farther and farther apart. I thought I loved him, I truly did, but . . .' I chose to love him, I chose him, and he rejected me. She couldn't say it, she couldn't even bring herself to think it. Crystal had never been rejected in her life. Suddenly she began to cry, more in anger than in sorrow, gusty irregular sobs tearing at her chest. Mona stroked her damp hair and murmured soothing trivia. The doorbell rang but she made no move to answer it.

Crystal struggled to recover her self-possession. 'You'd better go,' she said. 'It's probably only more journalists; still . . . Anyway, I won't see them. I won't see anyone. Unless it's Richard.'

Mona got to her feet. 'Richard's a nice young man,' she remarked.

In the prison van Vincent, as Crystal had surmised, was not thinking about her. Richard was. He considered staying with his uncle, if only to show solidarity, but when John dived into Piers Percival's chauffeur-driven Rolls somehow Richard was left behind. He eluded roving photographers, hailed a cab, and gave Crystal's address. There was nothing he could do for Vincent and not much for John, but Crystal needed him. In the past months that had acquired an overwhelming importance. Crystal needed him. The taxi, suitably encouraged, sped him to her side.

4

Vincent served six months of his sentence, six months that he would later claim changed him forever. But he was wrong. Character does not change, it merely develops: strengths grow stronger, weaknesses weaker, fundamental qualities and defects which have been present from birth become more dominant under pressure. Cut off from the insulation of wealth and class, isolated and alienated, Vincent was forced to draw on resources from within himself, to learn at last who he really was. He was taken initially to Wormwood Scrubs, and because his sentence was relatively short the powers that be decided to leave him there. He had little idea of what to expect. Even in the van, he did not speculate: he was too numbed by events to do more than exist, minute by minute. During his earlier sojourn in a police cell he had been on his own, and without further reflection he assumed it would be the same in prison: he would be locked away in solitary splendour like a latter-day Edmond Dantès in a rather more civilised version of the Château d'If. He visualised a cell large enough to allow for restless pacing, bare walls, a hard bed, a few extra amenities suitable to the twentieth century. He would look out through a barred window at 'that little tent of blue which prisoners call the sky' and think his own bleak thoughts, undisturbed by any intrusion. Instead, he was taken to a room so narrow that the two beds inside it almost overlapped; the walls were decorated with girlie pictures and the amenities supplied by a bucket. 'No private suites and chilled champagne here,' said the screw, who didn't like his Oxbridge accent. His cellmate stared at him out of matt-black eyes with practised unenthusiasm. He looked a couple of years older than Vincent and three or four inches taller, overfilling his share of the living space, long legs folded on the bed, enormous shoulders stretching almost from wall to wall. He had a sort of Cockney alertness superimposed on the statuesque features of the Caribbean, the bone structure of a steel pylon, hair cropped against his skull. He did not say hello. Vincent, who was not easily daunted as a rule, felt daunted. Presently, his companion lit a cigarette and began to smoke with quiet concentration. He did not offer one to the newcomer and, with no appreciation of the barter system which underpins prison life, Vincent assumed he was being unfriendly. Since there was nothing else to do he lay down on his bunk with his hands behind his head gazing at the ceiling. His reason told him this was it, this was reality, he must adapt or perish, but his unreason still screamed in protest. This could not be happening to him, not to *him*, locked away in a sliver of a room between a hostile black giant and a picture of Chesty Morgan, with outside guards and grids, walls within walls, clanking keys, clanging doors. Soon, surely, someone would come and let him out, apologise profusely, tell him it was all a frightful mistake. But no one came. Footsteps passed down the corridor and died away. No one came.

'What's your name, then?' his companion enquired eventually.

'Vincent Savage.' It didn't seem the moment to roll out the whole lot.

'They call you Vin?'

'No. I can't stand it.'

The other appeared to consider for a minute. 'Hello, Vin.' The intention might have been offensive or merely mischievous; but he did not look mischievous. He was too large and too black.

Vincent waited in vain for him to proffer some corresponding information. At length he felt impelled to ask: 'So what's your name?'

'Hannibal Barker. My friends call me Han.'

'Hello, Han.'

'I didn't say you was one of my friends.'

It was not a promising beginning. Much later, Vincent tried to drift off to sleep, but such relaxation cannot always be achieved by trying, and although he drifted sleep would not come. He lingered on the borders of oblivion, in the penumbra of a shadowland where locks and bars meant nothing. Every time he began the slide into the shadows some shift in the pattern of his floating dreams would snatch him back into consciousness, once so violently that he thought the bed rocked. He felt both drained and tense, as if his nervous system was stretched taut over an inward emptiness. He had ceased to think about past or future: he functioned only in the present, in a dim region midway between sleeping and waking. He thought he heard an owl hooting somewhere nearby, a sound he associated with Weatherfray, not with London; certainly not with jail. Then the call was answered by another, and another, the fox's bark, the jackal's howl, the hyena's shriek, and soon the whole building echoed with animal cries, mimicked, distorted, magnified by the human zoo all around him. He heard monkeys yammering, parrots screeching, feet drumming, the clatter of mugs against the bars. It was a phenomenon he came to recognise later, the younger prisoners exhausting their pent-up energy in an outburst that was half protest, half mere pandemonium. But that first night Vincent thought it was the final insanity: he had left the rational world behind and now here he was, trapped in a menagerie of madmen crying with animal voices, a lost note of lucidity in a bedlam. The din died away at last to be replaced by another irritant: Hannibal was snoring. His huge chest rose and fell and from his nostrils there came the deep gurgling of a subterranean torrent. In the end, abandoning caution, Vincent reached out and gave him a shove, then a punch. Hannibal rolled over and grunted; the snoring simply changed its tune. Vincent lay wakeful far into the small hours, wondering how in all the circles of hell he was going to endure.

He endured because he had no choice, of course. At Gordonstoun he had learned to compromise with discipline; here, he could do the same. In some ways the environment was very similar: an authoritarian regime, petty restrictions, the inevitable frustrations and below-the-belt humour of a single-sex society. As at school, Vincent found an outlet in exercise, working out in the gym every day in the company of assorted thugs who were hoping to graduate from GBH to armed robbery. He held himself aloof out of habit and at the start most of his fellow prisoners regarded him with suspicion and hostility: he was arrogant, snobbish, an upper-class ponce; he read too many books, he chewed with his mouth shut, he picked up his aitches. The warders occasionally harassed him, possibly for the same reasons. 'A couple of the screws have really got it in for you,' Hannibal remarked. 'You know why?'

'Bugger,' Vincent said. 'I forgot to tip.'

Hannibal laughed. 'Nah. You act posh, see. Kind of high and mighty. That's the trouble. You take Claud along the passage, Claud the creep. He talks posh but he don't act it. He sucks up to people, he don't look down on 'em. You do. The lags don't like that but the screws bloody hate it. You got to ask yourself why a bloke wants to be a screw. We're in here because the judge said so but he isn't. He's here because he likes it. He likes putting on a uniform and giving orders and acting big. Same as the pigs. There's a few decent ones but in a place like this most of them are just bullies. They got all the power and we get all the shit. You want to be careful, Vin. A friendly warning. You think you're smart but you're as innocent as a bleeding baby.'

'Are you threatening me?' Vincent demanded flatly, closing the Len Deighton he had borrowed from the library.

'No. You aren't listening. If I wanted to do you over I wouldn't waste time talking about it. You're all right. I thought you'd be a real pain in the arse to begin with but I'm getting used to you. I'm even getting used to the way you talk. Maybe I'll walk out of here talking BBC too. At least you don't fart all the time like Evans, or pick your nose with a teaspoon like Dooley. I told him, it's fucking bad manners. My mum brought me up proper. I won't have bad manners.'

'Did he reform?' Vincent said.

'You bet he did.' Hannibal spoke without false modesty. Vincent, who was also getting used to his cellmate, found himself grinning.

'Read a lot, don't you?' Hannibal resumed presently.

'It passes the time.'

'You good at reading?'

Vincent, baffled by the question, looked up from his book with a frown. '*Good* at it?'

'I mean, can you read handwriting, or just print?'

'Depends.'

'I got this letter from my girlfriend, see. She don't write so good. Since you're so clever, maybe you can read it.'

There was a spurious scepticism in Hannibal's tone which did not deceive Vincent at all. He took the letter and glanced through it: there were two pages of lined paper, covered in a laboured, schoolgirlish script which seemed to him particularly clear. It was signed Lexy.

He read it aloud without further comment.

'You read good,' Hannibal declared at the end, offering judicious approval. 'S'pose you went to a posh school?'

Vincent grimaced. 'Very posh. But it wasn't academic. I was bright, so they thought I must be a freak.'

'You know what? My teacher said I was a freak, too. I was twelve years old and six inches taller than him. You're all brawn and no brains, he said. So I hit him.' After a moment's reflection, Hannibal added: 'He didn't teach me nothing.'

'I'm not surprised.'

'Yeah, well, I didn't have much time for school. I was into other things. All the same, I think kids ought to be taught proper. Some teachers, they think you're a tough, they give you a bad name, so they just can't be buggered. If I'd been taught proper, I'd have read as good as you. Here, you want to try this one? This is from my other girlfriend. She writes *really* bad.'

There was some justification for this assessment. Jayne, unlike Lexy, had dispensed with lines: her handwriting wriggled across the page in a worm-like fashion, sloping in every direction at once. But the sentiments thus expressed were very similar: passionate love in passionate cliché, interspersed with random bits of news. Judi had had her baby. Doll had been arrested for soliciting, it wasn't fair, just 'cos she was a black girl in a short skirt. The fryer at the Chinese takeaway had caught fire and burned the place down. Missing you dreadfully. Vincent's lip curled: he tried to imagine Crystal writing such a letter; but she hadn't written at all. He had thought about her more often lately, usually at night. His lip uncurled again; he knew the stress must be affecting him, making him emotionally vulnerable; suddenly, even the banalities seemed oddly touching.

'What have you got that I haven't got?' he quipped, mocking himself.

Hannibal grinned broadly. 'You guess. Black guys have more of everything.'

He had, it transpired, three girlfriends, Jayne, Lexy and Di. They each wrote once a week and visited in turn, causing Hannibal continuous anxiety in case their schedules got mixed up. He was, he said, in love with all of them, but for different reasons: Jayne for her easy-going manner, Lexy for her romantic fervour, Di for her looks. Photographs were forthcoming. Jayne was plump with an enormous smile and glossy conker-brown breasts. Lexy was skinny with a complexion more sallow than black and short hair, ruthlessly straightened, standing up like wire on top of her head. Di was an improbable blonde with a Barbie Doll figure who was supposed to resemble Diana Ross. 'That's why I call her Di; her real name's Helen.' Jayne had a baby by a previous boyfriend; Di a husband. Vincent preferred Lexy, she of the legible handwriting, according to Hannibal because she had no tits. 'Your sort are all the same,' he averred. 'You want girls to look like blokes. It's the bleeding public schools. You're all queers underneath.'

'Better watch out, darling,' Vincent murmured.

'In here,' said Hannibal, 'that's not funny.'

Vincent flicked through the photographs again. 'Do you write back to them?' he said. 'It must keep you pretty busy.'

'Nah. I'm the one in stir, aren't I? I need the letters. I need cheering up. They're on the outside; they got plenty to do without having letters writ to them.'

Vincent hesitated for an instant, then plunged.

'You can't read and write, can you?' he said.

'It's my eyesight, see. I—'

'Bullshit. Your eyesight's as good as mine. You can see Chesty Morgan well enough on a dark night to count the creases in her nipples. You can't read and write. You got right through school without even learning the basics, didn't you? So much for state education.' Vincent had heard of adult illiteracy but he had never met it before and certainly never thought about it. He was shocked – the way his grandfather had been shocked at desertion and his father at fraud. The three Rs were something he had always taken for granted.

'You don't tell no one,' Hannibal said, leaning forward. 'Your bleeding word of honour, mate. I'm telling you, same as I told Evans the Fart. You start shooting your mouth off outside this cell—'

'Don't be an idiot,' Vincent snapped. 'I'm too high and mighty, remember? I act posh. I don't talk to people.' And he added, deliberately ungrammatical: 'I won't say nothing to nobody.'

In those restricted surroundings he was prepared to bet everyone knew already; they either didn't care or were too wary of Hannibal to mention it.

But Hannibal cared. That much was obvious. He sat back on the bed, slowly relaxing. He said: 'Yeah, well,' and 'You're all right, Vin.' Eventually he continued: 'Would you help me to write a letter, then? I mean, if I wanted.'

'Sure.' Vincent reopened his Len Deighton, then closed it again. 'Now?'

Hannibal knew most of the alphabet, getting muddled around MNO. He could recognise a few simple words. That was all. Vincent refused to write the actual letter for him, insisting: 'Even if you just copy me, you'll start to learn.' And so Hannibal started to learn and Vincent, willy-nilly, found himself starting to teach. He had little patience and no spirit of philanthropy but, like the Len Deighton thriller, it passed the time. And time crawled in prison. Bouts of furious exercise filled him with restless energy but he had no way of expending it. The two of them were banged up for hours, sometimes silent, sometimes talking, swapping anecdotes of their different lives, comparing their curiously similar brands of cynicism, until the last of the conversation petered out and there were only the creeping seconds and the lagging minutes and the grey boredom fading into insidious despair. Then Vincent would reach for pen and paper and say: 'Come on, let's try another letter. Jayne this time,' or Di, or Lexy again, pushing Hannibal into unwanted effort, unaccustomed concentration, unexpected results. So the days passed, a whole month of days, ticked off on the wall calendar with the Raquel Welch lookalike in leopard-skin crotchless briefs. It occurred to Vincent that endurance was both easier and more difficult than he had anticipated. It was easy to get on with Hannibal – despite the snoring – difficult to struggle through those endless, sleepless nights, when all the thoughts he did not want to think would come slithering out of their holes to pester him. 'How come you sleep so well?' he asked Hannibal once.

'Been here longer than you, haven't I? I'm used to the place. Getting used to things: that's the secret. I keep telling you. Anyway, I always sleep well. Clear conscience.'

Vincent contemplated enquiring what he had done to be sent to prison but refrained; he had already learned that was something you didn't ask.

Hannibal read his mind. 'Knife job,' he said. 'Mind you, the other bloke went for me. I didn't have no choice. But you try telling that to the judge when you're black and on the dole and the pigs insist you give the arresting officer a fat lip.'

'The man you knifed,' said Vincent, managing to sound non-committal, 'did you kill him?'

'Course not. He was too big; the knife was too small. He had a belly on him like a darts player. I just let a little blood. Probably did him good.'

There was a pause while Vincent absorbed this. Then Hannibal went on: 'You're in for fraud, right?'

'Yes.'

'Fraud's no good. No class. A knife job, that's class, see. I get respect from the other blokes. Not like a blagger or a cop-killer, mind; that's the big time. But I get respect. Fraud, that's borjwar. That's crime for clerks.'

'It was a big fraud,' Vincent offered.

'I should bloody hope so. I won't have no piddling little crimes in here.'

Vincent laughed. 'I didn't really do anything wrong,' he said. 'I just did it in the wrong way. There's a fine distinction which escaped me. I was – honestly dishonest, overtly covert. If I had been a hypocrite they would have clapped me on the back and told me to get on with it.'

'You're as innocent as the driven snow,' said Hannibal. 'I know. We're all bleeding innocent in here. House rule.'

Later, when they got back to letter-writing, he remarked: 'You don't get many letters.'

'I won't have them,' said Vincent. 'This is a rest cure. Doctor's orders: I mustn't be disturbed.'

Richard was a bad correspondent: they had agreed he wouldn't attempt to write. Phrases like 'The weather is fine' and 'I hope you are well' had formed the gist of all his letters from school. 'Don't bother,' Vincent had said lightly. 'What's the point?' – not realising that a time might come when even those simple expressions could have constituted the high point of his day. John had written once but that letter Vincent had returned unopened. There was still no word from Crystal. Jolanda, hearing belatedly of her son's situation, had sent a ream of scrawled notepaper, affectionate, tearbesplotched, eloquent and incoherent. Much of it was in Italian, and since Vincent had forgotten all but a few essential swear-words this left him as baffled as was Hannibal by his correspondence. A pocket dictionary, borrowed from a crooked antique dealer who was trying to break into Europe, only confused the issue still further. 'I'm damned if I'll answer it,' Vincent had said on receipt of this tome; but a week later he wrote back, a single page, cool but not cold, his only epistolary effort to date.

'You don't get many visitors, either,' Hannibal persisted.

'None.' Vincent was brusque. 'I told you: I'm incommunicado. I've already embarrassed my family and now I won't have them embarrassing me. Besides, I don't want my girlfriend exciting the screws.'

'You never said you got a girlfriend,' Hannibal observed. 'What's she like?'

'I *had* a girlfriend,' Vincent said.

Another month passed, no quicker than the one before. Vincent waited for the days to speed up but they didn't: time spent in tedium cannot accelerate, it can only plod. However, he was beginning to feel at ease, even at home, to have a sense of belonging if not actual camaraderie, bickering with the other convicts, beating them at Monopoly, absorbing the ruthlessly practical mores of prison life. As for Hannibal, they had become friends almost without his noticing it. Vincent told him things he had never even told Richard, shameful fears and angry hopes, poured out in a moment of weakness, a spasm of despair, usually in the evenings when he was at a low physical ebb and the sense of desolation seemed to suck his willpower away. He wished his relatives had not taken him quite so literally when he claimed he did not want visitors; yet when Elizabeth wrote as one in duty bound to ask if she should come he sent back an immediate refusal, frigidly worded, icily polite. His inflexible façade was maintained for the benefit of all but Hannibal. But there were still some prisoners on whom his dark good looks made a softer impression: one Higgs, a chunky, muscled, pimpled individual with gangster connections, offered two ounces of tobacco and a quarter of marijuana for sexual intercourse. When Vincent declined, he threw in a pot of jam. 'I suppose that bloody nigger's getting it all,' he said after a final negative.

'He's not my type,' said Vincent. 'Nor are you. Frankly, even if I was as bent as a hairpin I wouldn't want your smelly little prick near my arsehole. God knows what I might catch.'

His audience sniggered and Higgs retreated, muttering. Vincent thought no more of it.

'You want to be careful with Higgs,' Hannibal said when regaled with the incident. 'He's big and nasty and some of his mates are even bigger and nastier. He's the kind you want to let down sort of gentle.'

'What does it matter?' said Vincent.

A week later he found out. He was in the showers when they came for him, Higgs and two others, one of whom, Vincent knew, was a murderer with a sentence so long that he didn't give a damn what he did. The screw on duty was the man who had sneered at Vincent the night he arrived. He simply turned his back; perhaps he had been bribed, perhaps his dislike of the Oxbridge accent had undermined his few principles. The three men surrounded Vincent, blocking his exit, cornering him, ponderous and threatening. Higgs was sweating with eagerness and wiping his hands on his clothes, leaving visible patches of damp. 'You won't give, I'll take,' he muttered, swallowing the words in his haste as though he did not wish to waste too much breath on talking. Vincent had realised at once what they wanted but he was still too disgusted to be afraid. His main disadvantage was that he was naked; he considered reaching for a towel but it would waste precious seconds and provide no protection. He reminded himself that the ancient Greeks had gone into battle nude, at least according to their statuary. The men advanced, he backed away, looking for weaknesses, trying to ignore his own exposure. Then the wall was behind him and he could back no further. Higgs moved in, actually licking his lips, small pink tongue poking out to explore pallid labia. With the part of his mind that was still detached Vincent registered a kind of aesthetic contempt at such stereotyped behaviour. When Higgs was near enough for him to count the pimples on his cheek, he moved. He grabbed his opponent by the balls and squeezed. Hard. Higgs yelled, the other two pounced, and then there was no more time for thinking. The worst thing about it was the impossibility of shielding his own genitals while trying to hit back, preferably at theirs. But they were three to one and all heavier than he; it was no contest. There came a moment when he knew he could not fight his way out. A kidney punch doubled him up and then somehow he was on the floor. They pushed him on to his stomach and one of them seemed to be kneeling on his back. He decided that this was a good time to call for assistance but they had smashed his face on to the tiles and his mouth was full of blood. He thought: this is how women feel during a rape, this frustration, this terrible helplessness. He had not known physical helplessness since babyhood. The inner core of anger which had always made him stronger and more vicious than any rival seemed suddenly a small, inadequate thing, the battering of a moth's wings against a lighted window, violent but futile. He strained every muscle, tried to struggle, to twist, to kick, but the weight on his back pressed him to the floor and his legs were pinioned. Hands fumbled between his thighs in a gross parody of a caress. Nausea filled him. He knew fear – fear not of pain but of invasion, defilement, the ultimate obscenity. He heard a fly unzipped, felt groping fingers between his buttocks. He was helpless, useless, weak as a woman. He would have broken his own neck if he had been able.

Such was the blackness of his mind, it was an instant before he was aware of the change. Running footsteps – a sudden silence – an angry voice, deep as a growl. Hannibal's voice. The pressure on his back shifted slightly and he jerked his body free with flick-knife speed and scrambled to his feet. Higgs also stood up, adjusting his clothes and glancing from Hannibal to Vincent and back again. His thought processes were clearly legible: he and his henchmen would tackle either of them alone but not both together. That would be too much like a fair fight.

Hannibal ignored him. 'You all right?' he asked Vincent.

Vincent merely grunted. He was dressing quickly, keeping one eye on the opposition. When he came to the fastenings he hoped they would not see his fingers trembling. He did not say anything because he knew his voice would give him away.

Hannibal was having words with the screw, unfriendly words consisting mostly of four letters. Vincent didn't listen. He wanted to get back to the safety of his cell, to the closeness of protective walls, the privacy of a locked door. He maintained his taut façade by instinct but his control felt brittle: the lightest touch would have broken him. His self-image had been exposed in all its vainglory: he was not the tough, enigmatic, untouchable anti-hero of his own life-story but as defenceless and ineffectual as other men. It gave him no sense of kinship with the rest of humanity; instead, he saw himself belittled, one victim among many, a creature of less significance than the lowest of his fellow convicts. He remembered his father on morality, and the judge's piously expressed hope that in prison he would reflect on the error of his ways. He thought: they're living on another planet; and a bitterness rose in him like bile, giving him strength. It occurred to him that it is only the darker emotions which make you strong. Bitterness would rebuild the outer casing of his ego, restore his dignity, revive his spirit. But for now, he only wanted to lick his wounds, and hide.

In their cell, Hannibal said: 'You sure you're all right?'

'Fairly.' Vincent took refuge in a rather shaky sarcasm. 'At least I didn't suffer a fate worse than death.'

The memory of total helplessness was not something he could put aside without an effort.

Presently, he demanded: 'How did you know about it?'

'I heard, didn't I? You know what this place is like: you hear everything two days before it's happened. Someone said Higgs was looking for you with a couple of his mates. So I went looking for Higgs.'

Vincent said awkwardly: 'Thanks.' He wasn't used to being grateful.

'Nothing to thank me for. You done me a favour with my letter-writing; now I done you one. A favour for a favour. Makes us even.'

'I didn't help you with your writing as part of a trade,' Vincent said sharply. 'I thought we were friends.'

'Course we're friends. I told you. You done something for me; I done something for you. Now it's your turn again. In here, that's the way it goes. Out there, too, if you ask me – only here we're straight about it. I don't go for the emotional stuff. Friendship, it's a deal like any other. You scratch my back, I scratch yours. See what I mean?'

'So that's what we are.' Vincent was beginning to relax again; he even managed a faint smile. 'Back-scratchers.'

Later, they discussed the screw whose duties had placed him so conveniently for turning a blind eye. Vincent wanted to make an official complaint, but Hannibal vetoed the idea.

'You don't want to do nothing official. It don't look good. You take care of yourself in here; you don't ask the bleeding authorities to take care of you. It's us against them, see. The other blokes, they mostly think you're one of us now. You start making complaints and talking official and you're acting like one of them. That don't go down well. Anyway, Higgs isn't hardly going to back you up, is he? It'd be your word against the screw. You'd be wasting your time.'

'It makes me sick.' Vincent was recovering his anger as well as his humour. 'That bastard is a public servant. My taxes pay his wages. If he doesn't do his job he ought to be fired.'

'My taxes pay his wages! Fucking hell!' It was Hannibal's turn to be amused. 'You're in prison, Vin, not in Parliament. I never heard nothing like it! Tell you what: one of these days, when you get out of here, you ought to stand for election. You got my vote, anyway. Power to the bleeding people!'

'I don't see what's so funny,' Vincent argued. 'I'm still a citizen, even in jail. I've got the same rights.'

'Rights,' said Hannibal profoundly, 'aren't what you got. They're what you take.'

When Vincent was in his fifth month, Hannibal was transferred. He had served a year of his sentence in Wormwood Scrubs and the authorities in their wisdom had decided a change of surroundings might be beneficial. He said goodbye clumsily, evidently feeling a display of emotion was unsuited to his macho image. Vincent was equally uncomfortable.

'You ain't got long left,' Hannibal said. 'You'll be out in a month.'

'Mmm.'

'I'll miss you, you know. I got used to you. Getting used to people, that's the main thing.'

'I was better than Evans the Fart?'

'Yeah. Well . . . yeah.'

'Hope I don't get him now.'

There was a pause – an elephantine pause heavy with swallowed words and stifled feelings. Hannibal's Englishness was solely a matter of upbringing; Vincent had only a half-share of Anglo-Saxon genes. Yet the warmth of the Caribbean and the ardour of Italy were both submerged under traditional British stoicism. At length Vincent said: 'I'll see you some time – when you get out.'

'Nah. You'll be the smart-arse fixing the stock market and I'll be the yob who steals the radio out of your Roller. What d'you bet? You got to face things. What've we got in common? This place. On the outside, nothing. We live in different worlds. You got to be real-istic . . .'

Vincent said curtly: 'You're my best friend.'

It was Richard who belonged to a different world, a long ago fairy tale of two boys growing up in their own private kingdom, untouched by the coarser side of life. Blurred with distance, Weatherfray and all its shadows appeared as a castle in a fantasy, a nostalgic vision darkened with rejection and betrayal, sweet tainted with bitter. But for Vincent, the bitter would always have the stronger flavour. He thought: 'Richard should have visited me, no matter what I said. He should at least have written . . .' Resentment had grown in him unnoticed: he did not want it but he could not drive it out. His own gall was too much for him.

'All right,' Hannibal was saying. 'In here we're mates. Outside, it's another ball game. I'm telling you—'

'I won't change,' Vincent said.

'Nice thought.' Hannibal kept it flippant. 'Anyway, it's the bleeding thought what counts, innit?'

'Fuck off.'

They shook hands on the phrase. No farewell, no *au revoir*. Just 'fuck off'. That night, Vincent had a new cellmate, a ginger-haired fence from Birmingham who didn't snore. The gentle rhythm of his breathing seemed unbearably irritating after Hannibal's tigerish rumblings. Vincent lay awake in the unnatural hush, almost wish-ing the menagerie would begin its midnight chorus, rerunning old trains of thought. In prison, he reflected, there is nothing to protect you from your own feelings – helplessness, loneliness, affection, they are all there waiting to catch you off guard. The physical bar-riers are in place but the mental barriers are torn down, the prisoner is stripped naked, deprived of the carefully chosen settings which give him cover, the public image which conceals him, the *bella figura* to which he clings. There is only the man, isolated and defenceless. Vincent missed Hannibal with an ache which he knew to be weakness, yet the pain had an edge that stung his eyes as if with tears. Childish folly. He might have wept for his mother when he was four years old, though he could not remember it, but an adult does not cry in the night because his friend has been taken away. He felt as if he had been flayed, laid open to every emotion which might choose to rampage through his spirit. Irrational pangs of longing jabbed at his heart – not merely for Hannibal but for Richard, Crystal, even his father. Hannibal had been his friend indeed but he believed he would never forgive the other three, not just for their desertion but because he could not stop loving them in return.

The night dragged by like all the other nights. One month left. It would be the longest month of all.

PART III

A NECESSARY POISON

1

At Vincent's own injunction no one came to meet him the day he was released. He had sent instructions to his lawyer, piling bitterness on bitterness, yet when the prison doors finally closed behind him he was genuinely glad to be alone, savouring that first taste of liberty. It should have been a spring day, with a high sun and birds singing and leaves fluttering on the trees. Instead it was a grey English summer, treeless streets, chattering rain, smoking traffic, umbrellas jostling for position on the pavement. He took a cab to Chelsea, thinking idly of Richard, his rancour half melting in the pleasure of simply being free. They would go for a drink together, a pint of tepid beer in the fug of some drab city bar. Later, there would be dinner, underdone steaks oozing blood and wine to match. Last of all, he would find a girl – if Crystal was not available, any girl would do – and fuck himself to sleep. He did not want to make plans, not yet; the future was too full of uncertainty. But for the moment, this one small plan did not seem over-ambitious.

At the house, he received his first check. Richard had moved out.

'Your room's still empty,' said the new tenant. 'I think your father paid the rent.'

'Big of him,' said Vincent. 'Where's Richard?'

'He's got a flat with some girl. I'll give you the number.'

'Which girl?'

'Just some girl.'

'*Which girl?*'

He knew the answer. Against logic, against loyalty, he knew. He forgot that before the trial he had effectively repudiated her and remembered only that she had been his. The thought of her black chocolate hair and white chocolate limbs had formed his nightly dessert for the last six months. He had run through every detail of her anatomy, every aspect of her mystery: the secret workings of her mind, the seamless mask of her face. Surely, too, he had said he loved her, in those far-off Cambridge days – once or twice when the poetry of Yeats or the size of his erection had carried him away. Even though she hadn't written he had told himself she would be there when he came out; he had sought reassurance in remembered words, fragments of midnight conversation; if he had imagined her with other men they had always been transients, escorts for an evening or an hour, no one important. No one like Richard. Yet he knew. Immediately, impossibly. Only Richard could have taken her from him, only she could have stolen Richard. Only Crystal.

He obtained his cousin's address from the new tenant and went straight round there. Richard opened the door. They stared at each other as if it had been six years, not six months, since their last meeting. Richard wore tattered jeans, unironed shirt, unshaven chin. Yet in Vincent's eyes he looked somehow the picture of domestic bliss, as if the carelessness of intimacy had crumpled the shirt and neglected the razor. He said: 'You'd better come in.' There was no irresistible smile, no conventional welcome. A sneaking hope that he might say: 'I've met this wonderful girl' died unborn.

Over coffee, Vincent said: 'Well?'

'I assume you've heard.'

'Heard what?' Vincent was not going to make it easy for him. His face was tight, as though the features had finally become set in his habitual expression of inflexibility, skin taut, muscles locked. Richard thought he seemed indefinably older, not through the addition of lines but from some internal hardening process. The thought hurt him, but there was nothing he could do.

He said: 'For God's sake! You know, don't you? Let's not piss around.'

'Know?'

'About Crystal and me.'

Vincent said nothing at all. In fear, in distress, in pain, it is your voice that gives you away. He wanted to lose his temper, to swear and curse and smash his fist in Richard's face, but he could not. His reactions were numbed.

'We couldn't help it,' Richard continued after a short pause. 'Sorry: that's bloody trite. We couldn't help it, we didn't mean it, it was just one of those things. All the classic excuses. The truth is, she was unhappy and very alone. She needed someone. I didn't realise I was falling in love with her until it was too late. And she—'

'Fell in love with you?'

'*You* didn't love her,' Richard observed. Like the childhood toys Vincent hadn't wanted, until his cousin tried to play with them.

With an effort, Vincent said lightly: 'You always told me I could pull the girls but I couldn't keep them: wasn't that it? At least you've proved your point.'

'Do you seriously believe that's why I did it? Look, you didn't care about her; I did. You lost all interest in her after your arrest. You didn't even write to her while you were in prison. It would have been ludicrous for Crys and I to go through some sort of noble renunciation just so that when you came out you could fuck her and forget her like all the rest. I know our timing was bloody awful, but do we have to make a high drama out of it? After all, we've shared a girlfriend before. The only difference is that I love this one and I mean to keep her. You'd have traded her for a newer registration in a month or two. Come on, Vincent. Tell me I'm a rat – hit me if you like – and then I'll pick my teeth off the floor and we'll go for a drink.'

A drink with Richard: phase one of Vincent's project for the day. The old charm was there now, the familiar grin. But they were not schoolboys any more, fighting and making up over schoolboy issues. Vincent, in his turn, thought his cousin looked older, both stronger and somehow more solid, a self-asssured, self-centred adult, using his own wants and needs to justify his perfidy. In the past Vincent had always been the selfish one, unconsciously dependent on Richard's altruism, Richard's generosity, Richard's love. Without thinking about it, he had known he would come first. But this time, Richard had put himself first – himself and Crystal. Vincent had been betrayed in absentia by the person he trusted most, and now he was supposed to shake hands and say it didn't matter. Let us drink to friendship, cousinship and domestic bliss. Worst of all,

there was a part of him – a loose thread in his nervous system, a
weak link in his heart – which urged him to succumb to Richard's
charm, to dismiss Crystal for the sake of old affection and a pint of
beer. That sickened him. Anger dispelled the numbness, a black
controlled rage which turned everything to wormwood. He got to
his feet.

'Keep your teeth,' he said. 'Also your drink.'

He thought of other things to say – I'll never forget this; I'll
never forgive you. One day I'll even the score. Send me a bill for
the coffee.

All of them sounded ridiculously melodramatic.

Richard followed him to the door. 'Give it a few weeks,' he said.
'Get used to it. Then call me.' His words were hopeful but his
expression was unhappy and unsurprised.

Vincent just looked at him. Then he walked out of the flat and
down the stairs to the street without looking back.

That evening he found a girl. Any girl. He made love to her clumsily, fury translated into passion, with none of the fiery sweetness he
had been anticipating. Afterwards, he fell asleep, exhausted if not
fulfilled, while she lay awake, wondering why her flatmate had told
her he was so special. The next morning, he began to think about
leaving England. He had no job, no immediate prospects, nothing
to do but crawl back to his father in contrition and beg for
clemency – for help in his career, money in his bank account. It was
impossible. In London, he had grown apart from his social circle;
former friends had become mere acquaintances; without Richard,
there was no one to whom he was close any more. Inevitably, he
thought of his mother. She had continued writing to him, assuring
him in a motley of languages and grammatical forms – Italian,
English, American – that she had always loved him, she had never
willingly abandoned him, it was all John with his cold British manners and that sly *traditrice* of a nanny. Vincent recalled Dixy with a
vague affection, yet the discussion he had overheard in the shadows
of Weatherfray had left an ineradicable aftertaste. He was too old
now to believe his mother and he had never believed his father, but
it did not matter. Come and stay with me, Jolanda begged him, in
letter after letter; here in Italy which is your true home you will
rediscover yourself – the warm southern vitality which John had

tried so hard to suppress. Vincent distrusted her effusions on principle, looking for the catch, but she seemed to offer him something he needed: unquestioning allegiance, unfailing devotion, or simply a change of scene. It was a chance for a new life, a way of escape. He would not admit to himself that he wanted to escape.

He did not go north to Weatherfray. He did not revisit Richard or attempt to see Crystal. Both John and Elizabeth wrote but John's letter was returned as always, Elizabeth's directed to the wastepaper bin. By the time John came to London himself, Vincent had left the country.

At Malpensa Airport, Vincent was accosted by a pale young man who spoke hesitant English and offered to carry his suitcase, only to find he could scarcely lift it. Vincent assumed he must be a chauffeur or manservant of some kind, but he wore no uniform and his air of embarrassed friendliness did not accord with the role. His name, he said, was Sebastiano Dandolini, on which announcement he essayed a hopeful handshake.

'I have much trouble to recognise you,' he explained carefully. 'La Signora, she have no photograph since you are *bambino*. She say: "You will know him *subito* because he is my son. He look exactly like me." You see: it is very difficult.'

'Do I look like her?' Vincent asked, genuinely curious.

'I think – maybe. A little. But also you look *molto inglese*.'

'In what way?' Vincent was obscurely displeased.

Sebastiano made a series of haphazard gestures no doubt intended to convey Vincent's intrinsic Englishness. '*Espressione – maniera—*' He ended on a helpless shrug as if defeated by his own inarticulateness.

In the car park, they got into a Lancia which had seen better days, probably around 1960. Sebastiano drove away, making halting conversation about Vincent's flight, the weather in England, the weather in Italy, the beauties of Milan. He gave his passenger far more of his attention than the road ahead or the other drivers. Definitely not the chauffeur, Vincent decided from the tenor of his small talk. He had thought at first that Sebastiano must be only a few years older than he was, but a closer scrutiny showed little bunchings and scrunchings around the eye-pockets, a drawing-down of the mouth, a blurring of planes that had once been clearly defined. He was good-looking in that soft, pretty-boy style which normally wears out all too quickly, but in his case the wearing process seemed to have been arrested, at least in part, perhaps by a lack of corresponding mental maturity. His diffidence, his friendliness, his gaucheries were all incongruously youthful, teenage mannerisms sitting awkwardly on a man of over thirty. Vincent concluded, rather dubiously, that he might be some sort of secretary. It was not an explanation which satisfied him.

They drove for over an hour, winding up in a little village with a long name – Mirafiore-Tripodina – on the edge of which Jolanda had a house. 'A big house,' declared Sebastiano, attempting suitable gesticulation. 'Much room. I have one part; Mariangela and Tommaso another; la Signora have all the rest.'

A slight frown drew Vincent's brows together, but he said nothing. He had always taken it for granted that his mother must be very wealthy; now, he was beginning to wonder. It was a long while since the days of her superstardom.

They swung off the road and into a lane. Jolanda's house stood on the right, a crumbling villa behind a crumbling wall. To Vincent, brought up in Weatherfray, it seemed small for a country house and not particularly impressive, merely rambling, flaking, fading, gradually sinking into a decline. Thick twists of vine straddled the porch like the petrified coils of some ancient boa constrictor – glimpses of apricot stucco showed between limp-wristed leaves and pendulous bunches of grapes. The garden was a wilderness of roses. A huge cedar cast its glimmering shade across the front of the house. The whole façade was a collage of sagging shutters, chipped tiles, bleached paintwork, matted hangings of wisteria and jasmine, all petal-starred and shadow-flecked, an artist's dream and a gardener's nightmare, a chaotic commingling of natural growth and domestic decay. Vincent looked in vain for signs of architectural restoration or even regular maintenance. He had left Sebastiano to struggle with his luggage and as he walked up the path he saw a flicker of movement beyond one of the windows. Then the front door opened and she was there. His mother. She ran towards him and embraced him with a fervour that he knew must be familiar; it occurred to him that no one had embraced him like that since she left. Suddenly, he felt strange: the sunlight dazzled him, the heat suffocated him, he needed to go indoors where it was cool and sit down. 'Vincente! *Caro!*' Jolanda's formerly melodious voice had acquired a husky note, the hint of a rasp, a crack in the bell. 'Come into the house. I will make you some tea – not dull English tea with much milk, all pale, pale, like mud in the rain – no, no. I make you iced tea in a long glass to refresh you – or would you rather have champagne? I have iced tea, I have champagne, I have English gin and tonic . . .' He was studying her upturned face for a feature he recognised, but there were none. His childhood memories were too distant for him to have retained more than a dim recollection of laughter and sparkle, warm round cheek, warm round breast, plump arms enfolding him; but he had seen her on screen, a tempestuous creature who could switch from vestal to virago in the flick of a baton, and that Jolanda, too, had vanished. The woman who gazed up at him was smaller than he had expected and thin to gauntness, burned out, sucked-in cheeks under out-thrust bones, every change of expression etched in premature lines; smile lines, scowl lines, storm lines, the intaglio of a thousand lightning moods. The spicy perfume which he missed had been replaced by a whiff of Chanel applied in his honour; her clothes were expensive but out of date and out of style, the wrong colours and designs all jumbled together; if it worked, it was because she had a style of her own. The happiness that lit her eyes was unmistakable, but he did not recognise it.

She took him into the living room, sat him down on the sofa, clasped his hands awkwardly between her own. Her fingers felt like bird's claws, little bunches of fragile bones with crimson nails too long for them and several rings whose big stones knocked together. He thought: This is ridiculous. We don't even know each other, but Jolanda, undeterred, managed to shed a few tears in the pauses between bawling at Sebastiano and a heavily built woman in rustic black, the live-in Mariangela, who appeared to be housekeeper, butler and maid-of-all-work. Presently Sebastiano, having dragged Vincent's luggage into the hall, produced a bottle of *spumante*, Mariangela a set of Venetian wine glasses badly in need of a re-polish.

'Now you are in Italy,' Sebastiano said, 'you must drink Italian wine.'

Vincent duly drank, and experienced a secret yearning to be back in England. Jolanda said: 'We should have had champagne:

Krug is best. Why did you not buy Krug? This stuff – it taste like lemonade' – and she proceeded to drink it in appropriate quantities. Mariangela, who evidently belonged to the dour class of peasant, took a mouthful, deposited her glass on the tray with a significant clang, and retreated to the kitchen. Sebastiano alternated between polite forays into English and rather more voluble Italian, both of which Jolanda ignored. Later, they graduated on to gin and tonic: Jolanda had most of the gin, Sebastiano most of the tonic. Dinner materialised far too late to do any good.

Why did I come to this place? Vincent wondered, halfway down a bottle of Barolo. I don't know these people: my relationship with my mother is a genetic accident. I don't speak the language. I don't have a job. What the hell am I going to do here?

By the bottom of the bottle, his doubts had been reduced to a single phrase, this time without a question-mark: Oh, what the hell.

He staggered up to bed long after midnight carrying his unopened suitcase, with Sebastiano shouting directions from the rear. 'More stairs . . . yes, more stairs. *A destra* . . . along the corridor. No, not that door. *That* door.' Vincent stumbled inside and reached for a light switch. There was a flash, and the darkness continued unrelieved. '*L'elettricità*,' Sebastiano murmured, by way of explanation or apology.

'Perhaps you need a new bulb,' Vincent suggested.

His companion agreed but did not offer to fetch one. Instead, he bumped around in the dark until he found a bedside lamp. In its limited radiance the two men surveyed each other: Vincent, who was still not yet sure of Sebastiano's precise position in the household, thought he looked both nervous and anxious, tentatively friendly, tentatively hostile. However, all he said was: 'I hope you sleep well. Is not very comfortable, but . . .'

'It's better than prison,' Vincent said carelessly.

Sebastiano began to laugh and then checked himself, clearly considering whether he had committed an error of taste. 'You intend stay long?' he hazarded.

He thinks I'll say no, Vincent deduced. He wants me to go home. That settles it. I'm staying.

Aloud, he was noncommittal. 'Maybe. I'll see how I feel when the hangover wears off.'

'Hangover?'

'The one I'm going to have tomorrow.'

'Oh – I see. English joke.' This time Sebastiano laughed without a check, conscientiously. He went to the door, and then turned. Vincent formed the impression he was trying for a Parthian shot. 'La Signora, she is very happy to see you. But she is an artist; she have many *umori*. You must not mind, if tomorrow she is not so happy.'

'I'll remember,' Vincent said. 'Thanks for the tip.'

He endeavoured to keep the sarcasm out of his voice but was not entirely successful. Sebastiano went out, shutting the door behind him; Vincent heard his wavering footsteps retreating down the passage and faltering on the stairs. He took off his shoes, lay down still in his jeans and T-shirt, and switched off the lamp. The bed, as Sebastiano had said, was not very comfortable: several broken springs gave vent to eerie twanging noises whenever he shifted his weight and the stuffing in the mattress appeared to consist mostly of lumps. But although his brain was sufficiently lucid to notice such details, he was not sober enough for them to keep him awake. The last thing he registered was the sound of a cricket tuning up somewhere inside the room; then he slept.

He awoke before dawn with a reeling head and a bursting bladder, only to realise he had no idea of the whereabouts of the upstairs loo, and the downstairs one, according to his recollections of the previous night, was in Sebastiano's part of the house. In the end, he pissed out of the window, narrowly missing Mariangela's husband Tommaso, who had risen early to go about his horticultural duties before the heat got underway. Vincent closed the shutters on a string of graphic oaths and went back to bed.

It was nearly a year before Vincent found out the truth about the hierarchy at the Villa Mirafiore. He took a temporary job in a Milanese bar run by a distant cousin of Mariangela's and Italian lessons from an Englishwoman married to a local count who was a friend of Sebastiano's. The bar work had the charm of novelty, also the charm of the cousin's *fidanzata*, who helped out when they were busy. The Italian lessons, consisting initially of the most basic exercises, reminded him of Hannibal's efforts at learning to read, and eventually he found himself telling his instructress something of prison life while they walked in the beautiful gardens of her beautiful house, arm in arm, hand in hand, cheek to cheek. Sebastiano was appalled, Mariangela furious. Vincent merely claimed that after six months of sexual isolation he needed the practice, and did his best not to think about Crystal. For the most part, he succeeded. The situation at the villa might have become untenable but Sebastiano lacked the stomach for a confrontation and Mariangela, for all her fury, proved to be one of those grim female retainers with a soft spot for the family scapegrace. As for Jolanda, she was delighted, laughing at Vincent's adult adventures even as she had laughed at the peccadillos of a three-year-old infant. 'Is he not wonderful, *mio figlio?* So big, so handsome: all the women are in love with him. But he, he love only his mother.' Do I? Vincent asked himself, in the privacy of his own mind. Jolanda was adoring, maddening, possessive, passionate, no longer beautiful, always unreasonable, given to cyclones of tears and manic outbursts of happiness, yet Mariangela bullied her with real affection, Sebastiano worshipped her, and Vincent, despite his misgivings, had slipped back into their relationship without a second thought. So might a man resume some old familiar garment which has been lying in mothballs for several seasons, only to find it feeling as warm and fitting as snugly as ever. In theory they were strangers; in practice, they understood one another by instinct. Jolanda insisted as a matter of course that she was the most important person in his world and Vincent, equally jealous of rights he had never paused to consider, also expected to come first with her. Hence the conflict with Sebastiano.

He knew, of course, that Dandolini was effectively her boyfriend: that disagreeable fact had filtered through in the early days of his stay. He did not like it, but he supposed it was necessary to be tolerant. He thought of his father, of Frank Cavalcanti, of other men with whom her name had been coupled – a film star, a famous baritone, a gangster, a conductor, a senator. It seemed something of a comedown that she should be reduced to Sebastiano, with his wilting prettiness, his uncertain manners, the chest problem which, Vincent was told, prevented him from singing or lifting heavy objects. Angry at the idea that he was sponging off Jolanda, Vincent was slightly mollified to learn that he had an inherited income which he used to subsidise his love of opera. He had an ambition to be a composer and was, Jolanda declared, outstandingly talented, but he needed an impresario with the boldness and imagination to finance him, and alas, there were no such men in the business any more. Nowadays, they were all *affaristi*, interested solely in a guaranteed dividend, the same old Verdi and Puccini, nothing daring or different. Sebastiano, however, was working on a new opera, with – by coincidence – a starring role for Jolanda, which could not possibly fail to impress even the most soulless producer. When it was completed, Sebastiano would make his name and Jolanda stage her comeback in a shared triumph. Jolanda's comeback was always talked of as an immutable certainty, the way communists in the West used to speak of the Revolution. It will happen, no one knows when but it *will* happen: it is unavoidable, ineffable and always tomorrow.

Meanwhile, Vincent grudgingly permitted Sebastiano to sit at Jolanda's feet and admire, to consult her on the arrangement of an aria or the drama of a duet, and to run errands for her, fuss over her, and tell her, usually at dinner, that she must stop drinking so much. Jolanda paid little attention to his concern whereas, at least in the beginning, she appeared to accept her son's diktat. It was some while before Vincent realised that when she did not drink in his presence she would make up for it behind his back, and that Sebastiano, far from sitting at her feet, frequently slept with her. A distressing scene ensued where Vincent criticised his mother's taste, Jolanda had hysterics, and Sebastiano, intruding at an inapposite moment, lost what little command of English he had ever possessed in an unexpected explosion of rage. 'You not love her!' he accused. 'Twenty years you not see her – you not phone, you not write. Now, you think you can come here, change everything, run her life. Shout orders like bloody *fascista*. You not give one single damn about her. *I* love her, *I* care for her, *io, io, io!*' He sounded fervent, incoherent and vaguely pathetic and Vincent, who wanted to hit him, could not bring himself to do so and slammed his way out of the room instead.

'He does love her,' Mariangela explained later. 'You must quarrel with him in Italian: your Italian is quite good now. It will be much easier in Italian.'

'He loves her,' Vincent echoed sardonically. 'So what? She doesn't have to put up with every spineless wimp who becomes infatuated with her. It's degrading.'

'You don't use your head.' Mariangela, who was chopping vegetables, briefly halted the rhythmic motion of her knife.
'Sometimes, Vincente, you are very young. Your mother, she is not
so young, not so beautiful any more. *La voce*, it is gone. There are
few men who want to be in her bed now. But Sebastiano wants her.
He loves her both for what she was and for what she is. He believes
in her. And so she believes in him, and they are both happy with
their illusions. In her eyes, he is a great composer; in his eyes, she
is a diva still, a star. Together, they are content. They survive.'

'She drinks too much,' said Vincent.

'Without Sebastiano,' opined Mariangela, 'she would drink a lot
more.'

For a month or two, Vincent let the matter rest. An old friend of
Jolanda's had found him a job with a property company, and after
the initial shock of regular hours and regulation clothes he was
enjoying putting rusty brain cells back into action. Helped by a
loan from his mother, he bought a second-hand Motoguzzi 750 on
which to roar through the streets of Milan, deafening the unsuspecting populace. One day, he took Jolanda for a ride on the
pillion, provoking Sebastiano, who had quite as many *umori* as his
Signora, to an outburst of protective anger. Vincent found his imitation of the alpha male asserting authority over his little herd so
unconvincing as to be ludicrous, and said so. Sebastiano, stammer-
ing even in his own language, said a good deal in return. The bike
wasn't safe, Vincente wasn't safe; he would get his mother killed,
speeding round the bends on the wrong side of the road while she
clung on behind him without a helmet, looking like one of those
tarts he was always picking up. If he loved her . . .

'Either he goes,' Vincent told his mother afterwards, forgetting
Mariangela's words, 'or I go.'

'But Vincente!'

'How you can bear to have him here?'

'Vincente . . .' Jolanda turned away, hiding her face, picking at
the frayed hem of her Gucci scarf. 'You must try to like him. Please.
I, your mother, I ask this of you. It is not such a hard thing, to like
someone. He is a nice boy. And I – I cannot send him away. I cannot.'

'Why not?' Vincent was blunt.

For once Jolanda, too, was blunt. 'This is his house.'

'*What?*'

'I did not want to tell you. You see, I am not rich. Once, there was much money, but it is all spent, all gone. Sebastiano said to me: "My home is yours. I give you whatever you want. I look after you." So I live here. He have his own rooms. We pretend.' She turned towards Vincent again, extending her hands in a gesture half pleading, half penitent.

'And I live here,' Vincent said slowly. 'In his house. Am I supposed to pretend too?'

Jolanda did not attempt to answer.

'What about the money for the bike? Was that also a loan from Sebastiano?'

'Oh no.' Jolanda appeared relieved at a question to which she could give an acceptable answer. 'For that, I sell my pendant. You know: the big sapphire Franco give me because he say I sing *Traviata* to break his heart. His heart it break only temporary but his bank account it grow fat for a long time. So he give me the pendant. Franco, he is very sentimental about his bank account. When he leave me I am angry, I send back the chinchilla coat and the Lamborghini and many, many diamonds, but I forget about the sapphire. So when I need money for something, I sell. I have glass now; not so good but who notice? See!'

She fished in her shrunken cleavage and produced a costume pendant with a glaring blue stone which might, on a dark night, have passed for a sapphire. But Vincent was not looking. Under his Mediterranean suntan, he had gone rather pale.

He said: 'You shouldn't have sold your jewellery just to help me. The bike wasn't important. Anyway, I could have borrowed the cash somewhere else.' His father had always had plenty of money; he had merely been – in his son's view – a little capricious about parting with it. It was a shock adjusting to seeing things in different terms.

'No, no.' Jolanda dismissed his qualms. 'Is right you come to me. I am your mother. Besides, I often sell my jewellery. How else I have money of my own? Sebastiano want to give me an allowance, but that I will not have. To live in his house, that is one thing; to take his money as well, that is the action of a *puttana*.'

'Does he give you jewellery?' Vincent found himself asking.

'Of course not! What is the point of that? If he give me jewellery that I cannot sell, that is a big waste. He is not a millionaire, Sebastiano.' She took Vincent's arm, gazed up at him with those huge eyes that could still flash like Tosca or melt like Violetta. 'Please, Vincente. Try to understand. You are my son, I love you most of all, but I am fond of Sebastiano. I – need him.'

Vincent said nothing, lips clenched not on rage but on some other, more complex emotion, an unfamiliar mixture of indignation, exasperation, pain. His father had angered and hurt him but had never made him feel defeated; Jolanda, with her garbled logic, her self-confessed failings, her tragic eyes, stood in front of him like a wall. A broken wall maybe, with flaking mortar and gaps between the stones, but he could neither surmount nor demolish it.

'Besides,' Jolanda went on, in an altered voice, 'he have a very special talent. I who have worked with the best, I tell you this. One day, he will be acknowledged as a great composer. Then everybody will realise how clever I was to encourage him, to promote his career. You will see. *Caro*—'

Abruptly Vincent shook off her hand and stalked out, unable to cope not just with his mother but with himself. At dinner, he and Sebastiano were carefully polite. Vincent thought the food would choke him, prepared as it was in Sebastiano's kitchen, but Mariangela's Tuscan cooking tasted as edible as ever. Afterwards, Sebastiano approached him for a word alone.

'La Signora love you very much,' he began in English. He invariably tried to speak to Vincent in English, as though doing so would somehow keep him at a distance, an outsider, not a part of the household. 'She is afraid you go away, because we have stupid quarrel.' He did not say which of them he thought had been stupid. And finally, with clumsy brevity: 'Please stay.'

Vincent managed an ambiguous movement which might have been a shrug or a nod.

'If you stay,' Sebastiano continued, 'I try not to . . . not to . . .' *I try not to be jealous*: that was what he meant to say, but either his resolution or his vocabulary petered out midway.

Vincent understood, but he did not yet appreciate that he might have to make a similar effort.

'All right,' he said.

*

In the succeeding weeks, Vincent thought a good deal about the problem – he still saw it as a problem – of his mother's dependence on Sebastiano. Jolanda seemed to have become his responsibility, and although the idea dismayed it did not daunt him. Responsibility for another person was something new in his experience: it held the charm of novelty. But the novelty wore off; the responsibility did not. In an attempt to cover all the angles, he asked Jolanda about her Italian relations, and was not surprised to learn there had been a disagreement. The Scapare – Jolanda's real name was Giulia Scapara – were a wine-growing family, Catholic and conventional: her mother had nudged her into a singing career and then expired too soon to enjoy her daughter's success; her father, brothers, uncles and aunts had merely been horrified by her eventual notoriety. 'When I leave John, *mio padre* write to me. He say I am entirely cast off. After that, every time I am in the newspapers, he write to me again. Every time, I am entirely cast off. He is very religious: his God is strict, disapproving, a schoolteacher of a God. I tell him, my God is more human. He make mankind fallible, so He is not *stupito* when we fail. I make mistake, He forgive me. I make many mistakes, He forgive me many times. He is a real Christian God: He is good at forgiving people. *Mio padre* does not forgive anybody. It is ten years now since we write. He does not even cast me off any more.'

'Maybe he's dead,' Vincent suggested.

'I do not think so. When he die, they tell me. I go to his funeral with Borsalino hat, black veil, expensive wreath. More expensive than anyone else's. Then *I* forgive *him*.'

Faced with this project, there seemed little point in seeking the assistance of the Scaparas: even if they offered any, Jolanda would certainly reject it. Vincent reflected that although the problem might vary the solution was always the same. He needed money. Big money. Quick money. A high-risk gamble on long odds and loaded dice. He had learned from previous errors; all he required was a second chance. In the Milanese office, he did his job, assimilated information, kept his thoughts in his head. Increasingly, he was re-examining his relationship with Judas Carson. In his anger against his father, the judicial system, Richard, Crystal, he had somehow forgotten to be angry with the primary traitor. Carson, after all, had been virtually a stranger, owing him nothing, a tutor at the gaming table who had instructed him, crudely and effectively, in the basic rules of the game. Never sign anything, never trust anyone. 'Judas by name and Judas by nature,' Vincent thought without originality. A philosopher might have speculated as to the influence of that long-ago bureaucrat on Ellis Island, who had provided the foreign urchin with a label to live up to; but Vincent was uninterested in fruitless philosophy. What he wanted was a business guru, a guide in the world of fast deals and fast bucks. Carson had the experience and the know-how – and Carson, Vincent suspected, had enjoyed playing the role of Svengali, dropping pearls of wisdom into Vincent's ear, initiating the eager apprentice into the secrets of his trade. No doubt it had pleased his vanity: vanity is always easy to please. 'No matter how this deal works out,' he had told Vincent, 'I really like you.' Idle words – the sugar on the pill – but Vincent pondered how he could make use of them. Liars believe their own lies, dictators their own propaganda; Carson, challenged with sufficient bravado, might yet be persuaded to recall the sentiment. Vincent liked the idea of hooking him with his own bait, but he knew he would have to supply more than effrontery. Jolanda must have contacts in Hollywood; if not, he could always bluff it out. But he needed capital. Carson would never take him seriously without capital.

He had come full circle back to the original problem. Money. To make money he needed money. His present employment afforded only limited prospects, transactions were on a modest scale, the patter of tiny lire did little to quicken his blood. Selling his bike might pay his air fare to Los Angeles but would hardly set him up in funds. Spare-time research gave him Carson's office and home addresses and a few details of his personal life, and frustration drove him to brooding and bad company. Sebastiano was worried about him, Jolanda declared one afternoon when they were alone.

'Is he?' Vincent said dangerously.

It did not occur to him or his mother – or, presumably, to Sebastiano – that he might have more ascendancy over Milan's young tearaways than they would ever have over him. Vincent was not easily influenced, and his prison record, his habit of riding the Motoguzzi *ventre-à-terre* through the city streets, and what Richard had once called his fuck-off manner were all guaranteed to impress the impressionable. But Sebastiano's attitude riled him, as Sebastiano's attitudes usually did. The paradox, he thought, was that Sebastiano, who wanted him to go, would beg him to stay for Jolanda's sake, while he stayed to annoy Sebastiano, although to achieve his ambitions he needed to leave. It was a ludicrous state of affairs and, facing facts, Vincent knew he would be stupid to let it continue.

In the end, he took Jolanda out to dinner for a serious discussion.

'I'm getting nowhere here,' he told her. 'I won't waste any more time sitting behind a desk that belongs to someone else, making someone else's money – or spending it. If I'm going to be a millionaire before I'm thirty I have to start now. There's a hell of a long way to go.'

'You will be a millionaire!' Jolanda decreed confidently. 'You are so clever, *caro*. You will be a *real* millionaire – in dollars.' Lira millionaires are understandably common in Italy. 'But, Vincente, why you not stay in Milan? I find you a better job. I have other friends, old friends. Some dead, some not. I have one old, old friend—'

'Do you have friends in Los Angeles?' Vincent interrupted.

'Of course. Not for several years do I see them, but I was a very big star. *In verità*, I am still a big star! In Hollywood, I had a house with swimming pool, many clothes, many servants. Also many friends. *Naturalmente*. But I do not know if they give you a job. I will write letters, lots of letters. Then we see. But why you want to go to America? Are you not happy here? We have much fun together. America . . . America is a long way.'

'When I'm rich,' Vincent said, 'you can come and live with me. In a house with a swimming pool.'

'I – do not know. Maybe Sebastiano would not like that.'

'Sebastiano—' Vincent bit off short what he would have said, and there was an uncertain pause.

Then: 'I could not leave Sebastiano,' Jolanda said unhappily. 'I am his inspiration. Without me, he cannot write the opera. And I do not think he would be comfortable, in America. If he is not comfortable, he cannot write. It is the artistic temperament.'

Vincent had had enough of the artistic temperament. 'Mamma, all this is pure hypothesis: there's no point in worrying about it. When I've made my first million, we'll worry. Listen. There's a man in Los Angeles who might – *might* – be induced to help me, if

I can offer him something in return. Perhaps if I can show him I have contacts . . . It's a risk, but it's better than sitting on my arse going nowhere. I've nothing to lose by trying.' Only his nerve, he thought. And the air fare. 'Write to your friends; tell them I'm coming. I don't want a job: just contacts. Something to interest this man Carson. I know he's wealthy and successful but I'm prepared to bet he doesn't move in film-star circles. It's the kind of thing that'll go down well with him. He'll see money in it.' Judas had seen his father's name as an asset; surely Vincent could convince him that his mother's name, too, could be useful.

'I will do whatever you want, Vincente,' Jolanda sounded doubtful. 'This Carson – he is a friend of yours?'

'No.' Vincent smiled a suitably twisted smile. 'An enemy.'

'But that is *stupido*! If he is your enemy, he will not help you. *Caro*, I love you, but you are quite mad.'

'My friends didn't help me,' Vincent retorted. He had told her a part of his story, the part concerning his father and Richard, though nothing about his criminal naiveté and nothing much about Crystal. 'I'm through with my friends. With an enemy, at least I'll know where I am.'

'You are mad,' Jolanda repeated, staring at him in bewilderment.

She emptied her wineglass; absently, he refilled it. 'Maybe I am,' he said. 'Anyway, we're still in the realm of supposition. If I'm to go, I must have money. That's the difficult bit. Money breeds money, but you have to start with something. Even getting rich is expensive. Mamma, do you know anybody who could give me a loan? I'll pay interest, naturally. I just need some capital.'

'A big loan?' Jolanda asked.

'Well . . .'

'Of course it must be a big loan.' Unexpectedly, Jolanda seemed to have become both practical and shrewd. Vincent knew she was capable of such quirks, but one had rarely been more opportune. 'For a friend, you need only a little money, or no money at all. But for an enemy, you must have much money. Then he see you are important – he will not turn you away.'

'I hope not,' Vincent affirmed.

'*Allora*,' Jolanda took a deep breath and gazed up at him with beaming confidence, 'I do not properly comprehend what is your plan, but it does not matter. I trust you. You are my son: I know it is for me that you wish to do this. I will arrange the money. Not a loan: *non è necessario*. I still have jewellery—'

'No.' Vincent spoke too loudly, giving himself no time to hesitate. The possibility that Jolanda might suggest this had been in his mind, but he had resolutely thrust it to the back. He did not want to be tempted.

'Now you are being *molto ostinato*. You do not have to borrow money, pay interest: why you insist on it? Your father tell me: he who borrow never get rich. Is better—'

'He may have done,' Vincent interjected. 'It's the sort of thing he would say. But I won't let you sell more jewellery. You can't have much left.'

'I have a ring, John's ring that he give to me when we are engaged. Marquise diamond, very good quality, many, many carats. It is the engagement ring of John's mother, *tua nonna* – also, I think, of her mother. Long time in family, very old, very traditional. I am not Signora Savage any more but you, you are a Savage. So it belong to you more than me. If I sell, it is right that you have the money.'

'*Stronzate*,' said Vincent. 'My father *gave* it to you; it has nothing to do with me. If you want to get rid of it, buy your own house with the proceeds. Property's cheap *in campagna*.'

'I do not want my own house. I like the Villa Mirafiore. Besides . . . I am happy with Sebastiano.'

Until he quits, Vincent thought, but he did not say it.

'Anyway,' Jolanda went on. 'I want you to become a famous tycoon. Like Agnelli. If you think there is no opportunity for you in Milan, then you go to America. It is decided. We will not argue any more.'

'No,' said Vincent, 'we won't. Keep your bloody jewellery; drink your bloody wine; we're going home.'

Jolanda sold the ring without telling him a month later. The diamond, although not quite as many carats as she had averred, was of respectable size and quality, the setting antique and ugly, the sum realised certainly adequate to give Vincent a start. He took it because he needed it, and because it was too late to refuse. Beneath his surface resistance he had always intended to take it, if she sold the ring herself, but having a conscience to fob off was, for him, an unusual experience. He said: 'I'll buy you something else from my first big deal. Something very special.' Jolanda laughed, kissed him, cried a little. The day he left, she cried a lot more.

'I love you,' he told her, to his surprise, against his will. He could not recall saying it before.

Her face glittered. 'When you come back,' she said, 'you will be a millionaire!'

'*Magari*,' said Mariangela.

He gave her a brief hug and the corner of a smile, and submitted to a further embrace from his mother. At the last moment, he turned to Sebastiano. 'Look after her,' he said, to the man he did not like or trust, whose ability to look after Jolanda he had so often decried. But the words came unforced, conjured by circumstance, sincere at least in their plea. They shook hands for the second time. Then Vincent got into the waiting taxi and was driven away to the airport.

2

Vincent's initial feeling about Los Angeles was one of bewilderment. He had been expecting a modern cityscape something like New York, with towering cliff faces of glass and concrete and streets cloven like chasms in between, down which traffic and pedestrians poured in a seething, churning, rushing torrent. But Los Angeles at a first glance appeared less like a city than a vast sprawling holiday village, with endless rows of bungalows, a palm tree on every corner, wide dusty roads, empty pavements. For all its size it had an air of impermanence: the bungalows looked flimsily built, little more than prefabs; fragments of the original desert showed here and there like glimpses of canvas in an unfinished painting. The villas in Santa Monica and Little Venice had a toytown quaintness, gingerbread houses made of marzipan and roofed with coloured icing, while in the wealthiest areas – Beverly Hills, Bel-Air, the Canyons – there was a hotch-potch of architectural fantasies from every style and period, a rose-pink trianon next to a Moorish palace, a cluster of powder-blue turrets protruding like a fairy-tale castle from a belt of cultivated woodland. The gardens were as artificial as the houses, impossibly green, iridescent with sprinklers, burgeoning with exotic plants. It was like an enormous film set, all cardboard and plaster and paint, burlesque, haphazard, collapsible, carpets of lawn that could be rolled up and stacked away, mansions, courtyards, colonnades, shacks and shanties all easily dismantled and moved on at a word from the director. There was no subway, no city centre, few skyscrapers – no tradition, no history, no roots in the past, no time but the present. A gipsy capital with a floating, drifting, migrant population, who had abandoned their origins and their heritage to pitch their tents here and start again, unshackled, footloose and fancy-free. As Vincent became accustomed to the atmosphere he began to feel that he, too, was freed, a contemporary pioneer who had come to dig for gold, leaving behind class and family, mistakes and commitments. Here, the rules were changed, the cards unmarked: anything could happen.

But the past still had its uses. Old friends of his mother welcomed him, for the most part, with the famed enthusiasm of Angelenos, an enthusiasm no doubt assisted by his good looks and the poise engendered by a combination of public school and prison. He had cocktails on a mountainside terrace with the Valley spread out below him, blue with nightfall and misty with distance and spangled with enough lights to out-glitter the Milky Way. He had dinner in a Malibu beach house built on stilts over the rocks while the waves rushed and thundered underneath. He had lunch at Chasen's with Frank Cavalcanti, whose worldly smile had sunken into sardonic lines in his cheeks and whose black and silver hair represented a triumph of trichological understatement. Everyone asked after Jolanda, even Cavalcanti. She was so lovely – such personality, such screen presence, and the Voice – darling the Voice! Of course, it might not be so powerful now, but surely it would still have the depth, the resonance, the passion. She must return to Los Angeles and they would have a wonderful party and she could sing for them all again. They were thrilled to meet Vincent but why hadn't she come with him? When would she be joining him? She must not bury herself in Europe for the rest of her life. Vincent responded with courtesy rather than information. In all the time he had spent in Italy he had never heard his mother do more than hum a tune or trill a few notes that would falter for want of breath and potency. At the back of his mind there was a picture, a picture of Jolanda being fêted by these glossy Californians, with their carefully preserved complexions, their exquisitely casual clothes, their faces hitched up behind their ears – Jolanda with her haggard eyes and leathered skin, dressed at random with fake jewellery clinking at wrist and throat, drinking too much champagne against the terrifying moment when they would ask her to sing. It was a picture he could not bear and he did his best to put it out of his thoughts. 'I hope she'll come soon,' he said. 'Once I've got my own place –

somewhere for her to stay. She hates hotels.' He had no idea if she hated hotels or not, but it made a good excuse.

'Oh, but she can stay with *us*,' everyone assured him (except Cavalcanti).

'I'm selfish,' Vincent said lightly. 'I want her to stay with me.'

He had been in LA a week when he went to see Judas Carson. It was long enough for him to get the feel of the city, long enough to bolster his nerve and revive his system from its initial trance of culture shock. He arrived at the offices on La Cienega around eleven. He had calculated the time to a nicety: earlier would appear too eager, later might overlap with a lunch date. In the event, Carson wasn't there. A secretary of the plain but serviceable variety informed him crisply that Mr Carson would be back by half past three and requested his name and his business. Vincent, who wanted to keep the element of surprise, gave neither. The secretary became even crisper, appraising him with a disparaging eye as if he were a beach bum who had just arrived by surfboard with his qualifications in his swimming trunks. Mr Carson, she intimated, was a very busy man. He did not see people unless they had either an appointment or an introduction.

'He'll see me,' Vincent asserted with a degree of confidence he did not feel. 'I'll be back later.'

It was four o'clock when he returned. Carson was in residence and Vincent duly gave the secretary his name, wishing he had provided himself with business cards. Then he waited. She was absent for about ten minutes – one to give the information, Vincent guessed, nine for Judas to think about it. Then she came back.

'This way.'

She showed Vincent into the main office, closed the door behind him. Carson rose to greet him and they stood face to face for a long, cool moment, assessing and reassessing each other, warily hostile. Then Carson smiled. The gentle crocodile smile. 'Well, kid,' he said, 'what can I do for you?'

'Offer me a drink,' said Vincent.

The smile broadened. Carson opened the cocktail cabinet, clinked ice cubes, splashed Bourbon into a couple of tumblers. 'You're looking well,' he remarked conversationally.

'I've been in Italy.'

'Holiday?'

'I was living there. My mother's Italian . . . Jolanda Scarpia.' Carson hesitated over the Bourbon; evidently, even with him, the name rang a bell. 'She's an opera singer.'

'Yeah. I've heard of her. I didn't know she was your mother. Quite a classy mixture, ain't you?'

Vincent ignored the comment, accepted the drink, and sat back in his chair. Now the preliminaries were over he felt more sure of himself, if not of Judas. 'My parents split up when I was four,' he explained. 'I hadn't seen her in nearly twenty years.'

'Sad, sad.' Carson shook his head. He would have put flowers on his own mother's grave if he could have remembered where it was. 'Still, you got to see her in the end. I bet that was some reunion. Where's she living – Rome?'

'Near Milan.'

'Beautiful country, Italy.' Carson sounded nostalgic. Possibly he was recalling the black market he had operated there in the war. 'Beautiful people. Warm.'

Vincent was growing tired of this protracted waffle. 'She wrote to me when I was in jail,' he said. 'I went to see her when I got out.'

If Carson felt embarrassed or uncomfortable he did not show it. 'I heard you went to jail,' he admitted, as if this distant fact, floating across the Atlantic towards him like a message in a bottle, had been of only detached interest. 'That was a tough break. You should have gone to your father: he'd have bailed you out. I told you, kid, you can't live off pride. Still, I guess I wasn't surprised. I always had you figured for the stubborn kind. A real old-fashioned British aristocrat.'

Vincent, who was neither old-fashioned nor aristocratic, did not contradict him. Nor did he elucidate his father's attitude. 'Prison didn't do me any harm,' he said carelessly. 'Six months of boredom – a few fights, that's all.'

'You can look after yourself in a fight?'

'Fortunately.'

'What you been doing since?'

'Not a lot. I was working for a property company in Milan but it was all rather low-key and . . . very respectable. There were no real openings for the future. That's why I came here. In the fifties and sixties my mother starred in several film versions of major operas – *Tosca*, *Carmen*, that sort of thing. You might have seen one of them.' He was quite certain Judas hadn't seen any of them, but he knew the whiff of culture would impress him. 'She still has a good many friends in Hollywood, some powerful, some just famous. They've been very kind to me. Anyway, you always told me to capitalise on my assets.' He took a mouthful of Bourbon and the necessary deep breath before the plunge. When he spoke again his voice was skilfully tempered, artistically cool. 'I listened to your advice, you know. I had a lot of time to think, when I was in prison. Learn from your mistakes, you said. I learned.'

'Well?' said Judas.

'When I decided to come to California, I knew I would need help. A colleague, an adviser, someone who can teach me the business. You were the first to spring to mind.'

'I like your cheek,' Carson said after an appreciable silence. He looked surprised, nonplussed, but hardly responsive. 'Sorry, kid. If I wanted a junior partner you'd be top of my list, but as it is . . .'

'Don't forget, I have contacts,' Vincent reiterated. 'I also have intelligence, resilience, and experience – very varied experience. And capital, naturally. If you won't take me on, someone else will. But—'

'But what?'

Vincent shrugged, grinned. 'Better the devil you know.'

Judas laughed. 'That's straightforward enough. Hell, kid, you almost tempt me. The problem is, see, when two people work together, they got to trust each other. Not all the way, maybe, but they got to have some kind of basic mutual . . . integrity. Like a kind of faith. They got to be honest with each other if not with anybody else. With you, after what I done to you, you're gonna be out to get me. I'll have to keep looking over my shoulder all the time. So I'm gonna be out to get you. We just won't have no trust at all. See what I mean?'

'Balls,' said Vincent. 'You had a partner here after the war. You double-crossed him and elbowed him out of the business without any provocation whatsoever. You can stab me in the back only if I present you with a back to stab. I shan't.'

'When I was a kid,' Carson said, 'my old grandmother had a saying: "There are more ways than one of cooking a chicken."'

'I'm not a chicken,' Vincent retorted. Nor did he believe that Judas cherished the sayings of his old grandmother, if indeed he had ever possessed one.

'OK, kid, OK. Look, I'll think about it. That's the most I can promise you. And it's quite a concession.'

'For old times' sake?' Vincent suggested blandly.

'I like your cheek,' Judas said, 'but I don't need an overdose. I got work to do. Come back in a couple of days. I tell you what, we'll have lunch. Yeah, why not? Thursday, twelve-thirty.'

'I'll see if I'm free,' Vincent said.

They lunched, talked, and a few days later, Vincent was invited to dine at Carson's Bel-Air mansion, where he admired the paintings, listened to the anecdotes and murmured suitable appreciation of the history of the Corot. From guarded amusement and genial distrust Judas slipped easily into his former role of professional mentor, driving Vincent miles to admire potentially valuable patches of desert or the nascent walls of factories and apartment blocks. His presence at the La Cienega office became familiar, the crisp secretary softened, in due course he acquired a desk if not a partnership. 'When I first got here I thought the streets of Los Angeles were gonna be paved with gold,' Carson would say, conjuring up an improbable vision of himself as a callow youth leaping down from a covered wagon while defeated Indians fled in the distance. 'And you know what, kid? They are. Every square metre of sand and rock, that's gold. The Russians got wheat and the Arabs got oil but America is God's Own Country and here, here the dirt beneath your feet is worth money. How's that for a thought?' Vincent, soaking up these gems of wisdom with more scepticism than formerly, was nonetheless inclined to give them credence. 'Look at that,' Judas declared one afternoon, pulling over on a mountainside bend to indicate a long-range vista of arid wasteland. 'Dry as the Sahara. Fit only for snakes and bugs. But you add water, kid, and you got the Garden of Eden. Everyone wants a piece of Eden.'

'The guy with the water tap,' Vincent remarked, 'must be a powerful man.'

'You said it.' Carson looked pleased, as he always did when his pupil seized promptly on the most important aspect of the situation. 'They don't call it the Department of Water and Power for nothing!' It was an old joke of his and he laughed at it himself, the familiar silent laugh.

Vincent smiled on a reflex, without humour. 'So what we need,' he said thoughtfully, 'is a contact in the department who will either arrange for them to bring water to an area we have already bought up, or . . . who will let us know in advance where the pipes are going to be laid, so we can go shopping before everyone else.'

'The general manager – the guy with the water tap – is the highest paid civil servant in the state. He's supposed to be Mr Clean. Pure as his own water. But I like your reasoning.' Carson restarted the engine and prepared to drive on. 'You know, I was right about you, kid. You're a quick learner. I thought you would be.'

This time, Vincent's amusement was genuine, but he kept it to himself.

He had Carson's words in mind when, some months later, he met Richmond LeSueur.

He saw her across the room at a party, making an entrance, a woman of medium height dressed to look tall with an older man on one arm and a younger man on the other. An acquaintance told him who she was and added that the older man was her lover, the younger her lawyer. Or vice versa. Vincent, who had heard of her, spent much of the evening assimilating gossip. Other girls came to LA to get into the movies; Richmond LeSueur was only interested in real estate. She had arrived ten or fifteen years earlier, a failed streetwalker with no looks and less charm; the arms of a navvy, a broken nose, a heavy jaw, assorted features revealing assorted racial ancestry. Some said she was Hispanic, others Italian, others part black, part Chinese, part Apache. She had bought up the slum where she was living on behalf of a developer, alternately bullying and persuading the other tenants to get the best deal. She took her cut and put it in the bank to grow fat. The developer went bust and many of her neighbours found themselves homeless but Richmond LeSueur made money. She was rumoured to be impossibly mean, selfishly extravagant, rapacious, sadistic, nymphomaniac. No one knew if Richmond LeSueur was her real name. Her friends called her Rich, her enemies called her LeSewer. The latter far outnumbered the former. Now, she had notched up two lucrative divorces and had recently sold off her own agency. Like Judas Carson, she had acquired an interest in art; unlike him, she had a real appreciation of the objects she collected, as if resentment at her own ugliness had given her a deep secret hunger for beauty, a yearning to possess it and gloat over it like a Wagnerian dwarf with a treasure hoard. They said she owned pictures that were never shown, a Borgia cup stolen in Italy a decade earlier, a Goya that had once been the property of Herman Goering. The legacy of a prostitute who had only done business with men who could not afford a prettier girl.

Not that she was ugly any more. She had become a Hollywood product: dieting, exercise and silicates had given her a perfect figure, cosmetic surgery had adjusted her jaw and remodelled her nose. Bi-weekly sessions in a beauty salon kept a slight moustache at bay and transformed her coarse dark hair into a variegated blonde mane, artfully shaded from a silvery brown through several beiges to highlights of platinum. Her clothes were understated and very, very expensive. Vincent saw a woman who was striking if not actually handsome, with Red Indian cheekbones, an inflatable pout, the complexion of a crème caramel, and the poise of a boxer before a fight. He talked to her and found her brusque, plainly considering him too young to be important, her gaze flickering round the room in search of someone more interesting. She declined to have lunch with him automatically, without pause for thought.

'All right,' he said, as one making a concession, 'shed your escorts and we'll make it dinner. Tonight.'

That caught her attention: she looked at him for the first time, laughed abruptly. 'Sorry. I like your nerve' – Carson's favourite line – 'but not that much.'

'I don't want to make love to you, you know,' Vincent explained. 'I prefer my women very young, very pretty, and not too bright. I want to talk business.' He stared her straight in the eyes as he spoke – small eyes, hard as basalt, elongated with kohl, softened with shadow. A little to his surprise he found their very hardness sexy. He sensed, under her smooth synthetic exterior, a core like a lump of rock, all roughness and jags. He was conscious of an urge to fuck her into a state of surrender, to force her into an unaccustomed gentleness, melting away all the hard edges. He switched off the stare quickly, feeling he had been too blatant, too arrogant, unnecessarily crude.

Richmond played with her champagne glass, flexing metallic nails. She had been stared at in that way by too many men who wanted to pick her brains or worm their way into her bank account. Usually, it was she who had ended up with the pickings, both informational and financial. 'What can you offer me?' she asked bluntly, with a faint stress on the 'you'.

'Investment.' Richmond had plenty of capital but was notoriously careful with it, rationing herself on every venture, preferring to share the risk even if it meant sharing the profit. Perhaps she had learned from the fate of her first associate in the property business.

'Mom and Daddy's money?' She was openly contemptuous.

Vincent merely smiled. 'It's all the same colour.'

'You're Carson's bright boy, aren't you?' Richmond said after a pause for a further scan of the party. 'I suppose he told you to chat me up.'

'He said I should avoid you at all costs,' Vincent said. 'He doesn't want to get involved with someone who's too quick, too sharp, and always takes the cream off the cake before anyone else can get their spoon stuck in.'

The abrupt laugh again. 'I can believe he might have said that!'

Since Vincent had made it up, he was gratified.

'What's your accent?' Hers, despite the efforts of a speech therapist, was a sort of corncrake drawl with more than a hint of the south.

'English.'

'I heard your Mom was an Italian opera singer.'

'I speak Italian, but I was brought up in England.'

'I hate opera. Fat men with double chins who are meant to be dashing young lovers. And those long dreary parts where they just sing and sing and nothing happens.'

'You're going to do business with me,' said Vincent, 'not my mother.'

'So what's my part of the deal?'

'I was thinking of a partnership. You, me, Carson. If a big enough prospect were to turn up, of course . . . in a suitable area.' He did not want to mention straight out what he had heard, but he wished to be sure that she knew that he knew. The item in question still came under the heading of restricted data, not available for general gossip. He had obtained it from Carson's lawyer, a specialist in real estate intelligence, who had heard it from his secretary, who had heard it from the office cleaner, who was a friend of the girl at the florist who had dispatched the first red roses and giveaway message from the gentleman to the lady.

Richmond LeSueur was having an affair with Carson's Mr Clean, the general manager of the Department of Water and Power.

'I've had a couple of offers of that kind lately,' said Richmond. 'Why should I take up yours?'

'Why not?' said Vincent.

Their acquaintance proceeded along the customary lines for such business negotiations – lunch, informal meeting, more lunch, drinks, dinner – with the added ingredient of sex. Vincent didn't hurry, deciding that delay was good tactics, showing the leisurely nature of his interest, keeping her – or so he hoped – in suspense. When he finally did take her to bed he found her practised rather than perfect, mentally resistant, physically accommodating, shuddering obligingly in the aftermath of his own orgasm. On the second occasion, he said: 'Tell me you enjoyed that.'

'I enjoyed it.'

'Then stop faking it.'

She let her voice fall to a purr. 'Honey, I wouldn't fake it. Not with *you.*'

'Don't bullshit either. Mutual orgasm is bloody rare, and nobody's timing is that good, particularly at the beginning. Maybe you've been used once too often; maybe you just like being detached. It must make you feel superior, in control, watching some poor mug panting away while your brain is on ice. Anyway, whatever the reason, you don't do it with me. The women I screw come or they don't come, but they don't have to fake. If you do it again, I'll beat you.'

'You motherfucking *bastard*—'

'Shut up. You've been a whore too long and it shows. Let go. Don't be – don't be *afraid* of it.'

Exercise classes had made her strong but Vincent was considerably stronger. He twisted her arms under her, holding them with one hand while with the other he pushed her legs apart. The weight of his shoulders pinioned her thighs. She went on swearing but he ignored it, licking her slowly and thoroughly until she grew quiet and he felt her body softened, gentled, hesitating on the verge of submission. When she was very close to orgasm he would sense the tension in her muscles and draw back for a moment or two, murmuring: 'Soon, darling. Don't rush it. Very soon.' Then he would start again, exploring her with his tongue, opening her labia and sucking her to the point where she could hold back no longer.

Afterwards, he said: 'That was the first time you ever climaxed with a man, wasn't it?'

'Yes,' said Richmond. She was thirty-eight years old and had had more pointless sex than she could remember.

'Have you always faked it?'

'Sometimes I didn't bother. Lots of men don't notice either way.'

Vincent did not comment. Arousing her against her will, having total dominance over her, had stimulated his own desire to a point that was almost unbearable. He wanted to penetrate her, deep and hard, to fuck her and fuck her into exhausted subjugation, but he knew that a very little friction would precipitate his own orgasm and self-restraint was becoming difficult. He let her get her breath back before rolling on top of her and entering her without further preamble. She felt different after coitus, not greased with Vaseline like the earlier times but wet with her own moisture, warm and yielding. The surrender about which he had fantasised occurred immediately. 'That's better,' he said, pushing himself right into her, feeling her tight and soft around him, internal muscles rippling in response to his thrust. 'Yes . . . better . . . much better . . .' He could not contain it: the climax came quickly and subsided slowly, butterfly shivers running through his penis for some time afterwards. He stayed inside her, spreading her improbably firm breasts to avoid crushing them, relishing intimacy, possession, takeover.

Later, they talked business.

'I'm damned if I'm going to fall in love with you,' Richmond said. 'Sex is too useful to do it just for pleasure.'

'Anyway,' Vincent pointed out, 'we need your friend from the Water Department. Why else do you imagine I'm in bed with you? I don't do this for fun, you know.'

'OK: let's say I get to hear of something interesting. Something too big for me to handle on my own. Between us, we corner the market – you, me, Carson. But I'll need a reason to choose you rather than somebody else. A percentage of your profits, for instance.'

'Like hell.'

Under the silk sheets which she considered a suitable accompaniment to intercourse, Richmond shrugged. 'That's the deal. Take it or leave it.'

'I could bribe some underpaid official for less.'

'If you could, you'd have done it already. I do the dirty work. I earn my cut. If he was gay, would you have him up your fanny?'

Vincent ignored this. 'You wouldn't consider taking your percentage in bed?'

'You must be kidding.'

'What is this, then?'

Again, Richmond shrugged. 'A sweetener.'

'Ah,' said Vincent, 'but for whom?'

It was that same week when he received the invitation to Richard and Crystal's wedding. It had evidently been wandering round the world in pursuit of him for some while, having been forwarded from his old address in London to Jolanda Scarpia, c/o La Scala, Milan, where it had presumably sat on the desk of a baffled secretary until it was eventually passed on to the Villa Mirafiore. From thence it had been redirected, in Jolanda's own hand, to California. It had been opened once, without subterfuge, and resealed with sellotape. No other mail had followed him from England and Vincent did not doubt that curiosity had proved too much for his mother. He had always known he should have sent his father or cousin his current address but he had felt a profound reluctance to extend even so tenuous a feeler of communication. He had left the past behind him, several thousand miles behind him, and reaching out meant reaching back, regressing, reawakening the possibility of pain. It was a long time since he had had to concentrate on distracting his thoughts from Crystal. Scanning the invitation with a mechanical sneer on his lips, he tried to picture her, probably in white, flowing hair under a flowing veil, a soft-focus fantasy in a blur of silk with an armful of orange blossom. The fantasy had to be in soft focus because he realised without any particular pang that he could not clearly recall what she looked like. Her image retreated into a heart-shaped silver frame on a cluttered mantelpiece surrounded by other such images, the scrapbook of a predictable lifestyle: the new baby, the older baby, the besotted grandmother, the dog. And Richard. Richard beside her in the silver frame, dressed incongruously in top hat and tails, gazing out at his cousin with a smile that did not alter or fade. Vincent's sneer deepened: he went to tear the invitation in half, then checked himself. As an exercise in nonchalance he placed it upright on the table, half open like a birthday card. The table was opposite the front door and it would catch his eye every time he came in. It had taken so long to find him that there were less than two weeks left till the wedding. At the church in Ridpath, he noted. Reception at Weatherfray. A feudal occasion, complete with admiring peasantry. On the back of the card Crystal had scrawled: 'Please come. We would really love to see you.' Crystal, not Richard. Doubtless that was the correct etiquette for such things. The Farrows were the official hosts despite the location but Crystal must have vetted the guest list, scribbled any personal messages. 'You do it, darling,' Richard might have said.

Vincent left the card there until the day of the wedding. It was ridiculous, he reflected, that a scrap of cardboard could come between him and sleep, eat its way into his dreams. When the day came, he burned it over an ashtray, knowing the gesture was futile, feeling a fool for his futility, his impotence, his hurt.

'One day,' he promised himself, 'I'll go back. When it doesn't matter any more.'

But the bitterness and the folly had worked like splinters deep inside him, and although on the surface he was whole and unscarred the splinters remained, buried in his heart, twisting at a memory. To divert himself, he applied his energies to real estate, and Richmond LeSueur.

Judas, in whom he had confided, was rather entertained at his method of approach.

'You watch out, kid,' he recommended. 'You're a good-looking boy but LeSewer isn't the kind to lose her head. You'd be safer in bed with a snake.'

'A zoologist at Cambridge once told me, if you tickle a python's tail in the right place, it won't constrict,' Vincent said.

'Fine if you're dealing with a python,' Carson responded caustically. 'LeSewer's a rattlesnake. You ever tried tickling the tail on one of those?'

But when Vincent heard of the project at Poco Hondo, he knew Richmond had not let him down. It was an area of land on the outskirts of the city, as dry as its name, which means Little River. In fact, the Little River which had been there when the Spanish missionaries arrived had evaporated long ago. The missionaries had moved on to greener pastures and the Indians they converted had followed them. In the sixties the land had been bought by a rich hippy who set up a commune there, without mains, water, electricity or other pollutants, in an attempt to return to nature and isolate himself and his hapless followers from the lamentable influence of society. He had subsequently died from a surfeit of such natural substances as alcohol and heroin, bequeathing the commune and attached acreage to his disciples. They lingered on, their numbers growing less over the years as the corrupt world lured many back, trying to farm the parched ground and growing nothing with success except cacti and marijuana plants. They had not heard about the new pipeline when Vincent arrived with his chequebook, looking reassuringly young and long-haired, getting out of a battered Mustang in jeans which had seen better days. Only two or three did not want to sell, determined to uphold the noble aims of the Master, at whose instigation they had taken root there. Possibly it was a coincidence that shortly afterwards the police came to inspect the marijuana plants and the social workers to test the children for worms and truancy. Next time Vincent dropped by with his chequebook, there were no dissenters. The price seemed high to the hippies, who had lost touch with inflation. They probably never learned about the water that was brought in after they left, turning their desert acres into a residential suburb. Vincent had no qualms about them. Life, he knew, is what you can grab; wealth and prosperity do not come looking for those who sit on their backsides and wait. The coup led to an official partnership with Carson and cemented his relations with Richmond, both business and sexual. In later years, as Carson grew older, Richmond would also become a partner, until she and Vincent realised that two sharks could not comfortably be accommodated in a single fishpond. And until then they continued to share a bed on a regular basis, without commitment or fidelity, discussing business in the aftermath of pleasure with the competitive edge they would have brought to a boardroom.

'I always knew you had what it takes,' Richmond told him over a celebration dinner at the Beverly, after the Poco Hondo site had been resold for a staggering profit. So says the director who promoted an extra on the off-chance, only to find he has actually become a star.

'No you didn't,' Vincent said. '*I* knew. That's what counts.'

The following morning, in her bed, he studied the face on the pillow beside him, naked without its make-up – the real Richmond LeSueur, ugly and defenceless, the sallow skin, the elflock tangles, the plumped-up lips. He knew, when she awoke, she would be prickly and pugnacious, pulling her hair forward in an oddly vulnerable gesture to hide her unpainted eyes, and then tossing it back again with sudden brashness to show she did not really care. This was the time he liked her best, though he never stopped to analyse why. He could not imagine Richmond in soft focus, under a flowing veil, her image fading from his memory into a silver photo frame. She would always be herself, tough, devious, greedy, unrepentant. He looked down at her for a few moments with an emotion he did not recognise, something akin to tenderness. Then he climbed on top of her and entered her, without effort – she was still wet from the activities of the previous night – waking her to sex. She swore at him as usual, more in annoyance than anger, trying to push him away. Vincent only laughed, desiring her most in her bad moods.

'Asshole! I need a piss.'

'All right, but be quick. And don't clean your teeth.'

'My mouth is furred up.'

'So's mine. Come back to bed.'

'I hate sex in the mornings. You know I do. I hate mornings.'

'Come back to bed.'

The next day, he went to a jeweller's on Rodeo Drive and bought his mother a black pearl pendant which he had had his eye on for some time. He took it with him on a trip to Italy that summer – the first since he'd left, though he had telephoned with reasonable regularity and Jolanda had written frequently in her normal verbose, haphazard, multilingual style. At the airport he collected a hire car – an Alfa Romeo Spider – and drove to Mirafiore-Tripodina. His welcome was predictable. Jolanda clung to him and wept. Mariangela and Sebastiano surveyed the Alfa, the former grimly appreciative, the latter with resolute admiration; and

Tommaso disappeared round the back of the house, reportedly in search of an umbrella.

'Nice car,' Sebastiano said politely.

'Nice toy,' said Mariangela. 'Always the loud motorbikes, the fast cars. Boys never grow up.' She added, with routine scepticism: 'I hope you can afford it.'

'Of course he can!' Jolanda was indignant. 'He is very rich now, very successful. Soon, he have a car at every airport, just in case. Come into the cool, *caro*, and we celebrate. We have champagne, French champagne. Best quality Krug. Sebastiano!'

They had *spumante*. Vincent gave her the pendant, temporarily halting the flow of smiles and tears. 'It is false, no?' she insisted, large-eyed.

'No.'

'But a black pearl – it is too expensive! To buy this, you must be real millionaire. Vincente, never, never in my whole life have I had anything so wonderful, but—'

'Good.' He kissed her cheek. 'Don't sell it.'

Sebastiano, his resolution already strained by Vincent's evident affluence, looked resentful. When, later that week, Vincent restocked the cellar with vintage Krug the inevitable row ensued. Jolanda had gone to bed early, worn out by her own transports, leaving the two men in her life in a perilous *tête-à-tête* over the last of the wine. 'You must not buy this stuff,' Sebastiano said accusingly. 'La Signora, she drink too much, get pissed, pass out. Is very bad for her.'

'She drinks too much anyway,' Vincent said, wearily aware that that was a problem he could not resolve. 'She might as well enjoy it. And good champagne will do her less harm than cheap *spumante*.'

'Is not cheap! You, you are *ignorante*, you know nothing about Italian wine. Is very superior Berlucchi *spumante*!'

'If you say so.'

'You come here, you throw money around – where you get this money? Maybe you steal it.' By this time, Sebastiano had reached the most irrational stage of inebriation.

Vincent, a slow drinker with a harder head, maintained his thinning self-restraint. 'I don't steal, I deal,' he said curtly.

Sebastiano did not hear him. 'Before, you are in prison, you are *criminale.* When they let you out you are poor, you come to Italy, you sponge off your mother. Now, *subito*, you are rich again—'

'*I* sponge off my mother?' The restraint snapped. Vincent got to his feet and reached across the table for Sebastiano's collar, upsetting a glass and sending a plate spinning. The glass rolled around on the table for a while; the plate fell to the floor with a crash. '*You're* the parasite. You may have been paying the bills but you are still living off her, battering on her talent and her affections. Well, just listen. From now on it's going to be different. I'm making her an allowance. I'm going to pay for everything. So where does that leave you? A failed gigolo whose looks are going clinging on in desperation to a woman who no longer needs him. What have you got to give her now, Sebastiano? Your operatic genius? Your fatal charm? Picking up the tab was all you were ever good for, and I'm putting a stop to that. Do you really think she's going to want you around any more?' He relinquished what was left of Sebastiano's collar and thrust the weaker man violently away, dislodging a chair. The glass gave up rolling and joined the plate on the floor.

The noise brought Mariangela with a dustpan and brush. 'If you fight, you fight in the garden,' she said briskly. '*Fortunatamente*, this is not the best crockery.'

'We're not going to fight,' Vincent said. 'He isn't worth it.'

'We see if I am worth it!' Sebastiano, despite his physical inferiority, was shaking with anger, not fear. As always, it made him incoherent. '*Bastardo – io ti ammazzo—*'

'I think you had better go to bed,' said Mariangela. 'You too, Vincente. It is good to have a big argument, it clears the air, but that is enough now. You must go and sleep and in the morning you will shake hands and this will all be forgotten.'

'Not by me,' said Vincent.

'Yes, Vincente.'

'Why?'

Mariangela looked at him with familiar meaning. 'Because of your mother.'

In the morning they did not actually shake hands, but the usual compromises evolved, without specific discussion. Jolanda continued to live in Sebastiano's home. Vincent arranged an allowance for her which he finally agreed to pay through Sebastiano, on the discovery that several cheques which he had sent her in the past were sitting in her dressing-table drawer, tied up with ribbon, to be exhibited to privileged visitors as evidence of her son's devotion and industry. 'If you wrote letters,' Sebastiano said accusingly, 'she would not need to keep the cheques.'

'I'm no good at letters,' Vincent snapped. 'I prefer the phone.'

The possibility of a return visit to LA was mooted, but Vincent knew in his heart that it would never happen. Old friends of hers and new friends of his regularly enquired after her, expressing the conviction that she must be as beautiful as ever, her *vibrato* as emotive. She was both a singer and an actress: like Callas, she sang not merely from her diaphragm but from her soul. But her performance conveyed a suggestion of contained fury, of dark fires, of self-destruction and danger which made her *Vissi d'Arte* – they said – more superb even than Callas's, while her voice, of course, was almost flawless, whereas everyone knew that Callas's voice had been far from perfect. And so on. The great debate as to which of them had been the most outstanding could still animate many a dinner party in Beverly Hills, in the interludes from movie talk. As the star they had adopted, for a while, as their own, most of them favoured Jolanda. Her current status as a recluse, residing – so they assumed – in some exotic *palazzo*, seeing only a few chosen friends for rarified conversation about the musical world, simply added an aura of mystery to the image. Vincent was indifferent to the prospect of shattering their illusions, but he knew Jolanda could not have borne to disappoint. 'Get her cosmetic surgery,' suggested Richmond, in whom he once confided. 'Have you tried a specialist for her voice? They can do anything these days. I should know.'

'Don't be ridiculous,' Vincent said. 'She'd stare at the mere idea of a face-lift. Besides, it would be like saying I don't find her beautiful the way she is – at least, that's how she'd take it. As for the voice, medicine can't cure that. She's soaked up too many lubricants already. When the bell cracks you can't paste over it. It's cracked and it's going to stay cracked – for good.'

In the end, he told Jolanda exactly what LA society said, how they longed to welcome her, to hear her sing again – knowing, from her reaction, that no further communication was necessary. 'It is true,' Jolanda admitted. 'Maybe I am not quite so beautiful, the voice is not quite so fine, but I am still a prima donna, a *femme fatale*, and in Hollywood – ah, it would all come back to me. It is sad that I cannot go. I know that they will be heartbroken, but I am too busy.' She did not mention with what. 'Anyway, I cannot leave Sebastiano. Perhaps next year.' Or the next, or the next. Now he could afford it, Vincent visited annually, often several times. Jolanda's return to America, he concluded, had fallen into the same category as her operatic comeback: it was going to happen, it was definite, an immutable certainty – one day.

However, although it never occurred to Jolanda to visit a doctor for her wrinkles, she did try professional help for her voice. The gentleman in question had a suave manner, dubious medical qualifications, and a black and silver coiffure to rival that of Frank Cavalcanti. He was also very, very expensive. The influence he acquired over Jolanda led to an unexpected rapprochement between Sebastiano and Vincent. Sebastiano wrote to him, vehemently and at length: the so-called doctor had insinuated his way into Jolanda's confidence; he was a crook, a *truffatore*, and worst of all, English. (Possibly because of Jolanda's connections with the British, Sebastiano was a convinced Anglophobe.) He, Vincente, must get on the next plane and speak to la Signora, if he cared for her at all, because she would not listen to her devoted Sebastiano. Vincent promptly telephoned his mother, who assured him he would be charmed with the *dottore* – such a brilliant man, so sensitive, so *simpatico*! – and he must not pay any attention to poor Sebastiano, who was a little bit jealous. Seriously alarmed, Vincent booked the first available flight. By the time he arrived the doctor had beaten a hasty retreat, presumably back to England. Forewarned by Jolanda, he had evidently found himself less than charmed to meet Vincent. Jolanda was incredulous: she could not believe his defection to be anything more than an unhappy coincidence. Vincent studied the staggering amounts she had paid out of the allowance he made her in growing fury. He left Sebastiano with an absent-minded handshake and an injunction to talk to Jolanda and got on another plane, this time to Heathrow. Jolanda was so breathless from his high-speed arrival and departure she actually forgot to weep over him.

It was more than five years since he had been to England. He arrived in the rain – real English rain, streaming incessantly from a livid grey sky, turning the world beyond the taxi window to a watercolour where all the paint was running. He knew it was stupid to feel sentimental about London in the rain – he had never been sentimental about anything – but its very familiarity caught him unawares, like a reminiscent pang of some awkward attachment which should have vanished with adolescence. It made him feel both unsettled and uncomfortable. At the Dorchester, he contacted a detective agency, Quidnunc PLC, which had been recommended to him by a friend in the States. He sent them on the trail of the spurious doctor and sat back to await results. He wanted to call someone who could tell him what his father was doing, whether Richard and Crystal had the requisite two-point-four children, if Weatherfray had been struck by lightning: but he could think of no one whom he trusted not to report back to his family afterwards. He had sent his address, in the end, to his father's lawyers, but there had been no further exchange of letters, even unopened ones, and he could not ask the ancestral solicitors for gossip. He was annoyed to find himself brooding over the problem: in Los Angeles he had been able – mostly – to distance himself from the past; in London it came back to him, vivid and immediate, as if the bitterness and hurt had been locked inside him all that time, merely waiting for the appropriate stimulus to re-emerge. He had intended to leave as soon as possible, yet even after Quidnunc had located the errant *dottore* and Vincent had dealt with him, briefly and forcefully, he lingered on for a few more days. The *dottore*, confronted by Vincent's thin-lipped self-control and the dossier on his earlier activities compiled by the private detectives, sighed, shrugged, and wrote out a cheque, pausing only to protest the validity of his efforts to help Jolanda. 'When the cheque's gone through,' said Vincent, 'you're off the hook. Not before.' He found it harder to let himself off the hook – caught by a curiosity that he called morbid, close to obsession. Eventually, he gave Quidnunc a watching brief, hoping to obtain from strangers the information he could not request from friends.

It was Quidnunc who told him his father was now Sir John Savage, apparently a reward for his charitable activities: there had always been plenty of those. The Savages were traditionally high-minded, conscientious landlords, dutiful officers: John had simply extended his sense of responsibility to include the modern underclass. The hungry villeins have gone from his back yard so he has to look for them in the city slums, Vincent thought derisively. The benevolent face of business. He has time and money for the name-less underprivileged, but not for his own son: there are no knighthoods in that. Vincent was viciously proud of his own achievements, gained in the teeth of paternal ostracism, without financial or moral support; yet the rejection still galled him, reviv-ing an old anger all the stronger for being irrational, a reaction from pain. He could not forgive or forget: it was not in his nature. He saw himself as a pragmatist, practical and unemotional, but in truth his few passions were powerful enough to distort both cold reason and clear vision. His father, in his view, had built his reputation on hypocrisy, accepting society's ultimate accolade in all the sincerity of self-deceit. He had supported the establishment and now the establishment was patting him on the back. Vincent sneered, though there was nobody there to appreciate it. Sneering had become a reflex with him: it did not make him feel better, but it was what he expected of himself. Knighthood: sneer. Honour, probity, principle: sneer. The anger which he would not acknowledge fed on the sneer, and the sneer fed on the anger, until all the luxury of his room at the Dorchester became another prison in which he felt trapped and useless. He went out, taking his anger with him, in search of a memory that would not taste sour.

Hannibal Barker must be out there somewhere, the black giant with the ready knife who had been, for a few short months, his clos-est friend. He would be a free man now – fighting, drinking, stealing, screwing Lexy or Jayne or Di. Vincent wished him luck. Hannibal had been the true pragmatist for whom every relationship was a deal, trust and loyalty were merely part of the coinage, noth-ing was for nothing. Vincent had not thought of him in a long while but he thought of him now. Hannibal had been right, of course: in the world beyond the prison bars they would have little left to say to each other. But at least the memory of his former inti-mate had no savour of betrayal, no aftertaste of loss. On an impulse, Vincent hailed a cab. He had a vague recollection of a pub Hannibal had mentioned somewhere in south London, the King's Head or the Queen's Legs or some such name. The cab driver might know.

He didn't, but on the offer of a tenner up front he drove Vincent to Brixton and made enquiries. Eventually they found a pub – the Queen's Head – which Vincent thought might be the one: a large building with three or four bars and a façade recently repainted the malevolent yellow of English mustard. A blare of music emerged from one end, a babel of voices from the other. Vincent, who had been expecting a small, quiet local where he could ask a few discreet questions, felt his enthusiasm ebbing by the minute. He paid off the taxi with some reluctance and went inside.

The interior was crowded, noisy, ill lit. The cigarette smoke, unable to find a means of egress, hung around on the air like a smog. Vincent made his way to a stretch of bar as far as possible from the jukebox and waited much longer than was usual to get served. He was conscious of being stared at, not in overt hostility – not yet – but warily and with suspicion. There were few other white faces in the room and those, Vincent guessed, were already known and accepted. He was a stranger, an alien, the creases were still sharp in his jeans, his leather jacket was customised, his wallet bulged with credit cards. The knowledge that his muscles were as hard as the next man's was scarcely reassuring: there were too many next men in the vicinity. But prison had given him an all-round assurance which it would take more than an unfriendly pub to daunt. Having finally acquired a drink he asked the barman if he knew Hannibal Barker.

The reaction was not quite what he had expected. Instead of easing, the atmosphere tautened. The barman ceased serving and glared, his expression icing over. Conversation within earshot ran down. Wariness condensed into active enmity.

'Who wants him?' The barman's tone, even more than the words, conveyed a sort of defensive truculence.

Vincent raised a supercilious eyebrow. 'I do.' He could think of no reason why his enquiry should provoke such a prickly rebuff – unless the clientèle of the Queen's Head was more than usually paranoid. And at least he knew he had come to the right place.

Two Afro-Cockneys seemed to materialise out of the crowd, flanking him to right and left. 'He ain't here,' said one, and 'He don't want to see nobody,' confirmed the other.

'If he's not here,' said Vincent, 'how do you know?'

He was aware of a stirring in the further bar, a rustle of whispers travelling below the level of normal chatter, a shifting in the solid formation of the crowd. A very large, very dark figure, standing head and shoulders above his fellows, extricated himself from the group where he had somehow been concealed. Vincent felt a sudden shakiness in his stomach which might have been secret relief or spontaneous pleasure. Hannibal's face wore the belligerent look which Vincent associated with inner uncertainty but when he saw his former cellmate the look disappeared, slowly, melting into a dropped jaw and widened eyes. Then a huge smile spread from cheek to cheek. 'Vin! Vin Savage! *Fucking* hell! Here, you two' – this to the right and left flank – 'back off, all right? This is my old mate Vin Savage. We was in stir together. Best mate I ever had.' And to Vincent: 'They don't mean no harm, see. They think every white face is trash. No sense of discrimination.'

'I got the idea,' Vincent said.

'Yeah, well . . . hey, man, look at this jacket. This is pretty cool. Where d'you nick it?'

'I had it made.'

'You're doing all right then? You would be. You always was a smart-arse. I looked for your Roller to pinch the radio but I ain't seen it. Saw one once I thought might be yours – big cream-coloured thing with a personalised number plate. VIN 100. One hundred, that's *cent* in French. I had a girlfriend from Martinique who taught me that. I thought that was just your style. VIN 100. Then this fat geezer gets in behind a chauffeur covered in enough gold leaf to repaper St Paul's. It was a bleeding let-down, I'm telling you.'

'So you didn't pinch the radio after all?'

'Nah.' There was a pause while they studied each other, checking recollection against fact. Then Hannibal hailed the barman by name and ordered more drinks. The Afro-Cockney back-up shook hands and the people around resumed their own conversations.

'So,' said Hannibal when they had retired to a corner and two nervous youths had vacated the only available seats, 'where you been?'

'California,' said Vincent. 'I went to seek my fortune. I'd had enough of this country.'

'Did you find it?'

Vincent shrugged. 'I got rich, sure. That was what I wanted. With money, you can buy most things, material things anyway. They're the only ones that matter.'

'What about love?' Hannibal asked. 'You buy that, too?'

'Hardly. What's the point, when there's so much of it around for free?'

Hannibal grinned. 'Same old Vin. You always thought the world was there to be screwed, one way or another.'

'That was what you taught me. Screw or get screwed. The neat little moral at the end of disaster.' He took a mouthful of beer. 'You were the one who was always banging on about it. "Get wise, Vin. Listen to me. Rights ain't what you got, they're what you take." Well, I listened.'

There was a silence during which Vincent sensed Hannibal fishing for something to say.

'What about that girl?' he asked presently. 'The one what didn't write when you was inside. Like your family what didn't write. You see her?'

'No.' Even if he had felt inclined to personal revelation, the pub corner would not have met Vincent's standards of privacy. 'Do you see Lexy and Jayne and Di?'

'Still see Jayne. She's got two kids now but neither of them's mine. Di moved to Birmingham.' From his tone of voice, it might have been Timbuktu. 'Lexy got religion.'

'Shit.'

'You said it.'

There was another silence, not the companionable silence of prison days but one prickling with unexplained awkwardness. Hannibal broke it. 'You hear about Claud? You remember – Claud the creep. He—'

'Stop it,' Vincent said abruptly. 'Stop all this matey let's-have-a-good-gossip bullshit. It doesn't suit me and it doesn't bloody suit you either. Of course I haven't heard about Claud the creep: I've been in California. What's more, I don't give a fuck. If there's something wrong why don't you just tell me? When I asked for you everyone looked as if I'd tossed a live grenade over the bar. Who were you expecting?'

'Nobody much,' Hannibal mumbled. 'I said I was sorry about the hassle, didn't I? You whites are all the same. If you don't get a red carpet you think it's a declaration of war.' Despite his aggression, some of the awkwardness had gone. He went on in his old manner: 'Anyway, you might have been interested in Claud the creep. He was inside with us.'

'Quit boring on about Claud. If he was that ginger-haired git along the corridor, I always loathed him. Look, if you don't want to tell me what's wrong then don't, but stop pretending there's nothing wrong at all. In case you've forgotten, I'm the one with brains.'

'I got brains too,' Hannibal retorted. 'I just didn't have your advantages. I'm not a bleeding privileged member of the bleeding upper classes. I come out of jail and go on social; I don't shove off to bleeding California to seek my bleeding fortune.'

'I taught you to read,' Vincent snapped. 'Isn't it time you acquired a few more bleeding adjectives?'

'Fuck off.'

'Fuck yourself.'

Suddenly, they were back on their former terms, their differences not forgotten but accepted. 'So what's wrong?' Vincent persisted. 'Maybe I can help.'

'Nah. Not your problem, mate. I can deal with it.'

In the end, Vincent extracted the story a trickle at a time. It was all fairly predictable. A debt to a loan shark, astronomical interest, a run of bad luck on the dogs. Hannibal didn't say what the original loan had been for and Vincent didn't ask unnecessary questions. 'I'll clear it for you,' he said briefly. 'I just need to get the cash. Tomorrow.'

'I don't want no favours. Thanks all the same.'

'*Cazzate.* You can owe me one – some day. It doesn't matter. We're not inside now.' He added, flippantly: 'It'll take the weight off my wallet.'

'I told you, no.' On Hannibal's dark face, stubbornness was transformed into a classic immobility.

'You're a pain in the arse,' Vincent said. 'Why not? You'd nick it without a qualm.'

'That's different. I don't stick my friends.'

Vincent drained the last of his beer and sat for a minute immersed in his own thoughts while Hannibal turned for a desultory word with someone else.

Then Vincent said: 'Would you take the money as an advance on salary?'

'*Salary?* I ain't got no salary.'

'Do you like it here?'

'What?'

'In this pub. In Brixton. In England. In the cold winters. In the wet summers. Do you like it?'

'It's all right. It's not bleeding California, but . . .'

'Exactly.' A flick-knife smile gleamed across Vincent's features. 'Chuck it. Come to California and work for me.'

'You're kidding.' Vincent shook his head. 'I mean, work for you? Doing what? You're into financial fiddles and fraud and all that stuff. I don't know nothing about that.'

'Actually,' Vincent said, 'most of what I do is superficially legal. What I need is someone I can rely on when the going gets bumpy. I have two colleagues, a man named Carson and a woman named LeSueur, and I don't trust either of them as far as I could spit. I want you as a kind of assistant – minder, chauffeur, henchman, whatever. No job description and no questions asked. If you have to get your hands dirty I'll pay you over the odds. What do you say?' After a moment or two, he went on: 'It's a nice place, California. Palm trees. Sunshine. Long yellow beaches. Blue sea.'

'I know,' Hannibal said. 'I've seen it on the telly.'

'And an infinite supply of beautiful women.'

'The thing is,' Hannibal said, 'we've been mates. You know. Equals. If you were my boss, it would be different.'

'You don't have to call me sir,' Vincent murmured.

'You bet your fucking life I don't!'

Fleetingly, Vincent thought of his father. *Sir* John Savage. No doubt both his social circle and his inferiors all dutifully called him Sir John. He said: 'Look, Han, I'm at the Dorchester. I'll be there a couple more days. Let me know what you decide, OK? Either way.'

Hannibal nodded. 'Don't get me wrong. It's a good offer: I'm grateful. It's just that I don't like—'

'Being grateful? Bugger that. I meant what I said. I need you.'

'I'll think it over.'

The following afternoon, Hannibal walked into the Dorchester and up to the reception desk. A certain awe at his surroundings made him very polite. The surroundings, equally awed, were even politer: the doorman held the door and the receptionist responded to his enquiries in a faint voice, wondering if she dared summon Security. In due course, Vincent appeared. They went into the bar, Hannibal trying to look nonchalant, leaving raised eyebrows in their wake. 'Well?' said Vincent.

'I thought about what you said. The palm trees, and the beaches, and the sun. Good money. Plenty of birds. All that stuff. Then I thought about you being my boss.'

'I see,' said Vincent. 'You prefer your independence.' He concluded, with something of an effort. 'I can understand that.'

'Bollocks,' said Hannibal. 'You think I'm missing out on a chance like this? I'm not a bleeding moron. Nice to work for you – *sir*.'

By the end of the week the loan shark was paid off, Hannibal's few possessions were either packed or in store, and they were on the plane to Los Angeles. Vincent had arranged with Quidnunc to receive quarterly reports on his relatives, since he could think of no better way to keep track of their activities. He had sent no letters, nor telephoned: they would not even realise he had been in England. He welcomed their ignorance but at the same time it injured him, as though they and not he were to blame for this neglect. Among other snippets of information Quidnunc had told him that Crystal was pregnant. He found it impossible to picture her in that state, yet curiously easy to imagine Richard aglow with the prospect of paternity. That was happiness, Vincent reflected balefully, a bourgeois, banal, everyday happiness, radiant father, radiant mother and grandmother, probably radiant great-uncle – complete with knighthood – all basking in their own radiance, while he, Vincent, the misfit, the black sheep, was cosily out of the way. Absent and forgotten. Perhaps it was not really an impulse which had sent him to find Hannibal, the friend who had not failed him, nor an impromptu gesture when Vincent had offered him a job.

He had no cause to regret it. Hannibal called him sir only in mockery and criticised him freely when he felt the urge, but the street-smart south London tough had no fault to find with Vincent's business methods and was prepared to engage in almost any activity, no matter how dubious, on his behalf. To the Angelenos, Vincent had produced him from nowhere, like a genie from a lamp, and accordingly they endowed him with the traditional powers of a genie: mythical strength, unswerving fidelity. Rumour credited him with deeds darker than anything Vincent had demanded, inclusive of murder. Meanwhile, to the women he picked up in bars and nightclubs rather more glamorous than the Queen's Head, Brixton, his massive musculature, god-like assets and financial and sexual prodigality made him something of an idol. Carson tolerated him, Richmond was wary of him – perhaps he brought back memories of her own downbeat past that were a little too vivid for comfort – but Hannibal did not care. He was having a good time. As he grew accustomed to his role he criticised Vincent less and felt less need to assert his independence. Eventually he set up house with a nightclub singer called Smokey Brown who gave up singing to have five children and cook wonderful food. Hannibal ate like a hungry tiger and worked out like a true Californian to counteract the after-effects. 'I'm a Londoner,' he would still say with pride when he had not been back to London in nearly a decade, but in fact he had become Americanised after the fashion of so many immigrants, making himself a larger-than-life caricature of a Jamaican Cockney, clinging to his accent in the teeth of the west coast drawl. His recollection of London had dimmed into a sentimental blur; so had the days when he and Vincent were cellmates, partners in a world where size and experience gave Hannibal the edge. Now, Vincent was always in charge. Hannibal was his sidekick, his supporting cast, his subordinate. It did not bother him. Nor would it have bothered Vincent, if he had noticed the change. After all, Hannibal still swore at him on occasion, still called him Vin, was still free to expostulate and admonish even if he no longer did so. Had he thought about it, Vincent would have found it perfectly natural that there should be an alteration in the balance of their relationship.

But he had brought Hannibal to the States because he needed a friend, an equal, not simply a supporter.

3

The years passed. Quidnunc duly informed Vincent of the birth of Penelope Snow Crystal and her brother Jonas, of the progress of Richard's career, of Sir John's entry into politics. When Elizabeth Savage's herbaceous border featured in *Country Living*, they sent him the pictures. He read the draft of his father's maiden speech to the Commons – a down-to-earth statement of old-fashioned Toryism, already out of date, sincere, heartfelt and elusively stodgy. 'More appropriate to the Lords,' Vincent thought. 'They should have given him a peerage on top of the knighthood and stuck him among the antiquities where he belongs.' While Crystal was still with Récamier he received copies of her ads but they did little to remind him of her, the photographs glossy beyond recognition, tinted, softened, shaded into anonymity. When he tried to visualise making love to her, all he could really remember was her wonderful hair. Even in LA, where the most beautiful girls in the world come to trade their bodies for a moment of celluloid, he had never seen hair so long, so thick, or so coldly silky. 'I bet she's had it cut,' he told himself with faint regret. 'They always do.' Forgetting Crystal had once been an effort; now, it was an effort to remember her. But he wasn't thankful. His recollections of Richard and his father may have distorted but did not wear thin, fed on the morsels Quidnunc supplied, a typed report, a sly snapshot, an extract from a newspaper or magazine. When Sir John's constituency duties led him to dine out rather frequently with the local party secretary, photographs appeared in the quarterly report. Vincent, observing that Hester Bradley had neither looks nor glamour, reserved his suspicions and ordered the agency to check her out largely as a matter of form. It was only after a conversation with Richmond that he revised his attitude.

They had dissolved their partnership when Richmond married yet again, this time to a bright young man who, Vincent opined, was out to take her for every cent. Since he expressed his opinion both frankly and forcefully, a business relationship which had already become strained promptly disintegrated and they embarrassed their entire acquaintance by not speaking for a year. The bright young man was booted out after six months when he claimed it was Richmond's meanness in refusing him access to her bank account which had compelled him to sell the *famille rose* vases. She would never have noticed the loss of the Paul Klee, he insisted, if that two-faced art-dealer hadn't welshed on him. Richmond, understandably far angrier with Vincent for being right than she would have been had she been able to prove him wrong, refused to consider a détente and continued to cherish her umbrage for some while. However, old habits die hard and they were now back on lunching if not bedroom terms. She remained the only woman in whom Vincent would occasionally confide or to whom he would turn for advice.

She took one look at the photos of Sir John and Hester Bradley and said: 'Watch out. If he hasn't got it badly he will have. Look at them. In every picture it's the same.'

'What do you mean?'

'He's talking; she's listening. See her face? All quiet and attentive. She's obviously a perfect listener. It gets them every time. Forget beauty and charm and sex appeal. The woman who sits there soaking up the outpourings of his ego and telling him he's wonderful – not too often, that's flattery, just once in a while when it fits in nicely – she's the one who's got what it takes. I taught myself to be a good listener, particularly when they talk about money, but this Bradley woman's a natural. She doesn't need make-up and designer clothes: just ears. If he's a normal vain, self-absorbed male he'll fall in love with her.'

'He's a normal male, certainly,' Vincent said, slightly defensive.

'Then he's vain and self-absorbed. It's all part of the package.'

'Time and sorrow have not sweetened you, have they?' Vincent remarked. But he had asked her opinion, it would be stupid not to give it due consideration. He sent Quidnunc a fax requesting further data on Hester Bradley immediately. The results included her childlessness, her invalid husband, and a long record as a conscientious citizen which Vincent knew would appeal to his father. The agency said that so far there was no evidence of a physical relationship: should he require more intensive observation it would be costly and might well prove fruitless. Vincent authorised it without hesitation. This was his family, his own back yard, no matter how distant and out of touch, and he had no intention of being caught off guard by any untoward developments. He knew his father was a man of strong principles, he guessed Hester Bradley was the same, yet he awaited the inevitable with a cynical conviction, a sort of black eagerness. So might Lucifer have waited behind the apple tree for Adam to take the fatal bite, seeking in the downfall of Man to justify his own downfall, salving his own loss with theirs. Such regression was as natural as breathing, as unavoidable as death, or so Vincent believed: show Adam an apple and eventually he would succumb and eat. Without defining his emotions he felt that in some way his father's fall from grace would be the end of an era, the completion of a circle, and once he had witnessed that final apostasy – once he had said to himself, in silence, thousands of miles away: 'I told you so', then he could reign in hell free from conscience or doubt. He might almost have said, with Milton's Satan: 'Farewell remorse: all good to me is lost. Evil be thou my Good.' Yet when the evidence arrived, it gave him a sombre satisfaction but no happiness. Even the words 'I told you so' lost their savour. It was a bore, he decided, always to be right about human nature: its weakness, its fallibility, its congenital hypocrisy. Sir John had bought a flat in Belgravia to use while he was at Westminster and on one occasion Hester Bradley had accompanied him. Only one, but it was enough. An aberration? Vincent wondered. An instant of passion, maybe, which carried them both away for an instant. He looked through the pictures and the careful accounts for a few more minutes and then put them in his private safe where he kept all such documentation, inaccessible even to his secretary. He had no plans to make use of it. His interest might be as obsessive as Lucifer's but it was also remote, aloof: he had done nothing to promote the case for eating the apple. The worst had happened without any encouragement from him.

Then came the letter. Neither anticipation nor intuition had prepared him for that. A letter from his father, in the language of cliché which Vincent had so often derided, suggesting that bygones should be bygones, that blood was thicker than water, that much water (or blood?) had gone under the bridge and flowed away and it was time to make a new start. Vincent did not know and never guessed that it was Hester Bradley who had nudged Sir John into writing, that childless woman who sensed that parenthood was precious and offspring, whatever their sins, should not be banished forever. He read the letter again and again, distrusted it, brooded on it. He discussed it with no one. When he told Hannibal and Carson that he was going to England, he did not say why. He flew into Heathrow, changed to a domestic flight to Newcastle. There, as usual, he picked up a hired car. He had not rung his father or aunt to say he was coming. He simply drove home.

Home. Weatherfray – Weatherfray on a grey afternoon, looking the way he had forgotten, ominous against a darkening sky. Stormclouds were rolling down from Scotland, gathering themselves together above the hills into wavering columns and billows and pendulous swags heavy with unshed rain. In the gap between cloud and land the falling sun blazed out suddenly, sending long rays slanting low across the countryside, stretching every shadow to preposterous lengths. The light touched the front of the house, sparked off the tip of a finial, picked out a tooth of carving here and there, but the façade was south-facing and the windows remained opaque and sombre. Home – the word was a meaningless reflex. Weatherfray had not been home to him since the day his father refused to help him, thereby condemning him to prison. The place was an ancestral white elephant, an anachronism in the modern world, oppressive, gloomy, draughty inside and windswept without, not mellowing into a graceful old age as such houses should but resisting time and weather with a stiffening of joists, a grumbling of ancient plumbing, a clenching of stone on stone. 'When I inherit,' Vincent found himself thinking, 'I'll sell it and be rid of it for good. I don't give a damn about family tradition. I always hated it.' He carefully omitted from his reflections any reference to himself and Richard, going on rambling adventures over stair and under stair, through cellar door and kitchen window, fighting dragons, hostile natives, each other. He had always hated it: that was official. He pulled up in front of the house and sat in the car for a couple of minutes while the sun dropped behind the hills and a cold grey shadow washed over everything. There was a faint drum roll in the distance which might have been thunder or a passing jugger-naut. Two or three isolated raindrops, the vanguard of the storm, splattered themselves against the windscreen.

Vincent got out of the car, mounted the steps to the front door, and rang the bell.

Nobody was expecting him. Sir John, secretly glad to succumb to persuasion and write the letter, had awaited a prompt answer with characteristic impatience and, when none came, had given up hope just as impatiently. He had spent the day in London, lunching at length with Piers Percival, in whom he chose to confide his pater-nal angst. At the time of Vincent's return he was still with Inter-City, being whisked from one delay to the next with custom-ary British Rail efficiency. Hester Bradley, who was occasionally to be found at Weatherfray, had gone to visit her doctor, while an agent from Quidnunc abstracted the remnants of the pregnancy testing kit from the depths of her dustbin. Elizabeth Savage knew nothing whatsoever about the letter.

It was Elizabeth who stared blankly at Vincent on the doorstep and who admitted him, with reluctance, after a minute or two. 'What are you doing here?' she asked with her usual bluntness, and then, realising she sounded far from friendly. 'Would you like some tea?'

Elizabeth was a great tea-drinker, Vincent remembered. He wasn't, but he accepted because, as he put it in his own mind, it would give her something with which to fidget, a reassuring little ritual to perform. She clearly needed that. He followed her into the kitchen and sat down at the table, long legs stretched out in front of him, an incongruous figure in the expensive clothes which he wore so indifferently. Elizabeth noted that a haircut was overdue and that his face, permanently sallowed by the Californian sun, bore the imprint of recurrent expressions, a habitual narrowing of the eyes, a hardening of the mouth, a tautening of cheeks already lean. There were no smile lines, no blurring of the jaw, no hint of laughter or softening. Time had not altered him, merely paring

away the residue of youth so that, in Elizabeth's view, his personality showed as sharp and hard as his bones.

'Tea,' he mused. 'The classic English reaction to everything.
Forget the champagne: come triumph or disaster, we'll open up the
tea canisters. The barbarians are at the gate: offer them tea. The
return of the prodigal: tea. The Second Coming: tea – presumably
made with holy water.'

'If you wanted a surprise party,' Elizabeth said, 'you should have
given us some advance warning.'

The faint irony was unlike the aunt he remembered and Vincent
glanced quickly at her. He didn't mention the letter. Faced with her
ignorance on the subject he was filled with a sudden insecurity, a
loss of confidence which appalled him. He found himself drinking
his tea for something to do.

Elizabeth made stilted conversation for a while on standard matters: Sir John's political career, her own admiration for Mrs
Thatcher, the impossibility of getting reliable domestic help. Then
she suggested, rather abruptly, that since she assumed he wished to
stay he might like to go to his room and unpack. She made up the
bed herself, doubtless due to the shortage of domestics. Vincent,
accustomed to the services of a Hispanic maid, did not offer to
assist her. When she had finished she hesitated for a minute, trying
to find something welcoming to say to this nephew she had never
been able to love.

'You should have come sooner.' The words, though brusquely
uttered, were well-intentioned and to Vincent, meaningless. 'Your
father missed you. I'm sure he did.' She didn't sound sure.

'Really.' Vincent had no idea how to answer her and turned
away, superficially bored. Elizabeth went downstairs, leaving him
alone.

On the Inter-City train, Sir John was thinking about his son. His
thoughts were not happy.

'So you've written to him,' Piers had said, contemplating his
exquisitely manicured fingertips. 'I always thought you would.'

'You don't sound as if you approve,' said Sir John.

'It isn't a question of approval or disapproval, dear boy. I'm not
sure you were wise, that's all.'

'At the time of the court case,' Sir John reminded him, 'you
made it pretty clear you thought I'd been unduly harsh, right from

the start. You've maintained all along that I mishandled the boy. Maybe you were right. But now, when I try to mend matters—'

'No, no,' interrupted Piers. 'I am convinced you have always discharged the responsibilities of fatherhood quite conscientiously. Probably far too conscientiously. I know nothing of such things, of course, nor would I dream of setting myself up as a judge. Any little observations I may have made have been in the nature of – how shall I put it?'

'Devil's advocate?' suggested Sir John.

'I wish,' complained Piers, 'you would cultivate a little subtlety. Understatement, evasion – these things are so convenient. Properly disposed, they smooth the rocky path of social intercourse.'

'All of which takes us a long way from the point,' resumed Sir John. 'Why do you think I was – what word did you use? – not *wise* in writing to Vincent?'

'One hears things.' Piers' usual eloquence appeared to desert him: he became unexpectedly cryptic. 'He's been away a long time. You don't really know anything about him any more.'

'What is that supposed to mean?'

'I've been in LA recently . . .'

'So?'

'Vincent has become a very successful entrepreneur. In real estate, I understand. Very successful, and very rich.'

'I'd heard,' Sir John admitted. 'He hasn't been in trouble again, either. He's obviously learned his lesson. You can't expect me to object because my son, on his own initiative, without any help from me' – a note of pride crept into his voice and was allowed to stay there – 'has become rich and successful.'

Piers did not attempt to contradict him. 'I came across one of his associates,' he pursued, returning to the examination of his hands. 'A certain Richmond LeSueur. Formerly a co-director with Vincent and still, I understand, closely connected with him. Something of a collector, Madame LeSueur: a rather notorious collector.'

'Madame? I thought you said his name was Richard.'

'Rich*mond*. I should imagine she made it up. Possibly from the French – *riche monde*. No doubt that would appeal to her. She is also known as LeSewer. Her collection is said to include certain items obtained . . . by somewhat questionable means. Of course, there are so many temptations nowadays. Difficulties with an export licence – you bribe the correct official. In some countries they expect it: it's not really bribery, purely a matter of courtesy. As for what was the Eastern Bloc, there's stuff coming on the market which should never be put up for sale, but what can you do? People are desperate for funds and much of it was stolen in the first place. The art world, alas, is stronger on greed than probity, and there is no greed like the greed for beauty. A form of lust, I always think, for those who consider mere fleshly appetites too easily sated. Where was I?'

'God knows.'

'Ah yes. Richmond LeSueur. To have a bad reputation in the art world you really have to earn it. There is a particular painting, a Palma Vecchio, stolen a few years ago – but I won't bore you with the details. Gossip in the trade says it is in her possession. Also—'

'What has all this to do with Vincent?' Sir John interjected.

'Nothing, dear boy, nothing. I am simply trying to avoid coming to the point. Richmond LeSueur is a collector whose methods would not bear close scrutiny. The same, I infer, is true of her business methods. And she is, or was, a colleague of Vincent's.'

'I am reliably informed,' Sir John said frigidly, 'that my son is a respected member of Hollywood society.'

'Oh, most definitely. But then, all sorts of people have been, at one time or another, respected members of Hollywood society. It is not a list outstanding for collective virtue. John, I have no wish to be a tale-bearer. You wrote to him; he did not respond. Before you write again there are certain things I think you should be told. It is better to know the worst already than to stumble on it without warning, as you undoubtedly would. From what I remember of Vincent, he is quite capable of hurling his activities in your teeth. That would not be pleasant. I do not want you to be hurt again, dear friend.'

'He has not broken the law,' Sir John reiterated doggedly.

'There are so many laws,' sighed Piers, 'and so many ways round them.'

If Piers had known Vincent was already at Weatherfray, he might not have spoken. But he did not know. Sir John arrived home in the midst of a rainstorm to find his sister in the hallway plucking at his wet sleeve and whispering in his ear words he could not hear against the battledrums of the thunder. There was no further chance to prepare him: he strode briskly into the sitting room and there was his son, rising out of a chair to meet him, pale with the onset of apprehension, taut-lipped from the fear of giving himself away. Sir John, his mind full of what Piers had related, was equally taut about the lips, clamping a firm hand on any upsurge of sentiment. Outside, clouds darkened the evening into night. The thunder rolled away. The room, like all the rooms at Weatherfray, was poorly lit; thick stone walls kept out the rush and clatter of the rain. The silence after the storm rumblings was sudden and dreadful.

'So you've come back,' said Sir John.

You invited me, thought Vincent, but he didn't say it. His throat felt tighter than his lips. He had expected some sort of a welcome, a reception in keeping with the mood of the letter, but his father's face was as harsh and inflexible as ever. He offered neither a handshake nor an embrace; Vincent, stiffening by the second, gave no indication that he wanted one.

'You *have* come back.' Sir John struggled with himself, moral fibre against emotional weakness. For an instant, weakness dominated, his expression changed and his voice shook; but the returning thunder obliterated any treacherous detail.

'Your suggestion,' said Vincent. The words held a challenge, not a plea.

'Yes,' said Sir John. 'Yes, I know. But I hardly supposed . . . that is, I had ceased to expect . . . You left it so long.'

'I'll go,' said Vincent.

'Don't be ridiculous.' Irritation overrode other, deeper feelings. 'You can't possibly go out in this. Anyway, it's far too late. We'll be having dinner at eight-thirty.' For the first time, he seemed to register that he was still wearing his overcoat and outdoor shoes, soaked between the station and the car, the car and the house. 'I must get out of these things. Have you had a drink?'

'Tea.'

'Elizabeth!' His sister had been waiting in the hall, restraining both curiosity and anxiety with a self-control as rigorous as Sir John's. She came in without comment. 'I've got to get changed. Tell Mrs Gurney there'll be an extra one for dinner . . .'

'I have.'

'. . . and for God's sake give the boy a whisky.'

Dinner was delayed since the current cook-housekeeper, returning from her afternoon off, claimed she was put out by the storm and the advent of an extra diner. Halfway through the meal the electricity failed. Sir John lit the candles. Vincent reflected that Weatherfray was living up to its normal neo-Gothic standards and found himself smiling at the thought, though it had never amused him before. Possibly he smiled, on this occasion, because there was so little else at which to smile. Neither his father nor his aunt noticed. Elizabeth appeared to be enduring the evening with fortitude – rather more fortitude, perhaps, than the situation warranted. Initially, Sir John kept the conversation, such as it was, on trivial topics, but every so often he would ask his son a question, listen assiduously to the answer, and then relapse into a fit of abstraction which might last some minutes. It did not take them long to get on to politics, whereupon the atmosphere warmed up by several degrees. Sir John, as ever, was vehement, trenchant, authoritarian, laying down the law with all the sincerity and conviction of a limited vision, while Vincent remained coolly detached, dismissing every assumption with familiar cynicism. The veteran bull pawed the ground, the designer cape whisked here and there. Old-fashioned ideology charged in vain at New Age unbelief. The girl from the village who came in to help serve the dinner and wash up afterwards remarked hopefully: 'They're at it hammer and tongs. D'you think they'll get violent?'

'No,' said Mrs Gurney, wiser in the ways of men. 'It's only politics.'

'You don't change, boy, do you?' Sir John commented rather grimly at the end of the meal.

'Nor do you,' retorted Vincent.

The exchange might have revealed a hint of mutual affection, even an underlying respect, if either of them had been able to see it. But they saw no further than the candlelight.

Sir John said: 'Come to my study.'

The ambience grew increasingly Victorian as they ascended the stairs, holding their respective candlesticks, a free hand shielding each unsteady flame. Vincent reflected in passing on the notion, popular with every bard from Shakespeare to Elton John, that a human life was best epitomised by the candle flame, doubtless because of its ephemeral nature, its frailty, its small brave source of light. He himself had always felt the life within him burning with a far greater fire, but for a moment, looking down at the tiny cone of brilliance which shivered uneasily in the shelter of his hand, the image touched him with a sort of truth. In that instant he was aware of an elusive significance, a forgotten word on the tip of his tongue, a flicker, perhaps of déjà vu, as if he were reliving something from a dream or dreaming something he had yet to relive; but the moment vanished as such moments invariably do, long before he could catch its meaning. In the study, he placed his candle on the mantelpiece; Sir Johns was already on his desk. Shadows came swarming out of the walls to meet them. Vincent, recalling another confrontation in this same room long ago, felt a resurgence of antagonism although there was little, as yet, to antagonise him. It was a beginning as unpromising as all their other beginnings. Sir John, fiercely resisting his own susceptibility, launched without preamble into the issue of Vincent's professional ethics, as culled from Piers Percival. Vincent, disdaining to defend himself, said it was none of his father's business. Sir John said matters of principle were every man's business, and Vincent was his son, his flesh and blood, the flawed product of his upbringing. His genes and his responsibility. 'It's a responsibility you've ignored for rather a long time!' Vincent flashed, goaded. 'I'm not a child any more for you to lecture. I've made money and I've done it my own way, without your backing or your bogus morality. People got hurt: so what? I don't care and I don't pretend to care. In this life you look after yourself. Some people will always get hurt. There's no such thing as natural justice, only an artificial concept invented by men like you to give you something to prate about. You like to call your ego your conscience and fatten it up on patronage and philanthropy. When you got rich other people got poor: that's the way it works – that's natural injustice – but you won't face it, will you? The only real difference between you and me is the charitable hand-outs.'

'I'd heard you yourself give generously to charity, on public occasions,' Sir John said painfully.

'It's fashionable.' Vincent was dismissive. 'If you're going to write a cheque, you might as well make it a large one. I don't give a damn about the recipients. It's a purely social habit. Like smoking or drinking champagne.'

'A social habit!' echoed Sir John. 'Dear God, what kind of a man are you? *My son!* Did I teach you nothing?'

'You sent me to jail!' Vincent retaliated. 'What did you expect me to learn there? Brotherly love?'

Right on cue, the storm which had wandered away east for a while came grumbling back, nudged from hilltop to hilltop, bad-tempered from continuous buffeting. A double prong of lightning split the sky beyond the uncurtained windows; for a second the room was filled with a dazzling glare. Thunder rolled directly overhead, so close the ceiling seemed to shake. The elements without and the dispute within mounted to a parallel climax. Vincent had long forgotten his resolve not to use the data gathered by Quidnunc. He wanted to pierce his father's veneer of self-righteousness, to force from him the admission that he was only a man, a man like other men, fallible, corruptible, open to temptation – a man like his son. Hester Bradley was the obvious weapon. 'What about your mistress?' Vincent taunted him. 'Does the moral code you're so proud of make special allowances for her? A married woman with a husband who's incurably ill – multiple sclerosis, isn't it? He must provide you with serious competition!'

'Who told you about her?' Sir John's expression froze, caught between anger and shock, suddenly terrible in its stillness – terrible even to Vincent, for whom a perfunctory qualm was only an additional spur.

'What the hell! I *know*. Information is survival. I make it my business to know. You have your mucky little secrets just like the rest of us. You're in no position to—'

'*Who told you?*'

'I've had detectives watching you,' Vincent said shortly.

'Detectives!'

'How else was I supposed to find out what was going on here? You could have got married without telling me!'

'You mean you've paid some sordid little agency to spy on me – on Hester? My own son!'

'Stop saying that as if it poisons you!' Vincent's rage concealed any trace of hurt. 'Yes, I'm your son. You're stuck with it; I'm stuck with it. You cannot eradicate my blood from the noble house of Savage – which, by the way, doesn't look quite so noble now. A sordid little affair with the sexually frustrated wife of an invalid is just the thing for a sordid little detective agency to investigate, don't you think?'

'Get out!' There was no more quibbling about the weather or the lateness of the hour. 'Get out *now*! I never want to set eyes on you again. Never: do you understand? *Never!*'

Vincent went – slamming the heavy door with the strength of fury, running perilously downstairs in the blind dark. Elizabeth heard him cross the hallway, started after him too late. A flash of lightning showed him the driveway, the standing yews, huge shifting masses of cloud jostling for position in the overladen sky. In another flash he glanced back at the house – a monster of a house, battlemented and gargoyled, forested with chimneys, ribbed and ridged and rutted with carving, a stonemason's nightmare, a film director's fantasy – a Savage's home. But not his home. That was a delusion which would not recur. He had come to a reconciliation and had found reproaches and rejection. And now his father had cast him out, finally and irrefutably. He did not look back again.

Afterwards, he wondered why he had not taken the car, but at the time it did not occur to him. He walked on through the rain towards the village, without direction or purpose. About twenty minutes later he arrived at Ridpath's principal pub, the Green Man, where there were two or three bedrooms to let. The pub was an ancient and largely decrepit establishment which matched its ancient and largely decrepit clientèle, with a single bar, oak-beamed and smoke-stained, populated long after hours by several rustics, including the local policeman. The landlord recognised Vincent at once and proceeded to mix him a hot toddy while his wife adjured him to take off them clothes or he would catch his death. He sat in the bar wrapped in her husband's dressing-gown, savouring the aroma of lemon juice, cloves and Lagavulin, while the last of the rustics departed in a mutter of speculation. Unusually, there was another guest that night, a southerner who claimed to be writing a book of regional history and who had been staying some time, buying rounds in a lavish way which made the landlady deeply suspicious. He joined Vincent in the bar, wielding an ingratiating smile and studying him with alert eyes unaffected by his intake of liquor.

'The name's Hibbert,' he offered, matily. 'Gerald Hibbert. My friends call me Gerry.'

'Bully for them,' said Vincent.

He drank his second hot toddy and went to bed. Gerry Hibbert, maintaining his geniality undiscouraged, tapped the landlord for village gossip and retired to his own room.

Vincent slept badly. The wind, having howled around Weatherfray, came down to the pub to moan and whimper under the eaves. Rain swept the countryside in waves, battering the windowpanes with the vigour of artillery fire and then relapsing into a steady drizzle until it was ready to resume the onslaught. The thunder grumbled around till morning. From trying not to think about his row with his father Vincent slipped irresistibly into other unbidden trains of thought. The sound of Gerry Hibbert snoring alternated with the thunder, not the deep, subterranean snore favoured by Hannibal Barker but a lighter, snuffling, whiffling sound, like a pig rooting in a rubbish heap. It annoyed Vincent but did not trouble him. In all his unwanted thoughts, no conjecture about his fellow guest ever entered his head.

Gerry Hibbert slept well – the satisfied slumber of a journalist on a cold trail who has at last found what might be a hot clue.

It was not till some time afterwards that Vincent pieced together the events of the following morning. He had risen early, too early, to collect his luggage and car from Weatherfray, since he wished to be sure of missing his father. To kill time, he walked up to the crest of Allweathers, where the lightning had scored a direct hit. There was a charred gap in the cluster of trees, as if a witches' coven had foregathered there as they were rumoured to do, and had been carried away by their own black magic. 'The Devil's hoofprint,' said a farmer who had come to inspect the damage, indicating a scorched area on the ground. Vincent recollected rites of passage with the Fat Cat in the secret hollow under the leaves, the only pagan rites ever to appeal to him. 'Call me Satan,' he said, but the man, thinking he must have misheard, did not answer. Vincent gazed bleakly at the familiar view for a few minutes before making his way back down the hill.

The courier from Quidnunc, reaching Weatherfray before seven, had already been sent on to the pub. Vincent's instructions had been precise: 'I will be in England for maybe a week. If there's anything important I want to know immediately. Put the courier on my bill.' At the Green Man, with no reception desk or similar facility, the landlord took delivery of a large brown envelope and placed it in Vincent's room. Gerry Hibbert had earlier found an opportunity to appropriate the key from the cleaner with a view to a quick search. He ripped open the envelope, read and photographed its contents, and sent the barmaid out for a replacement envelope which he typed on his own portable. When Vincent returned, Gerry blandly presented it to him. 'This came for you, old man. Thought I'd better hang on to it. Safer than leaving it lying around the bar.'

Vincent took it with brief thanks and read it with brief interest. Hester's pregnancy might once have threatened him; now, it did not seem to be relevant. His home, his life, his future were in America. He had missed his father as planned and bidden his aunt a curt goodbye, and henceforth he intended to forget Weatherfray and all it contained.

His intention was a cold angry force which stayed with him throughout the flight to California and did not evaporate even in the tranquilising sunshine. Using an inside tip-off about a forthcoming merger, he bought some shares low and sold high. Hannibal, under his instructions, ejected half a dozen Cuban families from their makeshift accommodation on a plot of land where he proposed to build luxury condominiums. He bedded a lovely young thing who had leaped to fifteen-minute stardom in a recent film and a lovely but slightly older thing who preferred critical acclaim to big bucks. None of it made him feel any better. The intellectual actress proved as empty-headed as the starlet and far more loquacious. The type of financial coup which had once boosted his adrenalin had begun to feel vaguely monotonous. Having convinced himself he was an American fixture, he felt a contradictory yearning for pastures new, though he did not particularise where. He and Carson had done business in Europe, mainly of the quick-profit cut-and-run variety on the French and German stock exchanges, but for obvious reasons they had not ventured into the UK market since their first unfortunate encounter. 'My father would try to stop me,' Vincent thought, and his intention altered, subtly, from negative rancour to positive impetus, from deterrent to determination. He had progressed no further than determination when Quidnunc sent him the tabloids.

Once he had registered Gerry Hibbert's byline it took little checking to assimilate what must have happened. Quidnunc promised to sack the courier but Vincent knew it was too late to signify. His father faced public humiliation and imminent disgrace, a state of affairs which should have pleased him but did not. His own exposure to the media at the time of the court case had been partially cushioned by the machinery of the law, by policemen and solicitors and barristers, by cries of injunction and sub judice, finally and most efficaciously by prison walls. His father would have no such insulation. He visualised journalists besieging Weatherfray with microphones and grappling hooks while Sir John stalked his study in futile rage and Hester Bradley was smuggled to a safe house in the outer Hebrides. Possibly there would be questions in the House from pious Labour back-benchers, editorials in the quality press citing the pressures of high office and bemoaning the disintegration of the family unit. The spectre of Cecil Parkinson would inevitably rear its ugly head. Fleetingly, Vincent considered writing a letter expressing whatever commiseration was appropriate in view of the fact that Sir John had just banished him from the ancestral home for good, but suitable phrases could not be found and he came to the conclusion there were none. There was nothing he could do at all, either in the way of constructive action or moral support. He lay awake at night wondering what was happening – whether Hester would have the baby, sell her memoirs, or become a nun – but it did not improve his frame of mind. The paparazzi took pictures of Sir John and Quidnunc took pictures of the paparazzi. Statements were issued of the terse and noncommittal variety; Sir John, scrupulously honest even in the face of catastrophe, would not deny what he knew to be true. His political colleagues despaired of him.

Another couple of weeks went by. The phone ringing in the small hours jerked Vincent from a fitful doze into irritable awakening. He murmured: 'Hello?' and heard his aunt's voice booming in his ear, unnecessarily loud since she automatically assumed it was a bad line. Elizabeth Savage was oblivious to satellite technology and always attempted to bridge the Atlantic on volume alone. Because he was half asleep, or because her strident accents produced an echo which confused him, it was a minute or two before he took in what she was saying.

'Your father.'

'What?'

'I'm sorry, Vincent – so awfully sorry.' Later, it occurred to him that one cause of her loudness was distress.

'What's the matter?'

'It was an accident – a car accident. They took him to hospital.'

'How is he?' Vincent was wide awake now.

'He's dead.'

You don't expect people to die like that, Vincent thought at the funeral. Not when you have quarrelled unforgivably, broken irrevocably, and an assortment of disasters are piling up in all directions like a leaf-fall in autumn. Death, in those circumstances, is too easy, a way of escape, a cheat, a quick drop through a loophole into eternity. The inquest had rejected the possibility of suicide but gossips continued to gossip and scandalmongers mongered scandal. Vincent knew his father would never have killed himself – Sir John considered suicide both spineless and immoral – but he still admitted to a nebulous doubt. Perhaps there had been something in his fathers subconscious which had aborted his concentration, that fatal night: a kind of deep-seated weariness, not physical but psychological, the weariness that comes from a surfeit of conscience, from a belated and hopeless love affair, from high ideals brought too low. Vincent remembered their last showdown, and the storm raging, and how when he gazed at the candle flame he had felt his own vital force burning with a fierce steady fire. Without giving the matter any serious thought he had assumed that his father's life, too, was fuelled by a blaze and not a flicker – a flame that could not, surely, be snuffed out so easily, on a lonely road at night by a moment's inattention and a passing car. But it seemed the poets were right after all. Out, out, brief candle! – and the flame vanished, presumably forever. Vincent did not believe in an afterlife. His father's death was an undignified exit, hasty and arbitrary, leaving only a collection of loose ends like a novel with the final chapters missing. His alienation from his son, his relationship with Hester, his blighted reputation and career – unfinished themes which would never be resolved. It was too late. In that moment, Vincent wished he believed in something, anything, a god whom he could curse, a heaven that would slam its doors on him, a hell from whence he might scream his defiance. But there was nothing. Only a glossy coffin under a cushion of flowers, a babble of obituaries. The end.

The church at Ridpath was full, of course. Locals, friends, politicos, press, they crowded every pew, knelt on every hassock, huddled three and four to a hymnbook. They had brought wreaths and handkerchiefs, Nikons and notepads. They sang 'Abide With Me' in a variety of keys or no key at all. The vicar, inspired doubtless by the size of his audience, held forth at length on the good qualities of the deceased, a subject which taxed his invention far less than is usual in such a situation. Vincent knew much of the eulogy was deserved but nonetheless he found it hypocritical, a banal effusion of cliché and cant which must nauseate any person of discrimination. Disdain held him rigid, keeping his face stony through song, sermon and prayer. Other mourners would almost certainly take due note of his lack of emotion, but he did not care. He had arrived at the last minute to avoid awkward meetings, spoken two words to Elizabeth, one to Piers Percival, none to anybody else. Hester Bradley was not there – an indication, Vincent assumed, of the prudence and discretion which Sir John had probably numbered among her many virtues. Richard and Crystal had formed part of the group which followed him to the front of the congregation: they now stood directly across the aisle. The cousins' eyes had met, the shadow of a familiar smile had crossed Richard's face – but only a shadow, picked up by the ready lines of frequent usage, fading swiftly. After all, a smile such as Richard's was hardly the correct wear for a funeral.

As for Crystal, Vincent had neither sought her gaze nor evaded it: he had scanned her automatically, sidelong, with a tiny pang and an idle curiosity. She had not cut her hair. It was meshed into a complex system of braids and piled on the back of her head, with a kind of nodule, presumably intended for a hat, affixed in front of it, sprouting two perpendicular feathers and a wisp of gauze. The effect was reminiscent of a Japanese flower arrangement. The gauze veiled her brow to the nose; below, the angles of her bone structure seemed to have become a little more acute, the pout maybe more determined. Her mystery had been refined into sophistication, polished into a perfect veneer. It struck Vincent on the way out, watching her avert her face gracefully from the cameras, that she was not at all the sort of woman he would have expected to hold Richard's affection. Of course, she had only given up work recently: most likely glamour and poise had become a habit which she had yet to discard. 'She must look after herself like a film star,' Vincent reflected. It seemed slightly inappropriate in Richard's wife.

After the ritual at the graveside they retired to Weatherfray. In the rear, the local constable enjoyed his finest hour defending the grounds against the pursuing journalists. The MPs and their myrmidons took their leave, pleading service to their country and the long road to Westminster. Selected friends and relatives were admitted to the gloomiest of the drawing rooms, where they were served with the very dry sherry and very thin sandwiches that Elizabeth considered proper to the occasion. 'Don't encourage them to stay,' Piers had said. 'It isn't a bloody party. John was a man in his prime – 'he had been seventy-one' – not a mass of aches and pains and grouches like me. It wouldn't matter a damn if I died: bits of me have been rotting away for years.' It was the only time Elizabeth had ever heard him allude directly to his war wound. 'But John – God knows, he had problems, but he was tough, he was fit, he had plenty to look forward to. Lizzy, don't ever let them tell you Providence is benevolent. She's a bitch with the head of a Gorgon who's got it in for us all.'

He hadn't called her Lizzy since she was a debutante, a gauche adolescent too shy for social small talk, and somehow it made her want to cry, as if she was young and vulnerable again. She said: 'The years go so quickly now, taking from us all those we hold most dear. Still, at least I have Richard. I have a stake in the future. Richard and Richard's children. That's very important.'

'Ah, like gold fall the leaves in the wind! And numberless as the wings of trees are the years,' Piers quoted, but Elizabeth was not listening.

'You should have someone,' she persisted. 'Someone for whom you too can – look forward. Richard's your godson. Maybe if you took more interest in him . . .'

'For John's sake,' asked Piers wryly, 'or for yours?'

'Neither,' she said. 'For your own.'

Over the manzanilla, Richard and Vincent came face to face at last. It was an encounter which should have been difficult but wasn't. There was a short interlude of stilted courtesy, routine enquiries as to health and prosperity, and then gradually, insensibly, they relaxed, remembered, began swapping confidences with the ease of long ago. 'I heard you came back here just recently,' Richard said. 'My mother told me you wanted to patch things up.' This was not quite how she had put it, but Richard felt entitled to use a little poetic licence.

'Then you also know he sent me to hell,' Vincent responded.

Richard made a characteristic grimace. 'He always was a pig-headed old bugger,' he said. 'Like his son. All the same, I'll bet it made a difference to him, even if he wouldn't admit it. He changed his will again, just before he died. Yes, I know what people are saying, but he wouldn't have – I'm sure he didn't . . .'

'I'm sure too,' said Vincent.

There was a moment of mutual agreement, mutual reassurance, all the more effective for being unspoken. 'Anyway,' Richard resumed, 'as I said, he changed his will.'

'Your mother told you?' Vincent interpolated.

'My spies are everywhere. The thing is, I rather inferred he'd cut you out of the original one – except for this place, of course.'

'I don't want anything,' said Vincent. 'I haven't done so badly on my own. I don't really want this place, either. What am I supposed to do with a Gothic monstrosity in the wilds of Northumberland when I don't even live in this country any more?'

'You could always move it,' Richard said. 'Dismantle it, pack it up in boxes, send it off to California and rebuild it there. I thought that was the kind of thing Americans went in for. One ancestral mansion, specially imported. Guaranteed to impress your friends. Should go down a bomb.'

'Frankly,' said Vincent, 'I'd rather have modern comfort than Victorian grandeur any day, no matter how ancestral it is.'

'Sacrilege,' Richard murmured, grinning, and their exchange was curtailed only by a request from the lawyer to come and listen to the reading of the will.

They went upstairs together. Elizabeth, Piers and Crystal were already in the study, plus a brace of solicitors, a clutch of co-directors from Silver Shield Insurance, and an isolated representative of the local Conservative party. It would be the study, Vincent thought, instinctively wary: if anything was going to happen it always happened in the study, scene of so many bitter

duels between father and son. Even by day and with electric light
the room was dismal, not impressively sombre as he used to imagine but cheerless and grey, smelling of old books whose pages had
never been cut, of leather upholstery, of furniture polish from a previous spring clean and dust beyond the reach of any hoover. The
will was full of legal phraseology which matched the setting. To
begin with it seemed fairly predictable, strong on charitable
bequests, with trusts for the infant Garoghans and a generous
allowance to Elizabeth. Piers was executor, along with one of the
lawyers. There was no reference to Hester Bradley; probably Sir
John had realised that inclusion among his legatees would embarrass and effectively inculpate her, at least in the public eye. He had,
however, made a large donation to the Conservative party: hence
the presence of a token recipient. 'A good cause,' Vincent remarked
to his cousin, in a voice even drier than the manzanilla.

'I should have thought you would have supported the
Conservatives,' Richard said. 'Private enterprise and all that.'

'All politicians are the same,' Vincent was caustic. 'They just
wear different colour ties.'

The residue of the estate, comprising the shares in Silver Shield
and the bulk of Sir John's fortune, had evidently been converted
into a species of benevolent fund to be administered at the discretion of the executors and their nominees for purposes too laudable
to specify. Vincent was unsurprised; Richard began to frown. Lastly,
almost as an afterthought, they came to the clause concerning
Weatherfray. The house, with an inflation-linked allowance for its
upkeep, was bequeathed 'to my nephew Richard Garoghan, who
spent his childhood there, to be his absolutely and uncondition-
ally'. There was no further comment or explanation. Richard went
white; Vincent, thanks to his tan, a sort of parchment yellow.
Nobody said anything. Vincent might not have wanted
Weatherfray but as Sir John's son he felt he had a right to it, a right
to acknowledgement, recognition, to a tardy gesture of paternal
affection. He was not sure if the sickening sensation in his stomach
was shame or anger. The lawyer's voice droned on; the will rambled
to a close without even mentioning his name. 'There is a letter
with it,' the lawyer added, 'addressed to Vincent Scarpia Savage.'

'Thank you.'

Vincent took the letter over to the window – not because he

required the extra light but because it enabled him to turn his back on the other occupants of the room. He opened it and read without a change of expression. For once there were few platitudes, no lecture. 'You yourself admitted to me that you had paid a detective agency to pry into my personal affairs,' Sir John had written. 'While staying at the Green Man in the company of a journalist named Hibbert you clearly saw fit to pass on the information thus obtained. Whether you received any payment for this – whether you erred out of malice or greed or both – I neither know nor care: the motives that could lead you to such an act are beyond my comprehension. Aside from what I myself have had to endure, the suffering you have caused an innocent and honourable woman is something I can never forgive. I have too often overlooked your total lack of heart or principle but your conduct this time has been so despicable, so dastardly, that I find it almost impossible to believe you are in truth my flesh and blood. I cannot prevent you bringing the name of Savage into disrepute and no doubt you will do your best to injure and degrade the rest of the family in the future, but I can at least make it plain, both to them and to the world at large, that I repudiate you utterly. My business you cannot touch; my home will never be yours. You are no longer worthy to be called my son.'

When he had finished reading Vincent refolded the letter with hands that did not shake and placed it in his inside pocket. He turned to the lawyer and said: 'Thank you' again in a quiet voice with no inflexion. Then he walked out of the room, down the stairs, out of the house that would never be his and into the garden. He leaned against a low stone wall for a while, his hair whipped into his eyes, staring at the empty sky and the invisible wind. Richard watched him from the hall but did not have the courage to come near him.

4

Vincent thought it would have been easier to bear, if he had not loved Richard. He would have been less humiliated in his own eyes if there had been no emotional involvement; if they had not experienced that instant rapport, when they met at the funeral; if Richard had not come to him afterwards, open-handed, open-hearted, horrified by his uncle's attitude, offering to give him the house, should he want it. 'I don't want it,' Vincent said. 'I told you so, remember?' He showed the letter to no one. He knew that the sense of burning injustice which possessed him was both commonplace and futile: life was naturally unfair, he had said so often enough, you grabbed the prizes and took the knocks, there was no court of appeal, no balancing of the scales, no universal laws of redemption and retribution. Human beings fell into two categories: the deceivers and the deceived. He was a deceiver; his father had always been one of those most easily deceived. It was folly to succumb to shock or distress. When his anger would not go away he turned it inwards, as he had done before, into his subconscious mind, into the darkest corner of his heart. There it could be nurtured unseen, fed on memories and tidbits, little gestures, morsels of behaviour, fragments of thought. His father was gone where no anger could reach him but there was still Richard, the nephew Sir John had always preferred. The old myth returned to haunt Vincent like a ghost in whom he only half believed. When he was a child deserted by his mother, Richard had stolen his father's love; when he was in prison, at the nadir of his fortunes, Richard had taken his girlfriend; when he was an exile, Richard had taken his home, his rightful inheritance. And all through that inimitable charm, without effort, independent of his own volition. Richard smiled at life and life smiled back; a wink at fate, and fate winked in return. If he had schemed to seize his cousin's patrimony, if he had flattered and crawled like a latterday Uriah Heep, then Vincent might have felt free to despise and disregard him. But Richard did not scheme. It appeared to Vincent, seeing him through the rose-tinted spectacles of jealousy, which exaggerate every grace and every quality in the envied object, that Richard had always been the epitome of gilded youth, favoured by destiny, born in poverty to grow up in comfort and inherit wealth. The woodcutter's son whose fairy godmother had magicked him into the shoes of an unpopular prince. He had not even been required to slay dragons: the princess had simply rushed into his arms without any particular inducement. In the weeks following the funeral, Vincent saw himself increasingly as the satyr to Richard's Hyperion, and the image ate into his spirit. Love, he concluded, was the most essential ingredient of hatred.

He made no specific plan for revenge. It was rather as if revenge arose naturally from an evolving situation, the inevitable product of a concatenation of circumstances. There were times when he felt as if he were in the middle of one of the heavier Greek tragedies, treading fatalistically towards his doom: he had nothing to do but speak his lines and assume the masks allotted to him and the plot would unravel virtually without his assistance. Richard seemed to welcome the renewal of their friendship, unable to perceive the darkness behind his cousin's façade. Vincent began to visit England more regularly – had he not resolved to seek pastures new? – making contacts in the City, even communicating with old acquaintances of his father who might not know his history. He bought a few shares here and there, sold there and here, sniffed at a development project in Kent which could be of interest in due course. And when time was available, he had lunch with Richard and listened to his future aspirations and objectives.

'My mother's a bit shocked I'm selling the place,' Richard confessed one day. 'Heigh-ho for family tradition. She likes to think I'm a true Savage with no contaminating genes from outsiders. When I do something like this she blames it all on my hapless father. Poor sod. Or on herself for having married him. Bit like you and my uncle, I should think. I'm sure he blamed all your shortcomings on your Italian side. They're a funny pair, the older Savages. Let's hope we don't take after them too much.'

'They *were* a funny pair,' Vincent said. 'You're forgetting: he's dead.'

'Sorry.' Richard tugged at the lock of hair which, having got into the habit in childhood, still flopped over one eye. 'I can't get used to it.'

'Nor can I,' Vincent admitted. 'He was a good father to you. wasn't he? Much more than to me.'

Conversational eggshells, Richard thought. 'No,' he said. 'But he was a bloody good uncle.'

'What about your real father?' Vincent enquired idly, the awkward moment past. 'The hapless Mike Garoghan. Do you still write to him?'

'Once in a while. I haven't seen him in years. I never loved him; I never had a chance. But after all, he's my family. Family is important. Not all that stuff about tradition and hanging on to a useless barrack of a house just because your ancestors lived there: I don't mean that. But the *people* – the living people – they're what matters. There's a sort of bond, even if you go to opposite ends of the world, if you lead different lives, if your children speak different languages. The bond endures.'

'Blood,' said Vincent. 'Is that what you mean?'

'Not exactly.' Richard fumbled for the right words. 'Empathy. A kind of intuitive understanding. The kind you can't have with people who are merely friends.'

'*Stronzate*,' said Vincent. 'Do you and I understand one another intuitively?'

Richard picked up the gauntlet without hesitation. 'What do you think?'

He must know, Vincent thought. He must know what I'm feeling. Richard's gaze met his, unwavering, alert, both challenging and affectionate. 'I hope not,' Vincent said lightly, and, reverting to the original issue: 'About Weatherfray: I know *you* don't want it, but my aunt still lives there, doesn't she? Perhaps that's why she clings on to family tradition. She can't be all that eager to move.'

'As a matter of fact,' said Richard, 'she'll be much happier with a little place of her own in the village. She's got no turn for domestic management and Weatherfray takes a hell of a lot of work. Even when she can get the staff – which these days she usually can't – she has to instruct them, oversee them, run after them. My mother's no good at that; she never was. All right: I'm inventing selfish reasons for doing something that suits me, but it's justified. You'll see. She's got her eye on a pair of cottages. A few minor alterations, new kitchen, new bathroom, and she'll be far more comfortable than she ever was in that draught-ridden mausoleum.'

'I rather imagined she liked the draughts,' Vincent commented.

'If necessary,' Richard said with a grin, 'I expect the cottages can be rendered sufficiently draughty. Anyway, there's a big untidy garden at the back: she'll enjoy playing with that. She's always got on better with plants than with people.'

'Why didn't you suggest she moved to London? Like you and Crystal?'

'That would be a little too close for comfort,' Richard said candidly. 'She and Crys don't get on too well. You know my mother: she tries very hard *not* to think I'm perfect but she can't help it. The blessed delusions of parenthood. No woman would ever be good enough for me. I believe she decided Crys was a social climber who married me because she couldn't get you. She didn't say it in so many words but it sort of filtered through whenever Crys's name entered the conversation. Even after two kids and more than ten years of marriage her attitude hasn't softened much. She makes an effort and Crys makes an effort and the atmosphere in between creaks with the strain of it. I couldn't handle that full-time. Besides, my mother's a country person. Her home's always been in Ridpath; most of her friends live round there. She'd hate the city life.'

'Maybe.' For the sake of argument, Vincent looked unconvinced. 'But with Weatherfray going to strangers . . .'

'It's her decision,' Richard contended. 'If you imagine I pressured her you're wide of the mark. For one thing, I wouldn't do it; for another, it wouldn't work. My mother's tough enough to withstand any amount of pressure. She says, if you please, that if I'm going to sell she ought to stay around and keep an eye on things. I suspect her main worry is What People Will Think. I heard her on the phone the other day telling someone the allowance my uncle left really wasn't adequate and Weatherfray would have been too costly for me to maintain. She's a great one for family solidarity, my mother. It's all baloney, of course. I need the capital. But she wouldn't say that: it isn't the kind of thing her county chums would appreciate.'

'Will it be enough?' asked Vincent.

'Capital? No. For this type of research you need the latest equipment. It'll cost a fortune. If I'm to make a go of it, I can't afford to cut corners; My old firm had more computers than NASA. In order to be competitive – sorry, I'm talking shop. How boring. It doesn't take much encouragement, I'm afraid.'

'If everyone has the latest thing in desktop simulators,' Vincent said, 'what gives you an edge?'

'Brains.' Richard's face brightened with a mixture of real confidence and a faint, self-deprecating self-mockery. 'Ideas. I'm working on a totally new concept in aerodynamic design. Lord – it's the biggest cliché around, isn't it? I'm working on something *totally new*. All the same . . .'

'Go on,' Vincent prompted.

'Well, you asked for it. Like R.J. Mitchell, I'm going back to nature for my inspiration'

'R.J. Mitchell?'

'Designed the Spitfire. He looked at the clumsy aircraft of the time and decided to get back to the birds. Me, I'm interested in fish. Think of a skate, or a manta ray: the grace, the streamlining, the way they slice through the ocean. At the kind of speeds we can achieve today air becomes as thick as water. It churns along the wings, pummels and tugs at every square inch of the fuselage. Naturally, the superstructure has to be incredibly strong. If air becomes like water, water becomes like . . . well, put it this way: once you exceed Mach one a single raindrop can have the impact of a bullet. But what concerns me most is the effect of all this pressure on acceleration and fuel consumption. My idea is to alter the whole basic shape of the wings. Except for military aircraft, the only attempt in recent years to try anything different has been Concorde, and nobody seems to have learned from that. Aerodesign is stuck in a rut, trapped between old-fashioned theories and short-sighted companies. I mean to try to change all that.'

'Will this make money?' Vincent enquired blandly.

'Reduce fuel consumption and you reduce the cost of flying. The first airline to do that will steal the market. It's self-evident – but you'd be surprised how many banks can't or won't see it. I've tried to get financing before but they always said it was too risky and demanded collateral. Now, once I've sold Weatherfray, got myself some capital, sorted out the new premises – it's only just out of London: you must come over one day – then I'll be halfway there and hopefully someone will cough up the other half.'

Vincent recognised his cue but he did not take it immediately. He ordered coffee, rejected an offer of dessert.

'It's bloody difficult,' Richard said. 'Bloody banks.'

Vincent was still holding back, hesitating or deliberating. 'Why didn't you ask my father?'

'I don't know.' Richard sighed. 'Crys used to push that one. Because he was your father, I suppose. Because he was my uncle. I didn't want favours. Like you, I wanted to go it alone. Besides, to be honest, I wasn't absolutely sure he'd go for it. He didn't object to my plebeian passion for engines – not like my mother – but not objecting is a long way from investing.'

'What about your godfather? He's pretty well-heeled.'

'We don't have much of a relationship, but even if we did, same thing applies. No favours.'

'If I choose to invest in you,' Vincent said, 'I wouldn't be doing it as a favour.'

'I won't take your help either,' Richard snapped, with more vigour than courtesy.

'Don't be stupid. You said this idea of yours could make money. Making money is my favourite pastime. Cousinly sentiment doesn't enter into it.'

'The risk is too big,' Richard insisted.

'Tell that to the banks.' Vincent was amused. 'I like risks. The bigger the risk, the bigger the kick – also, Deo volente, the bigger the profit. Life's a gamble. Who dares wins. There is a tide in the affairs of men – or in this case, there is a tide in the air fares of men—'

'Stop,' said Richard. 'I don't trust you when you're flippant. Someone or other said lightness of mind betokens darkness of heart.' But he wanted to trust his cousin, Vincent sensed it, just as he trusted everybody else in his friendly, well-disposed universe. 'I'll think about it.'

No,' said Vincent. '*I'll* think about it.'

In the months that followed neither of them thought about it at all. The decision was taken without further reflection or discussion: all that remained was to work out the details. Richard finalised the purchase of his new premises and lined it with glittering stacks of equipment. Screens blinked, consoles chattered, and all the gadgetry of modern technology chirped, shrilled or bleeped according to temperament. Youthful secretaries and almost equally youthful engineers hurried to and fro, filled with the thrilling conviction that what they were doing was innovative and worthwhile and certain to succeed. It was the late eighties, everything was booming that possibly could, the rich were getting richer and so was everyone else (except, of course, for the poor, who, inscrutably, were getting poorer); stockbrokers, manufacturers, merchants, manipulators, they were all on a high. Analysts analysed, inventors invented, economists forgot to economise. The whole world was upwardly mobile and was never going to come down. Vincent stared dutifully at diagrams of aircraft in 3D which pirouetted before his eyes, at long, incomprehensible equations and little green figures jumping in and out of endlessly shifting columns. He listened to several disquisitions in technical jargon which meant nothing to him, making comments which he hoped were relevant. Afterwards, he and Richard generally repaired to a neighbouring pub for a drink which Vincent, for one, badly needed. There, Richard would talk for another half-hour on his plans for the future of aviation before cutting himself short to apologise and change the subject, at least for five minutes. In due course drinks began to overlap dinner, initially in the pub restaurant, later, in town, at Le Caprice, Langan's Brasserie, Orso's. Vincent had borrowed a Chelsea flat from a friend in the film industry and on one occasion they awoke on parallel sofas, uncomfortable, unshaven and hung-over, with only the haziest recollection of a long-winded philosophical argument the previous night. 'Next time,' Richard said, 'you'd better come to our place. For dinner.'

'So I should think,' said Vincent. 'I was beginning to wonder if I was persona non grata there. All right on neutral territory but don't bring him home.'

When he saw Crystal again, he understood. She was cool and unwelcoming, a scrupulous hostess who cooked and served flawless *nouvelle cuisine* on plates considerably warmer than the social ambience. Exquisitely thin slices of some meat which had been boned, rolled and marinated out of existence adorned one side of the Crown Derby; the rest of the space was taken up by the pattern on the china. Seasonal vegetables, conscientiously green, posed in different segments of a regrettably naff porcelain dish at the centre of the table. The conversation was as sparse as the food. Vincent decided Elizabeth Savage might have been right, or partly right: Crystal was a *petite-bourgeoise* on the make, trying too hard to keep up with the Sinclair-Joneses. He did not realise that her culinary efforts, as much as her chilly demeanour, were entirely for his benefit. Richard, conscious of a stomach seven-eighths empty and knowing his wife would be upset if he fetched crackers and low-grade cheddar to supplement the meal, endeavoured to line the void (he could not fill it) with mint crisps and opened a third bottle of wine. Nobody got drunk. Crystal had had far more alcohol than was her custom but it did not defrost her manner or bring a sparkle to her eyes. By the end of the evening Vincent had arrived at the judicious conclusion that she was more beautiful than ever but it had very little effect on him: she was overdressed for the occasion in the ensemble of a Ginochetti peasant and her hair, falling from a high knot in a single thick tress of sable, was unnecessarily sophisticated. He had no desire to kiss her except for research purposes but he would have enjoyed pulling down her hair, smudging her make-up, disarranging those affected clothes. He tried to remember her, all those years ago, looking like other girls, panting, hungry, ruffled, wrecked; but he could only recall a sort of misty pre-coital languor, succeeded normally by a misty post-coital languor, with the temporary blip of orgasm in between. Richmond LeSueur, for instance, had been far more energetic, even in the mornings.

He left before midnight, taking Crystal's cold hand in his and kissing her unresponsive cheek. Richard saw him to the door. 'Sorry,' he said, when Crystal was out of earshot. 'I suppose she must have been nervous. The trouble is, she thinks she jilted you.

I'm too tactful to tell her that you lost interest too. Anyway, it's all so long ago . . .'

'Too long ago to matter.' Vincent's expression was unreadable. 'It was a lovely meal. A bit meagre, but lovely. You have a lovely wife. I expect you make a good husband. I'd have made a rotten husband.'

'Probably,' Richard averred. 'But then, who wants a good husband, these days? They went out with the horse-drawn carriage.'

Vincent was not quite certain how far he was joking.

Over subsequent dinners Crystal allowed herself to thaw very slightly and the cuisine gradually lapsed from its *nouvelle* standards. Vincent found himself collating a string of minor incidents – hardly more than glimpses or impressions – shuffling and reshuffling them in his mind, watching them fall into place. The first time Crystal smiled at him, blue forget-me-not eyes staring straight into his with a message half bold, half shy, all hesitation. Crystal looking at Richard, unsmiling, her pout accentuated, not petulant but perplexed, as though Richard were a locked door on which she had been battering for a long, long while. Elizabeth Savage's opinion, as quoted by her son: 'She married me because she couldn't get you.' Crystal averting her face at the funeral, Crystal averting her shoulder at the dinner table, the impudent flash of a diamond engagement ring worn, he was sure, to remind him that it might have been his. It should have been his. Their fingers touched over the bread rolls and she shivered; he could feel the shiver travelling slowly down into his loins. Watching her, he knew she had taken Richard, not in the outdated cause of social advancement, but as a sort of sly feminine revenge. Vincent had failed her – the unforgivable heresy – and she had married Richard to spite him, sensing, with unerring instinct, that this was the surest way to stab at his heart. And now at last Vincent was back, in her home, in her life, and her pulse quickened against her wishes; even Crystal, with her sphinx-like face and her feline flair for self-preservation. So we all make fools of ourselves, Vincent thought. Even Crystal.

One afternoon he came to the house without Richard. Crystal was alone: her daughter, she explained, was visiting a schoolfriend, Jonas on an excursion with his nanny. Vincent had not given the children a thought; she had, for the most part, kept them out of the way when he was there, and he would have been surprised only by her failure to do so. She offered him tea; he declined. They sat in the drawing room, Crystal on the settee, Vincent on a chair, nearly two yards apart. Perhaps due to apprehension, Crystal appeared less perfectly posed than usual, rearranging her hands every few minutes as though sitting for an artist who was particularly difficult to please. Vincent was annoyed that he had not managed to catch her with her hair loose.

'What can I do for you?' she asked with obligatory courtesy.

'I was hoping to see Richard,' Vincent lied. 'He said he was lunching with a client. I assumed he'd drop in here afterwards.'

'No,' said Crystal, baldly. There was a moment when the combination of nervousness and candour made her seem very young, a trembling teenager who wanted to take the plunge and couldn't find the right gesture or the right words.

Vincent said: 'I'd better go. I'm in your way. I'm sure you have things to do.'

He did not move.

'No,' said Crystal.

The silence stretched out, tingling visibly. 'Shall we talk about the weather?' Vincent suggested.

'I don't know what to talk about.' Crystal's voice was soft but it sounded like a cry.

'Why did you marry Richard?'

The question took her by surprise, as he had intended. Behind a mask no longer incalculable he saw her trying for honesty, defeated by a lack of self-knowledge. It struck him suddenly that her celebrated poker face was merely a shortage of animation. 'You have no right to ask me that,' she said at length.

'None at all. So what? I'm asking anyway.' He got to his feet and stood over her, half threatening, half casual. She did not look up. 'Why did you?'

'I was in love with him.'

'Liar.' Vincent's tone was curt enough to be taken for anger. 'Was it worth it, for all this?' He indicated the photographs on the desk, the photographs he had guessed would be there. Many of them were in silver frames. The wedding, the grandparents, the children in infancy and childhood, decorous images of a conventional existence.

'I've been very lucky,' Crystal said colourlessly. 'I've had everything I wanted.'

'You know, you're like one of those wives in the ads,' Vincent observed. 'Nice house, handsome husband, one daughter, one son. The perfect family unit, as commissioned by Saatchi and Saatchi. You've even kept your looks. Nothing to worry about but which soap powder to use and whether the new Volvo is environmentally friendly. Crystal Winter, ex-model, housewife and mother. Are you happy, Crystal? Are you – what's the classic phrase? – emotionally fulfilled?'

'Fuck off,' Crystal said unexpectedly.

'Look at me.' He tried to pull her up but she resisted, shaking her head, keeping her gaze on her knees. 'Come on: admit it. You were in love with me but you married Richard. Why?'

She was mesmerised by his arrogance and his certainty, by the proximity of his body, by the aura of Hollywood glamour which hung about him like an aftershave. The passion and turmoil of nineteen returned to her with a nostalgia so vivid she thought it was real. She let him drag her on to her feet, looked up into his face. For good measure, he removed the elastic which confined her ponytail, tugging her long hair out of bondage and letting it slither down her back in a slippery fall of silk. In that moment he wanted her – because she was Richard's wife, because she was helpless and defenceless, because she had surrendered not just her physical but her mental reactions into his control.

'I *did* love Richard,' she insisted, 'in a way. He made me feel safe. Comfortable. I never felt safe and comfortable with you.'

'So you settled for this.' A jerk of his head designated the photos, the room, the house, a whole lifestyle. 'Safety and comfort. Did you really think I would be jealous?'

'I don't know.'

'Was that the only way you could get back at me, by marrying Richard?'

'I *don't know.*'

'We all want to hurt the people we love. The two things go together. Love and hurt. Hurt and love.'

'Do you want to hurt me,' she asked, 'now?'

It was an invitation and he took it, kissing her long and hard, exploring the familiar contours of her body, small round breasts, small tight buttocks, thighs parting under a rumpled skirt so he could feel the wetness of her briefs in between. He wanted to take her in situ, then and there, on the settee, on the carpet, under the watching eyes of the silver-framed photos, mingling pleasure and vengeance in a single act of consummate urgency. Pleasure and vengeance, hurt and love: he did not know what he felt nor did he care. He wanted to possess her, to despoil her, to come inside her and all over the shiny new upholstery and the expensive Wilton. He began to pull down her briefs, touching the moist warm entrance of her, the quivering clitoris, sensing he could bring her to an instantaneous climax whenever he was ready. But not yet. Not yet . . .

'The bedroom,' she gasped. 'Upstairs.'

'Here,' he whispered. *Here*.

They did not register the rattle of the key in the front door. But they heard the door open, footsteps in the hall, Jonas's high childish voice: 'Mummy, Mummy, I fell over in the park. There was a big boy and he pushed me. I wanted to push him back but Tilda wouldn't let me . . .'

In the few seconds while the nanny retrieved him to remove his jacket Crystal straightened her clothes with a speed that would have broken Olympic records and Vincent remembered why he had always eschewed married women with young children. 'Say hello to Uncle Vincent, Jo,' she instructed with barely a quaver when her son burst in.

Jo stood with his mouth open offering no comment. Uncle Vincent surveyed him laconically, ignored the nanny, and announced he was just leaving. His gaze met Crystal's with a message she thought she could interpret. 'You don't look well,' said the nanny when he had gone. 'You're awfully pale.'

'It's nothing,' Crystal said. 'Nothing at all.'

Vincent told Richard the truth in his borrowed flat, in the room with the parallel sofas where they had fallen asleep side by side.

'I'm pulling out.'

He watched the blood drain from Richard's face, taking with it not merely colour but expression, humour, character, leaving him washed out with shock. In that sudden blanching Richard looked older, the laughter lines transformed into lines of care, the smile dead on his lips. 'You can't,' he said. 'You don't mean it.' He said other things too, all the things Vincent had anticipated. The pleas, the recriminations, the banalities. 'I'm ruined. I'll never get other backing now: you must know that. I'll have to go bankrupt. You can't do this to me. You're my cousin. We've been closer than brothers.'

'I told you,' Vincent said, 'that doesn't weigh with me. You didn't want favours: remember?'

'Don't,' said Richard. 'Do what you like but don't – don't dally with words. Don't treat this as if it were all a clever little game and I lost because I didn't read the small print.' He added, abruptly: 'You make me sick.'

'It is a game,' Vincent said sombrely. 'Life's a game. You'll go bankrupt. Throw a six and pay one hundred grand. I once picked a card marked "Go to jail".'

'For God's sake,' Richard shouted, 'that's hardly my fault! Is *that* what this is all about? Some ludicrous pseudo-Gothic concept of revenge? You've been watching too many soaps. What have you done – made a tally of all your grievances and decided to send me the bill? I knew you were vindictive but I didn't think you could be so petty. I would have *given* you Weatherfray—'

'I never wanted anything you could have given me.'

'You can't be serious about this. We're not in some damned TV saga. Where's your sense of proportion? Where's your sense of *humour*?'

'I'm laughing,' said Vincent, who wasn't. 'Your turn to slip on the banana skin.'

Richard paced the room in frustration, colliding with a low table and staring at it in amazement as if it had cast itself in his path in a deliberate attempt to impede him. Vincent, noting his every move, knew revenge was not sweet after all: it was bitter, a draught of wormwood, absinthe to an alcoholic. A necessary poison.

'What about all the others?' Richard said. 'My employees – *your* employees – whom you're booting out so casually? You've talked to them: you've seen their enthusiasm, their high hopes, their confidence. Don't you care?'

'They'll find other jobs,' said Vincent. 'Don't be hypocritical. You don't care any more than I do.'

'You really believe that, don't you?' said Richard. 'You poor bastard.'

'Have a drink,' Vincent offered, bored. 'You must have run

through most of the protest lines by now. All we've got left is Crystal and the kids.'

'So that's it.' At the mention of his wife, Richard's pallor faded; his face set in a kind of dreary resignation. 'Crystal. I might have guessed. The girl you dumped whom I married. Disgraceful, wasn't it? I should have left her out on a limb in case you emerged from prison needing a casual fuck. Is that what this is about? Crystal?'

'Hardly.' This time, Vincent laughed – a brusque laugh with no amusement in it. 'You're welcome to her. The packaging is Van Cleef and Arpels but the contents are from a dime store. Still, no doubt you like her cooking.'

'I ought to hit you.'

'You can try.'

'You aren't worth it. You aren't worth the bruise on my knuckles. Let's get through the last of the clichés, shall we? It doesn't matter what I say or do, after all. You've closed your ears and your mind, shut yourself away in an empty little world of your own. You're all alone there and by the time you've realised it'll be too late. Do you know, I really wanted to trust you. I suppose I was a fool – I'll probably be a fool again – but I *made* myself believe in you. We could have built something together, something special. Your company, my company. A piece of the future. I dreamed about that. Because we were kids together – schoolmates, students, allies – I was sentimental, I wanted that to continue. That's what you'd call it, isn't it? Sentimentality. Softness of the heart. Softness of the brain. Imbecility.'

'I'd call it bollocks,' said Vincent. 'I opened my wallet and you stuck your hand in. Sentiment doesn't enter into it.'

'My God, I'm sorry for you,' Richard said. It wasn't true but anger had come and gone and the note of lofty pity was all he had left. He felt disillusioned and hollow inside. An elusive nausea had come to fill the gap.

'No you're not,' said Vincent churlishly. 'You've got enough to do being sorry for yourself.'

All the answers that Richard could think of were in four letters, and beside the point.

He went.

Crystal received the bad news in total silence. The next day she went to see a solicitor. She was not impetuous, she would not rush upon disaster. Instead, she picked her way, one careful step at a time. The savings from her highly paid career were in various private accounts; Richard had no access to them. The new house was in her name, a precaution he himself had suggested at the start of his business venture. There was a safety net below the precipice, should she miss her footing. But Crystal did not think she would fall. It was ten days since the kiss, ten days since she had seen Vincent. Every vacant moment had been filled with the thought of him. There were many vacant moments in Crystal's current routine. Whatever Vincent's original motives in financing Richard, she knew now that he had destroyed her husband out of jealousy, in revenge – an act of chagrin on his part that made her heart beat faster and set her blue eyes aglitter. She even contemplated begging Vincent to bale Richard out, if only for her sake. What need for revenge, now she had come back to him? The solicitor warmed to her lambent gaze and anticipated a staggering divorce settlement. A woman as lovely as Crystal Winter deserved the best of everything.

That evening, she sent Jonas and Penelope Snow to her mother's house under Tilda's jurisdiction and took a taxi to the flat in Chelsea. She had obtained the address from Richard's Filofax, ten days earlier. There was a letter for him on the desk in the empty drawing room, beside the silver photo frames, telling him where she had gone. She was sorry, she was truly sorry, she had never wished to hurt him – you only wish to hurt the people you love – but it had always been Vincent, right from the beginning. It was best for all of them, this way. She was taking the children. Meanwhile, she was his sincerely, Crystal. Afterwards, when the unthinkable had happened, every line of that letter would be branded on her ego, burned into her pride.

Richard read the letter and remembered Vincent's laugh, and the tiny cold pang inside him was not for his own loss.

Crystal went upstairs to the flat with a pounding heart and came down with no heart at all.

'Come in,' said Vincent. 'What can I do for you? Have you come to plead?'

He knew why she had come.

'I've left Richard,' she said. 'I was wrong, playing safe, opting for security. It was stupid and cowardly. I can't go on. I can't pretend any more. It's always been you, Vincent. Since I was nineteen. Only you.'

Vincent laced her gin with tonic and handed her the glass. 'How unfortunate,' he remarked.

'*Unfortunate?*' Crystal was baffled – but he had often baffled her. 'Don't you see? I've come back to you. I know why you ruined Richard. I know it was for me.'

'For you?' The laugh that Vincent considered appropriate was even harsher than his previous effort, mirthless, derisive. 'For you!'

'You do love me,' she asked – Crystal who had never needed to ask for love, who had only to take, and take, and take – 'don't you?'

'What is there to love?' Vincent was deliberately careless. 'Spoiled, selfish, superficial' – he flicked her cheek with the tip of his finger – 'a decorative exterior but unfurnished within. I know a slag from a Los Angeles back slum who's made herself queen of the heap: she owes her looks to the beauticians and her bank balance to double-dealing and she's worth a million of you. I could find a tart on a Soho street corner with more sincerity and a dead rabbit who was better in bed. Love you?' His voice had hardened and he checked himself sharply, reverting to flippancy. 'Don't be ridiculous. I don't love an imitation champagne, or a maggot in an apple. I spit it out and move on. Finish your drink; you seem to need it.'

She was shaking so badly the ice cubes knocked against the side of the glass.

'I don't . . . understand,' she said faintly.

'I know,' said Vincent. 'That was always your problem. Look, I'd love to chat but I'm flying home in the morning and I've got a lot to do. You'll have to go now. Drink up.'

Crystal screamed. She threw the gin at him, then the glass. She had never experienced an all-consuming rage in her life and she did not know what to do with it. She had no words for such anger. She could only scream. Vincent went to the door and held it open. She bit the scream off short, struggling for her long-lost self-control, the Siamese kitten turned into a wildcat, eyes slitted, lips thinned. Her whisper was as intense as a hiss. 'I'll pay you back.' The script, he concluded, was unoriginal, but the delivery superb. 'One day. I'll pay you back!'

A polite nothing, he thought when she had gone. Second-rate

melodrama. He poured himself a bourbon – more than a decade in the States had given him a taste for it – and downed it in one long, slow draught. The affair was over, the vicious circle complete. Time to write *finis* at the end of the story. He felt neither satisfaction nor regret but only a dull fatigue and a vacuum inside. He lay down on the sofa but he could not fall asleep.

PART IV

DANCING IN THE DARK

1

I arrived on Dominique at the fag end of a long, dreary day. The transatlantic flight was delayed by the usual ructions at air-traffic control. The movie was one I had seen before. The small child behind me kicked me persistently in the back despite ineffectual protests from its mother and the man in the seat next to me suffered from BO. Such are the hazards of travelling by air. When I got out at Barbados, where I had to transfer to a local flight for the Grenadines, the heat and humidity enveloped me like a clammy blanket. It was worse than London. 'Hurricane weather,' someone said cheerfully. The bar, in contrast, resembled the interior of a refrigerator, and the iced drink with which they served me lowered my body temperature so rapidly I felt physically ill. I should be inured to the tedium and frustration of such journeys, I know, but I'm not. I just wish that everyone – stewards and stewardesses, airport personnel, the moron who chose the movie – wouldn't go to quite so much *trouble* to make your trip a bore.

By the time we reached Praline Airport it was growing dark. The brief tropical sunset had melted rapidly into a violet sea and the sky was filling up with stars. Phyl had come to meet me in a topless car with Janáček blaring out of the stereo: the car belonged to the Ashleys and the taste in music to Win. We darlinged each other in the accepted manner and I loaded my suitcase into the boot. 'Is this all?' Phyl said, scandalised.

'You know I always travel light,' I said. 'I'm a journalist, not a society girl. Normally I only have hand luggage. This is a lot for me.'

'That suitcase wouldn't even take my face creams,' Phyl observed.

She did not look in need of much face cream. At school, her complexion had been the envy of less fortunate teenagers plagued with acne, grease and open pores; now, it still had that bloom-on-a-peach quality which usually only comes out of a tube. She had the eyes and eyelashes of a Walt Disney gazelle and a quantity of hair which at our last meeting had been Summer Harvest Gold and was now Autumn Chestnut Bronze. At five foot nothing her figure resembled a double ice-cream cornet and she exuded an aura that was not so much sexual as edible. We got in the car and she drove off briskly, looking at me more than the road and talking all the time. The stars were twinkling away in earnest and the soft air, night-cooled, fanned over us. The few other drivers we encountered avoided Phyllida without rancour; possibly they recognised her. This was the kind of Caribbean island I had dreamed of, an idyllic little kingdom, cluttered with princesses. Unstiffening limbs cramped from too long in economy class seats, I began to feel better. Too soon.

'It would be a wonderful thing,' I remarked, 'if they could come up with somewhere to sit other than on your arse.'

Phyl wasn't listening. 'So I rang Deirdre this morning,' she said, evidently picking up the threads of a conversation the early part of which had been addressed to someone else. 'I didn't ask her anything bluntly, Micky, of course – I knew you'd want me to be subtle – but I'm *almost certain* Vincent will be there. Deirdre loves to reel off her guest list in advance – all the big names, you know, what Farzad calls financial muscle and celebrity nerves – and she assured me—'

'You said Vincent always comes,' I interrupted in sudden horror. 'Do you mean to tell me I've travelled halfway round the world at the company's expense to attend this bloody party, and bloody Vincent Savage might not even show up?'

'You came to see *me*,' said Phyl, hurt.

'Alun will kill me.'

'Don't be silly, Micky. Think . . . think *positive*. Deirdre said Vincent was one of her Practically Definites. She says he was going to borrow Irving Blum's house on West Point for at least a week. Barring an upset stomach or a missed plane or an act of

God he'll be at her party. And God is on your side, isn't he? I
mean, you're supposed to be one of the good guys. Anyway, if the
worst comes to the worst you can always make something up.
Your producer won't be there to know the difference.'

'I can't make up a tape,' I pointed out.

'You don't mean you're going to be wearing one of those wire
things?' Phyl demanded.

'No, of course not. I'll have a small tape recorder in my shoulder bag, that's all. I couldn't wear a wire with my best dress
even if I wanted to: it's that black Roland Klein, skin-tight and
cut away at the sides, you know the one. If I had a flea in my
knickers it would show.'

'*You've still got that dress?*' said Phyl, diverted from the main
issue. And, in the voice of Cassandra: 'I knew it!'

'For Heaven's sake, Phyllida, I hardly ever wear a posh dress.
What would be the point of wasting money on a new one?'

'Don't call me Phyllida in that disapproving way: you're just
trying to distract me.' She switched a furious glare from me to an
approaching car without discrimination. The car flinched visibly.
'You bought that dress a decade ago, probably in a reject shop—'

'Five years, actually. And it wasn't a reject, precisely: just
slightly imperfect. It's quite all right. I've only worn it twice.'

'All right! *All right*! And you've worn it *twice*! Words fail me!'
They didn't. 'We are going to Deirdre Langelaan's summer
party – and although Deirdre is a professional toad-eater with no
taste, no sense of humour and an utterly loathsome husband it
will be a Major Social Event – last year she had Madonna,
Warren Beatty, and that bond-dealer whose name I can't remember who's just been sent to jail – where was I?'

'At a Major Social Event.'

'. . . and you are planning to wear your antique slightly dam-
aged Roland Klein because it's *all right*! Micky, if you weren't
one of my best friends I'd drop you. It won't do, darling. It
absolutely won't do. People notice things like that.'

'Let them,' I said. 'I don't care that much about my image.'

'I'm not worried about *your* image, darling,' Phyl wailed. 'I'm
worried about *mine*!'

When we reached the house, she lost no time in enlisting the
support of Win Ashley. Win, in his middle thirties, had an air of

fixed youth, a porcelain complexion on which the glaze was just beginning to crack, and loose waves of slightly gilded hair (Ombre d'Or No. 3). He had the languid manners of a hothouse plant and a sense of irony so finely tuned that it was beyond most people's range of hearing. I had met him once before, despite my telephone denial, an event that he recollected with gently flattering promptitude. His charm was of the low-key variety, mercifully free from sparkle or gush, which made me feel that Phyl and I were on a secret list of his favourite people and would always be accorded that unobtrusive preference. He did not scintillate or fascinate; he merely offered wonderful cocktails and sympathised over the discomforts of my journey. Inevitably, I found myself liking him very much.

It was equally inevitable that he would concur in Phyl's attitude.

'*That* black Roland Klein,' he said, as Phyl, rummaging in my suitcase, produced the offending garment. 'No, Micky, I'm afraid not. Phyl's quite right: it won't do. You're supposed to look inconspicuous at this party: isn't that the idea? To blend with the crowd? You cannot possibly expect to blend with the crowd when everyone else is wearing this year's registration and your little number is practically a veteran. If it were merely cheap you might get away with it; at least nobody would recognise it. But I saw Dorothia Von Glynd in that dress at the Princess's birthday – it must be all of six years ago. She looked frightful: everyone will remember it. You'll just have to have something new.'

'That's settled then,' said Phyl. 'We'll go into Praline tomorrow. There's this little boutique . . .'

I reflected that a little boutique on an island populated predominantly by millionaires would almost certainly overstrain my most flexible credit card. 'I can't afford it.' I told her. It was no use. Phyl, having decided that I was a latterday Cinderella clinging masochistically to my rags, was determined to force me into crystal slippers and a pumpkin.

'I'll pay,' she insisted. 'Don't, *don't* be proud, darling. It's not as if I were being generous and unselfish, after all. I'm acting from motives of the purest egotism. I won't be seen touting you round a party in that tatty out-of-date dress. My reputation would never survive.'

My actually quite presentable Roland Klein seemed to be deteriorating by the minute.

'Let her enjoy herself,' Win told me, in an aside. 'It would be ungracious of you to refuse her.'

In the end, partly from exhaustion and jet lag, partly from an uncomfortable inner conviction that Win's last comment was justified, I gave in.

Eleven o'clock the following morning found us outside the 'little boutique'. It had a window display so understated as to be virtually non-existent and a glass door that opened on to a waft of air-conditioning and a swathe of carpet. A haughty shop assistant who called Phyl Madame gave way to a glamorous manageress who called her Phyllida darling. The situation was explained; the party little more than thirty hours away. Was this enough time for the agonising operation of selecting a Dress? The manageress assured us that it was. The haughty assistant came and went with a succession of garments and I, stripped of my T-shirt and jeans, dutifully wriggled, struggled, squirmed and wormed my way in and out of them all. As Phyl was picking up the tab it was she who chose the dresses, ordering me into anything that caught her fancy, from a disastrous effusion in peacock-blue sequins to a brainstorm in multilayered chiffon. It was years since I had been shopping for anything more exciting than a sweater and the outing which I had anticipated with a sneaking pang of pleasure was rapidly becoming an ordeal. 'Not black,' Phyl had said firmly. 'Black is for the winter. I hate black at summer parties.'

'You're not wearing the dress,' I said. 'I like black.'

'What you like is irrelevant,' declared Phyl witheringly.

Eventually, we settled for a Karl Lagerfeld, a sinuous silver sheath which made me look, I observed, rather like an eel. As I moved the changing light sent long dull gleams slithering from thigh to ankle like ripples in a twilit river. The manageress eulogised and Phyl, at her most critical, bestowed judicious approval. Win studied me with the dispassionate appraisal of the confirmed homosexual. 'Too effective,' he opined, gently massaging my ego. 'You'll never be able to blend with the crowd looking like that.'

*

The next evening, complete with crystal slippers by some Milanese magician and a shoulder bag large enough to accommodate my tape recorder and elegant enough to satisfy the most exacting fashion standards, I was ready to go. Phyl and Win clearly thought they were taking part in a sort of glorious game, and unfortunately some of their misplaced exuberance appeared to have rubbed off on me. I told myself sternly that I was supposed to be working, but it was no use. There was a butterfly in my stomach which hadn't been there since my teens, the cicadas were tuning up like a frenetic jazz band, and a faint breeze ran like a tremor through the warm air, ruffling the topmost tufts of the palm trees with careless fingers. I felt I was in an expensive modern fairyland, where the lotus was eaten for breakfast and by dinner anything might happen. The party could only be an anticlimax.

'Do we bring a bottle?' I enquired innocently.

'Darling, don't be *common*,' said Phyl.

'You might take a raincoat,' Win suggested flippantly. 'If that hurricane should get here it will really blow the fun away.'

Dominique, I inferred, for all its exclusive status, did not escape the occasional hurricane, but such weather usually confined itself to the off season when the richest residents were safely out of the way. This year, however, Hurricane Anneka, a small but energetic storm from some Aeolian cauldron at the ocean's heart, had arrived on the scene a little prematurely. Win had been following the meteorological reports all day and we were assured it would pass just to the south of the island. Besides, Phyl contended, Deirdre Langelaan was capable of outfacing any number of hurricanes. I found myself wondering if Vincent would be deterred from attending the party – presupposing he planned to attend in the first place – and whether Alun would accept a hurricane as an excuse for my failure. I was unsure about Vincent but I had no doubts about Alun. He wouldn't.

'Do you think it will?' I asked Win. 'Get here, I mean?'

'No,' he said easily. 'Dominique is not exactly large. Any hurricane seeking to make a name for itself will find something bigger to devastate.'

A little cloud, as fluffy and innocuous as a handful of feathers, emerged from behind the island's central mountain and began to drift casually across the sky like an understated note of warning. But the car was waiting – a pale lilac Cadillac, with a chauffeur uniformed to match – and it was time to go. En route, I forgot the hurricane to prime the others on my background. I was to be introduced as Michelle Annesley, an old schoolfriend of Phyl's whom she rarely saw. I worked in television, no specific job to be mentioned but they might hint that I was just about capable of inaccurate typing or making the tea. 'Keep it simple,' I said. 'It's safer.' The two of them were yearning to elaborate but I was severe. Should anything I discovered produce unpleasant repercussions I didn't want them involved. Not that I believed I would make any dramatic discoveries: even if Vincent braved the weather reports and showed up, I could not visualise him dragging me off into the hibiscus bushes to tell me the story of his life.

We reached the Langelaans' beachside house in less than twenty minutes. It was a mansion in the colonial style, with almost as many French windows as Versailles and a sweeping terrace with a band at one end and a bar at the other. The garden was full of tropical plants with large fleshy leaves and bright-coloured flowers from which phallic stamens poked suggestively. The beach lay beyond it, with the sea murmur providing an incidental music which hardly anyone could hear. The guests swirled about the terrace and eddied round the garden, maintaining a conversational din that varied from a quiet buzz to a chattering cacophony according to how near you stood to the vortex of the party. Phyl presented me to my hostess, who wasn't interested, and my host, who was. It is a melancholy fact that whenever you dress to dazzle at a social occasion you always find yourself dazzling the wrong man. I tried to elicit something useful but whenever I turned the small talk to real estate Pete Langelaan simply leered at me and told me how charming it was to meet with such an acute business brain inside such a pretty little head. He was not pretty. His shocking pink suntan contrasted unhappily with fading orange hair and at close range I noticed he had bad breath. Unfortunately, we were at close range. Not far away I could hear Phyl telling someone that I was a researcher for Wogan (he was the only British TV presenter she had heard of) while Win, adopting a more esoteric approach, claimed I was the girl who varnished the food on the cookery programmes to make it look more appetising. My worst fears were being realised. Needless to say, there was no sign of Vincent Scarpia Savage.

He arrived much later, when the sun had set under a cloud like a snarl of yellow wool and the fairy lights were switched on among the tropical plants, illuminating an assortment of floral genitalia. I saw him at once, not because he made a spectacular entrance but because Phyl, at her most unobtrusively helpful, broke off a flirtation she was having to roll her eyes in my direction and gesticulate wildly. Following the sharp end of her pointing finger my gaze fell on a man talking – or rather listening – to Deirdre Langelaan. His face was so immediately recognisable that I was disconcerted: I had leafed through his photographs often enough but I was unaware of how familiar these features had become – the haughty nose, the lowering eyebrows, the habitually unsmiling mouth. I identified him with a sense of shock, as if he were a close aquaintance whom I had not expected to see, an intimate enemy who had been a part of my life for some time. I remembered a John Dickson Carr novel I had read as a child: *The Devil in Velvet*. Vincent Savage might have posed as the Devil in Armani: where most of the men wore variations on a black tie and tuxedo he was expensively casual, unconcernedly elegant, with a style that was all Italian and an aloofness that was distinctively British. He did not look like his father but the arrogance of the Savages was there, unsoftened by any gentler qualities. It was impossible to tell if his contempt was for his hostess, the whole party, or simply for himself for bothering to come. He did not look actively wicked, of course, but then, very few people do. Adolf Hitler resembled a rather twitchy bookie's clerk, Stalin a genial peasant, and even Genghis Khan owed much of his diabolical aura to those oriental moustaches. Vincent's chilly expression might have concealed both strength and courage but it was clear, at least to me, that if he had a code of honour it was inexcusably different from the accepted norm: he was a nonconformist who was prepared to sacrifice anyone to his own private rebellion.

For the rest, as Phyl had said, he was polite in a minimalist way. I watched him brush off his hostess, completely ignore a

ravishing brunette, swallow two glasses of champagne with no
effect on his mood and get into an argument with a passing senator. When I came within earshot I noted with a sinking
sensation in my stomach that Vincent's fluency in debate
reminded me of Patrick. But whereas Patrick had dazzled with
the passion of the moment I felt that Vincent's vicious eloquence
sprang from a deep-seated conviction of cynicism, a paradox in
his very nature – unbelief as a creed, a ruthless negative force. I
did not want him to sound like Patrick. I had anticipated finding
him a villain, but not a cheapskate.

Presently, thanks to a certain amount of manoeuvring on
Phyl's part, we were introduced. Vincent nodded curtly and
looked me over without interest. I said what a lovely evening it
was. End of conversation. He moved off in one direction; I was
drawn (by Pete Langelaan) in the other. 'Micky!' Phyl hissed in
admonition, somewhere near the back of my neck. But there was
nothing I could do: those inscrutable currents which circulate
round all parties were sweeping me irresistibly from my goal. My
tape recorder must be enjoying itself, I concluded: a nice little
trip in a nice new bag and no work at all. It was not a satisfactory
thought.

In due course we moved into the house for dinner. 'Deirdre
has a horror of crumbs,' Win explained. 'She won't allow anybody to eat in the garden since the regrettable incident when she
ordered one of the maids to vacuum the lawn. It took a year to
recover.' I didn't believe a word of it but the change was welcome. The fretful breeze had strengthened, blowing in irregular
gusts which set the fairy lights dancing among the leaves and
chilled bare arms and shoulders into gooseflesh. Long tongues of
cloud were licking at the moon; half the sky was starless. The
very air felt uneasy, as if the storm, passing to the south, was
brushing the island with its heaving flank. Indoors, there was
muted lighting, small tables where guests vied discreetly for the
best places, and a seafood buffet that resembled the chorus line
from *The Little Mermaid*. I sat on one side of the room eating
lobster; Vincent sat on the other side eating crab. Since the
evening was clearly going to be a disaster as far as work was concerned, I abandoned caution and began to make serious inroads
into Pete Langelaan's champagne.

The band had moved inside with the guests and servants had unobtrusively closed windows against the scurrying draughts. The music and the chatter drowned out external sounds. A long time went by before anyone noticed anything wrong, and even then there was no instant panic, no dramatic announcement of danger, rather a ripple of anxiety spreading slowly through the crowd, a hiccup in the conversation, a faltering in the music, and suddenly the voice of the wind could be heard, no longer merely uneasy but a raging neurotic, battering its fists against the windowpanes and shrieking its traumas to the night. Staring out into the garden, I saw the fairy lights had gone: flying wisps of moonlight showed plants clinging to their roots and grass that trembled like racing water. The major domo emerged from the hall reeling off the latest from the meteorologists; I learned later that Deirdre Langelaan had been ignoring his bulletins for hours. The trickle of departing guests became an exodus. Our lilac chauffeur came in search of us, his normally chestnut complexion as pale as coffee. 'Come on,' said Win. 'Since this hurricane has the bad taste to be heading our way after all, I think it's time we went home. I only hope it's still safe to drive.' He laid an imperative hand on my arm.

I had had far too much champagne. I had passed the bubbly stage and the muzzy stage and the change of atmosphere seemed to bring my mind back into focus, engendering that unnatural clarity of vision which is too easily mistaken for returning sobriety. In that condition, recklessness becomes logic, an act of insanity the product of unclouded common sense.

I said 'I'm not coming.'

'Don't be silly!' Phyl sounded agitated. 'You don't want to stay *here*, Micky, surely?'

'I have other plans.'

Across the room Vincent was still sitting at his table. His dinner companions had gone. His feet were on a chair. There was a glass at his elbow that looked like brandy and a bottle in the offing to which he appeared to have solitary title. His hair was ruffled; his expression wasn't. The surge of people on their way out tugged at his sleeve and spoke to him with visible urgency, presumably exhorting him to follow, but he disregarded them. He looked blasé to the point of boredom, brooding to the edge of depression, and very very drunk. 'The Marquis of Vidal with a dash of Heathcliff,' Crystal had said, but in that state, for all his pantheresque beauty, Vincent did not present a genuinely attractive figure. The inky brushstrokes of his brows, the hooded eyes, hollow cheeks, snake-like tendrils of sweat-soaked hair, all belonged more to some dissolute rakehell from the pen of Edgar Allan Poe rather than to a conventional hero of romance. It was only too easy to imagine him dismissing the advice of his conscience to steep himself in dissipation, or sealing his worst enemy in an oubliette on the pretext of offering him a vintage sherry. There was a delinquent quality about him which would have set the most gullible Mills and Boon virgin on her guard. I was visited by the fancy that here was a human being with no behavioural restraints, none of the built-in braking system developed by centuries of civilised conditioning. The storm outside might well trigger a corresponding violence in his spirit, and his current mood might be merely the preliminary lull.

Intuition should have made me cautious. I should have known better. I didn't.

'This is my chance,' I told Phyl. 'You go, you and Win. Don't wait for me. And don't worry. I'm used to taking care of myself. Anyway, it's a small island. I shan't get lost.'

'Micky!' For all her earlier schemes, Phyl was frightened.

'It's a small hurricane,' said Win. 'You might still be blown away.'

But there was no time to waste in persuasion or argument and he knew it. After a few minutes they went, Phyl clasping my hand in farewell like a heroine in a war film. I was left behind to play my part. When the room was almost empty I wandered over to Vincent's table. There was a queasiness in my stomach, excitement or nerves, but I knew from experience that my voice would be steady enough. This was my chance. My moment. My fight.

On reflection, I must have been as pissed as a maenad at a bacchanal.

'May I?' I indicated the brandy bottle.

'Sure.'

I poured some into my glass and sat down on one of the vacant chairs. By now, all the other guests had gone. The huge room, deserted by its glittering populace, already had the tawdry, morning-after air of a room with a hangover. The dismembered remnants of the buffet sprawled on the main table; a debris of plates, crockery, tall champagne glasses and short liqueur glasses littered its lesser satellites. Staff hired for the occasion had presumably fled. Beyond the French windows, two of the remaining servants were defying the elements in a gallant attempt to close the shutters. From the hall came the unmistakable sounds of a society hostess in hysterics.

Vincent paid no attention to any of it. He barely glanced at me and I, determined to match his indifference, varied the direction of my gaze between the amber depths of the brandy and the black depths of the night outside.

Presently, Pete Langelaan came in. He seemed surprised to see Vincent and completely nonplussed by me. He had palpably lost all desire to flirt. 'Michelle! What are you doing here? I thought everyone had left. Christ, what a mess! Deirdre's gone up to bed, but—'

'I'm afraid,' I rose to my feet, 'I seem to have been abandoned. Phyl must have rushed off without thinking when the panic started.' If she should object to my sacrificing her reputation so ruthlessly, that was her hard luck. There are penalties to being involved in journalistic endeavour.

'Shit! What are you going to do? You can't stay here. At least – I suppose we *could* put you up . . .'

The house was palatial and could comfortably have accommodated an army, but he spoke as if he would have difficulty finding me a couch. I paused long enough to allow the full impact of his discourtesy to sink in before turning to Vincent as one forced at gunpoint.

'Perhaps you could give me a lift somewhere?'

Vincent surveyed me as if I was a racehorse whose prospects for the Derby he considered uncertain.

'Where?'

Fortunately, Pete Langelaan had been diverted by the two men still wrestling with the shutters and had moved towards the windows, trying to give largely ineffectual guidance in mime.

'Anywhere,' I said.

'I'm going home,' said Vincent, also getting to his feet. 'Unless

I dump you under a palm tree on the way you'll have to come with me.'

'Do you have a spare bed?' Beneath my champagne-inspired precipitance it occurred to me that I ought to make my position clear. 'This place,' I added, 'evidently doesn't even run to a palliasse on the kitchen floor.'

Vincent's lip curled in an expression half smile, half sneer, as if he could not quite decide his own humour. 'I expect I can find you a palliasse,' he said. 'Pete! I'll look after – Michelle, is it? Get someone to bring my car round. Your man has the keys.'

Pete, distracted, took a few seconds to absorb these instructions before relief showed plainly on his face. 'Great,' he said, several times, and to me: 'You'll be fine with Vincent' – a triumph of wishful thinking over incontrovertible fact. He bustled off to summon the car and I was left reflecting that no female would be fine with Vincent, particularly in his present mood. I asked: 'Are you sure it's all right to drive?'

'No,' he said. 'On the contrary. But frankly, my dear, I don't give a fuck.'

'If your chauffeur doesn't like the idea—'

'I'm driving myself,' Vincent interjected. 'No chauffeur. No chaperone. Just me and the hurricane. Would you like to change your mind?'

'No.'

'Also,' Vincent concluded, 'I'm bloody drunk.'

'So am I,' I said. 'Or I wouldn't be stupid enough to go with you.'

This time, he was startled into a half laugh, reluctant but spontaneous. 'Didn't you hear your host?' he said. 'You'll be fine with me.'

'Like hell.'

We went into the hall, Vincent preceding me. Evidently he was a believer in sexual equality: he made no concessions to the double standards of old-fashioned good manners. Pete was waiting for us. 'Your car's here,' he said and, with belated and grudging concern: 'Sure you'll be OK? It's pretty rough out there.'

Vincent made no reply, shrugging off the query with the contempt I felt it deserved. He took the keys from the Langelaans' chauffeur, who was looking windswept and far more anxious than his employer, and we stepped out into the storm.

The first shock was the noise. Within the house we had been partially insulated; outside, we had to shout to make ourselves heard. The wind howled and shrieked and yammered, as if several packs of wolves were being slowly roasted alive somewhere in the vicinity. The normally insubstantial air had acquired body and muscle: invisible forces tried to pluck me off my feet, while the stationary car shuddered as demented molecules hurled themselves against the coachwork. Every so often there would be a brief pause, a microsecond of quiet, while the wind drew its breath for further efforts, and then the decibels would be redoubled. Overhead, I could make out the shapes of huge clouds breaking and reforming as they poured in a floodtide across the sky. It was cold. My thin silver dress glued itself to my anatomy, showing every goosepimple. But my main worry was the car. It was a long, low Italian model, as red as the scarlet woman, fast, flash, phallic and so predictable an automobile for a man like Vincent Scarpia Savage that I was hardly surprised to learn, some time later, that it belonged to Irving Blum. Vincent made no attempt to close the top, merely vaulting the door into the driver's seat and leaving me to shift for myself. 'If the wind gets under this,' he yelled, 'it'll flip over like a pancake!'

'Are you nervous?' I yelled back. It was an idiotic thing to say, but his blatant nonchalance was beginning to annoy me.

Vincent smiled – a wide feline smile utterly different from his former imperturbability. His bared teeth gleamed in the light from an unshuttered window and his eyes, narrowed to slits against the wind, shone with a glow of their own, or so it seemed, green and luminous as the eyes of a cat. Had we been in a vampire film, this would have been the moment when I saw his elongated incisors. I told myself firmly that it was too late to turn back. He switched on the ignition, slammed the engine into gear. There was a screech of tyres audible even above the clamour of the air, a sputter of gravel thrown up in our wake, and then we were wheeling into the driveway, swerving to avoid whiplash trees and flailing shadows, cutting across cherished corners of lawn, the car rocking perilously with every gust. Ahead, the drive plunged between stone gateposts to join the passing road. I shut my eyes, cursed, opened them again. Vincent negotiated the gap without hesitation or prudence and much too fast. We swung on to the tarmac surface, the beam of our headlamps ricocheting off leaf edge and road verge. I felt Vincent's foot go down on the accelerator, felt the surge of power in both man and vehicle, violent yet helpless against the superpower of the elements, and then the car leaped forward and we went hurtling into the dark.

There was no point in calling out: Vincent would not have heard or heeded. I clung to the side of the car and thought seriously about prayer. Our Father which art in heaven, I don't wish to join You just yet. Vincent drove as though he were trying to outrun the hurricane; the designer chassis shook and rattled like a bag of loose bolts and broken springs. Bodiless Furies, belling on our trail, buffeted and pummelled us, manhandling the car as if it were no heavier than a toy, nudging us carelessly on to the verge one minute, sending us careering back across the road the next. We rode the storm like a spun leaf, skimming the tumult of the night on three wheels, on two wheels, on luck, on lunacy, on hope. Vincent's face was barely discernible in the darkness but I thought I could see the remnants of his feral smile still pinned to his features. It was as if the storm were inside him, a part of him, the Furies within and the Furies without, fighting him, filling him, lashing him on. I was a lone note of sanity in the heart of chaos, driven by the Devil and pursued by every demon in hell.

Disaster came suddenly. The road dipped and veered abruptly to the right. At the same moment, I was conscious of another noise, beneath the ululation of the wind, the deeper, more ominous thunder of the sea. On the left, there was a swift glimpse of beach, the dull sheen of sand, black sharp rocks, white spume sucked downwards into the wave mouth. Ahead, the tarmac gleamed wet. Vincent did his best to turn with the road but it was impossible. Our wheels aquaplaned and we were skidding sideways, backwards, out of control. Towards the beach. Towards the sea. There was an instant of absolute terror when I saw a vast wave rearing above us, so high that the spray plumes appeared to mingle with the rolling clouds and all the universe seemed to come crashing down on us at once. And then the impact of water obliterated everything else. Somewhere at the back of my mind there came an instant of clarity, a tiny flicker of indignant thought. This is it. What a bloody *waste*.

It was the wave which saved us, hurling us back across the road. From the fire to the frying pan. Vincent might be far from sober but his reaction time could not be faulted. He yanked the steering wheel round and revved the spluttering engine into a crescendo, pulling us out of reach of the sea. Unfortunately, he missed the bend. The tarmac slithered beneath our gripless tyres and a particularly violent gust of wind propelled us headlong, off the road, into the unknown. A tree loomed up – not a palm: something more solid – and we came to a grinding, scrunching, juddering halt. I remember thinking, with a mixture of relief and surprise: 'I'm still alive.' It felt like an achievement. The long bonnet was crumpled into a concertina of expensive metal. One headlamp still functioned, the beam tilted uninstructively towards the sky. I had been protected by my safety belt but Vincent had naturally dispensed with this unmanly device; only the steering wheel had prevented him from being flung straight through the windscreen. He was slumped forward, apparently unconscious. I decided it would not have been inappropriate if he were dead.

The first thing was to get out of the car. The wind was already shaking us loose from our anchorage against the tree, the ravening sea was much too close for comfort, and to cap it all there was a disquieting smell of petrol. On television, crashed cars always explode promptly just as the star has scrambled out of range; I only hoped real life would allow me a little more leeway. I wriggled my legs and found them intact, but when I attempted to extricate myself from my seat a portion of mechanical innards jabbed into them, and it took more wriggling and several bruises before I was clear. The sensation of rending material would have had Karl Lagerfeld digging his grave in order to turn in it. One of my silver sandals had already been lost in the depths of the car and I kicked off the other, leaving myself barefoot, a disgruntled Cinderella; tottering on high heels would in any case have been hopeless in the prevailing weather conditions. Vincent, meanwhile, was showing signs of reanimation. Not dead this time, I thought, resigned. Physical toughness and a flair for survival were probably typical of him. He groaned, lifted his head, tried to push the wet hair back from his eyes but the wind whipped it forward again. There was a dark trickle beside his mouth where he had smashed his lip on the rim of the wheel but no other visible injury. 'Get out of the car!' I bawled in his ear. '*Petrol!*'

He seemed to understand, pulling himself together faster than I had done and beginning the extraction process with much grimacing and several oaths which I could only lip-read. His door was jammed but he climbed over the top and stood leaning against the buckled wing, clearly dizzy and struggling to recover his strength. 'What now?' I asked, still in stereo.

'Walk!'

I pointed to my shoeless feet; he shrugged. He was right, of course. We could hardly stay where we were. He set off and I followed, pausing only to retrieve my bag from the interior of the car and sling it diagonally across my body. The instincts of a journalist or the reflex of a woman: I didn't know which. Then I stumbled back to the road.

The walk, predictably, was a nightmare. If the car had exploded behind us, I would not have noticed: staying upright, keeping moving, occupied all my attention. The wind seemed to be coming from every quarter of the compass at once, but the main force of the blast was behind us, thrusting us forward, sometimes almost lifting me off the ground. If it had been against us progress would have been impossible. Vincent gripped my wrist, my arm, my waist, whenever necessary, evidently aware that our combined weight offered more chance of stability than if we each struggled on alone. His hold braced me against the onslaught of the gale, half supporting, half dragging me when my steps flagged, while occasional insults in the vernacular were doubtless intended for encouragement. Chivalry obviously did not enter into it. Somehow, we maintained a steady if precarious course; I hoped Vincent had a sense of direction as I had lost mine long since. I was wet through and shivering with cold and the rough tarmac tenderised the soles of my feet. Presently, the rain began, a sudden squall walloping us from the rear with the vigour of a water cannon. Stray palm fronds went flapping past like enormous bats. The trees themselves survived on flexibility but other species were suffering; heavy branches too stiff to bend snapped off like twigs and were sent spinning through the air. Eventually I reached the point where I knew I could not go on any longer, but since to stop would not solve my problems or alleviate my woes I carried on regardless. I reached that same point again, and again, gave up, kept going, spurred on by Vincent's freely expressed contempt. A measureless period of time went past. The wind skirled, the rain slashed at my legs, a windswept glimpse of moon showed the billowing outlines of great clouds streaking across the sky. I thought the nightmare would go on forever.

I missed the gates, which were wide-spaced and fixed open, so the house loomed up on me almost without warning. Automatic lights flicked on at our approach, showing a seething border of tropical undergrowth and a silhouette of geometric concrete, starkly modern and reassuringly solid. Then at last, a door – a door out of the wind, out of the wet, into warmth, shelter, sanctuary. Vincent took what seemed like an age to find the key. Then the door opened and I fell thankfully across the threshold into the house.

2

I emerged from the shower about half an hour later, helped myself to a bath robe hanging on the door, and went in search of Vincent and liquid restorative, not necessarily in that order. I found both in the living room, which was the size of a small amphitheatre and surrounded by a daunting acreage of window. Steel shutters, electronically operated, protected the glass from the hurricane. The weather was outside, we were inside, my sore feet sank blissfully into rugs both thick and thin. Vincent was lying on a stretch sofa next to a heartening collection of bottles, drinking what proved to be Wild Turkey with a sublime disregard for the state of his liver. His hair was still damp and he was dressed for comfort not style, in jeans grown floppy with age and a black sweatshirt faded to grey from much washing. Only a fleck of dried blood and a slightly swollen lip betrayed his injury. The violence of his earlier mood seemed to have burned itself out; he looked both exhausted and alert, like a tennis player who has just won a particularly strenuous Centre Court final. 'If you're looking for your bag,' he remarked, 'it's on that chair. You eventually parted company with it in the hall. Why *do* women cling so faithfully to their handbags, anyway? Through desert and jungle, battle and war, they clutch that pouch of Gucci leather as if their soul was rolled up inside.'

'No woman is entirely lost while she has her handbag,' I improvised, too worn out to be profoundly unnerved.

'Who said that?'

'Margaret Thatcher.'

'What do you find to put in it?' Vincent continued idly. 'What's so essential that you can't leave it behind when you're off to a party? That bag of yours feels a little heavy for a spare lipstick and a powder compact.'

I was ready for that one. 'Wallet. Comb. Hand mirror. Personal stereo.' There was a lead and a set of headphones wound round my tape recorder to deceive the unwary. 'Make-up kit. Nail file. Piece of string. Pearl-handled revolver. Hatstand.'

'I believe you,' said Vincent. 'My mother's handbag invariably contains all that and more. Grand piano, case of champagne, you name it. Have a drink. Whisky? Gin? Scotch?'

'Tea,' I said.

'Tea. Of course. You're a true Brit, aren't you? Under that painstaking suntan you have the milk-and-water complexion of the upper classes. Sorry: milk-and-roses. A nice piece of English Spode. You're not my type at all.'

I grinned at him. 'I'll survive.'

'The servants live out. The kitchen's through there. I doubt if there's any tea.'

However, I found a packet of Twinings Earl Grey – unfortunately the milder blend made especially for the American palate – and a saucepan to use by way of a kettle. Back in the living room, I added a generous dollop of Scotch. It wouldn't go well with the champagne and brandy I had already consumed, but I needed it.

'Where does your friend keep his candles?' I asked.

'*Candles*? What do you want – romantic lighting?'

'We're in the middle of a hurricane. Sooner or later the power will go off. We may as well be ready.' I was remembering the 1987 hurricane in Britain, when parts of the south-east were without electricity for days. 'How strong is this house? Are we likely to lose the roof?'

'I shouldn't think so. Irving suffers from galloping paranoia: he thinks the whole world is out to get him. This place is probably built to withstand a direct hit from an atomic bomb.'

'Seriously.' I sat down on the end of the sofa beside his feet.

'I *am* serious.' On his own and relaxing after his earlier exertions, Vincent was becoming more communicative. 'Irving is short, balding and as Jewish as gefüllte fish. He's riddled with angst from generations on the run and whether it's terrorists or World War Three he *knows* he's a prime target. Worst of all, he has an obsession with tall blonde *shiksas* from Germany and Scandinavia. That gives him a guilt complex into the bargain.'

'Doesn't he have therapy?' I enquired.

'Of course he does. He's an American. At the last count he had five shrinks. The Americans are all mad.'

I took an invigorating swig of whisky and tea. 'So,' I said, 'the Americans are mad and the English are milksops. Where does that leave you? I detect an echo of perfidious Albion in your accent.'

'I'm a mongrel,' said Vincent. 'English father, Italian mother. I live in LA.'

'A citizen of the world,' I murmured. 'Don't tell me, let me guess. You graduated from the University of Life.'

Vincent registered the sarcasm with a narrowing of his eyes and a slow-down on his easy flippancy. 'Cambridge, actually,' he drawled. 'And Wormwood Scrubs.'

'How unusual.' I sounded politely bored. 'What did you say your name was? I didn't catch it.'

'Vincent. Scarpia. Savage.' He spoke through shut teeth – an interesting phenomenon, since I had not thought it possible. There followed a lifted eyebrow. 'And – er – I'm afraid I've forgotten yours?'

'Michelle Annesley.'

'Michelle. Every bimbo on Sunset Strip is called Michelle. Which diminutive do you favour, Misha or Shelley? The pretentiously exotic or the nauseatingly cute?'

'Micky.' Regrettably, I was enjoying myself. So, I suspected, was Vincent. It was a predicament spiked with dangerous possibilities. 'I suppose you're generally called Vince. Yes – Vince . . .' I savoured the name with airy distaste. 'It sounds like a second-hand car-dealer.'

'No one,' his voice crackled with frost and dripped acid, '*no one* calls me Vince. My friends call me Vincent, my mother calls me Vincente. *You* may call me sir.'

I laughed; after a moment, so did he. He had moved along the sofa towards me and we were sitting much too close. His sex appeal was of the most basic variety, a species of crude animal magnetism laced with the brand of machismo fashionable at the time of Attila the Hun. Only a capacity for self-mockery and a latent sense of humour made his company tolerable, or so I decided. If I was attracted, it was by the situation, not the man: the challenge, the risk factor, the zest of conflict. Vincent had never been beaten, Jan Horrocks had implied. Certainly not at his own game.

Casually, more as if he were fondling a pet than making a pass, he inserted an exploratory hand under the collar of my bathrobe. 'Nice breast,' he remarked. 'Not too big, not too small. Just a comfortable handful.' He took my nipple between thumb and forefinger, massaging gently, and a thin trickle of heat ran down through my midriff into my lower abdomen. What price detachment now, I thought.

'Recollect that I'm not your type,' I reminded him. 'Too wishy-washy. Too English. A porcelain vessel filled with luke-warm tea.'

'True,' said Vincent. 'But right now I'm not exactly spoiled for choice. Under such restricted conditions, a sensible man makes the most of what he's got. You're not ideal but I'm prepared to compromise.'

'Too generous of you,' I said. 'Unfortunately, I'm not.'

We swapped a smile which went from eye to eye without touching our lips. He leaned forward, kissing me, not passionately but with a certain deliberation, sampling the wine prior to giving his approval. I could feel the knot of dried blood where he had cut himself, taste the bourbon on his tongue. There was a pause when, as if by mutual agreement, we both pulled back, studying each other, Vincent's face unreadable, mine (I hoped) as cool as wish power and duplicity could achieve. Then we returned to the kiss. This time, he was rather more insistent, his breath quickening and his treatment of my breast growing pleasurably rougher. At length I pushed him away with a resolution I did not feel and removed his hand from inside my bathrobe.

'Candles,' I said.

It was too late, of course: it had been too late right from the start. I told myself that my starved libido had turned my brain, that this was against every unwritten rule in the book, that the very truth I pursued would be invalidated by such an act of dishonour. But my principles were scattered by the wind and my conscience merely laughed. My weariness had faded: I felt suddenly and exquisitely alive, high on the sheer magic of existence, capable – deplorably – of anything. I was bewitched by my own ingenuity, ensnared in my own machinations. For as long as I could remember I had set myself impossible standards to fall short of; now, I was horrified to discover the satisfaction that comes from behaving badly. Conscious virtue had often left me feeling inadequate and unfulfilled; conscious wickedness gave me a warm inner glow of the kind no martyr could have experienced while burning at the stake. Hellfire in my belly, no doubt. To be complacent about personal merit negates any claim to goodness, but it is allowable to gloat over depravity. The Devil is less particular than God. Blame it on the hurricane – blame it on the tropics – blame it on Pete Langelaan's champagne and Irving Blum's Scotch. I did not have an ethic to my creed and it felt wonderful.

I found the candles in a cabinet in the dining area. Vincent, having bestirred himself to indicate the geography of the room, watched me wedge them into holders and deposit them on the table with matches to hand. Outside, Hurricane Anneka was rattling the steel shutters, buffeting its way from wall to wall in search of eaves to give it some leverage on the roof. But it found only implacable surfaces of concrete, aerodynamic planes, smooth-sided intersections where it seethed and boiled with impotent fury. Within the house, thanks to the chronic insecurity of its owner, we were enclosed in a spacious cell, with armour-plated windows and unshakeable doors. The air, despite subtle conditioning, was still. The temperature was temperate. We might have been at the epicentre of the storm, sealed in a nucleus of unnatural quiet while all around us were the whirling winds. It was an impossible, inconceivable position: Vincent the predator, at ease in his borrowed lair, seeing in me, very likely, only a prospective dinner, and Micky Murphy, journalist and smart-arse, bereft of morality and judgement, come in from the cold to take a deadly and seductive gamble. The lamentable influence of knicker-and-dime literature on modern society. It felt like a Hollywood soap opera and I acted accordingly. Real life with all its grim consequences would catch up with me in the end, but for the moment it could wait.

The lights went out, with perfect timing, in the middle of our next kiss. We were standing thigh to thigh if not quite crotch to crotch, since Vincent was several inches taller. In the sudden dark he loosened my bathrobe and slid his hands round my naked body, cupping my buttocks, pulling me hard against him. His denims were rubbed into silkiness and washed into emaciation and I could feel everything there was to feel forcing itself on my attention. I had betted that either his entire career was an attempt to compensate for under-endowment or else he had no excuse whatsoever: there could be no middle ground. It was as I feared. He had no excuse whatsoever. Nor had I. His embrace tightened around my ribs, his tongue was halfway down my throat, my hormones leaped up and did a war dance. I could sense the strength in his muscles – that same strength which had kept me going on our trek through the hurricane – used no longer to sustain but to dominate me, driven by an innate ruthlessness and the lust of mastery. I should have been alarmed but I knew only excitement. Ruthlessness, the real thing, the wanton shutdown of the imagination that thrusts pity aside, is always frightening. But I believed brain could outwit brawn any day. We were in a duel to the death, and if Vincent had the only weapon – currently pressed urgently against my pelvis – I had the advantage of being the only combatant who knew there was a fight in progress at all.

I broke free with some difficulty, caught my breath. 'Light.'

'Where did you put the bloody candles?'

'On the bloody table. You saw me. You can find them: you know the room better than I do, so you're less likely to bump into things.'

There followed the sound of Vincent bumping into things, swearing fluently in Italian when he stubbed his toe on a piece of furniture. With the shutters down it was pitch-black and rather horrible. I realised that the air-conditioning must have gone off too and felt suddenly claustrophobic, trapped in a dark hole with the oxygen running out. There came the zip of a striking match and a tiny flame sprang into being a short distance away; its subdued glow limned Vincent's face and sent a vast shadow straddling the room behind him. He lit two of the candles and retrieved a bottle, fortunately capped, which he had knocked on to the nearest rug.

'Don't you want to say I told you so?'

I obliged. 'I told you so.'

'Satisfied?'

'Hardly.'

'Then let's go to bed. You take the candles; I'll take the bottles. You're not bringing that damned bag along, surely? Even Margaret Thatcher doesn't need a handbag during sex.'

'Of course she does. She beats Denis over the head with it if his cunnilingus doesn't come up to the mark.' I hooked the strap on my shoulder and picked up the candlesticks with complete sang-froid. 'Condoms,' I elucidated. 'Somewhere between the nail file and the hatstand. I forgot to mention them.' I always carried a packet, if only to prove my status as an intelligent human being, since I rarely had occasion to make use of one.

'Good,' said Vincent. 'I've got some of Irving's kosher specials but if the hurricane damage is bad we could be stuck here for ages and we don't want to run out.'

'Dear me,' I said drily, 'is this virility or wishful thinking?'

'Upstairs on the left,' he dictated, ignoring provocation. 'I'll follow you.'

The main bedroom boasted a huge skylight directly above a wide bed. The builders had omitted to protect it with a shutter but Vincent assured me it was probably quadruple-glazed. I could see little through it but a formless night and the reflection of the twin candle flames, two teardrops of gold apparently floating in the darkness, unattached to any stem, each surrounded by its own halo. Vincent and I were indeterminate shapes beyond the periphery of their radiance. I put one on each bedside table, shed my bathrobe on the floor, and got into bed, while Vincent went for a piss, a chancy operation in the unrelieved gloom of the adjacent shower room. On his return he stripped hurriedly, then paused for a minute looking down at me. His body was a tracery of bone and sinew under a sparse mantling of flesh; his penis stood upright, an impressive column, straight and thick and very solid. There was a nuance in his attitude, as if were allowing me the leisure to admire, to gasp and stretch my eyes. 'Stunning,' I commented dutifully, running a finger up and down the object in question. 'Tell me, what did my predecessors say at this juncture? Honey, you are simply colossal? Signor, you offer me a make I cannot refuse? *Cheri, quel truc que tu as?*'

'In a moment,' said Vincent, torn between appreciation and pique, 'I'm going to teach you a lesson. In manners.'

'I didn't know you had any manners to teach,' I retorted.

He pulled on a condom with the deftness of extensive practice. 'To hell with foreplay,' he said. 'We can get back to that afterwards. Come here.'

I remember thinking, with a sudden pinpoint of lucidity: 'I can't possibly be doing this.'

But I was.

Here there was no ebb of desire, no irresistible chill spreading from my brain down to my loins, no mental withdrawal, no fear, no guilt. I had expected guilt. I waited for guilt, but it never materialised. Maybe I was mellowed from alcohol, just drunk enough and not too drunk, suspended in a magical hinterland on the borders of intoxication. Maybe I was warmed from the tropical clime, fevered from my struggle with wind and rain, inflamed with unaccustomed lust. Vincent parted my thighs almost immediately and began inching his penis into me: it felt gargantuan, inflexible, unstoppable, prising me open, stretching me, forcing a passage deeper and deeper inside me until I imagined he would split my womb and penetrate to my very core. Such an invasion should have hurt but there was little pain, only a sense of exhilaration, a kind of freedom even in total submission. No more restraint, no holding back, no furtive dabbling in passion: this was enthusiastic and absolute, an eight-course banquet, a sleigh-ride down the Cresta Run. In the candlelight I saw Vincent wincing with pleasure, wrestling with his own impatient urges, caught in the hiatus between impending heaven and failing self-control. But his penis was too eager for him: I felt him starting to succumb, felt every muscle tensed, every nerve racked, felt him soaring and shuddering with a species of ecstatic sensual implosion. Afterwards he lay and panted, biting me from time to time, very gently, without breaking the skin. I sighed, not with fulfilment but with a different satisfaction, still speared on what was left of his erection, yet paradoxically conscious of possession and conquest.

Sex is power. That was a lesson I learned too late for Patrick and had never seriously applied to anyone else. Unaroused, the male organ is a vulnerable little creature, pathetic and faintly ridiculous, like a loose end of piping which has escaped from Man's internal plumbing and dangles uselessly between his legs. But oh, what a transformation is there! I have only to look at it and it perks up, its eye brightens, its head swells, it becomes a tower of strength, a tree trunk in girth, the pillar that sustains the universe. Confronted by this phallus I thought I could understand why primitive tribes had worshipped such a miraculous device, building statues of it and wearing its likeness for every aboriginal rite. All through history we have immortalised it with Nelson's Column, Cleopatra's Needle, the Empire State Building, the Apollo moon rocket, the cruise missile. This weak soft thing which can suddenly leap up in beauty and splendour is the symbol of Man's enterprise and evolutionary drive, the handle to his ego, the master key to his soul. With Vincent's penis in my mouth I tasted power. The essence of his maleness was between my lips, at my mercy, offered to me in helpless surrender. Vincent lay on his back, a willing victim, alternately moaning and gasping, letting me do what I pleased. This was the ultimate in gamesmanship, outrageous beyond fantasy, erotic beyond the limitations of pornography. I revelled in it.

I had not really expected Vincent to respond in kind. Sexual generosity usually springs from a generous spirit, loving and giving, as the poem says, and Vincent, I was sure, rarely loved and gave nothing. But some men have an aptitude for sex, a form of extra-sensual understanding as instinctive as an ear for music: their timing is almost infallible, their fervour comes not from the heart but from the gut. Vincent had obviously learned at an early age that you did not gain ascendancy over a woman merely by sporting a finely chiselled profile and designer jeans. He, too, was aware of the potential for power, and he must have exercised his megalomania whenever possible, coaxing the hesitant, compelling the reluctant, subduing the strong. He went down on me with a slow hunger, taking his time, disclosing my clitoris with a practised touch and the absorption of a gourmet sampling a rare delicacy. If the erect penis is a prodigy of lust, inflated far in excess of its normal size and bursting with a vitality often unrelated to that of its possessor, the female equivalent is a closed bud, a kernel of super-concentrated sensitivity, drawing threads of pleasure from every erogenous zone in the body into a single knot of blissful delirium. Victorian Man, though he frequently took his penis for a walk to the nearest whorehouse, had never even heard of it. His twenti-eth-century successor is better educated, broad of mind, caring, house-trained, genitally numerate and hopelessly confused. Vincent, however, was not a New Man; he was a Neanderthal with the curiosity of Casanova and the detection rate of Sherlock Holmes. By experiment, by intuition, he knew exactly how to use his tongue, when to pause, when to savour, when to suck and suck until I screamed in silent frenzy. I had not anticipated it and I was caught off guard, too enraptured to resist, yielding almost before I had realised what was happening, giving myself, taking his gift, drifting into a post-coital euphoria with a faint, cold warning whis-pering at my heart. *You shouldn't have done that.*

Too late.

I slept before dawn, briefly and lightly, waking to find myself gazing up at the glass ceiling and the reflection of the candle to my left. The other had already gone out. I slipped into a state half dream, half imagining, where the solitary flame became the lost spark of my soul, unquenched by the storm, burning on in steady tranquillity while in the background the night blew away in a flurry of wind and cloud. There came a point when I knew I was asleep: I struggled to reawaken, aware of urgency and danger, fighting my way out of the smothering darkness like a drowning man floundering for air, summoning all my resources of strength to break through the thin skin of slumber into consciousness. I sat up: the bed was on fire. My inmost spark had got out of hand, igniting the duvet. A dazzle of flames shone full in my eyes. I opened them, really awake now, to discover that I had rolled over towards the bedside table, and the candle flame, flaring up as the last of the wax melted, filled my vision. Even as I watched it shiv-ered and sank, expiring gently into the grey glimmer of morning.

We finally got up around noon. The hurricane was on its way to Haiti but the electricity was still off, which meant we could not raise the shutters and the unconditioned air was going stale. The smell of sex permeated the bedroom like yesterday's oysters; the

living room, though unperfumed, was a dark stuffy box, both dry
and dank. We opened any doors that we could find but owing to
Irving Blum's paranoia there weren't many. Outside, the garden
resembled a giant's stamping ground, battered and flattened in all
directions, but nature is by definition adaptable and already stalks
and stems were flexing themselves for the process of revival.
Tropical plants are used to such winds: they shake their leaves
and get back to photosynthesis. Human beings are restricted by
their own technology. The phone lines were down (I hoped Phyl
wouldn't worry); the hot water was cold; the fridge was defrosting. 'If there's a freezer somewhere,' I said, 'it should be all right
for a bit longer, but after that we'll just have to empty it and eat
the contents.'

'In the storeroom,' said Vincent, 'there are three freezers, all
full. We couldn't possibly eat our way through one of them.
Irving likes to lay in stocks in case of siege or famine. It never
occurs to him that when disaster strikes the power supply will be
the first thing to go.'

He gulped down an Alka-Seltzer; I followed suit. There is
nothing like a mutual hangover to help you skate over the initial
gêne of waking up next to a first-night stand. Vincent, however,
seemed unaffected, too preoccupied with the practical aspects of
our position to waste time on embarrassment. As for me, my
mind was on my tape recorder. I had run a tape in the bedroom
but the mere thought of playing it, even to myself, made my
blood run so cold I expected Vincent to hear ice chinking. I had
rewound the tape and was ready to start again, determined to
obtain something of use before I quit. Conversation rather than
heavy breathing. In the circumstances, it would have been ludicrous for me to enact the blushing English rose.

My bag was in the living room; Vincent had ceased to comment on its ubiquity. I suggested we should salvage a salad from
the fridge and retreat to the sofa, instead of standing in the
draught from the back door. The weather was still cool and over-
cast; sporadic gleams of sunshine crossed the garden too swiftly
to warm it up.

'I want some coffee,' Vincent said. 'Shit! Why does everything
have to be electric? What's wrong with gas?'

'There might be a camping gas somewhere about,' I ventured.

There wasn't, although Vincent's investigation of storeroom and garage did elicit one large torch, one small one, spare batteries, and a can of paraffin with which, he claimed, if the worst came to the worst, we could light a bonfire in the garden and have an improvised barbecue.

'Could we?' I said sceptically. 'Do you know how? I bet you were never a Boy Scout.'

'A revolting idea,' said Vincent, adding, with malice aforethought: 'I naturally assumed you were a Girl Guide. You look the type.'

We sat down to our salad, accompanied, for lack of coffee, by a bottle of wine. The skin of the grape, if not the hair of the dog. 'If your friend Irving is going to cultivate the siege mentality,' I remarked, 'he could at least get it right. Even if we take food out of the freezer we can't cook it. You might interest him in getting his own generator – for the future, you know.'

'Bolting the stable door after the horse has been shot,' Vincent said scathingly. 'Think of something we can do now.'

'Boil a kettle on his car engine?' I proposed. 'Or rather, a saucepan?'

'I doubt it. In any case, that was his car I was driving last night.'

'Oh Lord.' I paused for thought. 'Are you – are you *very* good friends?'

'I hope so.'

'How do you think he'll react?'

'Wave his arms around like Woody Allen. Heave his shoulders like Jack Benny. "What is it with you, Vincent?" he'll say. "I lend you my house on Dominique: the island is devastated by a hurricane. I lend you my car: you reduce it to a heap of iron filings. Remind me never to lend you my mistress: I'd probably find myself paying palimony after *you've* walked out." Then I'll give him the cash so neither of us has to ruffle the smooth waters of our respective insurance policies and that will be that.'

'How do you know him?' I asked, mindful of my tape recorder and trusting the oblique approach was going to lead somewhere.

'Business. He's in real estate; so am I. In LA there are only two areas of work: real estate and movies. Irving does both. He produces films which are long on action and short on script and owns a street or two in Beverly Hills. Shops pay him astronomical rental and charge astronomical prices. He makes a few million; so do they. A cosy situation.'

'What about you?' I said. 'Do you make films too, or do you prefer to reserve your drama for real life?'

'Invariably,' said Vincent.

I teased him to talk about real estate, although strictly speaking that was Alun's sphere of interest. Vincent was cryptic. 'I buy cheap and sell dear. That's all there is to it.'

'You mean you know in advance when property values are going to go up?'

'Mmm.'

'How?'

'Various underhand methods. You're too English; you wouldn't approve.'

'No, I wouldn't,' I said through a mouthful of lettuce. 'Tell me more.'

The spectacle of a person eating lettuce is deceptive: I appeared as unalarming as a friendly rabbit. 'For example,' Vincent expounded, 'a former associate of mine made a point of involving herself with the personnel of the Department of Water and Power. Richmond always knew when they were going to lay down a new pipeline to some desert outpost and transform it into a habitable environment. Very useful.'

'Richmond?' I remembered the name. Alun's contact; he had allowed me to believe it was a man. Alun being deliberately misleading, his favourite pastime.

'Richmond LeSueur,' said Vincent. 'Generally known as LeSewer. Slum-spawn whore turned power-pussy. And you needn't look so superior. Compared with Rich, you're cold tea after neat meths. It's nothing to be proud of. If you had a tenth of her guts you might be worth noticing.'

'It's dark in here,' I said. 'You couldn't possibly tell how I looked. Anyway that sounds like insider trading to me. The same principle – or lack of it.'

'It isn't a question of principles. If you've got information, it's stupid not to capitalise on it. Information is the lifeblood of business. Anyone with brains is going to try to glean whatever he can. Insider trading is just a prurient term for common sense.'

'Didn't they teach you to play cricket,' I said, 'at the expensive public school you undoubtedly attended?'

'Gordonstoun. Yes they did. I always thought it one long doze.' He refilled my wineglass. 'So what do you do, Micky? When not partying in the Caribbean?'

I ignored the sneer, which, since he was also partying in the Caribbean, was peculiarly unjust. 'I work in television.'

'Oh God.' To my relief, Vincent yawned. 'I should have guessed. The smart job for Sloanes. What are you, exactly? Director of telling drama documentaries? Make-up girl on a low-budget soap? Teasmade?'

'Teasmade,' I said. 'It's Breakfast TV. Actually, I rush around with a clipboard obeying the futile orders of my ineffectual producer and fantasising that one day Michael Grade will walk in and say: "Micky, let me take you away from all this."' As I spoke, I found myself picturing the girl from the studio above, who was always dashing in and out of the lift, clipboard clutched to a panting bosom and a frown of permanent anxiety on her youthful forehead. I wasn't sure what she did but she was just the person I wanted. As far as Vincent was concerned, I was a Caroline Portly-Smythe. If you are telling a lie it is always a good idea to base it on some form of truth.

'You know,' said Vincent with perception, 'you're too intelligent for that sort of thing. You won't get anywhere unless you screw your way up, and you're not the type for that.'

'How do you know?'

'Don't act the fool.' His eyes caught a stray flicker of light, gleaming in the dimness. 'I slept with you: of course I know. It's the kind of thing you can sense. Sexual honesty. Chamberpot virtue. You could never be a whore – and it's not a compliment. You haven't the nerve. I use sex like everything else; you couldn't. You'd fuck for love, you'd fuck for pleasure, but you'd never fuck for a promotion or a pay rise or a bigger slice of the company car. I know your class: I grew up in it. You'll take everything from Daddy but you won't go out and grab for yourself. You'd call it high ideals. I'd call it easy living and always expecting your dinner on a silver platter.'

Whatever I do to him, I thought, my skin prickling, he

deserves it. For his arrogance, his effrontery, his brazen assertion of crooked practices. For despising humanity and underestimating me. He deserves to stew in his own jacuzzi, to choke on his own medicine. He deserves to get screwed.

'From English Spode to the family silver,' I said. 'You're obsessed with crockery. Excuse me: I must go to the loo.'

What I meant was, I must change the tape.

We talked all afternoon. There was nothing else to do. In normal conditions there would have been competition from television and video, CDs and cassettes. ('For God's sake don't use that damned Walkman,' Vincent had said. 'I can't stand them.') But without electricity, civilisation as we know it comes to a full stop. Even the radio was a part of the music centre, so we had no news. We could not burn a piece of toast or chill a bottle of champagne. The last of the ice cubes had melted. Indoors, the light was too poor for reading. Outdoors, a wicked little breeze rustled the pages, losing your place the minute you turned away, and the garden furniture was still too damp for comfort. You cannot have sexual intercourse twenty-four hours a day and so we were reduced to conversation. I did not want to ask too many questions; instead, I contradicted him, argued with him, probed and prodded, employed the gentlest of irony, the smoothest of sarcasm. I even allowed myself to be drawn, offering an opinion for an opinion, a confidence for a confidence. After all, I conjectured, whatever Vincent learned about me he would as quickly forget. His memories emerged piecemeal, a scattered jigsaw which I could reassemble at a later stage. A childhood without a mother, a nanny who broke her promise, school, college, mortgage fraud, prison. The friendship of Hannibal Barker and the wisecracks of Judas Carson. 'But he cheated you!' I protested. 'Didn't you want to get even? I thought you were the kind for whom getting even was a priority.'

'You don't understand,' Vincent said. 'It wasn't Judas who let me down; he simply taught me some unpleasant but valuable facts. I considered some sort of revenge, once in a while, more by way of a mental exercise than a serious proposition; but by the time I was in a position to ruin him it didn't matter any more. Without his backing, I might not have succeeded. The credits outweighed the debits. Besides, revenge is bloody melodramatic.

Also time-consuming. You would have to care a great deal about someone to expend effort and imagination on a scheme that did not guarantee any material gain.'

Richard, I thought. He's referring to Richard. Melodrama and all. But I didn't say anything. It was too soon to press him on an issue clearly so close to what passed for his heart.

In the early evening the sun reappeared in earnest, finding its way through the occasional chink in the shutters to strew microdots of brilliance across the darkened room, pouring through the back door and bathing the kitchen in a glow of soft gold. Vincent and I crawled out of the gloom like moles, blinking in the sudden light. It was not merely warm but hot: the garden, too long chilled, sighed with relief, insects and other tiny creatures crept from their hideouts to bask in the resumption of summer. Most of the clouds had dispersed, leaving only a few stragglers trailing behind. The orb of the sun hung low over the horizon, swollen to enormous size and floating in a sky of yellow chartreuse. The sea beyond West Point was dimpled with fire.

'Well,' said Vincent, 'how about a swim?'

At the end of the garden there was a stair, descending a low cliff to Irving's private beach. The tempest of the preceding night had left flotsam at the top of the cliff as well as the bottom, but the sea was quiet now, endeavouring to atone for its tantrums, demure waves breaking gracefully on the virgin sand. We both went in naked: I had no swimwear, Vincent could not be bothered. The water lapped my body like silk, washing away the frowstiness and lassitude of the long day inside. 'Tell me I look like a mermaid,' I said to Vincent. 'That's the customary line.'

'I never heard of a mermaid with short hair,' Vincent retorted. As we made our way back to the house he continued, a little to my surprise: 'You look like yourself. A nymph of the modern school, all slender and streamlined. No untidy locks to detract from a silhouette of scrupulous simplicity. It's effective. I might even come to admire it, in time.'

We made love in the sunlight on the kitchen floor, spreading a rug and a couple of cushions on the tiles, taking advantage of the only part of the house where the day could penetrate. I had refused to do it on the beach since I did not want sand between my buttocks. A lizard watched us from the wall, a green dragonet no longer than my thumb and as vivid as a piece of jewellery. Suddenly, I was carried back to England and the memory of Penny Garoghan – 'Daddy says there are lizards in his *bedroom*' – and an uprush of irrational emotion and a promise I must not break. I could hear the exact inflection of her voice, see her slanting silver eyes. The impossible vow became linked, in my mind, with the promise Vincent's nanny had broken to Jolanda, all those years ago, teaching the child eavesdropping in the shadows that the best of us can break our sworn word. He had been too young for such a lesson; that was something only adults should ever find out. It had become my responsibility – my painful responsibility – to ensure that Penny, at least, did not lose faith in her fellow men until she was old enough to understand them.

Vincent and I made love. Already since the previous night something had changed, we were learning each other not just physically but mentally, a dangerous game for a dispassionate journalist. I had gone too far, much too far, not always in the same direction, and now I could not turn back. 'I want to see you,' Vincent said, touching me with his finger, a soft persistent massage, even while he was inside me. 'I want to watch you come.'

Afterwards he kissed me, glorying in his power; I could feel the thrill of it coursing through his veins like adrenaline. It was not love but it felt like love, for a few seconds of coitus, a brief lapse into tenderness: two bodies locked in cliché, two hearts with but a single throb – a deception, a cheat, a manoeuvre on the chessboard, a skirmish in the battle. A web of lies with here and there a strand of truth, entangling us both in its seductive tendrils.

I shivered under the shower for a hideous minute to rinse off the salt and went into the bedroom. 'I don't suppose it's possible to open the skylight?' I asked Vincent.

'Oh yes, it's possible.' His voice held a grim satisfaction. 'Unfortunately – can't you guess? – it's operated electronically. Like everything else in this house. Isn't technology wonderful?'

'Shit.' I sat down on the bed. 'Incidentally, I want to dress for dinner. Is there a change of bathrobe?'

'Is there a change of dinner?'

I had raided one of the storeroom freezers for bread, chopped liver and polyunsaturates, but it would all take hours to thaw out. There was some frozen yoghurt and two flavours of ice-cream, one with chocolate chip calories, one with low-fat extract of pounded-up biscuit and sugar-free syrup. I produced the salad remaindered at lunch time and Vincent, as usual, opened a bottle. Happily, the wine cellar went on more or less forever. With the aid of a torch I had applied a little make-up and I wore a shirt of Vincent's long enough for decency and sashed in round the waist with a Dior silk tie which he said he preferred on me. 'I hate ties,' he observed. 'It's like wearing a garotte around your neck. I only have them for business.' He had nicked his chin trying to shave with a cut-throat razor, but the damage, as I pointed out, was only superficial. We sat round the coffee table, passing a carton of ice-cream to and fro and dipping in with a long-handled spoon of the type recommended for supping with the Devil. 'Tomorrow,' I said, 'if the electricity doesn't come on, do you think we ought to do something?'

'We could light a beacon on West Point in the hope of attracting the attention of a passing galleon,' said Vincent. 'You can semaphore a message. Marooned on desert island. Total power-cut. Freezer defrosting. Please help.'

I laughed perfunctorily. 'I know we're not desperate,' I persisted, 'but we can't sit here indefinitely living off lettuce leaves and booze. Don't you have to be somewhere? Won't the real estate market in LA disintegrate without you?'

'I took a week's holiday,' Vincent explained. 'This isn't quite what I'd planned but it could be worse. Much worse. How about you? Weren't you supposed to be staying with somebody?'

'Phyllida Khorman,' I said, 'but I don't think she'll miss me.' I proceeded to massacre Phyl's reputation for the second time. 'We were at school together – I hadn't seen her for years – then I ran into her just recently. She invited me here in that gushing way people do when they don't really mean it: masses of enthusiasm and no specific details. I shouldn't have taken her seriously, but I needed a break so badly and it seemed like a heaven-sent opportunity. The hurricane, I suppose, was just my luck. Anyway, Phyl didn't seem quite so enthused when I actually got here. She's been sweet but aloof, as if my presence was a minor irritant which it behoved her to bear with courtesy. She's probably only too thankful I've absconded.'

'I know her,' said Vincent. 'A decorative miniature with family money and a penchant for marrying more of it. Present incumbent Farzad Khorman. One to watch. I shouldn't have thought the little Phyllida was your style at all.' He looked me over with careless consideration. 'What's the problem, Micky? Does my company pall?'

'It does rather,' I admitted, 'but I'm too polite to say so. About that stuff in the freezer: when do the servants come in?'

'In the aftermath of a hurricane, God knows. But when they do you can satisfy your urge to distribute largesse among the peasantry. Meanwhile, I'm tired of the subject. Do you play backgammon?'

'No.'

We found a set of Trivial Pursuit in a cupboard and played a couple of games. Vincent won both. I pleaded mitigating circumstances since it was an American edition. Later, the conversation relapsed naturally into personal matters, needing little encouragement from me. I found myself talking about my father, his poetry, his war record, his infinite capacity for compassion, the philosophy which had shaped my own.

'How old were you when he died?' Vincent asked.

'Eleven.'

'You were lucky. Mine hung around till I was nearly forty and then proceeded to cut me out of his will because he thought I'd leaked his love-life to the tabloid press. The stupid bugger. He knew – he *knew* I wouldn't do that. Or at least, he should have known, if he'd ever troubled to try to learn what sort of a man his undesirable son really was. He even wrote to me, a charming little posthumous missive explaining why I was being disinherited. Words like "despicable" and "dastardly" featured prominently. It was pathetic. As if I were some disgusting brat of a schoolboy, sticky-fingered and dripping snot, who'd run to the housemaster to sneak on his friends.' He shivered – I could have sworn it – with anger and revulsion.

'How *did* the story leak out?' I enquired.

Vincent told me about the Quidnunc file, and Gerry Hibbert.

'You must have loved your father very much,' I said, 'to feel so bitter. Even now.'

'You sound just like my cousin Richard. He always wanted people to love each other, an unlikely development at the best of times. My father was an antiquated bigot. Also a hypocrite. He thought he could get rich and still stay Mr Nice Guy. *Fesserie.* One man's wealth is another man's poverty: that's economics. But he wouldn't face facts – he blethered on about morality and integrity and the playing fields of Eton. I'll bet he became an MP out of sheer community spirit – and that must have made him a rarity at Westminster. He believed in Church and country and all that crap but worst of all he believed in Man.'

'And you don't,' I said. It wasn't a question.

'Adam and Eve were booted out of Eden because of a hunger for knowledge, an act of celestial insanity that set a permanent trend. We've been going downhill ever since, evolution in reverse. Look around you, Micky, look at the senseless wars, gluttony and famine, environmental catastrophe, all the issues you probably care about and love to protest. What do you do? Nothing. What *can* you do? Nothing. Man the Ape, Man the Bonehead is set on the road to annihilation. His stupidity is too strong for you. I should know: I've lived off it.'

'So,' I said, 'you saw from the start that civilisation was a dead duck. You didn't attempt resuscitation; you just robbed the corpse. How clever of you.'

He was growing accustomed to my critical attitude: he seemed stimulated rather than offended by it. 'Listen,' he said, 'all that really matters is survival. Snatching whatever you can get in the scrum. A little orange sauce for the dead duck. One of these days, probably without prior notice, I'm going to drop dead too. And then the total pointlessness of it all will finally become clear, though I shan't be there to see it. A life, a death, a journey into nowhere. No one to weep over me, no kids to disinherit. I invite you to my funeral, Micky. You'll say a prayer for me, even though you're not quite certain there's a God around to hear it. You're just that sort of woolly-minded pseudo-irreligious liberal.'

'Just,' I said. 'I disagree with everything you've said, of course, but you know that, don't you? Anything else would bore you to sleep. When I was a child my father used to tell me his version of that Eden affair. The way he told it, Man was a sketch on the drawing-board when a particularly nasty, flea-ridden, bum-scratching band of apes climbed over the wall and pinched the apples intended for Adam and Eve. So God showed them the sketch and said: "You've stolen Man's destiny: now it's yours. Get out there and turn into Men." And they stood up on their hind legs and looked God in the eye and went in search of their future. We haven't got there yet, we're still more than half ape, but it's important – it's *necessary* – to have hope. When I die the world will keep turning. That's immortality.' I added: 'What's more, you think so too. Otherwise you wouldn't ask me to your funeral. You like the idea of me standing at the graveside—'

'Urnside,' Vincent interjected.

'—dabbing my face with a black lace handkerchief. You need to indulge your ego after death. Continuity.'

'You're an optimist,' said Vincent. 'You want to find cause for hope in everyone, even me. I'm a realist. I refuse to cheat myself with lies – even yours.'

I saw him very clearly in that moment, circled in candlelight, a precise image against the shadow-blurred vastness of the living room. He was lying on his back with his hands behind his head, and his profile was cut into the darkness like a cameo, fine-drawn and palely gold. The scene imprinted itself on my memory with a ruthless poignancy. I knew that it would return to me later, much later, when the case was closed and the job was done and I did not want to remember at all. A moment when truth and deceit intermingled, the one merging with the other until the normal dividing lines were lost.

I said: 'You're a nihilist. Your own ethos doesn't matter because nothing matters any more. You've written off civilisation, you've written off humanity. What's left on the menu? Armageddon?'

'Hardly. Reality is a series of anti-climaxes. Mankind, no doubt, will quit not with a bang but with a fizzle. Slow-poisoned with pollution. Killing and being killed in a string of petty wars. The world will keep turning until it goes into a flat spin. Armageddon is a grotesque idea. Think of it: Good versus Evil, the last great battle at the end of time. But if it's the end, what's

the point? The eternal clock is ticking and there are only a few
seconds left. Hey, guys, we won! We finally won! The ultimate
victory.' He snapped his fingers. '*Finis*. So the good guys made it:
what for? So the bad guys licked them: why not? The everlasting
conflict is over as if it had never even started. Meaningless.
Personally, I have always thought existence not only a freak but
a nerve. It would be nice if there was a God to blame for it.

> 'What, without asking, hither hurried *whence*?
> And, without asking, *whither* hurried hence?
> Another and another Cup to drown
> The memory of this Impertinence!'

He suited the action to the words and I laughed.
    'The alcoholic tent-maker.' I identified the quote. 'I like that.
But supposing for the sake of argument, that Armageddon did
arrive, and among the multiple battalions of the two armies you
and I came face to face—'
    'On opposite sides, I infer?' Vincent lifted his eyebrows.
    'Naturally. Just guess who's on which team.'
    'You with your shining sword, me with my Kalashnikov?'
    'Exactly. You define yourself as a survivor. Would you shoot,
there at the end of the universe, for the last minute, the last
heartbeat, the principle of winning? Would you kill me? You
would, wouldn't you?'
    'Probably, yes.' The answer was light enough but Vincent's
tone was oddly sombre. 'Does it matter?'
    'Only to me,' I said.

We went for another swim in the small hours, taking a torch to
help us negotiate the garden and the steps down to the beach.
The moon had gone and the sky was full of stars, far brighter and
more numerous that the stars of an English night, twinkling
fires whose brilliance cast an ethereal shadow behind plant and
rock, and beyond them remote clusters, nameless and numberless, glittering faintly like the dust of diamonds. The waves
breaking on the sand were fretted with luminous foam; the black
water was as warm as a bath. Vincent swam farther out while I
drifted with the swell, rocking gently as if in a hammock, gazing

upwards at the wonder of the sky. It occurred to me that the situation was idyllic enough for any Hollywood fairy tale, a cinemagoer's dream of romance; and for the first time I began to appreciate the irony, the lunacy of my cold-blooded professional assignment juxtaposed with this brief sojourn in a treacherous Elysium. It was a paradox both magical and terrifying. I felt like a gambler on a winning streak: the turn of a card, the fall of the dice, is purely a matter of chance, yet once in a lifetime along comes that unforgettable hour when you cannot go wrong. Fate had sent the hurricane to whirl me into Vincent's arms and had cut off the power to make him talk, and now all the heavens were lit up for our benefit. There had to be a catch in it somewhere: fate plays no game but her own and is never so untrustworthy as when she appears to be on your side. But I didn't care. Not yet. The next day, or the next, the electricity would come on and existence would slip back into its old familiar rut, and then I was going to care, I knew it; but that was all the more reason not to burn my heart now. I floated with the tide and the stars watered me with their tears and nothing but that moment endured.

Back in the house, we lay in bed in a post-coital euphoria while the night, undimmed by candlelight, looked down on us through the glass. 'Vincent,' I said softly, 'you know what we were saying earlier? About the end of the world?'

He gave the statutory grunt that men give when they are more than half asleep and not really attending.

'Armageddon,' I persisted. 'The last great battle between Good and Evil. You and I locked in mortal combat.'

'Is that what it was?' murmured Vincent. 'Who won?'

'Idiot,' I said. 'We were discussing *Armageddon*. Remember?'

'That,' said Vincent. 'Small talk. What of it?'

'How can you be sure,' I whispered, 'that *you'll* be the one with the Kalashnikov?'

For answer he rolled over and pulled me closer, settling me into the hollow of his shoulder in a position virtually guaranteed to give him cramp later on. I had warned him – for no logical reason I felt I had to warn him – but he didn't listen, he didn't hear. The stars wept on uncaring.

3

The sun, rising above the skylight, reached me first, and I opened my eyes to see it winking at me over the frame. Vincent still lay in shadow, the sheet crumpled to his waist, one shoulder hunched against the advance of morning. His averted face was half buried in the pillow in an instinctive attempt to evade the uncurtained glare. Day two, I thought. It felt like a month or even more, a period outside time, outside morality. Two days in fairyland equal two hundred years on earth, and when I returned, like Rip Van Winkle, I would find everything changed irrevocably. The San Andreas fault would have swallowed up Los Angeles. Phyl would be on another marriage. Alun Craig would be producing game shows. It was a cheering prospect. I got up, since it was already disagreeably hot under the skylight, and went into the shower. Still no electricity. The shock of cold water revivified the sleepiest corners of my brain, reminding me of a problem which had been niggling at me since the preceding evening. I was running out of tapes. Hopefully Irving Blum would have some blank cassettes somewhere which I could appropriate: I would have to find a minute when Vincent's back was turned to search downstairs.

With this in view, when he awoke I let him go for a swim on his own. 'I'd like to sunbathe for a bit first,' I said. 'I'm supposed to be on holiday; sunbathing is part of the schedule. I'll look out some oil and join you shortly.' The oil was easy to locate; the cassettes weren't. The shelves beside the music centre were stacked with discs and tapes of everything from Izaak Perlman to *Fiddler*

on the Roof, but none of the cassettes were home-made and there
were no blanks. I might have abandoned all ethical considerations
but it did not seem right to me to record over any part of Irving's
music collection without at least looking for an alternative.
Presently, I discovered that the entire unit slid aside to reveal yet
more shelves laden with CDs, a stockpile of vintage LPs and
singles, and an assortment of tapes labelled in biro. Some of them
bore only girls' names: Ilse, Marika, Birgit, Inge. Irving's *shiksas*,
I deduced; compilations of their favourite tunes for seduction
purposes. Anyway, the labels were worn and smudged and the
shiksas in question must have succumbed (or not) long ago. With
an anomalous pang of guilt I helped myself to Ilse and Inge, slid
the unit back into place, and went down to the beach.

We stayed there till nearly midday, swimming and lazing on
the sand. Conversation was desultory. The sun beat down as it is
wont to do in the tropics, deepening Vincent's somewhat casual
tan to a colour which I rudely described as lifeguard bronze and
injecting a faint, injudicious note of rose into my subtle gilding.
Sunbathing in that climate is more of a penance than a pleasure:
you plunge into the sea to cool off, lie in the sun to dry off, oil
yourself religiously all over, fry, and five minutes later you have
to go back in the sea again. I found myself wondering how the
ozone layer was getting on, and whether there was a nice thick
sandwich of it between me and all that ultra-violet. The cold
shower up at the house acquired a new attraction. As the shadows shrank towards noon rock and sand bleached and baked,
while the sea seemed to be no longer water but liquid light, dancing in shimmering ripples across a golden floor. Irving's beach
parasol had literally gone with the wind and there was no proper
shelter anywhere. We retreated to the house and spent the
hottest part of the day in shuttered gloom, sprawled on sofa and
armchair, drinking tepid champagne. Much more of this, I
thought, and I really would have literary liver, the well-known
affliction of writers and journalists everywhere. It was incredibly
easy, in the dark, to fiddle with my bag, flick a switch on or off,
keep the microphone exposed. Frighteningly easy. I coaxed
Vincent to talk about his mother, offering details of mine in the
usual trade-off, one childhood memory for another, my adult
hang-ups for his. It was a high-risk poker game in which I would

toss little bits of myself on the table in order to up the ante. If my mother was merely *fatale* Jolanda, it was clear, was a *femme formidable*, a creature of unbridled passions and misdirected ardours whose inner fire had scorched everyone around her and all but consumed herself. Vincent spoke of her with a cynicism which belied the rueful warmth in his voice.

'You adore her,' I said.

'I have to,' he retorted. 'I'm all she's got. The friends of her heyday have gracefully faded out. There are one or two antiques still hanging around who kiss her hand and tell her she's beautiful, and are old enough and sentimental enough to mean it, but the rest – they'd be kind to her, of course, given half the chance. Out of pity, because she can't sing and she's lost her looks. I won't have that.'

'You think she's wonderful,' I said. 'Sebastiano obviously thinks she's wonderful. Why shouldn't they?'

Vincent made a sound somewhere between a snort and a sigh. 'She wouldn't like you,' he said with apparent irrelevance. 'She'd classify you as one of those bloodless English girls who are so well bred and so polite and so boring in bed. I could tell her you're responding to tuition, but she wouldn't believe me. "Vincente," she would say, "you must find yourself a real *Italiana* with a heaving bosom, a throbbing voice, and a light hand at pasta. Or an American girl with a big smile and a big heart. Not this insipid *Inglese* with her pale cold eyes and her pale cold emotions." She hates the English.'

For an instant, hearing him bracket me with Jolanda, I knew an extraordinary sensation, as if the bottom had dropped out of my stomach. Surprise, or something similar. I pulled myself together. 'My mother would love you,' I said. 'She'd find you too, too utterly charming. It would put me off for good.'

He laughed; I laughed. It meant nothing. Frivolous speculation. It wasn't even true: my mother, almost certainly, would detect Vincent's moral deficiencies with her usual unerring flair. 'Fascinating,' she would say, 'but not to *live* with. When you pick a man for life, darling, you want someone *reliable*. Like one of those car adverts. Someone with a good steady engine who doesn't go too fast on the bends. This one is beautiful but he isn't safe: I can sense it.'

No brakes, I thought. Too much power under the bonnet. Trouble.

'What next?' Vincent asked, with an acuteness of perception that both disturbed and stimulated me. 'We've covered most of the ground. Parents, principles, my dubious past, my equally dubious present. Anyone would think you were doing a thesis. Why the interest?'

'Why not?' I countered. 'When you wake up in a strange bed, it's fairly normal to be interested in the other occupant. Besides, there's nothing else to do. You make quite a good soap opera.'

'Better than *Dallas*?' Vincent suggested in dulcet tones.

'Well, I wouldn't go that far.' I grinned at him. 'Actually, I'd rather be listening to Mahler, but I don't have much choice, do I?'

The electricity came on again in the early evening. We lifted all the shutters and the falling sun flooded in through every window, its long rays filling the room with dust-hazed light. The air began to circulate, the fridge to hum. The telephone, it transpired, had recovered consciousness much earlier, but Vincent had promptly switched it off again. 'Irving will have heard about the hurricane,' he said. 'He'll call wanting to know if the house is in one piece. Hannibal will call wanting to know if I'm in one piece. I don't need the hassle. Did you wish to phone your anxious friend?'

'No thanks,' I said. It was too chancy. Phyl would have to trust me, and wait a little longer.

Vincent went off to enjoy the luxury of a power shave and I liberated some salmon and petits pois from the dripping freezers, emptied out the rest of the contents on principle (it was too late for them to re-freeze), and set about decoding the various cooking appliances in the kitchen. We had not eaten all day – it was too hot – and the prospect of a proper meal made me realise I was starving. I decided to do things in style, laying one end of the dining table and adding a tall vase with a single scarlet flower to my culinary efforts. We had chilled a bottle of Montrachet and a priceless Château Yqem 1959 for dessert. There was nothing else since the last of the ice-cream had dissolved beyond any possibility of reconstitution and the two gateaux I had unearthed from the murky depths of the third freezer were distressingly soggy. By the time we sat down to dinner the sky was turning green and darkness was stealing softly and swiftly over the land, though the sea still mirrored the afterglow of day. '*Saumon medusé*,' I told Vincent. 'Shipwrecked salmon. Friday potatoes – pre-peeled from a tin in the store room.'

'Peas Ben Gunn?' Vincent offered. 'Why the candles? We don't need them now.'

'I'm economising on energy,' I said. 'I've been worrying about the greenhouse effect all afternoon. Besides, they're so romantic . . . don't you think?'

Vincent did not deign to comment. Instead, he jerked a thumb in the direction of the music centre. 'Mahler?' he queried maliciously.

'Not with dinner.'

'We were always having power-cuts at Weatherfray,' he remarked towards the end of the salmon. 'The wiring must have been prehistoric. Even when the electricity did work the place was so vast and gloomy any sort of lighting seemed to shrivel, as if it was afraid to try to disturb the shadows. On reflection, the real solution was probably very simple. My aunt was given to false economies. It would have been just like her to insist on forty-watt bulbs.'

'Were you poor in those days?' I asked. 'Growing up in aristocratic penury?'

'My aunt was poor,' said Vincent. 'It took her that way. Anyhow, she's the sort of person who considers luxury – or indeed comfort – rather bourgeois. My father, as I think I told you, was indecently rich. And incidentally, *not* aristocratic. His title was earned, not inherited. However, we don't tell the Americans: they don't know the difference and I should hate to disillusion them. They think I'm a maverick offshoot of the nobility: the feudal British class system tore my parents apart and I was cast off for no other crime than my black hair and Roman nose and an excess of red corpuscles in the blood.'

'Sell the movie rights,' I quipped.

He didn't react. 'I was remembering . . . the last time I saw my father. In the words of the painting. There was a storm, and a power-cut. Much like now. The storm wasn't up to hurricane standards, of course, but it was still pretty effective: lots of percussion and strobe lightning. Weatherfray always provided the right background for a row. I looked at the candle and thought of that soliloquy from *Macbeth*—'

'Tomorrow and tomorrow and tomorrow?'

'—yes, that one – and relapsed into the usual trite meditation about the frailty of human life—'

'As one does.'

'Shut up, Micky – but I never imagined it could be snuffed out so abruptly. Not my father's life, anyway. Like *that*.' He pinched one of the two candle flames between thumb and forefinger: a thread of smoke rose upwards from the blackened wick. 'We both said various unforgivable things and I strode off in a fury, out into the rain. I didn't know he would die. When I heard it, it seemed so . . .'

'Meaningless?' I supplied, relighting the candle. 'A life, a death, a journey into nowhere. Wasn't that it?'

'Precisely,' said Vincent. 'Sometimes, Micky, you're too smart for your own good. You should cultivate stupidity: it would make you much better company.'

After dinner, we left the washing-up and took our Sauternes into the bedroom. 'It saves time later,' said Vincent. We lay on the bed sipping the nectar of the gods and let the talk meander where it wished. Or, given a little manipulation, where I wished.

'It seems to me,' I asseverated, 'that you have a problem with love. The few people you've loved, you also hated. You can't love without hate, you can't hate without love. Except for your mother. Have you ever loved any other woman?' As a question, it was perilously direct and might put him on his guard, but I was relying on the wine. 'You can't be completely obsessed by your Oedipus complex, surely. There must have been someone, some time. When you were an awkward adolescent with spots and teenage angst. Who was the first woman you slept with?'

'God knows,' said Vincent vaguely. 'It was after a party. I must have been twelve, thirteen. I was very drunk on two glasses of cider and I thought I was so bloody daring. She was somebody's sister. I don't remember her name.'

'You wouldn't.'

'I remember the first girl to whom I gave an orgasm,' Vincent went on, looking at me sidelong from under lowered eyelids. 'Catherine, Katrina – Catriona. They used to call her the Fat Cat. She was a not-so-innocent village maiden. The sultry, sensual, earth-mother type.'

'You mean big tits?'

He laughed. 'That's it. I shared her with my cousin Richard. As far as I can remember, we both had a hand in her knickers at once. The results were stunning. The earth mother moved. It changed my whole view of the sex act. I went home and threw D.H. Lawrence on the fire.'

D.H. Lawrence . . .? But Vincent had given me the opening I required, and I was forced to pass up this tempting byway. 'You keep mentioning this cousin of yours,' I said. 'This is the one you were brought up with, right? Do you still see him?'

'No.'

The monosyllable was brusque, intentionally off-putting but – I was used to Vincent's manner by now. I paused, topped up his wineglass, and refilled mine for good measure. 'Were you very close?' I asked.

Vincent's lips thinned in the faint grimace which I had come to associate with the moments when, for whatever reason, he felt the need of self-mockery. 'Leave it, Micky,' he said. 'It's a dull story and you've probably heard it all before. Let's fuck.'

'Not yet. I don't know the name for a complex about a cousin but you've evidently got one. To add to the Oedipus complex. I'm intrigued. This is the one you won't talk about: it must be serious. Lie down on the couch – oh, you are – and unburden your soul.'

'I haven't got a soul,' said Vincent. 'You know, I'll bet Pandora was just like you. I don't suppose she really cared about the contents of that famous jar; she simply couldn't resist prising off the lid.'

He kissed me and I ceased to press him, mentally crossing my fingers. In due course my patience was rewarded.

'We were like brothers, Richard and I,' Vincent said with a slightly self-conscious brand of sarcasm. 'Predictable, isn't it? If you see that phrase on a film poster or in the blurb on the back of a novel you know immediately what's going to happen. They'll end up on opposite sides in a civil war, or fighting a duel for love of the same woman, or cutting each other's throats at the conference table over control of their father's steel empire. It's as inevitable as fate. They were like brothers – the most essential ingredient of twentieth-century revenge tragedy. Yes, Richard and I were just like brothers. Cain and Abel. I had brains but he had morals. I won fights; he won friends. I got the girls; he got the Girl. In this case, my girl. Well, you ordered a girl, didn't you?'

'What was she like?'

'She was so pretty that clocks stopped at the sight of her. One of those clocks was our brotherly affiliation. We had been ticking away comfortably since childhood and then along came Crystal and boing! there was nothing left but a few busted springs. While I languished in Wormwood Scrubs Crystal moved in with Richard. They got married and lived happily ever after, at least for a while. It was all tedious beyond belief.'

'Did you love her?' I demanded.

'Hardly. I just stopped. Like a clock. When the ticking started again I could scarcely recall what she looked like.'

'But you remembered Richard,' I said. 'I see.'

'I'd known him longer,' Vincent said with something of a snap. 'Good old Richard. He's that kind, you know. A chip off the old block, the salt of the earth, one of the best. I should have found it tiresome but I didn't. I'm told he has charm, whatever that is. Anyway, it's something I haven't got.'

'The best definition I ever read was by Margery Allingham,' I affirmed. 'Charm is the ability to make people believe you like them. No wonder you haven't got any.'

'Richard really does like people,' Vincent said. 'That's the trouble. He likes people too easily and too often. No discrimination, let alone prejudgement. He's never heard of loathing at first sight. He even liked me, poor bastard. And I presume he liked Crystal – if there was anything there to like. It's strange: I was totally fascinated by her, for about five minutes – I daresay it's a record for me – but I couldn't tell you if she was clever or dumb, what she thought, what she felt. She was as mysterious as a waxwork, and almost as lifelike. Her mind was as unfathomable as a puddle reflecting the stars. It wasn't until long afterwards that I dipped a finger in and found half an inch of water and two inches of mud. I doubt if she ever cared much for me or anyone; her principal motivation was the comfort and well-being of Crystal Winter. With Richard, she must have thought she was on to a good thing. My father had always – how can I put it – *appreciated* Richard more than me. When I blotted my copybook beyond redemption Crys probably hoped Richard would scoop the pool. She must have been pissed off when he only got Weatherfray. I expect that was when she first thought about giving him the push.'

'And you?' I said. 'What did you think about?'

'Hell knows.' He was silent for what seemed like several minutes. 'What do you think about when your father dies and manages to spit in your eye even from the grave? And my dear cousin – my brother-cum-best-friend – having pinched my girl when I was temporarily out of the game, proceeds to pinch my bloody ancestral home to boot. In this case, a steel-capped boot straight in the balls.' He paused, the muscles of his face flexing and hardening. 'I thought about getting even. Teaching him a few of the lessons life had taught me.'

'Revenge,' I said. 'Time-wasting and melodramatic. Unquote.'

'Bugger that. He'd always had everything easy. Fate had smiled on him, a big sunny smile that probably echoed his own. I decided to show him that even the smiles of providence are full of teeth.'

'What did you do?'

'He was going into business solo. Aircraft design: some sort of engineering consultancy. I offered to back him. I knew he'd take me up on it: he thought it was natural for me to help him out, in spite of everything. The smile of providence. Anyway, at the last moment I pulled out. He went bankrupt. Served him right for giving me those interminable lectures on aeronautics every evening.' The words were flippant but there was a kind of pain in his face, as if he were deliberately punishing himself, in some twisted way, driving red-hot needles under his own fingernails. Or maybe I was seeing only what I wished to see, through the distorting lens of an insidious personal bias.

'And Crystal?' I whispered. 'Did you say – she left him?'

'Of course she left him. She could hardly wait.' A glimmer of sadistic amusement lit his features. 'I didn't even have to try. She bolted into my arms like a homing pigeon, straight into the pie.

"Oh Vincent, Vincent, it was always you. Only you." I almost think she believed it herself. She was beautifully convincing. The trouble is, once you've solved the mystery it isn't mysterious any more. I simply wanted to take her from Richard. When you've plumbed the depths of the puddle . . .'

'You threw her out,' I concluded quietly. Crystal's curiously ambivalent attitude during her interview – the flashes of frankness, concealment concealed – was suddenly explained. I had never imagined I could feel sympathy for her but I experienced an impromptu flicker of insight: the glimpse of a fragile ego, carefully cherished, shielded from harsh realities, shattered into smithereens by a single ruthless gesture. Poor Crystal. Where would she go, without her ego? What would she do? She did not have the innate toughness of coarser mortals. I sensed that she must be both vulnerable and desperate, a potentially dangerous combination.

But Vincent had not given the matter a thought.

'We had unfinished business,' he said. 'I finished it. You can call it revenge if you like. It was . . . an inevitable ending.'

'Did you enjoy it?'

'What?'

'*Did you enjoy it?*' I wanted to hurt him. I wanted to smash my fist wherever I thought there might be a weakness or a bruise, plunge a knife into every old wound. 'Did you laugh out loud? Did you open a bottle of champagne? Did you give yourself a fucking medal?'

'Micky—'

'What did you expect me to say? Oh Vincent, aren't you clever? Aren't you wonderful? So devious, so cold-blooded, so petty-minded – obsessive – destructive – puerile – *futile*. Revenge isn't a splendid achievement: it's an act of self-annihilation. An eye for an eye for an eye until the whole world has gone blind. Am I supposed to respect you, because there was no profit motive, because you actually put yourself out for a principle? You wouldn't know a principle if you sat on one and it bit you in the arse.' My limbs seemed to be shaking: incomprehensible tears started in my eyes. 'Dear God, is that the only thing you can find to do with all that energy and intelligence? Shabby little plots, nursery jealousy puffed up into an enormous bubble full of nothing? You have so much – brains, imagination, passion – and it's all wasted, wasted. You talk about your mother burning herself up from within but what about you? You're poisoning yourself with your own bile, feeding the worm that's eating you. You despise Sebastiano but at least he loves Jolanda. When you've alienated anyone foolhardy enough to care for you you'll envy her Sebastiano: do you know that? You'll have nothing but your own bitterness. No one could ever love you. No one.'

I didn't know why it was so important to emphasise that but I said it anyway. I said it again and again. He was as he had made himself, vile, loveless, unlovable. No one could ever . . .

'What about you?' Vincent's voice was hard and strangely raw. 'You with the high ideals. Couldn't you manage it? The angel redeeming Satan: that kind of thing. The formula is a little banal but don't let that stop you.'

'Angels are on Christmas cards,' I said. 'I can't live up to my ideals and I couldn't live down to yours. There isn't a formula for love. I don't know what love is – I wish I did – but I do know what it isn't. In any case, you don't want to be redeemed. You want me to adore you uncritically, to stand by my man like it says in the song. I can't, Vincent, I can't. That sort of woman went out with the manual typewriter. I can't change and you can't change and come Armageddon we'll be on opposite sides, just like I told you. That's destiny. I'm not sure what exactly it is you're asking—'

'I'm not asking for anything!' The violence in his tone startled both of us. 'All this is hypothesis. You're crying. You're crying over a hypothesis. Stupid girl.'

He smudged the angry tear under my eye with one finger and at that same instant we were both conscious that we were lying on a bed, that he was naked to the waist, that I was wearing a loose shirt – *his* shirt – and very little else. His bare torso was all rib pattern and muscle pattern; under his threadbare jeans the ridge of his erect penis was clearly visible. I didn't know precisely what had stimulated his erection: the behaviour of the penis has always been a mystery to me. As an emotional gauge, it reacts to much more than elementary desire. All I knew was that, for whatever reason, copulation had become necessary and urgent. There was a pause while we looked at each other, and then he was pulling my knickers down and I was tugging at his zip, frantic and clumsy, the bulge in his pants swelling and straining against my fumbling hands. He split the first condom, yanked on another with awkward haste. We were rolling around so that I was half on top, half underneath, caught in a muddle of elbows and knees, tangled thighs, misplaced kisses. Then Vincent located the appropriate hole and thrust himself into me, thrust deep and hard, like a sword in its sheath, like a spear in my heart, like possession, like rape, like love. I did not think about power any more, nor the tape that was still running, nor the game of truth and lies, but only of the absolute and overwhelming importance of his penis inside me, *fucking* me, the breathless essential act. His pleasure; my pleasure; there was no other priority. Just short of a climax he withdrew, sliding down to thigh level, turning over, turning me with him.

'Sit on my face.'

'You'll stifle.'

'*Sit on my face.*'

I obeyed, letting him spread my legs, lowering myself on to his tongue. Although I was in the dominant position I felt oddly helpless, my whole body surrendered to the control of his mouth and his hands. Vincent was both ungentle and ungentlemanly, grasping my buttocks and forcing me down on him while he burrowed into me, nibbled me, devoured me at his leisure. Eventually I came – and came and came and came, coaxed and coerced to a pitch of agonised bliss, gasping, softly screaming, clutching the pillow like the drowning man with the proverbial straw. Afterwards, Vincent re-entered me almost immediately, taking me from behind as I lay limply in a state of anti-climactic prostration. He penetrated cautiously, struggling to delay imminent orgasm, arms and legs locked around me in a grip that was part embrace, part wrestling hold. I felt boneless, resistless, willingly subjugated. At last he could contain himself no longer; his body stretched and stiffened, quivering with the onset of ecstasy like the throb of an arrow in the bullseye, or the vibration of a harp string after a note of unendurable sweetness. Then there was a long time when we didn't move and barely spoke, clinched in mutual exhaustion, laved in each other's sweat.

'Micky . . .'

'Yes?'

'You're a pain in the arse.'

'So are you.'

'I like you a lot.' His voice was very low, a murmur scarcely audible, so reluctant that I wondered when he had last said it, or if it had ever been said.

I responded automatically. 'Don't be ridiculous.'

I like you a lot, Vincent. You're a crook in legal armour, an emotional vandal, an educated barbarian, wantonly vindictive and as harmful to all around you as a radio-active leak. If I reduce you to a balance sheet, credits versus debits, you deserve everything that Alun Craig and I can possibly throw at you. But I like you. I wish I didn't but I do, I do. I enjoyed the fight, the risk, the hurricane, the bed. I respect you, as I never respected any of *Quest's* other targets. I like the drive which you misuse, the nerve you should have lost, the irony with which you dismiss your own shortcomings. In your crooked way, you're honest. You don't pretend, you don't try to impress, you don't give a damn. A human being is more than a balance sheet, more than an equation of good and bad. I like you for the soulfire whose existence you deny, the flame which fuels your strength and corrodes your heart. Sooner or later – probably sooner – I shall walk out of here with those damned tapes and set about the process of destroying you. But I shan't win. You'll fight back; you'll survive. I know that, and I'm glad.

Oh, *bloody* hell.

'What did you say?'

'I said: *bloody* hell.'

Vincent eased himself out of me and rolled sleepily away. 'Why?'

'I felt like it. What were we talking about?'

'When?'

'Before.'

'You were telling me you couldn't adore me uncritically.' He smiled faintly. 'You got quite worked up about it. After that, you started boring on about the end of the world again. You obviously have a fixation with the subject.'

'You have a fixation with crockery, as I recall,' I said. 'It's clear we're totally incompatible. I always thought so.'

'*Stronzate*,' said Vincent. 'Come the last great battle, we can throw plates at each other.'

He pulled me into his arms, cradling me, as usual, against his shoulder.

'If you sleep like that you'll snore,' I pointed out.

I think it was the last thing I said.

I awoke before dawn, knowing it was time to go. The knowledge was there waiting for me as soon as I opened my eyes, as if the decision had been made in my subconscious long before and while I slept it had worked its way to the surface of my mind. Time to go. A realisation as harsh as a command; a tightening of the stomach which I could not explain. I had the information I needed; the job was done. The previous night I had come to the edge of something I could not see, a mountain or an abyss: a step further was a step too far. I must go *now*.

I slid out of bed as quietly as I could, half afraid Vincent would wake, half wishing for it. He stirred slightly, shifted his position; I tugged the duvet up to his breast. Goodbye, Vincent. I wish you good luck, and bad. I picked up his shirt, my under-wear, my bag and contents. From the spare room across the corridor I collected the crumpled remnants of my silver dress: I wanted to leave nothing of myself behind. In the suite of wardrobes there I found a pair of trainers, presumably Irving's, only two or three sizes too big for me. I salved my conscience with the assurance that I would just be borrowing them: I could return them by post or leave them with Phyl. I dressed in the living room, in the dark. Everything was so quiet I imagined I could hear Vincent's breathing, slow and even, filling the whole house. There was no other sound but a solitary bird, somewhere in the garden, piping in the dawn. It struck me as faintly ominous, a whistling herald announcing sunrise, departure, the opening of the door back to reality.

Have you not heard

that Silence where no birds are, yet something pipeth like a bird?

I stood by the door – the front door – shivering a little, though it was not cold. Vincent had neglected the internal locks; all I had to do was turn the handle. I bit my lip at an echoing click, but at least the hinges did not squeak or groan. I listened; but nothing moved, no one woke or called, there was only a sigh that floated down the stairs, the whisper of my fancy, like a sleeper whose dream changes. I slipped out into the twilight like a matutinal ghost, closing the door behind me, and sped as fast as my flapping shoes would allow down the drive to the road.

It took me nearly an hour to get back to the Ashleys'. I walked for some time, heading east – from West Point, there was little alternative – before two policeman in a jeep pulled up to ask me where I was going and did I need help. I explained I had been concussed in a car accident during the hurricane, had been cared for by kindly strangers, and was now trying to get home. When I mentioned Win Ashley the police became very helpful indeed, insisting on driving me the rest of the way although, in the aftermath of meteorological disaster, they must have had better things to do. I saw scattered damage but they assured me it could have been much worse, with only one death from a falling tree and six at sea. They were plainly veterans of many hurricanes and adopted a connoisseur's attitude, reminiscing about devastations they had known. I responded automatically. At the gates I got out, thanked them, and went up to the house.

I was admitted by a maid who instantly set up a screech as if I had returned from the dead instead of a three-day absence. The din started a chain reaction which presently produced Win, in embroidered silk pyjamas worthy of a Noel Coward play, and Phyl, too distracted to remember her negligée, hurtling downstairs into my arms with a squeal like an air-raid siren. She reached up to kiss me; Win embraced me with genuine relief.

'Micky, darling' – Phyl's words came tumbling off her tongue in even more of a rush than usual – 'what happened to you? Where have you *been*? We were so worried – I wanted to call the police but Pooh wouldn't let me, he said we might spoil your plans and if anything awful had happened we'd hear soon enough, and he went to see the Langelaans and Pete said you'd gone with Vincent, and you were drunk, and Vincent was drunk, and he – Pete – he was so stupid, so *stupid*, he didn't seem to care at all. I've been so anxious I couldn't sleep all night for thinking of you—'

'Which night?' I asked in an attempt to stem the flow.

'Last night, the night before, any night. Darling, what *happened*? You look tanned, only sort of pale too. A bit green. You're not well. You must have some tea . . .'

'She looks faint,' said Win. 'Come on, Micky.'

He took my arm and they swept me into the breakfast room, ordered tea, coffee, and anything else that occurred to them, and Phyl's maid, who was unwilling to miss the story, was dispatched forcibly to fetch the forgotten negligée. I said: 'I'm all right,' but nobody paid any attention and in fact I felt, if not faint, rather weak about the knees, like someone in shock after a bad accident.

'Phyl,' I said when she finally sat down beside me, 'you must tell Patrice to pack my things. I've got to go. I've got to get off the island. If there isn't a plane I'll take a boat, or swim, or something, but I must get away.'

'*What happened?*' Phyl wailed. 'If you don't tell me *immediately* I shall go mad. Do you want to be responsible for putting me in an asylum? What happened? What happened?'

'Calm down,' said Win. 'Let her tell us in her own time.'

'I went with Vincent,' I said, 'like Pete told you. I suppose we were both pretty drunk. I mean, I know we were. Vincent crashed the car, and we had to walk to West Point. And then I – I went to bed with him.'

'Was it good?' Phyl demanded with inexcusable eagerness.

'He's a repressed homosexual,' Win asserted, assuming a wistful mien. 'I'll bet he's into sodomy.'

'He isn't into sodomy,' I said. 'He's into cunnilingus. Lots of it.'

'It was good,' Phyl confirmed with a sigh. 'What next? Why didn't you come home?'

'No transport,' I said. 'The power was off. The phone was off. We were stuck. There was nothing to do so . . . we talked. For two days, we just talked. He told me all about himself and I taped it like Mata bloody Hari. It went perfectly. Like a dream. Even the hurricane was perfect, just as if we'd laid it on.' I added: 'I feel rather sick.' I did. Reality was beginning to hit me, in Phyl's rounded eyes, in the twist of Win's smile. The idyll was over; the brutal fact of what I had done stared me in the face and punched me in the stomach.

'You mean,' Phyl said, 'you got all the gen for your programme from Vincent himself?'

I nodded. 'He'll come looking for me,' I said. 'He'll come here. He thinks you're a featherbrain with just enough wit to marry money, so—'

'Thanks,' said Phyl indignantly.

'—so be vague, be scatty, be mildly surprised at his intrusion. You don't know me well, you haven't seen me. I did a flit. Oh, and give him these.' I kicked off the trainers. 'I think they're Irving's. Say I left them with the servants.'

'I suppose I shouldn't ask what happened to your party shoes?' Phyl remarked. 'And the dress? Did Vincent tear it off you in the extremity of passion?'

'No,' I said, pulling the silver tatters out of my bag. Phyl surveyed them regretfully. 'It got ripped in the car crash. I lost the shoes, too. I'm terribly sorry. I'll pay you back . . .'

'Don't be silly,' Phyl said. 'It's only a dress. And it did what we bought it for, didn't it? I think I shall give it a beautiful funeral. It died in the execution of its duty. Good: here's the tea. Darling—'

'I can't,' I said. 'I really have to go. I daren't wait. If Vincent finds me—'

'He won't.' Win got to his feet with an air of decision. 'Sit here; drink your tea. I'll call the airport and arrange a plane. Where do you want to go?'

'Barbados, but—'

'Fine. I said sit *down*, Micky. And don't start moaning about the money. We're in this together, as the saying goes. All for one and one for all. At least, I hope so: it would be very unfair of you to cut Phyl and I out when we've come this far. Think of us as the Three Musketeers; I always loved those frilly shirts and tight satin breeches.' He patted my shoulder with an exquisitely manicured hand. 'You stay here, I'll sort out your flight and when you're ready I'll drive you to the airport. If Vincent shows up too quickly we'll hide you in my mother's Oriental tea chest. He can hardly demand to search the house, after all.'

'Pooh,' I said simply, 'you're wonderful.' It was a regrettable lapse: I had vowed never to call him Pooh. 'It's just . . . you don't understand. When the programme comes out, he'll know. He'll know it was me. I don't want you two implicated. He must believe I duped you the way I duped him.'

'I appreciate that,' said Win. 'Stop fussing and eat your breakfast.'

He went out and I sat facing a slice of melon which should have made my mouth water, feeling as if my entire digestive system had gone on strike.

'What about bacon and eggs?' Phyl suggested. I blenched. 'Buttered toast? Muesli? Smoked salmon?'

'No thanks,' I said. 'I'm just not hungry, that's all.'

I added, rather pointlessly: 'I'm sorry. I mean, about everything.'

'Oh, Micky.' Phyl held my hand and stroked my hair. Seated, we were near enough in height to make this feasible.

'Farzad was right,' I continued. 'I had no business to involve you in all this.'

'But I had fun!' Phyl protested. And, after a pause: 'Did you?'

'That question is inadmissible.'

'It's *honest*.' Phyl studied me with the ruthless candour that can only exist between two women, never between men. 'Well, did you?'

I didn't attempt to answer. Presently, Phyl launched into a description of the side-effects of Hurricane Anneka, by way of a diversion. I exerted myself to eat a spoonful of melon. My tastebuds told me it was melon, but it went down like uncooked dough.

In due course, Win came back. 'It's all fixed,' he said. 'Patrice is packing your case. We laid out some clothes for you: I thought you might want to change.'

'Of course.' I realised, belatedly, that I was still barefoot and somewhat inadequately clad.

'Is that Vincent's shirt?' Win enquired. 'Giorgio. Very pretty. What are you going to do with it?'

'I'll keep it,' I said. 'Souvenir.'

'A scalp for your teepee?'

I smiled wanly. 'Not funny.'

Later, when I was changed, shod, packed and ready, Win preceded me out to the car and Phyl gave me an abrupt hug. 'You won't hurt yourself too much, will you?' she said with a perception all the more devastating because I was not quite sure what it was she had perceived.

We drove off, leaving her waving from the doorway. I wanted to cry, although I have never been the sort of person who weeps over my friends. I had tried to thank Win, and to apologise, but he would have neither.

'Just remember to phone,' he said. 'We want to hear the end of the story.'

At Praline Airport I had my passport checked at speed and got into the waiting Cessna. Up till the very last moment I had been expecting Vincent to materialise, like a demon in a pantomime, calling my name, calling me back. But the plane lurched into the air and the threat – or possibility – diminished with the runway. The island of Dominique receded, the roads shrinking, the mountain levelling out, until it was only a piece of vivid cartography against an aquatint of sea. The engine roar drowned out speech and thought. I sat in grateful numbness while the Cessna bumped over a cloud and climbed, like Icarus, towards the sun.

4

Vincent slept late. A blind over the window excluded the sunlight, all but a thin gold thread along the edge which crawled across the bed and climbed, like a luminous scribble, over the ridge of his body. Artificially cooled air belied the tropical heat outside. Around ten he began to wake, taking his time, as lazy as a cat, stretching, rolling over, lifting an eyelid a millimetre or so and then latching it down again to relapse into a doze. He realised he was alone but was not unduly disturbed: he could hear sounds of movement from downstairs, a tap running, padding footsteps, a door that opened and shut. When Micky did not reappear irritation roused him completely. He got up, ignored the presence of an attendant bathrobe, and descended the stairs, stark naked and optimistically erect, intent on requesting a replay of the preceding night's activities. The maid who had returned after the hurricane gave a muted shriek and stood staring with widened eyes, unable to drag her mesmerised gaze from Vincent's anatomy.

'Where's Micky?' Vincent said sharply, wasting no time on false modesty or embarrassment.

'Sir!'

'Micky. The girl who's staying here. Has she gone for a swim?' He was glancing round the room as he spoke and the sense of something missing slid into the back of his mind like a vague shadow of unease. Of course: the bag. That damned bag to which she had clung so persistently, through storm and sex, trailing it after her into every predicament. He couldn't recall seeing it in the bedroom and it certainly wasn't down here. His anxiety became irrationally acute. He brushed aside the bewildered maid and ran, still naked, into the garden; but there was no one there. Down at the beach the shadows of the rocks lay long and dark across the empty sand. The sea was like green glass, the moving ripples catching the sun, every so often, with a swift flash of reflected light. There was no abandoned clothing, no faithful bag. No Micky.

He went back to the house, showered, dressed. He couldn't seem to think clearly about the situation – about why she should have gone, without a farewell, a note, a forwarding address – he only knew that he had to find her. The maid had driven there in an ancient Volkswagen Beetle and he appropriated it in arbitrary fashion, removing the keys from her nerveless hold and allowing her no time for the court of appeal. On the way out he remarked, over his shoulder: 'Those three freezers in the storeroom thawed out; the stuff inside them can't be re-frozen. When you leave you'd better take it all down to the village. It's stupid to waste it.' And, as a concession: 'I'll be back with the car.'

It gave him the glimmer of a virtuous glow – or the quirk of a crooked smile – doing something of which he knew Micky would approve. Silly of her to worry, but she was that type. The kind of person who would agonise about anything: the environment, the state of the nation, the end of the world, the deteriorating contents of three overstocked freezers. Not his type at all. Rather like that woman he had bedded in connection with the Walmsley Village project, Jan Horrocks, wife of some fool on the planning committee. Only she had been angry and intense; Micky – thank God – was flippant, indifferent, subtle. Last night was the one occasion when she had shown anger, a swift sudden flame which had blazed up into violent love-making and subsided in tranquillity. Why the hell had she gone?

There was no point in speculation. He would find her, he was convinced, with Phyllida Khorman; she had nowhere else to go. He would tell her she was a bloody nuisance, dragging him out of bed when what he wanted was a long lie-in and leisurely intercourse. Whatever was wrong, he would diminish it with his sarcasm, tease it into unimportance, persuade or compel her into the Volkswagen and bring her back to West Point for the rest of his allotted holiday. Maybe longer. He felt so certain – yet beneath his confidence there was a vein of doubt, a fear, a question. Suddenly, even his certainties were only skin-deep.

He took several wrong turnings before he found the Ashleys' house. The butler opened the door, words of denial carefully rehearsed, but Vincent walked straight past him, through the living room and on to the terrace. Phyl was lying by the pool, her bikini straps under her arms, substantial breasts bursting from twin cups of ruched Lycra. Dark glasses spanned her nose and a copy of *Cosmo* lay open at her side, a scene-setting gesture to indicate the essential frivolity of her outlook. When she saw Vincent she sat up, dipping her glasses with one hand and scooping her falling bikini bra against her bosom with the other. It was a manoeuvre few women could have achieved without losing either their poise or their decency, but Phyl managed it. Her eyebrows flew upward, her mouth formed an artistic 'oh'.

'Vincent Savage,' she said. 'How . . . how delightful. I'm afraid I—'

'I'm looking for a girl,' Vincent interrupted.

Phyl succumbed to her worse self. 'Really?' she said on a note of baffled astonishment. '*Here?*'

'Not that sort of girl,' he snapped. 'The one I want was staying with you. Micky. Micky Annesley.'

'Oh . . . yes.' Phyl frowned as if chasing an elusive recollection. The event in question had clearly happened so long ago it was unreasonable to expect her to remember it. 'She *was* here, yes. I can't think why I invited her, but you know how it is. It kind of slipped out before I could get a hold of myself. Anyway, she sloped off after Deirdre's party. I expect she went with some man – although she isn't really *like that*, if you follow me. She was frightfully boring at school. Much more interested in swotting for exams than going out with boys.'

'You didn't worry about her,' Vincent enquired, diverted, 'going missing in a hurricane?'

'No. Why?' Phyl looked amazed. 'I *never* worry about people. It gives you wrinkles.'

There was a pause while she observed the rigidity about his mouth with private satisfaction. *Oh, Micky, Micky, what have you done?*

'Well,' said Vincent, 'you might like to know that she went with

me. I took care of her.' The small matter of the car smash was omitted or forgotten. 'She was bloody lucky: God knows what would
have happened to her if I hadn't. May I suggest that in future you
show rather more solicitude for errant guests?'

Phyl made a little-girl moue, as if she had had her hand slapped
for raiding the cookie jar.

'And now,' said Vincent, 'she's missing again. Have you seen
her?'

'People don't change, do they?' Phyl averred, seizing an opportunity. 'She was always running away when we were kids. She
bolted once after an RE lesson because the teacher told her off for
saying she didn't believe in hell. They found her hours later, just sitting in the middle of a field. She said she wanted to *think*. Can you
imagine that?'

Vincent, who was beginning to feel he had strayed into an alternative universe, or was trapped between the pages of a particularly
inane modern novel, did his best to jerk the conversation back on
course.

'Just tell me, has she been here?' he reiterated. 'Did she come
back? She must have had some luggage with her.'

'She picked that up this morning,' Phyl said promptly. 'I didn't
see her; the servants told me. I thought it was a bit off, myself; she
didn't even stop to say thank you. Oh, and . . . she left a pair of
shoes. Running shoes. I'm sure they don't belong to her. Are they
yours?'

'Irving's, probably. Didn't you—'

'Good heavens,' Phyl interjected. 'I had no idea she could be so
prolific. It just goes to show what my mother always used to say. No
matter how well you know people, you never *really* know them, do
you?'

'Profound,' said Vincent. 'Listen: I have to get in touch with
her. Do you know where she's gone? Do you have her address in
England?'

'Well, of course,' said Phyl, 'I did have. I wrote it down in my
pink address book. Or was it the blue one? I was looking for it only
yesterday and I couldn't find it anywhere. Is it very important?'

'Very.'

'Why?'

Vincent had had enough. 'She pinched the silver,' he said

shortly. 'Irving will be furious. A set of teaspoons: George the Fourth. Irreplaceable.'

'*No!*' Phyl fielded this latest ball with relish. 'Of course, there was an incident at school – but it was just after her father died, and they said she was emotionally disturbed and couldn't help it. She was sent to a psychiatrist. I wonder – my God, she had the run of this house for days! My *jewellery*! Win's Japanese prints! Patrice! Patrice!'

It was an entertaining position, Phyl reflected. She knew Vincent was talking nonsense, Vincent knew she was talking nonsense, but they both adhered resolutely to their unlikely fantasy. Vincent evidently had no suspicion that his hostess was being deliberately obstructive, doubtless attributing her vagaries to a single-digit IQ and a penchant for self-dramatisation. In the circumstances, Phyl went as far as she dared. It took twenty minutes to check her jewellery and other valuables, a further ten to search for non-existent address books.

'When's Win due back?' Vincent asked.

'I don't know.' Phyl's manner implied a brush with a boundless area of unexplored knowledge. She didn't know, she had never known, it was extraordinary – and impertinent – to assume that she would know anything.

Vincent drove off in mingled anger and exasperation.

He went to the airport. Exhaustive enquiry drew a blank on routine flights and the departure of the Cessna, thanks to the Ashley influence and Win's flair for comprehensive bribery, was mantled in a veil of discretion. Win had subsequently gone into town to have a word with the manageress of the boutique, determined to seal off any points of potential leakage. While he was leaving he saw Vincent driving past, much too fast for a built-up area, heading for the harbour. His thoughts ran on similar lines to Phyl's: 'Oh, Micky, Micky . . .'

Vincent had an unproductive morning, followed by an unproductive afternoon. Back at West Point he telephoned the airport for a further harangue, then the ferry, the coastguards, Hannibal in Los Angeles, and even Pete Langelaan. Unfortunately, he got Deirdre.

'Vincent darling, I can't remember every insignificant girl who turns up at one of my parties. You know what it's like: you try so hard to be particular but whatever you do *someone* always manages to sneak in. Oh, she came with a friend, did she? Well, they always say that. Phyl Khorman? No wonder. Phyl is an absolute darling – honestly, one of my best friends – but generous to a fault, as they say. She'd invite a tramp to dinner if he told her he was short of a sandwich. Who was this girl? The one with the blonde crew-cut? Yes I *do* remember her – she was wearing a lovely model, a Lagerfeld; she would have looked like two cents' worth of nothing without it. She never bought *that* on a PA's salary. Oh, television. Darling, what a drag. Ten to one she's in admin on one of the evangelical channels. Pete said he turned on the charm with her but she was very heavy going.'

'She's English,' said Vincent. 'English TV. Hardly evangelical. One of the few things to be said for my native country is that the Archbishop of Canterbury has yet to host his own chat show. No doubt it will come.'

He rang off with ill-controlled brusquerie.

His conversation with Hannibal was in some respects even more disheartening.

'You lost a blonde?' His henchman was obviously puzzled. 'Vin, what's got into you? We got more blondes in LA than there are maggots in a corpse. You lose one, you find another. There ain't no shortage. I'll wrap one up and send her out express – oh, all right, all right. Let's start again. You went to the party and you met this girl. You don't know nothing about her except her name . . . yeah, and her family history, and her boring job, and her – *what*? Her bleeding philosophy of bleeding life! Fuck me. OK, go on. You got off with her in the thick of the hurricane – you sure it wasn't *really* the earth that moved? – and she stayed around a couple of days, and then she did a bunk. Now nobody seems to know where she came from or where she went. Sounds like bleeding Cinderella. You seen a pumpkin lying around outside?'

'Don't be stupid,' said Vincent. 'Look, she works in television – one of those dreary programmes for masochists who switch on the box over breakfast. It shouldn't be too difficult to trace her. Start checking.'

'BBC or ITV?'

'Yes,' said Vincent unhelpfully. 'Michelle Annesley. Her father was a poet – Second World War. I got the impression he was quite well known.'

'You want me to put the agency on to it?'

'N-no. No, I don't. Do it yourself. It should be straightforward enough.' He poured a glass of Bourbon and drank it, absent-mindedly, without ice, although there was plenty in the fridge. 'I don't see why you're making such heavy weather of this. She's just a girl. All I want to know is where she went, and why. I don't like mysteries.' He had solved the enigma of Crystal long before, plumbing the depths of the puddle; but Micky seemed to be proving herself a bottomless lake. It was ludicrous. Even in such a little while, he had come to know her well – her dry humour, her careless taunts, her hopeless principles, the many facets of her mind and mood. There had been no sphinx-like stillness in her face, no mask to rip away, only the reflection of happiness and unhappiness, courage and regret, the varying imprint of her feelings. He could imagine no reason – no real reason – for her abrupt getaway.

I cannot adore you uncritically . . .

'Vin,' Hannibal's voice travelled effortlessly over the airwaves to reach him, 'you really keen on this girl, or just pissed off 'cause she walked out?'

'Pissed off,' said Vincent, and hung up.

He spent the evening drinking alone, a habit he had never acquired before. The television was boring and he had seen all Irving's videos. He selected a CD at random; it was only after he had put it on that he realised he had inadvertently chosen Mahler. The music came welling out of a dozen speakers as if the orchestra was in the room with him and Klaus Tenstedt was beating him over the head with his baton. He bore it in a spirit of self-flagellation, cursing all technology.

The next day he flew back to LA.

By the time Hannibal drew a blank at the TV stations Vincent had gone beyond surprise. He could think of no motive for Micky to lie – after all, she hadn't tried to represent her job as either glamorous or exciting – yet he felt instinctively that with her departure a door had slammed in his face which would not easily reopen. It was par for the course that there should be no bell or knocker, no letterbox, no door handle, no keyhole. Only an impassable barrier.

Meeting Hannibal's speculative gaze with an expression of stony disinterest, he insisted that it didn't matter, she was one blonde among many (and not even especially pretty); he had already dismissed her from his thoughts. Get London for him; they had work to do.

'Not pretty, right?' Hannibal scowled ponderously. 'Don't like the sound of that. If she's not pretty, why all the panic?'

'I didn't panic,' Vincent said coldly. 'I was merely curious. Forget it. And I didn't say she wasn't pretty, I said not *especially* pretty. She was all right.'

He went to a club that night with wall-to-wall blondes, all of them prettier than Micky. Or so he was able to believe in the Impressionist lighting which left most details of form and feature to the imagination. He bought a drink for one girl, danced with another, snubbed a third. None of them had anything original to say about it. He had a hazy recollection of Richard telling him, years ago, that it was he, and not the women, who lacked conversation, he who failed to communicate, to empathise, to build a relationship. Certainly he had never bared his soul for Crystal, though she had probed, clumsily, possibly considering it her duty to draw him out on his hang-ups. Anyway, his liaison with Crystal had been based on mutual ignorance: revelation had killed it. Since then he had confided only in Richmond, whose advice, at least on some subjects, he rated a little higher than that of Hannibal or Judas Carson. But such confidences were rare and growing rarer. Yet in Micky he had found the ideal listener, critical maybe, mocking, unsympathetic, an idle participant in an interchange of experiences, but never boring, never bored. His eyes scanned the room, wondering if there was another Micky among those California blondes. They must surely have their own tales to tell, their sagas of trauma and trivia, and it was his fault, entirely his fault, that all he could elicit from them was 'hello', 'thank you', and 'fuck off'. But it was no good: he could not be bothered to persist, to suffer their life-stories or their personae. Why ask the question when you do not want to know the answer? He left the club, taking his disillusionment with him. Outside he tossed twenty dollars to a beggar who looked like a junkie.

'Have one on me,' he said. 'Shoot up and die: there's fuck all else to do.'

The next morning, when he remembered, he was seriously annoyed with himself. The gesture had been futile, the words cheap. Normally, he never gave anything to beggars, and he was uncomfortable with his lapse, attributing it variously to weakness, stupidity, alcohol.

'Never deviate from a lifestyle of healthy egotism,' he instructed his startled secretary. 'Generosity can make you feel like shit, particularly if you're not used to it.'

'Are you OK?' she asked, assuming a hangover.

'Of course I am,' Vincent almost snarled.

5

After Dominique, Barbados looked busy, lively and to my eyes rather sleazy. There were fast food restaurants, bars blaring with music, vast hoardings emblazoned with familiar images – the Coca-Cola bottle and the cut in the silk – young men, ostentatiously handsome, sashaying down the sidewalk in search of visiting talent, groups of tourists chattering like starlings, flower-printed girls in twos and threes fingering sarongs, eating ice-cream, brushing off the young men. In some places the sugared-almond paint was peeling from crumbling colonial architecture and the natives stared after the flocks of starlings with the weary, resentful gaze of those who have been permanently short-changed watching those who, albeit without malice aforethought, have change and to spare. The best hotels provided havens of expensive quiet but everywhere else – in the street, on the beach, wherever you took a stroll or paused to rest – someone was trying to sell you something. I didn't blame them: I simply felt tired and harassed, my tolerance factor at a low ebb. Back on expenses, I booked into a hotel on the downside of luxurious, had a shower when what I wanted was a bath, and went to bed for a couple of hours.

In the early evening I returned to the airport and enquired for Windhover Air Taxis. I had decided to give their offices a miss since I had telephoned there several times without result and I was afraid the receptionist would recognise my voice and relapse into routine hostility. Presumably Elizabeth Savage had appealed to her son for assistance, telling him she had put me on the trail entirely for his own good, and he had replied loftily that he would have nothing to do with the sensationalist journalism of the small screen. An admirable attitude which I would have to overcome. I had never seen a picture of him or received an adequate description but I could not help visualising him as a Bogart character, embittered by his wrongs, spending his free time in seedy bars staring lugubriously into a tumbler of Jack Daniels and tossing the occasional caustic rejoinder to the barman. 'He was fun,' Crystal had said; but I could not believe that Richard Garoghan was fun any more. He probably carried her photograph and gazed at it every day, a cynical sneer, cousin to Vincent's, playing about his lips. His much-vaunted charm would have soured, his warmth of heart gone cold, his humour acidulated. Without realising it, I was recreating him in Vincent's image, the good side of the bad guy, a kindred spirit to whom I could really feel akin.

'I'm looking for Richard Garoghan,' I explained when I finally located a Windhover technician. 'I flew with him a few weeks ago and I think I must have left my address book on the plane. I hoped he might have picked it up.' It was a feeble excuse but it didn't matter; if he thought I had a more personal reason for pursuing Richard that would do just as well. Sex is an acceptable motive for almost anything, and on this trip I seemed to be playing the joker in every hand.

The technician was unhelpful, recommending me to try the office, but one of his fellows, having eyed me comprehensively to see if I passed muster, volunteered the information that Richard hung out most evenings in a bar in town. It did not appear to have a name but he gave me directions, adding as a rider that it was not a suitable place for whites or ladies.

'Richard's white,' I pointed out, 'and I'm not a lady.'

But Richard, it transpired, was a special case. The barmaid had adopted him. He was pally with the pal of somebody's pal. He went where he liked and everyone liked him. I had heard all this before. It was depressingly clear that Richard the universal pal lived on even in seedy surroundings, mothered by stray females and probably getting his lugubrious Jack Daniels on the house. I thanked my informant, wrote down the directions, and made my way back to Bridgetown clutching the piece of paper like a treasure map. It took me half an hour to find my goal.

The bar was of a type I recognised at once. There is one in every tourist resort, usually in a back street, entered via an anonymous doorway and undistinguished by any external sign or title. The decor is basic, the clientèle male and often decrepit. The barmaid has the garb and countenance of a recent widow. The jukebox, if there is one, displays a motley selection of music most of which was originally recorded on 78s. There is no fancy lighting, no ethnic dancing, no miniature parasols sprouting from rainbow-coloured cocktails. Even if you speak the native language with fluency, in this particular bar the accents will be as thick as porridge and the local dialect incomprehensible. Men cluster around the tables muttering and sipping the liquor of the region, which is deceptively colourless and invariably lethal. In this version the room was a little larger than usual, the counter a little cleaner. But the ambience was unmistakable. This was the residents' bar, their bolt-hole, safe house: furtive, shabby, and as exclusive as a masonic lodge. Richard, a relative newcomer, was presumably allowed in on sufferance, after making a few of the right friends. (Everybody said he had the knack of making friends.) When I walked in heads turned, muttered conversations stopped and then resumed at a different level. I glanced round. There were no tourists and, except for myself, only one white face. That simplified matters.

'Hello,' I said. 'You must be Richard Garoghan.'

He did not look anything like Bogart. Nor did he look like Vincent's cousin. He had the sort of face that is basically solid, reliable clay on which expression and experience have wrought both their best and their worst, moulding features, drawing and redrawing lines – smile lines, laughter lines, lines of doubt and concentration, quizzical little frown lines, crow's feet around the eyes, a butterfly quirk at the corner of the mouth. His skin was sun-browned and wind-reddened, his nose peeling, his hair bleached on the crown to the colour of straw. The forelock showed a tendency to impede his line of vision which would have made me slightly nervous if I had been an airborne passenger of his. His eyes were very bright against his tan, grey with a nucleus of hazel, so clear that I could see the actual graining of the iris like the weft in raw silk. The stubble on his jaw was probably undesigned, two days' growth of beard which he had been too busy, or too lazy, to shave off. He was not tall – perhaps five feet ten – stocky in build, with big, comfortable shoulders of the kind any damsel in distress would want to cry on. Maybe Crystal had once seen him that way – Crystal the clock-stopper, the mermaid with the Cecil Beaton tail who had lost her voice and thrown herself on to her own Borilous Rocks. I wondered if he knew, or, knowing, if he would care. He looked open to the point of candour, approachable and yet inwardly reserved, like a stately home where most of the rooms are on show to the public except for a few private apartments which are always kept locked. His face betrayed no cherished bitterness, no lingering rancour, just the spark of chronic optimism which is the only secret of eternal youth. I found his very approachability, his air of total and ruthless honesty, unexpectedly daunting. He did not look like a man whose clock was easily stopped.

He studied me with frank appraisal, his gaze pausing on the RAF cap which shaded my forehead.

'You must be my mother's journalist,' he said.

I hadn't intended to lie but it was disconcerting to find him quite so quick on the uptake.

'No,' I said baldly. 'Much as I respect your mother, she didn't hire my services. And in case you were wondering, she didn't send me here.'

'I know.'

'I sent myself. At the expense of Thames Television. Can I buy you a drink?' I pulled out my wallet. 'Or rather, can they?'

'Tell them thank you, but no,' Richard replied. The locked room. 'It was generous of them to send you such a long way for nothing.'

'Can I buy *me* a drink?' I asked. 'Or do I have to know the password?'

The barmaid, to date, had not given me a second look, let alone an offer of service.

'I'll buy you a drink,' said Richard with unscrupulous courtesy, thus putting me not only in the wrong but in his debt. I demurred unsuccessfully. The barmaid responded to his lightest command with a capricious smile and continued to ignore me completely. Two chilled beers arrived soonest. I am not fond of beer but there was bound to be little choice and at least it was wet and cold.

'I like the cap,' Richard remarked. 'It's a nice touch. Made the right impression on my mother. Do you always dish up your family history in the middle of an interview?'

'I prefer to talk, not interrogate.' He looked easier than Vincent. He was going to be more difficult. 'Mrs Savage' – like the people of Ridpath, I automatically called her Mrs Savage – 'told me about your father. It seemed natural to mention that mine was in the RAF too.'

'My father was a deserter, poor sod. No medals for the umpteen times he kept his nerve, ten thousand feet up in the darkness with aircraft dodging him and diving down on him and shooting at him from all directions. Just a big black mark for the moment when that nerve snapped. Still, *c'est la guerre*, I suppose. You don't get any points for trying. Your father, I gather, was a hero. It doesn't give them much in common, does it?'

There was no derision in his voice as there would have been in Vincent's, but the noncommittal tone left me free to infer either scepticism or contempt. 'Yes,' I said, 'he bloody was. He flew like your father and he was scared like your father and he of all people would have admitted that it was just luck his nerve didn't go too. When peace came he wasn't totting up points, for himself or for anyone else. He was trying to put his life together with only half a face and writing poetry about it all. It wasn't great poetry but it came from the heart and anyway, I like it. He believed in trying. In war he tried to fight and afterwards he tried to say something valuable about the whole mess and he always tried to understand. He would have understood your father – probably without trying. I don't know what a hero is but he did his best – and his best was bloody good – and that's heroic enough for me.'

I was suffering from an emotional hangover, losing control at the merest nuance of provocation. Like the morning-after drunk who swallows a glass of water which washes all the alcohol back into his bloodstream again. The events on Dominique had undermined years of habitual self-containment, chipping away at my iceberg façade until everything inside me seemed to be either melting or cracking up. I was overreacting, unstable, idiotically sensitive. The effect might have been planned. Richard softened immediately.

'I'm sorry,' he said. 'I rather assumed you'd been spinning my mother a line. Oh hell! Here, have a handkerchief. Mind the greasy bit. I'm afraid it's not really a handkerchief, just a piece of old rag, but it'll blot up the tears. You mustn't cry: you're not a weepy sort of girl, and besides, it's making me feel a complete bastard. I didn't mean to upset you. Journalists are supposed to be case-hardened, or so I always thought. My mother said you were different. Obviously she was right.'

'I *am* case-hardened,' I retorted, furious with myself. 'Anyway, I'm not crying. I didn't spin your mother a line because it wasn't necessary. If it had been, then I would have done. It's my bloody job.'

'What's your name? Murphy, isn't it?'

'Micky Murphy.'

'I like that. It goes with the cap.' This time, there was no elusive sarcasm. 'Look, Miss Murphy – *Miz* Murphy—'

'Micky.'

'All right then, Micky – though it doesn't change anything. You've wasted your time. My mother is a dear who loves me very much – I expect that's the formula for most mothers, even the bad ones – but unfortunately she really believes the old adage that Mother Knows Best. Her baby chick has grown up and flown the nest and made a cuckoo of himself all on his own but she still thinks she can sort everything out for him with a spoonful of cough linctus and a few pages from *The Wind in the Willows*.' I laughed, though the sound emerged as a kind of hiccup. 'I know she takes herself seriously but I must say, I didn't expect a sensation-hunting investigative team from a prime-time TV show to do the same. Not that you personally look much like a sensation-hunter – at least, not right now.'

'That's just my devious approach,' I explained. 'Normally, I wear a leather corselette with built-in camera, crotchless leggings and an Hermès bullwhip. It gets people in the mood.'

'It would.'

'About your mother,' I went on, opting to meet his brand of frankness with my own. 'When I interviewed her, she appeared to think my producer and I were involved in all this out of some kind of disinterested chivalry, to vindicate your good name. I don't have to tell you that's bullshit. So we're sensation-hunters – if the truth causes a sensation, that's the desired effect. But it's truth we want, not cheap lies which wouldn't last five minutes in a legal battle. That's why we need you. You may see your cousin simply as the man who ruined you but in fact he's a business crook on an international scale with a quasi-legal modus operandi and the moral scruples of a king cobra. His public profile has been carefully chiselled and the Americans are so dazzled by his antecedents they've left him well alone. Nowadays, he's operating more and more in the UK – or trying to. Homesick, probably. Anyway, he's freewheeled through California; we don't want him to have such an easy ride with us. You could help.'

'You weren't listening,' said Richard. 'I don't need anyone to fight my battles. No matter how good – or how bad – their intentions.'

'Who said anything about fighting your battles?' I countered. 'We want *you* to fight *ours*.'

'Nice angle,' Richard said with genuine approbation, 'but it won't wash. What you actually mean is that you want me to give evidence in a kind of trial-by-television where my cousin won't get the chance to speak in his own defence and the verdict is worked out in advance. That isn't my idea of a clean fight. Nor is it my idea of justice. I'm old-fashioned. I believe in the creak and grind of the legal system, not the flash and zap of the camera. Sorry.'

'Ouch,' I said. 'Yes. I daresay that was a reasonably accurate summary. Still . . . we don't pretend to be judge and jury: we just interview the witnesses and offer the evidence, pro or con. We won't try to pass sentence, if that makes any difference.'

'It doesn't,' said Richard. 'Just for the record—'

'Yes?'

'I don't see my cousin simply as the man who ruined me. I see him as a man. Also as my cousin. I doubt if your programme would appreciate that.'

'Just for the record,' I responded, 'I'm trying to see him as a man, too. A whole man, not just an outline, a drop of gall, a morsel of spleen. I'm not interested in cardboard villains. In *Quest*, we do make an effort to analyse motivation if we can.

What bends the bent cop, what goes on inside the insider trader, why does the millionaire put his hand in the till, what muse inspires the demagogue.'

'Greed,' suggested Richard. 'The lust for power. The usual stuff.'

I nodded. 'There's a dreadful sameness about the criminal mentality,' I admitted. 'I've noticed it much too often. People do good things for all sorts of reasons, but when they turn to the bad the reasons are depressingly similar. I sometimes think they have something missing, not merely their moral sense but something fundamental to humanity, some essential part of their being. They're like bodies without souls, clever, strong bodies pre-programmed for self-preservation and snatching automatically at other people's money, but with no core of feeling, no desire deeper than appetite. It isn't that they don't care about those they hurt: they don't *understand*. I know I'm generalising, but . . .' I paused, fishing for the right words, or the wrong ones, for an evasion, an appropriate phrase. 'Anyhow, Vincent – your cousin – struck me as being in a separate category. I've got some background on him – old interviews, taped conversations – which seems to indicate he has a depth beyond greed, a sort of negative ideology. It's as if he isn't so much morally disabled as deliberately warped. Self-corrupted. Self-destroying. Self-defeating.'

Richard was staring at me curiously. I knew I had gone too far, said too much. 'You surprise me,' he said lightly, 'again. Tell me: exactly what type of programme are you aiming to produce?'

'A tragedy,' I said rashly. Our lawyers were concerned exclusively with facts and Alun Craig thought tragedy was something that only happened in Shakespeare, but on this one, I had already decided I would be writing the script.

Richard's eyebrows lifted, wrinkling his forehead into a dozen sceptical question-marks. 'My tragedy?'

'No. Vincent's.'

The eyebrows subsided.

'We can make the programme without you,' I said finally, 'but I'd welcome your input. For a complete picture.'

'You won't get a complete picture,' Richard said. 'Vincent's character contains too many dark corners. You can't shine your spotlight into them all. However . . . we may as well talk. I have nothing else to do this evening and anyhow, as I said, I like your cap.'

'Can Thames Television buy you dinner?' I offered.

Richard's response was predictable. 'No thanks. I'll buy you.'

We ate cheaply, tourist food, in a small restaurant where Richard, clearly a regular, was served promptly while earlier arrivals had to wait. The menu was universal, and universally boring: hamburger and chips, chicken and chips, chips.

'Upmarket food is very expensive here,' Richard explained.

'My allowance would have survived the shock,' I said.

'If you want to talk to me,' said Richard with a grin, 'you do so on my terms, at my rates, and on my bill. Understood?'

I didn't run a tape. For one thing, I had neglected to stock up on cassettes and I had only about an hour left; for another, I sensed with Richard that it was vital to be as straightforward as possible. Honesty breeds honesty. Under his bright, disturbing gaze I felt attentive, unrelaxed, balanced on the knife-edge of conscience. With Vincent I had generally been at ease, tinkering playfully with the lighter subtleties of deceit. Truth is less facile, and therefore more demanding.

'I thought pilots were fairly well paid,' I remarked, several chips later.

'Fairly. I have a few debts to clear.'

The bankruptcy. Of course. 'Stupid of me,' I said. 'Are you – are you getting there?'

'Well, you know what banks are like. I keep paying, they keep adding on more interest. It's a long haul. Sometimes I feel like a character in a fairy tale. I have to move every grain of sand on the beach with only a pair of tweezers, and all before sunset, or I shall be enslaved to the wicked witch forever. So far, the witch seems to be winning.'

'Ah, but if you manage it,' I recalled, 'you get to marry the princess.'

'I already did that,' said Richard.

It was a leading comment, and I duly picked up the lead.

'Is that how you saw her?' I asked. 'Crystal the princess, with Vincent as the dragon – or the black knight?'

'Not quite.' The smile that gleamed on his face was both rueful and irrepressible. 'Vincent was the prince and I . . . was charming.'

'Tell me about it.'

'Inquisitive, aren't you? Yes, I know – it's your job. Is it relevant?'

'Tell me and I'll see.'

He hesitated, took a mouthful of his drink. I had graduated to rum punch, a reassuringly basic variety with plenty of alcohol and no umbrella; Richard was still on beer. 'Have you met my ex-wife?'

'I interviewed her.'

'Then you should understand.'

'She's very pretty' – I injected extra enthusiasm into my voice – 'very, very pretty. But you don't marry someone, you don't even fall in love with someone, just because of that.'

'Vincent did.' Richard's amusement lingered. 'She was the prettiest girl around so she was the one he had to have. I imagine he might have defined it as love. It took him longer than usual to get her into bed, so . . . As it was, after he was arrested he simply wanted her out of the way. I wish I could say it was chivalry, but I don't think so. He wanted us all out of the way. He couldn't bear anyone to witness his humiliation. I don't believe he ever really appreciated that what he'd done was *wrong*, you see. He knew it was illegal but he just thought of it as clever, a little crooked, slick, one jump ahead of the law rather than outside it. The way he saw it, his failure was in getting caught. If my uncle had helped him instead of rejecting him – oh, I don't suppose it would have made Vincent any different, but at least their relationship would have improved. Anyway, there was Crys screwing her courage to the sticking point, all set to be loyal and true, when he turned round and effectively slapped her in the face. She announced her engagement like a heroine in a story and he repudiated it like a minor nuisance. Poor darling, she was so hopelessly valiant, so utterly bewildered. I remember when I took her to Weatherfray how nervous she was, how hard she tried to behave correctly, to say the right thing. Posing without a camera, acting without a script. I was so damned sorry for her.'

'Disastrous,' I said. 'If you're going to be sorry for people you should pick orphaned babies, very old ladies and tramps. Being sorry for pretty girls will only get you into trouble.'

'You're telling me.' The grin flashed out again and then faded into the semi-detached smile of nostalgia. 'Vincent fascinated her,' he went on, 'but she was never comfortable in his company. He didn't really know her or she him. With me, she could be herself. All the glamour and sophistication peeled away and she blossomed—'

'Just like a dear little flower,' I said before I could stop myself.

'Don't knock it, Micky. It must have happened to you some time – and not so long ago, at that. Youth. Springtime. When you feel you have to knock it, that shows you're getting old.'

'I beg pardon,' I said. 'That was a cheap dig. I expect I'm jealous. Spring passed me by; I got frostbite while still in bud. But when I met Crystal she seemed so very reserved – an artificial personality – every gesture was studied. It's difficult to picture her unfurling hidden petals. You must have green fingers.'

'The magic works both ways,' Richard confessed. 'That's the catch. Having that kind of power over another person is a terrifying responsibility, but it's also a charm. It bewitched me too. Springtime can be very contagious.'

He showed no trace of disillusionment, no regret. 'Do you still care?' I asked. 'I mean, would you give it a second chance?'

'I *care*,' Richard said. 'You should never stop caring. But . . . we've gone beyond second chances. You can't reanimate the dead.'

'When she left you,' I murmured, tiptoeing among broken tulips, 'where did she go?'

'You know so much,' said Richard. 'Surely you know that.'

'I was attempting to be tactful.'

Richard mimed polite incredulity. 'She left me a note,' he said. 'I forget the exact words, but our marriage had been a mistake and it was Vincent, always Vincent. Her one true love.' He was silent for a minute or two. 'I couldn't stop her: she'd already gone. I knew what he'd do. He'd made himself despise her. I could imagine him, pulling off the hidden petals one by one and putting them through the shredder. Crys couldn't fight him; she couldn't fight anyone. She never really understood what was going on. She assumed Vincent bankrupted me for revenge, because I'd stolen her away from him. Paperback melodrama.'

'Actually,' I supplied, 'it was Crystal he hated, for stealing you.'

'Perceptive.' The look of surprise was not pantomime. He picked up a chicken wing and began to gnaw the bones, licking his fingers by way of punctuation. I had left most of my meal untouched, but Richard ate everything on his plate, even the piece of wilting lettuce and half-tomato intended for decoration which nobody ever eats. Afterwards, he still looked hungry, though not for chips.

'You and Vincent were very close, weren't you?' I said. The familiar approach. 'Like brothers.'

'I hate that phrase. Brothers don't necessarily like each other. We were damned good friends. When we were kids, I looked up to him: he was older than me, bigger, stronger, much more daring. He got me into trouble pretty often but he stood up for me too. He licked anyone who tried to bully me – he licked me too, once in a while. He had so many good qualities, he should have grown into someone fine, someone special, but . . . I don't know exactly what changed him. If he changed. Maybe he was just born that way, with a speck of darkness in his soul, a fatal flaw, a kink in the substructure. Maybe it was his mother, running off when he was too young to come to terms with it. Maybe it was my uncle, a bigot of the old school, stubbornly determined never to display either affection or approval. God alone knows. Whatever the cause, Vincent grew up afraid of love. Not simply romantic love, any kind – for father, lover, friend. He saw love as a weakness, an act of self-betrayal, casting your bread upon the waters when you are already half starved. If he found the emotion growing inside him he had to uproot it or poison it, even if it meant tearing his own heart out or dosing himself with cyanide. I don't believe he loved Crystal but he certainly loved his father and he used to love me. Once. So he cut himself off from Uncle John until it was too late and when the opportunity offered he ruined me. So much for love. For an intelligent guy he could be one hell of a fool.'

'If you knew him so well,' I said, 'why did you trust him?'

'I didn't.' The sunny smile with which he had challenged providence came and went. 'I hoped, that's all. We could have done so much together. I relied on his reason – but unreason was stronger. My loss. Also his.'

'He means a lot to you, doesn't he?' I hazarded. 'Even now. What did you say? You should never . . . stop caring. That's your problem, isn't it?'

A hunch, a flash of inspiration, a gamble. Richard's face grew still. 'I don't consider it a problem,' he said. 'So Vincent means a lot to me: why not? A lot of what? I'll tell you something. Vincent means so much to me that what I would really like to do is grab him by the throat and beat the shit out of him. It would do him so much good. Mind you, even if I had the chance I'd probably muff it. Like I said, if we had a tussle he always licked me in the end.'

'The essence of winning a fight,' I said carefully, 'is to choose your own battleground. Also – if you can – to make up your own rules.'

'I told you,' said Richard, 'I won't play ball.' But he paused before he said it.

I braced myself to apply subtle pressure, remembering my promise to Penny Garoghan with an undefined sense of guilt. This was the real world: I was back to guilt, to qualms, doubts, unwanted self-questioning. Light-heartedness – and light-headedness – had vanished with Dominique. But I did not mention Penny or even refer to her except in the most oblique fashion. Somehow, because I had seen her, talked to her, promised that promise to her, to turn it inside out and use it as a spur to her father had become unthinkable.

'Why did you come here?' I enquired at length, approaching the pressure point sideways and with caution.

'The job.'

'Surely you could have found something nearer home?'

'Probably.'

'So what was it then?' I persisted. 'Voluntary exile?'

'You could call it that.' As always, he tackled his own defects with comprehensive honesty. 'I wanted to get as far away as possible. I'd made a mess of things and I felt I needed to leave it all behind. A bit feeble, I suppose, but natural, don't you think? It gave Crys the space to rearrange her life. She's got plenty of money, you know; I don't have to . . . Anyway, I send maintenance for the children. My lawyers look after that. It's all worked out.'

'And when you've cleared your name of the stigma of bank-ruptcy – when you've finished moving the beach with the tweezers – you'll go back?' I said.

'That's the idea.'

I took a deep breath and plunged. 'I think it's ridiculous,' I said frankly. 'Like – like joining the Foreign Legion because you've been falsely accused of stealing the family diamonds. Crystal isn't the only one who's into melodrama. What do you want – to make a last stand against the native hordes and die gal-lantly, proving your valour to the world? Fat chance. You'll just stay on here indefinitely, quietly going to seed, and as long as you're making a financial contribution you can kid yourself you're suffering in a good cause. You have other responsibilities than debt – or do you expect the lawyers to take care of them, too? To hell with family and friends: you're set on nursing your wounded ego in splendid isolation. It isn't Crystal who wants space – of all the tiresome clichés – it's you. Not just space between yourself and the past but space between yourself and the *present*. You're running away, sticking your head in the sand. Yes, I know that's a muddle of metaphors but it's true. Expiation is all very well but you don't have the right to punish others for crimes *you* didn't commit.'

'Aren't you rather exceeding your brief?' Richard said with the gentleness of calculated restraint.

'I don't care.' I was retrogressing again, sliding downhill towards a dark tangle of emotion. It would have been convenient to blame the rum punch, but I had already spent three days blaming Pete Langelaan's champagne. 'You've made your decision so there's no point in wasting my breath on tactful persuasion. You're not going to weaken, you're not going to budge, you're going to sit on your arse and be frightfully stoic and no one's allowed to help you or hinder you. You know what I think? Deep down inside you're actually rather proud of yourself, being so noble and immovable in the teeth of adversity. There's noth-ing as selfish as a really pig-headed martyr. You're determined to stretch on the rack even if you have to work the lever yourself and your nearest and dearest will just have to lump it. When I came here to find you I thought you were a person I would be able to respect, whether you agreed to do the programme or not, but I hadn't considered – I hadn't understood – it's bloody diffi-cult to respect someone so self-indulgently selfless, so doggedly dogged, obsessed with doing his far, far better thing even though it's against affection, against common sense—'

I broke off, well after time, trying to halt my downhill slide. I had intended any disparagement to be moderate, low-key, not vehement and shattering. There was some quality in Richard – perhaps his very openness – which seemed to destabilise me, eliciting a response that was correspondingly open and increas-ingly fatal. I had no excuses, there was no hurricane to blow me over the rainbow, no sex to make me vulnerable. But somewhere along the line I had become involved, entangled, committed. My equilibrium appeared to have gone for good.

I turned my empty glass in my empty hands and felt uncom-fortable. When I looked up again, to my astonishment Richard had begun to laugh.

'Some journalist!' he said. 'If this is how you talk to people when you want their help, what on earth do you say when you've got it in for them?'

For a second I saw myself screaming at Vincent, barely twenty-four hours earlier – it felt like a year ago – but I blotted out the image and laughed too, thankful for his tolerance and suddenly too tired to care about the outcome of the evening.

'Come on,' he said. 'Let's get some air.'

I remember very little of what happened later. Fatigue dimmed everything to a blur, with here and there a focusing of the picture, a turning up of the volume. We went to two or three more bars, listened to the midnight tom-tom of the Caribbean pounding out of jukeboxes and steel bands. There were stars and fairy lights and gyrating figures, sun-painted and shadow-printed, with the reflections of whirling mirrors skimming their bodies like fireflies and their limbs moving to impenetrable rhythms. Dancing in the dark. There is nothing more sensual, or more magical. What man would I not desire, under the cloak of a tropical night with the voodoo drumbeat and the dizzy fire-flies, dancing in the dark, dancing in the dark? We did not dance. Richard asked me why I liked journalism and I asked him why he liked aeroplanes. I told him about Leo Sands of the *Ely Watchman* – prod, prod, prod with a sword-shaped cocktail stick – and extolled with the warmth of genuine fervour my cold-blooded creed of the pursuit of truth. Richard talked about the exhilaration of flying and man's need for mastery of the elements. 'Have you ever watched the sunrise at thirty thousand feet? Of course not: you were asleep with the blind pulled down or eating your pre-packed breakfast; one roll, one orange juice, one sliver of bacon, one rubber egg. You should see it – not from the porthole of a Boeing but in a small plane, up there alone above a shoreless sea of cloud as desolate as the Antarctic, with the sun lifting over the horizon like a single note of red fire into a sky that has lost its blue. And when the wonder fades you can drop a few thousand feet and see the sunrise again, and again. The sun rises to order; you have power not only over air and gravity but morning and night, space and time. There's no other feeling quite like it in the whole world.'

'Power,' I said dreamily, 'that's what drives us all. The power of money and the power of communication and the power of technology. Little pockets of power in towns and villages and vast networks spanning the globe. The country busybody with power over tea parties and church socials and the prime minister with one eye on the opinion polls and the other on the back-benches who finds he hasn't really got much power after all. The power you have over someone you love, and the power they have over you. Society is one huge powerhouse, an enormous complex of Heath Robinson machinery with a big wheel here and a tiny cog there, thumping and clumping its way through history. Bang crash tinkle bleep crash bang. Power. Yes, that's the secret. That's what it's all about.' My eyes were closing but I opened them again. 'If you *did* want to talk to me – for *Quest*, I mean – I can set it up out here before I leave. Or we could pay for your ticket home. Economy class, I'm afraid. Only one sunrise. Otherwise . . .'

'Otherwise?'

'I may as well fly back tomorrow. No: today. Later today. I've had an overdose of the tropics. I need some real English rain. Although, come to think of it, we're in the middle of a heatwave and a drought. Still, at least there won't be any palm trees, or hurricanes, or—'

'You go home,' said Richard. 'Pestering me won't get you anywhere.'

'It got me here,' I said. 'That's bad enough.'

'I'll see you to your hotel.'

We took a taxi. (Inevitably, Richard knew the driver.) He didn't kiss me goodnight, although I half hoped, half doubted he would. A fortunate omission. I had enough troubles.

'Well?' I said, on the doorstep.

Richard was leaning against the taxi with his arms folded. 'Maybe,' he conceded. 'I'll think it over.'

'You've got my number. If you need the air fare—'

'I'll pay for it myself. You should know that by now.'

There was nothing more to be said, but I said it anyway. 'Should you decide to come home, you do the programme on one condition. I buy *you* dinner.'

Richard laughed. 'I'll think it over.'

PART V

ARMAGEDDON

1

I got a flight home late the following evening, arriving at Heathrow around seven in the morning. The sunrise was obscured by the wing of the plane. On consulting my diary, I discovered it was Friday. Only a week since I left. One week which had hauled down my standards, mopped up my morals, changed me forever. But of course I had not changed, people don't change; I might have been weakened or strengthened, tempered or tested, but I could not change. In the final analysis I remained irrevocably, terminally me. I didn't know whether the thought was depressing or reassuring.

Back at my flat, I rang the office. Alun Craig, Fizzy informed me, was still in LA, due back the following week. Presumably he was filming his interview with Richmond LeSueur – Richmond whose guts, enterprise and lack of ruth Vincent had said he admired, Richmond whom he had obviously bedded and for whom he seemed to feel a residual liking. How would he react to her treachery, I wondered? Would he shrug, would he sneer, would he care? You're too fond of mixing pleasure with business, Mr Savage, I thought. This time around, it's your turn to get stung, your turn to find out how it feels.

'I'll be in on Monday,' I told Fizzy. 'Right now I'm exhausted, jet-lagged, and suffering from a surfeit of palm trees. I also have a stack of tapes to transcribe. It'll probably take most of the weekend.'

Did I want to talk to Jeff, Fizzy enquired conscientiously.

'Is he there?'

No.

I duly declined to talk to him, and hung up. I spent most of that day making copies of the tapes in case of accident and transferring on to the computer everything that might be relevant for the programme – every shade in Vincent's character, every twist in his ethos. I was working too hard to have leisure for thought, driving myself purposely to the extreme of fatigue. Once in a while an intrusive little memory would poke its head above the ramparts, stilling my fingers on the keyboard and sending my unseeing gaze straying into nondescript corners of the room. But I would shoot it down with steel-tipped arrows and drag my gaze back to the computer screen, narrowing my vision, closing my mind, forcing myself to concentrate on the task in hand. The job, the whole job, and nothing but the job. *Whatever happened to truth?* would come the question, sneaking into a pause in the tape, a snag in my industry, snaring me into searching for an answer, for some kind of self-justification, sucking me down into the irresistible quagmire of Doubts. Sooner or later they would have to be faced and outfaced, I would have to argue and agonise and look into my own soul, but not yet. Please not yet. I must find my way through the groundwork first, then I could lose myself in a maze of wider implications. I kept on until the words began to swim before my eyes, falling asleep inadvertently with the tape still running and Vincent's voice sliding into my dreams. 'Armageddon is a grotesque idea . . . the last great battle at the end of time . . . Armageddon . . .' And there we were, in the midst of opposing armies, Vincent in an Armani leopard-skin, claws and all, and a helmet plumed with a nodding palm frond. He was carrying a brazen spear of enormous dimensions which seemed to lengthen when tilted in my direction. 'Where's your Kalashnikov?' I screamed, but suddenly it was I who had the Kalashnikov, just as I had always known I would. The end of the world was here and I had to fire, I had to fire, and there was the blood blossoming on the leopard-skin, red spots among black . . . I awoke with a jerk as my head slipped forward on to my arms, my heart thumping and my mouth dry. The dream was so vivid it was a second or two before I knew where I was. I might have been on the plane still, or in a Barbados bar, or in Irving Blum's bed.

Then the computer blinked at me and my surroundings resolved
into a barricade of files, a cup of cold coffee, a painting of sunlight on the wall above. Home. The clock told me it was
ten-thirty, my muscles ached and my brain yawned. Beside me,
the tape ran out on Vincent's snore. Sleeping on his back again.
I switched off everything that needed switching off, went to bed,
and fell instantly into a slumber like a black gulf. If I dreamed,
I did not remember it.

I finished the transcription on Saturday night. I had hoped I
would be too tired for soul-searching, evading the Doubts by a
further plunge into oblivion, but I had drunk a lot of coffee and
although my body was weary my mind would not let go. There
came a moment when I found myself abruptly, unwillingly alert,
filled with a form of hyper-awareness, seeing every detail with
steely clarity, hearing every sound falling coldly on my senses.
My flat had shrunk to a single luminous cell in the dark, multi-
cellular organism of the city: London, a sprawling Leviathan,
sweating, breathing, alive with the secret, subterranean life of all
midnight things, watching with a million eyes – eyes of neon and
argon, bulbous lamps, yellow windows, gleaming slits between
closing curtains – stirred by the slow unrelenting pulse of foot-
beats, music, traffic. But somehow, I felt a deep sense of
alienation, an unreachable solitude. I was out of place, out of
time, a creature neither nocturnal nor diurnal, awake when
others slept, working when they played. The pulse of the city
stopped at my door: within this one cell there was only the chatter of the keyboard and, when that ran down, a hollow of silence
exclusive to me. I was a reluctant individual sticking to my
course as stubbornly, and as desperately, as Richard to his mar-
tyrdom and Vincent to his pointless revenge, alone, separate,
trapped in my Self. The voices of the Doubts began but I saw,
with this new and daunting perception, that although they imi-
tated the accents of my mother, my step-father, my father, they
were in truth merely aspects of my own psyche, dissenters from
my viewpoint wearing the likeness of others to carp, criticise and
accuse. All those voices were my voice, all those words the product of my inmost confusion. My father was long dead, my
step-father shortly dead, my mother a useful vehicle on whom to
place the burden of prosecution. In the flesh, very probably,

none of them would have adhered to the script I gave them. They were, I realised, nothing more than a way of cheating myself, giving my Doubts a capital D, different faces, different tones, dividing them from me. I was alone indeed.

I had always believed character to be a fixed thing, a painting on canvas where the colours set at an early age, and although time might daub a highlight here and there or add an extra detail the basic lines could not be altered. But suddenly it seemed to me, not that the picture had changed but that it had never been real, never other than a painting, a speed-sketch of strength, decision and principle no more substantial than the paper on which it had been drawn. The person behind it was unformed, without identity or palpability, bending with every wind, switching hues like a chameleon. With Vincent I had used my body and enjoyed it, playing at single combat with an opponent who did not even know war had been declared. With Richard I had scrambled back on to my pedestal, resuming the standards I had dropped so carelessly, playing at honesty with someone who did not tell lies. Playing, always playing. Games of convenience in which I marked the cards and tossed away a little of my integrity with every hand. Where in all this was the real Micky, the essence beyond character, the self within all other selves? Inevitably, irresistibly, I turned inward, seeking the void and the spark which, on Dominique, had burned so fiercely it set fire to the bed. But the ghosts of my uncertainties obscured my view and I found neither the darkness nor the light, only grey shades of apprehension. I emerged shaken, my blood fizzing from an overdose of caffeine, my skull leaden. Finally, I went to bed, if only for something to do. Sleep came reluctantly. The last thing I remember among the plague of phantoms in my head was the figure of Jan Horrocks, standing tall amid the Doubts. Jan Horrocks the crusader of Walmsley Village, discredited heroine of a lost cause. 'It's your fight now,' she had said. She at least would commend my actions, or so I believed, clutching at the thought on the edge of unconsciousness. I would drive down and see her some time.

I went the next day. It was a mistake and I knew it, well before I got there, when I was ten miles down the motorway and the air proceeding through the open window felt as arid as the

khamsin and did nothing to alleviate my depression. I had telephoned in advance to check she could see me and her
acquiescence had sounded like a reflex, without enthusiasm or
curiosity. 'David is out with the kids,' she explained when I
arrived. 'He didn't want me to see you: he's afraid you'll stir
things up again. We've sorted ourselves out since I talked to
you. He's happy; I'm comfortable. I really don't want to spoil
anything.' Much of the restless discontent was gone from her
expression, leaving her somehow lessened, as if her environmental campaigning and the affair with Vincent had infused
her with a temporary vitality, a turbulence that had since faded.
She was opting for middle age, for safety, for a policy of stay put,
stay at home, maintain the status quo. Any fancy I had cherished of confiding in her died at once. She would not approve or
disapprove, might not even care. Vincent was something she had
put behind her.

I wondered if I would be able to do the same.

'We're going to make the programme,' I told her. 'I thought
you'd like to know.'

'Are you?' She sounded resigned rather than interested. 'Do
we get a mention?'

I smiled faintly. 'No. You wouldn't talk: remember?'

'I'm not into public striptease. I've had my share of the limelight; now I want a little welcome obscurity.' In spite of the heat
she had made tea, Indian, dark and bitter. I drank politely. 'If you
don't want my testimony,' she asked, 'why did you come?'

I fished for a question, a spare from my repertoire, something
to justify a wasted journey.

'When I talked to your friend Miss Arbuckle,' I said – she
laughed at the word 'friend' – 'I got the impression there was
someone behind her. A manipulator or – I don't know, maybe
just an adviser. I realise this sounds like a conspiracy theory but
in this business you get suspicious of everyone's motives. It's
probably not important. Could be a local nimby worried about
the sanctity of his back garden or a rival developer with a scheme
of his own. All the same . . . I'd like to find out.'

'There *was* another plan,' she admitted. 'Ralph Planterose.
Fits the bill on both counts. Resident nimbie, calls himself a
developer – though I don't know if he's ever actually developed

anything. He had some idea of a hotel and bird sanctuary to attract ornithologists. We were very keen on it at the time but I don't think it was ever much more than an idea: I didn't see any drawings or hear any estimates for costs and financing. Ralph's always making wonderful plans and expounding them to anyone who'll listen but I must say, I can't visualise him as a manipulator.'

'Did he have any associates?'

'Not that I know of. There was a friend of his from London whom I met once or twice, but I'm sure they weren't in business together. This other man – Percival – struck me as being too intelligent for that. I think Ralph tried to involve him but he wasn't interested. He was one of those monk-like aesthetes who have apparently unlimited resources and spend them on paintings too valuable to hang and porcelain too fragile to use. I daresay poor old Planterose leaned on him rather heavily for advice.' She stopped, her attention caught by the choice of word, and looked at me with an interrogatory grimace.

But I had noticed something else. 'Percival?'

'That was his name. Percival . . . Percival Pierce? It was an alliteration, anyway. Do you know him?'

'Piers Percival?'

'Eureka.'

'Not exactly,' I said. 'It rings a bell, that's all.' An alarm bell. Piers Percival, Richard's godfather, the man I had decided not to interview, pulling strings in the background. Possibly he had gone even further. I still did not know the identity of Alun's informant, the insider who had been spoon-feeding him the data on Vincent, but Piers Percival seemed a likely candidate. I wasn't sure of the significance of my discovery – if I had discovered anything – but at least it served to divert me from my lingering Weltschmerz.

'Thanks,' I said on my way out. 'You've told me something I didn't realise I needed to know.'

We shook hands: she was glad to see me go. I doubt if she recalled comparing Vincent to the Great Storm – a metaphor which had incorporated a hint of prophecy – or passing her battle colours on to me. *It's your fight now . . . good luck . . . I don't suppose he's ever been beaten.* She didn't want to remember and

I didn't remind her. I drove back to London with other problems to think about.

Alun Craig didn't return to the office until Wednesday, which gave me two days to satisfy the legal department and get my own way with Jeff Salter. Our chief lawyer was a hard-line feminist and unswerving lesbian who abominated the opposite sex on principle and whose hate-hate relationship with Alun made any co-operation a perennial minefield. With me she was normally more amenable, though on this occasion I was unsure how she would react to the revelation of my sexual proclivities implicit on those sections of tape which I was required to play for her. However, the exploitation of the male, in bed or out of it, was an undertaking of which she approved (in the seventies, she had supported SCUM) and she vetted my transcript with less fuss than usual and something which might have been an appreciative grunt at the end. On this one, she asserted, she was prepared to stick her neck out. 'He won't sue,' she said, 'even if some flash professional shyster like Carter-Ruck tells him he's got a case. His ego would never stand it.' Probably true. She plainly believed I had endured my experiences with Vincent in a state of valiant resignation, and thought the better of me in consequence. What the *Quest* team thought I did not want to hear. Nobody outside the legal office was going to listen to those tapes: the transcript was all we needed, for evidence and quotation. I trusted the lawyer to conceal her copies from all comers, especially Alun; mine I had left at my flat, where I intended them to stay. Jeff's look of patent speculation I met with a chilly stare.

'There was nothing about the hurricane on the news over here,' he said.

'Really?'

'Must have been quite a breeze.' He paused, fumbling with his words. 'Micky – how did you get Savage to open up like that? I mean, you didn't . . . you couldn't have . . .?'

It was impossible, his manner indicate. I was not that sort of girl.

'I got the goods,' I retorted sharply. 'Are you complaining?'

Jeff lapsed into silence.

Derek was too diffident to venture on vulgar speculation and

Fizzy I squashed without effort. Our other two associates, Malcolm and Ranjit, had had no connection with this investigation: they had spent most of the last eight weeks commuting to Birmingham to uncover a local government corruption scandal which would keep them happy for some while yet. Alun, I feared, would not be so easy to deal with.

In the event, I found I had misjudged him. He arrived from LA on schedule, with the angry vestiges of sunburn on his cheeks and a reel of Richmond LeSueur in his flight bag. Protective glasses had left a livid stripe across his face, like a white mask in which his eyes shone with their habitual pebbly gleam. I told him that, thanks to meteorological catastrophe, I had managed to maroon myself with Vincent – just in time, I remembered to call him 'Savage' – and circumstances had put him in a confiding mode. I told him I had seen Richard Garoghan and he might or might not agree to take part in the programme. (This was greeted with predictable derision.) I sowed the seeds of my idea for portraying Vincent in tragic vein, insinuating by subtle means that such a presentation would enhance Alun's artistic stature. (He was particularly intrigued by this concept, since artistic stature was not something to which he had previously laid claim.) I told him I intended to write the script. Anything to forestall him from asking the wrong questions. But the man who had once suggested I should sleep with a witness was not going to quibble if I slept with a mark. Presumably he considered it a proceeding too natural to be worth a mention; at any rate, he had other preoccupations. He wanted action, he wanted Richard Garoghan, he absolutely refused to let me do the script and above all he must, he *must* have copies of the tapes. Immediately. I demurred; he raged, the patches of sunburn standing out on his face so that he resembled a fuming scarlet-cheeked raccoon meanly deprived of a choice morsel of garbage. Be reasonable, Micky, be sensible, be tractable, be deferential, be docile, be good. He switched from shrill harangue to oily persuasion and back again. I remained unmoved. Eventually he declared that whatever the opinion of our legal advisers, if he could not have the tapes the whole project was off.

Very well, I said. It was off.

I didn't believe him.

The argument went on all day. I dragged in Piers Percival by way of a distraction, threatening to interview him – a suggestion which produced a flat negative from Alun, thus clarifying the position. His informers always had a top secret status not accorded to anyone or anything else, including my tapes. I pointed this out at some length. In desperation, Alun invited Jeff and I to lunch, to preclude our evading further dispute by sloping off in search of nourishment on our own. I rejected pizza, hamburgers and curry out of hand, so we enjoyed a superior Chinese meal at Poon's which Alun would have to justify to the accountants. His tirade continued both between mouthfuls and during. I ate with unruffled calm and a daintiness calculated to irritate. Jeff made no attempt to umpire. That evening when I got back to my flat I bundled the tapes in a plastic bag and hid them in the hollow under the bath, behind a broken piece of casing. I felt as paranoid as Irving Blum.

The row persisted spasmodically over the next couple of weeks, but so did the preparations for the programme. It would be broadcast in September as the opening salvo of our new series, and although Alun had done the exposé into Vincent's business methods – interviews with victims of his west coast deals as well as Richmond LeSueur – it was pre-eminently my show. We had agreed to split the scriptwriting, with Alun doing the part relevant to his research. However, as I edited his material when his back was turned the final format was more or less what I had planned. 'The dramatic element works really well,' he said after rereading. 'There's a real flavour of Greek tragedy about this bastard. Great idea, Micky. Great television.' He didn't say: 'I'm glad I thought of it,' but it was clear he intended to take the credit. He always did. He was not consciously ungenerous; he simply had no understanding of generosity. He had the driving force of a Black and Decker and the emotional range of a termite, or so I told Jeff, who thought my input deserved more recognition. 'I don't want recognition,' I said, battering away at my computer. 'For all I care, he can relegate my name to some small print at the fag end of the technicians. He can call it the Alun Craig Show, produced by Alun Craig, directed by Alun Craig, additional material by Alun Craig. I don't give a shit. I just want to get it *right*.'

The following day I went back to Ridpath, to redo my interview with Elizabeth Savage on film.

'I gather you tracked down my son,' she said afterwards.

'Yes.' I didn't want to say much in front of the camera team.
If anything.

'He likes you,' she went on. 'I knew he would; You're our
kind of person.'

'He isn't supposed to like me,' I said. 'He's supposed to talk to
me.'

She didn't say whether he was coming back and I didn't ask. I
still believed, or hoped, that I had dissuaded him from exile, but
although the phone on my desk trilled with tiresome regularity it
was never Richard. It was a query from our lawyer, it was gossip
from Annabel Purdey, it was an expert in the city, it was an ama-
teur on the Street, it was Los Angeles, it was Milan, it was
Kensington, it was my mother, my cleaner, my nervous system.
'Go home,' said Jeff. 'Just one thing more,' said Alun. I lived off
sandwiches, fended off Doubts. The air-conditioning failed again
and an electric fan sat beside me sending a grateful breeze waft-
ing across my fevered brow. If I closed my eyes, I could imagine
it came straight from the tops of the palm trees. I didn't close my
eyes. My hair needed cutting, my tan faded to sere, and I went to
see Crystal Winter feeling as off colour as a wilting leaf.

I had forgotten how pretty she was. I had learned so much
about her since we first met that her personality had grown in my
imagination, the puddle had acquired depth, she had become
endowed with the vanity of Salome and the weakness of Eve. It
was something of a shock to find that perfect physiognomy still
flawless and expressionless, delicate but not brittle, unsoftened
by any hint of vulnerability. Broken defences, turbulence and
pain had left no perceptible trace. She welcomed me with her
beautiful smile, its brilliance instinctive, its warmth illusory. Her
blue, blue eyes were as vivid as butterflies' wings. I had already
told her what I knew, explaining that in this interview she would
have to be more forthcoming, giving her time to hesitate, back
off, adjust her poise and her pose, return to the fray as the moth
to the candle or the model to the camera. She aspired to be an
actress; she would never pass up the opportunity to dramatise
herself. With judicious flattery, I had intimated that she was to

be the heroine of the piece. She saw herself, I recollected belatedly, as a woman among women, so I threw in the jibe that she
was the victim of her menfolk and this was her chance to retali-
ate. Tell the truth and shame the Devil. Publish and be damned.
It was an unfortunate combination of platitudes, but happily
Crystal had missed their conflicting conclusions. She called back
and agreed. I found out subsequently that she had consulted her
agent, the elusive Brendan, and he had obviously told her not to
be naive, this was publicity and she was to play it for all she was
worth.

But Crystal was not an actress. She did not achieve dignity,
she clung to it. Any emotion in her voice sounded a false note, as
if she were simulating stock reactions, giving a demonstration of
what she thought she ought to feel. It was in a pale recital of her
woes, a slightly tremulous self-control, that she became, if not
sincere, at least effective, acquiring pathos, suggesting courage.
'Tell it simply,' I urged, Coppola to an inadequate Streep. 'Don't
elaborate. You don't need to break down: people will sympathise
without that. They'll be on your side.' They, not I. I couldn't say
to her *be yourself* because Crystal's self was still an unknown
quantity, a chamber of hidden damage double-locked against the
world. But I said what I could. 'Keep your nerve. Tell the story
straight. You'll be fine.'

She was fine. She kept her nerve. Her voice quivered once or
twice but did not crack. There was sensitivity in the curve of her
pout, pride in the elevation of her exquisite chin. I reflected
unkindly that thus did Nature's handiwork compensate for any
deficiencies of the spirit. But I was being unfair and I knew it,
castigating myself without conviction. 'I loved my husband,' she
told the camera, fixing it with an unwavering gaze. 'I loved him
very much, but . . . I'd never really got over Vincent. I'd been
madly infatuated with him – but infatuation doesn't last. I suppose it was the guilt which lasted. After his arrest, when he
wouldn't announce our engagement, I thought he was rejecting
me. I didn't understand that he – he wanted to keep me out of it,
to protect me from the press. I should have stood by him, I
should have waited for him. Deep down inside, I think I always
sensed that. When Vincent came back into my life – when he
and Richard went into partnership – I had to confront all those

feelings that I'd been repressing for so long. I was desperately confused – and Vincent seemed so sure. He was always sure about everything. He asked me to go away with him – he said he still loved me, he'd never stopped loving me. I believed him: why should he lie? I hesitated and hesitated . . . and then when Richard told me Vincent was making him bankrupt I saw I would have to do something. His work meant so much to Richard, much more than I did.' It was an excuse, it was trite, but it might be true. 'I knew Vincent was doing it for revenge: the way he saw it, I'd deserted him for Richard. He had this dangerous streak, Vincent I mean. Anyway, it sounds silly now but I thought, if I left my husband, if I went back to Vincent—' For the first time she let her eyes drop, studying the convulsive interlacing of her fingers. Visibly, she steeled herself to face the lens again. 'Vincent has a very strong personality, very charismatic. I must have been sort of hypnotised by him. Vincent and I, back together – I thought that was how things were *meant* to be. And I hoped, if he had no more reason for revenge, that he would change his mind about Richard, maybe go on financing him. I really hoped that.'

She was fond of the word 'really', though its use probably had little to do with reality. Finding she needed a prompt, I said: 'Go on.'

'I was a fool.' The shock phrase was unexpectedly harsh, a jarring note, a revelation. 'Vincent didn't need a reason to hate: it came naturally to him. He hated Richard but most of all he hated me. He'd never forgiven me. He isn't capable of forgiving. All those years he'd been nursing his hate, marking time, making plans. When he told me he loved me – when he kissed me – the hate must have been there inside him, behind the lies, behind the kiss . . .' She shivered with a kind of horrified disgust, as if recalling a moment when she had allowed herself to taste something unspeakably foul. But I was not deceived. The shiver, I thought, was not emotional fastidiousness but fear, the fear of continuing her story, of the next item, the next horror, of walking carefully over memories as sharp as broken glass. Tread softly, for you tread upon my ego.

I said very gently: 'So you went back to Vincent. What happened?'

'He didn't want me.' It was a stark statement of fact, pathetic and gallant. Yes, gallant. When she was gallant I was able to admire her. If she could have smiled at her own folly . . . But Crystal didn't smile. 'He just wanted to hurt. I thought he loved me, but he – he had no love in him. Only the hate. Ever since I rejected him, he must have been meditating revenge. Dreaming of it. I can't imagine that, you see. I can't imagine someone hating that much.' She sounded as if she meant it. There was a genuine bewilderment in her tone, an echo of appalled wonder. I remember it disturbed me, though I didn't know why.

It was a good note on which to finish.

Later, when the paraphernalia of filming had been cleared from the sitting room, I found myself glancing again at the photographs on the desk. Jonas, four or five at a guess, with his mother's pout reproduced on a visage of seraphic innocence. No small boy, I thought, could look that innocent without being Damien personified, and I warmed to him instinctively. And Penny, on Crystal's other hand, younger and rounder of face than the girl I had met, regarding me with angular eyes and an inherited inscrutability.

'How are your children?' I asked Crystal.

She stared at me in surprise, her expression for a few seconds an exact mirror of her daughter's. 'Of course,' she said, 'you met Snow, didn't you? They're both well.'

'They aren't here today?' I visualised Penny remembering my unkept promise, waiting with the short-term patience of childhood, and the eyes in the picture followed me across the room.

But children are unpredictable. She might equally well have forgotten.

'They're at my mother's,' Crystal said. 'I thought it was best they should be out of the way. I didn't want them getting under everyone's feet.'

Out of the way. Out of sight. Out of mind. I was being unjust to her again. No doubt Crystal loved them in her fashion, showed them affection where appropriate.

'Thoughtful of you,' I said.

The programme was taking shape, interviews and commentary falling into place. I let Alun do the voice-over, a concession

which moved Jeff to protest. 'I told you,' I said, 'it's not important.' I wanted anonymity, a background role, minimal
attribution, no plaudits. Vincent would know what I had done as
soon as he heard Alun's voice denouncing him with his own
words. Perhaps he had already sensed betrayal: he had a nose for
it, even without cause, and I was giving him cause enough. I did
not wish to shirk responsibility for my actions but I would not
capitalise on them, using them to inflate my reputation or boost
my career. That would have been treachery indeed. It was illog-
ical, I knew, but in making the programme, for all my inner
perplexities, I could not feel I was doing anything intrinsically
immoral. It was an inevitable move, fulfilling the oracle, accom-
plishing something in my own fate, in Richard's, in Vincent's. A
grandiose concept, my conscience mocked, pretentious, hypocritical. Vincent would see it for what it was and label it
accordingly. Betrayal was a part of his destiny. His father, his
cousin, Crystal, and now me. Even Richmond LeSueur. Not for
the first time, I wondered what had made her do it. I had
watched her on film, a woman of fifty-odd who had had her face
petrified around thirty-five, with a cloud of hair that was bouf-
fant rather than soft and eyes like silt. With such a woman,
Alun would have found no means to threaten, no arts to persuade. Vincent had spoken of her as someone with whom he had
shared both bed and boardroom, an old ally and continuing
friend. Alun had said she was aggrieved when Vincent and
Carson elbowed her out of the triumvirate, but as a motive it did
not ring true. The incident was history: even if Ms LeSueur
was another one with a penchant for bearing grudges she must
have found weapons to hand in the cut-throat business world
without hanging around for a stray reporter to show up with a
camera. Maybe she wanted her fifteen minutes of fame, but she
did not look the type. It was a loose end in a case that already had
too many of them. But I was no Poirot or Wexford: just a journalist with a job to do and one eye on the ratings. I was used to
living with loose ends. Every investigation left a hundred or
more, maddening little question-marks crammed into the filing
cabinet and consigned to posterity. I put this one in a mental file
and thrust it away with the rest.

But there was one loose end I would not leave. Having

checked which drivelmonger was currently employing Gerry
Hibbert, I rang the Daily Bombast and invited him out for a
drink. I needed to verify Vincent's claim that the press leak on
Sir John's private life had been accidental. It had been the accusation contained in his father's last letter which had pushed
Vincent further towards self-destruct; I must be sure it was
unjustified. For me, this had assumed a disproportionate significance, becoming an essential link without which the whole chain
reaction fell apart. So I bought Gerry two double whiskies in
rapid succession and commenced negotiations.

Gerry Hibbert was an outstanding reporter of his kind, a
tabloid hack who pulled no punches, barred no holds, and abandoned the chase only for opening time. He had Alun's shortage
of scruple but there any similarity ended: Alun was a rat with
ideals; Gerry was merely a rat. At fortysomething, he had thinning hair, a thickening waistline, a letterbox squint and varicose
veins in his nose. His manner had the spurious geniality of a
door-to-door salesman and the friendly curiosity of a peeping
tom. His only attractive quality was a tendency to wear his tie
askew. Among his compeers he had been given the soubriquet of
Beggar Hibbert, to cite the politer version; he was also known
by the pseudo-Spoonerism Hairy Gibbet. His most memorable
scoops had been run under such headlines as 'Four Gerbils
Dead in Superstar Sex Romp', 'Payne's Private Penometer', 'I
Married the Pope' and 'Prince Bites Corgi'. I had met him initially many years earlier when I was a Fleet Street freshman
whom he thought he could entice into bed. It was perhaps fortunate that he did not appear to remember the tenor of my
refusal.

'Micky, old girl,' he said, 'you're looking great.' He always said
that. 'What can I do for you? And what's in it for me?'

I didn't waste my breath on subtlety or evasion. With Gerry,
it would have to be a straight deal, a favour for a favour, payment
in kind. And I had very little with which to bargain. But
although the tabloids are theoretically at war with television
they often take their cue from us, picking up the fall-out from
our stories, pursuing the hares we started. I explained that we
were targeting Vincent Savage, pointing out that if he became hot
news in consequence I had given Gerry advanced warning and

thus plenty of time to dig up some extra dirt. He was not impressed.

'Savage,' he repeated. 'Vincent Scarpia Savage. I know him, Horace. Upper-class prick who looks like a dago. Yes, I know him. He operates in California, doesn't he? Nobody over here is going to give a toss about him. Your chum Craig has pissed way out of the pan on this one.'

'Alun doesn't make elementary mistakes,' I said. 'For one thing, Savage is shifting some of his business back to home base. We've also got a load of gen on his private life. Previously unpublished and so on. Believe me, by the time we've finished with him he's going to be a celebrity, whether he likes it or not. Far be it from me to suggest you jump on the bandwagon, but—'

'Chuck it.' Absent-mindedly, Gerry ordered the next round himself. Clearly he was growing interested. 'I'll jump on anything if it's going my way. Or anyone.' He leered on a reflex, without intentions. 'So what is it you want from me, sweetheart?'

Soft words butter no parsnips. Or some such rustic saying. 'That piece you did on the father a while back. The respectable Sir John Savage with his alleged mistress and her alleged pregnancy and his alleged blameless reputation . . .'

'No alleged about it. Not the first two, anyway. He was in and out, she was up the spout, ended in a rout. How's that for poetry?'

'Revolting. How did you get hold of the story?'

'Well . . .' He eyed me narrowly over his whisky. 'I'd been after the old boy for some time. Eventually, I caught up. Haven't you seen *Rose-Marie*, Micky? The Mounties always get their man.'

I demanded bluntly: 'Who talked?'

'*Name my sources?* Come on, Mick: you know better than that.' He gave an unsuccessful imitation of journalistic rectitude.

It was my turn to be unimpressed.

'Did *anyone* talk?' I persevered. 'Did you bug the butler in Sir John's ancestral pile? When his mistress went to the doctor's, were you hiding in the medicine cupboard? Off the record, Gerry. Give. It can't make any difference now.'

'Why so keen?' He was frowning thoughtfully, baffled, wary, scenting equivocation.

'I must know,' I said. 'That's all I can tell you.'

'What's it worth?'

'One on account?'

I didn't like it. I didn't like it at all. Beggar Hibbert was not the sort of man to overlook a debt, or take payment in casual coinage. But I had no choice. He nodded in agreement; I ordered more drinks. I remember feeling idiotically tense.

'So?' I said.

'You were right,' he conceded. 'No one talked. There was an envelope that – er – went astray. I was staying in the local and Vincent Savage came in. Rowed with his dad, according to the village grapevine. It was a filthy night: he was wet through and dripping all over the floor. The next morning he goes out, courier shows up, and the envelope was just . . . left there. I looked after it. Any responsible citizen would.'

'Responsible for what?'

He ignored this sally. 'I'm telling you, Micky,' he went on, 'when I opened that envelope, I was shocked. *Me*. D'you know, the slimy bastard had been keeping tabs on his own father? The woman, too. Private dicks, the whole works. It was a ruddy disgrace. Spying on Pater – makes you wonder where he went to school.' Gerry himself had been to the sort of minor public school to which socially ambitious parents send their sons when they cannot afford the fees of the top ones. 'He has the dirt sent up by special delivery, then leaves it lying about for anyone to read. He might just as well have given it to me. I ask you!'

'Your moral outrage,' I said, 'is about as convincing as a hammerhead shark dressed up in a sequined jacket telling me it's a shubunkin. But thanks anyway.'

'You owe me,' said Gerry, draining his glass.

I bought him another double. I didn't imagine it cleared the bill.

The summer dragged on. The programme was completed and sat on the shelves awaiting final amendments. The temperature in Soho climbed towards a hundred. London slumped in a greyish torpor, buildings hunched over steaming streets while walls cracked and pavements subsided. Shadow offered no solace, nightfall little relief. An unknown satirist in Kent immortalised the situation:

> *'Water your rosebuds while ye may:*
> *The reservoirs are shrinking,*
> *And this same hose with which ye spray*
> *Tomorrow you'll be drinking.'*

Meanwhile, Saddam Hussein invaded Kuwait. World War Three was imminent. The nations held their breath. At Grey Gables, my mother gave a lunch party, dishing up the son of a friend who was doing awfully well in Venezuela. *What* he was doing awfully well in Venezuela I didn't bother to enquire. In the office, Alun and I continued to skirmish, undeterred by climactic conditions. At least, he was undeterred, I was merely stubborn. He tried to relegate the Savage edition to second place in the series, moving the armaments engineer designing for Iraq into pole position. His arguments were unanswerable, but there were still several lines of enquiry to pursue on the arms scandal and he was forced to retrench. He had stopped demanding copies of my tapes, displaying a restraint which filled me with nebulous suspicion. One day, I returned home to find a note from my cleaner, informing me that a colleague had been round, in my absence, to pick up some cassettes. She knew better than to sabotage my careful disorder, hoovering and dusting around every file; Alun had not been so conscientious. Books had been shifted, tapes jumbled, videos scattered. Happily, it had not occurred to him to look under the bath. But I was taking no more chances. I lodged the tapes with the bank the following morning, remarking nonchalantly when I arrived at the office that I *never* kept my valuables in the flat – burglars could get in anywhere nowadays – and by the way, had Alun found what he wanted? I thought it prudent not to mention which bank I patronised; he was quite capable of organising an armed raid.

Less than a week before the programme was due to appear I was alone in the office one afternoon: Jeff had gone on holiday, Fizzy had gone sick, and everyone else had gone God knew where. I was sitting at my desk beside the electric fan, holding the fort, waiting for the phone to ring. Eventually, it did.

It was Richard.

The new series of *Quest* began in early September. We had sold the programme on Vincent to the Americans, a one-off deal not incorporating other editions, and they broadcast it in California actually on the same night. Synergy was the buzzword. I had been working frantically right up to the last minute, filming an interview with Richard, cutting, inserting, rearranging. I went home in a state of exhaustion and flopped into the bath. Richard had suggested I should buy him dinner as promised, presumably in celebration, but I was too tired and I didn't feel I had anything to celebrate. Every so often I glanced at the clock. The show started at nine. Thin black hands crawled round the clock face, a modern ovoid with only four digits and sharp accents marking the hours in between. There were no doom-laden chimes, only the tick-tick-tick of the inexorable seconds as time ran out. The tide had turned, the flow had become an ebb, the future was shrinking towards a single moment, a hiccup, a full stop. Nine o'clock. I was lonely without my Doubts, sitting in my empty flat cradling a deeper emptiness inside. My heart beat faster than the clock, faster than time. Five minutes left. Four minutes. Three . . .

I didn't watch. You don't watch an execution: only barbarians do that. I thought about Phyl, relishing conspiracy; Win's hand on my arm; twin candle flames reflected in a storm-driven sky. I thought about a lizard on a wall, Richard's smile, Penny's eyes, shooting stars, asparagus soup. And then my thoughts melted away and I could not think any more. The programme ran for an hour, with two ad breaks. At ten o'clock it would be over.

At ten o'clock I switched on the news.

2

Mid-August found Vincent sunning himself on the island of San Giulio in the middle of Lake Orta. Los Angeles had been enduring a heatwave so shattering that even the traffic stayed at home, working conditions were all but impossible and lunching worse, and Vincent had removed to Italy, exchanging the smog-hazed horizon of his adopted home for sugar-topped alps stacked against a shining arc of sky. He lay in a lakeside garden with a glass of cold beer and copies of *The Economist*, the *Financial Times*, the *Herald Tribune*, and yesterday's *Corriere della Sera*, all of which had been transported from Milan hot off the international press. His private motorboat was moored at his private landing stage only yards away. A little breeze came down from the mountains and ruffled its way across the water, pleating the silk-smooth surface into ripples as unobtrusive as the shadows on a mirror. Somewhere indoors he could hear his mother, ably assisted by Mariangela, upsetting the resident cook. The intake of pure air and the tranquillising sound of Italian altercation had almost lulled him to sleep.

He had bought and renovated the villa on San Giulio a few years earlier, as a surprise for Jolanda's birthday. Which birthday, she refused to specify. He took her to see it with no advance notice, telling her it was time she left the tumbledown house at Mirafiore-Tripodina for something more comfortable; she could bring Mariangela and Tommaso, also – if she insisted – Sebastiano; the building work was nearly finished; they could move in immediately. Jolanda was in raptures. 'It is *bellissima!*' she declared warmly. 'My Vincente, he gives the best presents. No mother ever had such a wonderful son – except for the *Santa Vergine*, *naturalmente*, and she is special case. Now I have house on the lake with the *aristocratichi* and the *arrivisti*. You make me *molto, molto contenta*, Vincente, but—'

'But?'

'I cannot leave Villa Mirafiore. You understand, I know you understand. I live there long time now – so many years I not count them – is my home, Sebastiano's home. Maybe I grow a little old. When you are old and you find place where you are happy, you not want to make changes. When I was young, I change *costantemente*, every year I change my house, my country, my lover. Now, I am not so *volatile*. Also, Sebastiano . . .'

'*Si?*' Vincent spoke through shut teeth, on a hiss. *Sssi?*

'I think he begin to like you now. *Si abitua a te.* He knows you are good son to me, he knows you love me. But he not like to live in your house. He is proud, *capisci*, he mind very much that he is only a little rich, but you, you are very rich, like Agnelli, like Berlusconi. It hurt him, that he cannot buy me this beautiful *palazzo*, that he can only afford Villa Mirafiore, with taps that drip and leak in roof—'

'I'll have the bloody roof repaired if that's what you want!' Vincent fumed.

'No, *caro*; the nephew of Tommaso will do that when he is free. Maybe next week. *Magari.* Is arranged. Sebastiano will pay for roof – and then we come *here* on holiday, yes? Whenever you visit, we all come here. Sebastiano not mind that so much. I will drink the best champagne and live like a d'Este! I am very glad you buy this place, Vincente. Is more fun for you than Mirafiore-Tripodina. With house like this, you visit more often, yes?'

So the villa on San Giulio stood empty most of the time, except for a couple of caretaker staff who took care of nobody. On rare occasions, it was loaned to friends or rented out. And once or twice a year when Vincent came to Italy Jolanda's household would move there – bar Tommaso, who had never forgiven Vincent for their initial encounter and contended that his joints were growing too stiff for him to move anywhere. Their behaviour followed a standard pattern: Jolanda exulted, Sebastiano sulked, and Mariangela upstaged the cook/housekeeper by preparing – at her Signora's instigation – delicacies of the Tuscan cuisine with which the hapless

Lombard could not hope to compete. It galled Vincent that his mother would not live there all the time, but he was too accustomed to her erratic temperament to waste much energy on protest. It was like the matter of her jewellery. He regularly bought her the genuine article, but she still wore some of her old glassware, paste and diamonds crammed higgledy-piggledy on to her claw-like fingers. 'When I was film star in Hollywood, I thought diamonds *molto importanti*. I was like Elizabeth Taylor, like Zsa-Zsa Gabor: a big star must have lots of jewels, real jewels with many carats. Imitation diamonds are for imitation star. Now, I am not so mercenary. Real or false, is all pretty. Besides, I forget which is which.'

He was thinking of her with a familiar glow of exasperation, the *Corriere* sliding from his hand, when he heard the distant bleep of the telephone. Presently, Jolanda called him indoors.

'Is for you,' she said. 'Someone from America. I think he is much distressed.'

Vincent picked up the receiver. 'Hello?'

'Bastard!' said the voice of Irving Blum.

'I beg your pardon?'

'Bastard! Asshole! Ganev! I lend you my home – my own home, my goddamned castle – and what happens? You whistle up a hurricane, you smash up my car, and as if that wasn't enough you rob me! This is what comes of trusting a goy. Hell, I knew about your business deals but I never believed you were a real crook. I'm such a warm-hearted, open-handed mug—'

'Irving—'

'Don't interrupt. Use my house, I said to you, be my guest, and you steal mementos – intimate, personal mementos – which I can never replace. *Oy vey*, if I wasn't such a warm-handed, open-hearted mug—'

'Irving, stop being so Jewish.'

'I *am* Jewish!' By a form of extra-telephonic perception, Vincent was conscious of violent gesticulation. 'You just don't understand what that means. OK, I have guilt, I have paranoia, but I also have soul. I care, I *emote*. You're a lapsed Protestant and a Catholic non-starter and you don't even feel bad about it. To you, that stuff is mere religion. To me, it's in my blood. You're just a chilled lump of British indifference. But I'm a Jew, I'm sensitive, I—'

'You emote. Yes, I got that. Listen, the house was fine, the hurricane was hardly my fault, and I paid for the car. We emptied the freezers because we had to; I told you that. I didn't take any-thing – of course I bloody didn't – unless you count the booze.'

'Booze! Freezers! My house is yours – didn't I say so? Eat what you like, drink what you like – but my tapes, Vincent, my tapes! They may have been only pornography to you, but to me they rep-resent poetry, romance. When I listen to them, I am with those girls again, I am *inside* them again – Ilse with her ice-blonde hair, Inge with the bosom of a Valkyrie and the legs of a racehorse. Sex is so transitory but with those tapes of my girls I could hold them, I could dream of them forever. You're not Jewish; you wouldn't understand. You lust, Vincent, but I *love*. Those tapes to me are like – like petals moulted from the rose of passion, like the scent of wine in an empty glass . . .'

Irving, it transpired, had been in the habit of recording his sex-ual encounters with the shiksas, secreting the cassettes in the house on Dominique to keep them as far as possible from his divorced wife. (She had spent the past ten years endeavouring, in a proces-sion of courtrooms, to prove his unsuitability as a father, while at the same time trying to increase her already lavish alimony.) Now, two of them were missing. Irving explained in some detail why they weren't in a vault: he liked to play them whenever he felt lonely, to – as he put it – reanimate his torpid heart. He often felt lonely.

'You recorded *yourself?*' said Vincent, taken aback. 'My God, why didn't you go the whole hog and use a camera?'

'Shlemiel! I don't want to appear in blue movies! Dirty films are just – dirty. You know your trouble, Vincent? You have no subtlety, no imagination, no—'

'No soul. I am aware. On reflection, you could be wise to stick to sound-effects. You don't exactly have the physique of Sylvester Stallone.'

'Physique shmysique! I am an intellectual. I don't need any physique. Stop changing the subject. *Where are my tapes?*'

'I told you,' said Vincent with emphasis, 'I never touched them. You can't seriously suppose I would. I had my own shiksa there – legs and all – and we were making our own sound-effects. We didn't need yours. Are you sure the tapes are gone? Maybe you mislaid them. Or the servants—'

'I haven't mislaid anything and nor have the servants. I already talked to them: the tapes were in the concealed cabinet and none of them would've had any reason to look in there. In any case, they wouldn't meddle with my things, they're not like that – hell they're loyal, they *like* me. Which reminds me, you schmuck, did you have to expose yourself to the maid? She's been in analysis ever since.'

'You're scarcely in a position to lecture me on sexual modesty!' Vincent retorted.

'Never mind that. What about this bimbo you had with you? Maybe she's kinky. Maybe she took them.'

'Impossible,' Vincent said shortly.

'Look,' Irving said, 'the tapes were there before you arrived; they were gone after you left. OK, you didn't pinch them. I accept that. Did anyone else get the chance? Any casual callers? That nosy bitch Deirdre Langelaan? She'd send those tapes to Esther just to stir shit: they used to be bosom pals. Vincent—'

'Calm down. She was never there. I had no callers, casual or otherwise. All I wanted was to fuck in peace.'

'So we're back to the girl. What d'you know about her? She could be some kind of a detective. She could be working for Esther. Didn't you say she picked you up?'

'Hardly.' Vincent spoke with an assumption of boredom. 'It was pure fluke. If anything, *I* picked *her* up. At least . . .' He reviewed the dying moments of Deirdre Langelaan's Social Event. With a tiny thrill of shock, he thought: she *did* pick me up. She must have known she could rely on Pete to be inhospitable. She planted herself at my table, she invited herself to my house. *She picked me up* . . .

'Irving,' he said in an altered voice, 'this line's terrible and I've got a dinner date with the local *capo*. I'll get back to you.'

He rang off.

Jolanda was waiting for him.

'Who is this girl?' she demanded. 'You not tell me about any girl.'

'You wouldn't like her,' Vincent said curtly. 'She's much too English. A salad without the dressing. An iced drink with no gin. She's not your type.'

'Ah, the English!' Jolanda was disdainful. 'I have enough of them with your father and my so proper *cognata*. Sebastiano, he hate them worse than I do. Sometimes, he call you Englishman, but I tell him no, he must not say that, you are *vero italiano*. *Di fatto*, he only says it when he is angry with you. I do not think she would suit you, this English girl. Who are you telephoning now?'

'Hannibal,' said Vincent. 'About the girl.'

He did not really believe that Micky was a professional snoop in the pay of Esther Blum and he could think of no reason for her to abscond with a couple of pornographic cassettes, but he knew now that he must find out the truth about her. The itch had become too much for him: he had to scratch it or go mad. He ignored the well-founded axiom that if you scratch an itching spot it will blister and eventually bleed. When Hannibal answered the phone Vincent, at his most cryptic, informed him that there were certain items missing from Irving's house, and in view of that it was time to put Quidnunc on to the job. They were to trace Michelle Annesley at once, expense no object. He hung up before Hannibal could offer any comment, unwilling to deal with either query or protest. Suddenly, he remembered his own tale of vanished teaspoons, invented for the benefit of Phyllida Khorman. She had said something about a comparable incident at school, when Micky was a child. He had dismissed it as fantasy, but . . . no, Micky could not possibly be a kleptomaniac. Kleptomaniacs, surely, did not steal compromising tapes. The idea was preposterous. He determined to thrust the problem from his mind and wait upon events.

It was Judas Carson who first got wind of the programme. An old friend currently involved with a TV network tipped him off, and he came to see Vincent on his return to LA. 'You've got trouble, kid.' Vincent was thirty-nine but Judas still called him 'kid'. 'This is a British outfit, a nasty lot: smear now and pay damages later. That kind. They say the producer's the meanest bugger in the business. I don't know exactly what he's got on you but it's bad. I'm trying to get hold of a video in advance: if we can see what we're up against maybe the lawyers can pick a hole in it, get an injunction, something like that. They're sitting on those videos like a squirrel on his nuts but I'll winkle one out of them somehow. There's just one thing you ought to—'

'So they want to sling a little mud.' Vincent's thoughts were elsewhere. 'Let them. It doesn't matter.'

'Sure it matters. What's got into you, Vincent? All these years on the grab and you're still sentimental. Take your smart friends. They like you 'cause you got class, OK, but they like you a lot more 'cause you got dough. You spend it pretty free, you give to their pet charities: that makes you their pal. They don't want to know where you got the stuff; maybe they guess, but they don't want to know. They got two faces, see, one with its eyes shut spouting morality and one all smiles and sweet talk with a hand outstretched. A show like this, it makes them open their eyes: they can't go on kidding themselves. Suddenly, your money's too dirty for their lily-white fingers. You've become bad news. And bad news is bad business.'

'You're quite a philosopher, aren't you?' The hint of sarcasm was automatic, the offshoot of fatigue. 'Listen: my so-called smart friends may shy off for a while but when the fuss dies down they'll come running back. Any I lose I can do without. They just go with the flow – public opinion – and public opinion isn't going to waste much hot air-time on me. Anyhow, whatever these creeps have found out can't be that revealing. My life is a closed book.'

'I was coming to that.' Judas did not look happy. 'The way I heard it, some of it's personal – family spite, that sort of thing' – Vincent's gaze flicked briefly to his ex-mentor's face – 'but in the business area guess who they got to shoot her big mouth off?' He paused, but Vincent was once more plunged in abstraction, occupied with the familiar time-spinner of swirling his drink around his glass. 'I always said LeSewer was a snake,' Judas concluded. 'You should've listened to me, kid. You cosy up to a rattler and in the end you get bit. That's nature.'

'Rich?' Vincent sounded mildly incredulous. 'Dishing the dirt on some crap TV show? It seems rather – unlikely.'

'Yeah. Dying of snakebite is unlikely, but it happens. What you got to ask is, who paid her? She's one who never did nothing for nothing. If we could prove money changed hands, we'd have the bastards by the balls.'

'Are you sure about all this?' Vincent said slowly.

'Sure I'm sure. Wish I wasn't. It's a tough break, whichever way you look at it.'

'If Richmond *was* paid,' Vincent frowned, 'it would have to be one hell of a bribe. This isn't – it's not her style. If she wanted to have a go at me she'd do it in the market – beat me on a fast deal, take me for a million or so. That I could understand. But this . . . We go back a long way, Richmond and I, to coin a phrase. You remember. I always thought—'

'I know, kid. I know what you thought. Like I said, you're sentimental. You don't want to be so trusting. I told you that from the start.'

In the aftermath of this conversation Vincent took his jet lag to bed and slept badly, his mind distracted with alternating worries. Had he been less weary he might have put two and two together and made six, but his plane had been delayed, he had had a violent row with Sebastiano the preceding evening, and he was in no state for mental arithmetic. In any case, he still visualised all journalists as either Hibbert-like opportunists latching on to any chance of a scoop, or camera-toting paparazzi swarming at the entrance to every courtroom, every party, every Beverly Hills binge. In his subconscious, the facts had computed themselves, the equation was complete, the answer fell into place. X equals Micky. Micky equals X. As sometimes happens his dreams of that night only came back to him a week or so later, a vivid jumble of images in which Richmond's face, distended by the TV screen, broke up and resolved itself into Micky, lying on the bed beside him holding what he thought was his penis but it had turned into a microphone. 'Just one more question, Mr Savage,' she was saying, and then the microphone ejaculated but it brought him no pleasure, and she was laughing and shaking her head and shouting at him. *No one could ever love you . . .*

He woke early, still tired and feeling worse than hung-over. His fortieth birthday was in November and it occurred to him that he was technically middle-aged, a depressing consideration. He had no desire to be young again and short of senility he could cope with growing old, or so he believed, but middle age sounded like any other median, middling tedious, middle rate, mediocre. He had made a great deal of money and paid off a tally of old scores but what else had he done? What did he intend to do? Nothing and nothing. Here he was in the middle of nothing, an existentialist in a void. It was his credo, the nucleus of his philosophy, but for the first time, or what he thought was the first time, he tasted isolation and found it had no taste. Looking in the mirror while he shaved he saw a forbidding ensemble of features, black brows drawn low over sunless eyes, lips long cured of the habit of smiling, cheeks lean to gauntness under the froth of shaving cream. But it seemed to him that the strength and ruthlessness of that reflection was only a façade, a flimsy mask, too easily torn away, barely concealing the true man in all his naked despair. It was a long while since he had felt so insecure and now, with brutal unfairness, the resurgence of youthful vulnerability was compounded by the weariness of middle age. The worst of both worlds. He rinsed off the froth, leaving his jaw semi-shorn, and went to the office.

The report from Quidnunc was on his desk. Michelle Annesley Cloud, born 1957. British subject. London address. Mother, Veronica Annesley, later Cloud; father, Michael Annesley. Poet. The agency had even included a few of his best-known lines.

> 'They march with blood-soaked banners
> into the fading sunset; the battle-talk of drum and gun
> dwindles to sighing sea and breathing wind:
> Night spreads her swift shadow
> over the damaged land.'
>
> From *The Last Battle*

The last battle. Vincent remembered Armageddon, pictured Micky, mounted on her white charger, silver chainmail rippling in the sun like the skin of an eel, Excalibur in her hand. X-calibre, the unknown sword. The memory hurt him. He read on, absorbing little, skimming details, impatient to reach the punchline. Her step-father, Jolyon Cloud. Sussex University. Her early marriage to Patrick Murphy and subsequent divorce. Her professional name, Micky Murphy, with accompanying photograph, neck bare of hair, peaked cap angled over one eye. God knew where they had obtained that. Her work in Fleet Street: photocopies of old news articles. Serious features, investigations, revelations. Finally, her present employment. *Quest*. Producer, Alun Craig. Summary of programme's aims and achievements. New series starting 5 September. Opening edition 'Vincent Scarpia Savage: A Study in Revenge'.

Vincent sat at his desk for a long time without moving. He knew he ought to be angry – soon, he *would* be angry – but for now he felt merely empty and stupid and faintly sick. He tried to recall precisely what he had told her, how far he had betrayed himself – betrayed *himself* – but his brain would not work properly, it kept stalling on a single thought. Micky. Her image stared up at him from the open file, steady-eyed, deceptively candid, good-looking in a cool, high-toned, fine-boned sort of way. A nice piece of English Spode. What had he said to her? 'Anyone would think you were doing a thesis . . .' He could not follow his thoughts any further. He felt numb with the imminence of pain; empty, stupid. Stupid. Empty. He needed anger. Blind rage, unflagging hatred, the lust of revenge, those were the simple passions that made life worth living, that kept you warm when the Ice Age set in. But the only anger he could find was directed obscurely against himself, like a whiplash on the recoil stinging his own flesh. *Stupid* . . .

His secretary knocked, entered, halted abruptly well short of the desk. 'The mail . . . ?'

'Get out.'

She got out. Without a word. Vincent was left alone with his stupidity.

He didn't tell Hannibal the truth. He didn't tell Judas. He didn't call Irving. He was sure now that Micky had taken the tapes, although he could not guess why. Still, she was a journalist, an occupational scavenger who would help herself to anything on anybody as a matter of course. That was reason enough. When the promised video arrived, one day in advance, he watched it through, listened to the commentary, recognised too many quotes. And at the end there was Micky, Micky *Murphy*, two down in the credits, bowing out of the limelight. As if her contribution had been a mere bagatelle, scarcely deserving a mention. Somehow, that only deepened his chagrin. If she had demanded top billing and large letters, boasting a victory, blowing her own trumpet, he could have borne it better. But no doubt she would assert she had acted on a principle, cheated for a cause, claiming a victory for right and justice and not for herself. His mouth sneered, though there was no one there to see. She was still clinging to the trappings of honour, still flourishing her shining sword. A hypocrite like all the rest. He imagined destroying her as he had destroyed Richard, a long wait for a dreary vengeance, but even in his mind he could not make her weep or rail. She had wept in his bed when they argued about love but faced with the ruin of reputation and career her eyes remained the eyes of the photograph, steadfast and fearless. 'I told you,' she said, 'you cannot change.' People don't change. He accepted it with resignation, with resentment, with an irrational surge of fury. He would keep the picture and one day, when by means unspecified she was broken, hysterical, screaming at him as Crystal had once screamed, he would taunt her with it, telling her: 'Look at this. Look. This is the way you were.' And the longed-for satisfaction filled him with such blackness he thought he too could have cried, *lacrimae rerum*, tears of anger and bitterness and loss.

But it was only a chimera.

He rang Judas, told him; 'It's a non-event. A storm in a teacup. A hurricane in a champagne glass. If I sue, I'd simply be giving them credibility. It isn't worth the hassle.'

'It's up to you,' said Judas. And: 'I hope you're right.'

After the programme came the headlines.

Hostesses crossed him off the A list. Former friends turned away. A beautiful starlet whom he had once screwed phoned to assure him she was his through thick and thin. Vincent barely noticed. He had already given Quidnunc their instructions, acting on a reflex with no thoughts in his mind, no plans to mature. In due course, he learned that Piers Percival had cleared Richard's bankruptcy debts, saying, according to the Sunday papers: 'He's my godson. I neglected him shamefully. I'm a lonely old man with no child of my own . . .' and so forth. According to Vincent's recollection of Piers Percival, such heart-rending banalities seemed highly improbable, but presumably they had some foundation in fact. Quidnunc had verified that Richard was staying with him in his house in Surrey, commuting to London to see the children and be interviewed for various responsible positions in the field of aircraft design. (With the exception of Sir John, Piers had usually shunned visitors, maintaining that he found his own company more amusing than that of anyone else.) There was even a picture, snipped from one of the tabloids, taken by an enterprising reporter on a dull assignment at London Zoo. Richard, with small boy and awkward-looking girl, and beside them 'Micky Murphy, the TV journalist whose painstaking investigation helped Richard

Garoghan to clear his name and start a new life. Is romance in the air?' Vincent had ripped the photo in half before he could check himself, the ragged tear dividing Micky almost exactly from his cousin. He stared at the pieces for several minutes. Then he summoned his long-suffering secretary.

'Book me a flight,' he said. 'I'm going to England.'

3

I ran into Shirley Prosser again about a fortnight after the programme was shown, not in Sainsbury's but in Harrods Food
Hall. Literally ran into her, this time. We both drew back,
plunged into apology, broke off as recognition set in. I braced
myself for further recriminations: I suppose my expression must
have chilled over. But Shirley had evidently suffered a radical
change of outlook. An eager smile swept across her face; she
seized my arm in case I had thoughts of flight. 'Miss Murphy! I'm
so glad to see you! I've been wanting a chance to apologise –
about the other time, I mean – I nearly wrote to your programme, only I wasn't quite sure . . . anyway, I really am *awfully*
sorry. I was so upset after what happened, everything was so horrible, and the way those disgusting kids treated Mark – well, I
don't care what anyone says, it's their parents' blame, isn't it? He
was just an innocent child.'

'I hope things are easier for him now?' I enquired opportunely,
pulling myself together after initial surprise. 'I see he's not with
you today.'

'Oh no, he's at his friend's house. Everything's been fine since
he started the new school. In fact, I think these kids are actually
rather impressed his daddy's in jail. One of them has a grandfather who was done for insider trading, and another one's uncle
was in some kind of bank fraud, so you see! Still, that's big business for you. Of course, it's a much better school.'

'Obviously,' I murmured, slightly dazed.

'I must say, it's really kind of you to take an interest, particularly after the way I behaved. I just wasn't seeing things clearly, you know: I didn't want to face the truth about Guy. He kept saying whatever he'd done was only for Mark and me, as if that made it all right, but of course, when I came to think about it, I saw that was nonsense. I mean, no child needs a father who's mixed up with *drugs*, does he? Steve says anyone can get into a fiddle over money – the law's so complicated sometimes you don't even know when you're breaking it – but when it's drugs, well, that's different, isn't it?'

'Steve?'

Steve, it appeared, was the new man in her life. She was in the process of divorcing Guy and moving up in the world, from St John's Wood to a commuter village in Bucks, from a BMW to a Range Rover, from a launch in Brighton Marina to a yacht in Marbella. Mark's Scalextric would doubtless be replaced by a section of Brands Hatch. Meanwhile, she was living in a flat in Knightsbridge until Mark was sufficiently accustomed to his superior new school to become a weekly boarder – and until her decree nisi came through. Steve was paying the rent. He was 'very big in the City, much more successful than Guy: he says if you're really clever you don't have to do anything criminal at all.' She had met him when he came to buy Guy Prosser's Porsche – for his daughter. It all sounded depressingly familiar. I couldn't avoid speculating, with a sneaking sense of mischief, if Steve Marchant, too, would repay investigation. Poor Shirley: she would never forgive me. She looked very pretty, her hair blonde to the roots, her mascara freshly smudged. She was the sort of woman who never learns, who always marries a particular type of man and is always aggrieved when his deficiencies are made clear to her. A permanently injured innocent who clings stubbornly to her naïvety through fair weather and foul.

Nonetheless, I wished her luck.

She released my arm to clutch my hand. 'You were so nice about it, that time when I got all worked up – I felt really awful afterwards – and now, honestly, I can't tell you how grateful I am. Everything's turned out so well, and I'm so happy, and if it hadn't been for you and your programme I'd still be with Guy in St John's Wood. I never really liked that house, you know: we had Arab neighbours on both sides and the kitchen was much too small. Have you seen my ring? It's a *marquise* diamond.'

I admired the diamond on cue and we parted friends. Happy endings, I thought, seemed to be the order of the day. The bad guys got their comeuppance; the good guys their reward. Guy Prosser was in jail; Shirley had a marquise diamond. Vincent Scarpia Savage had become a regular target of the tabloid press, the details of his love-life, factual or fictional, providing a welcome distraction from the phoney war in the Middle East. The latest publicity shots of Crystal stared down at me from every news-stand. Those broadsheets which had taken a lofty tone over the mortgage fraud long ago were only too pleased to pat themselves on the back and reiterate how right they had been. And Richard was returned from his self-imposed exile, reunited with his children, while Piers Percival, whom I visualised as a well-intentioned but faintly sinister *eminence grise* – perhaps an *eminence beige* – had evidently decided to assume the role of benefactor on a large scale. Fortune smiled on Richard once again, with no cutting edge to her teeth. It struck me that he could even be said to have got the girl, if I could be so described. If he wanted me, if I wanted him, if I could make up my mind. A plethora of ifs. We had dined out together twice – once on my bill, once on his – and spent a day at the zoo with the children. Jonas, as I had suspected, was an angel-faced urchin with eyes as blue as Crystal's and Richard's smile; he was into chain-sucking ice-lollies and had to be forcibly deterred from attempting to shake hands with a gorilla. Both he and Penny accepted me with a comforting degree of nonchalance. Richard, I trusted, was not so nonchalant, but he clearly believed in taking his time, picking his moment, or simply keeping the opposite sex in suspense. He still hadn't kissed me.

I turned my attention to the selection of a birthday cake, which was why I had come to Harrods Food Hall in the first place. Penny was twelve on Friday, and I had suggested a birthday tea at my flat – a drastic offer that meant virtually redesigning my living room, shifting many of the books, files, and cassettes which I had just got back into their correct disorder after Alun's strip-search. Life, I reflected, was intruding on me with a vengeance, not only stirring emotions long untouched but usurping my personal space, invading every nook and cranny of my existence. Several of my friends had children but I had never invited them to tea. It was a traumatic proceeding.

'Mummy usually gives me a party with my schoolfriends,' Penny explained, 'but this year she says it's too difficult. I think it's something to do with your programme. There've been reporters calling ever since. Brendan says Mummy wasn't as famous as this even when she was famous. She's going to sell her story to a newspaper but she can't decide which. They've offered her lots of money.'

'Did *you* watch the programme?' I asked.

Penny made a face. 'Mummy wouldn't let me. She said it wasn't suitable for me, because Uncle Vincent did such wicked things.' Such as refusing to elope with her mother, I thought. Penny was looking faintly wistful. Nameless wickedness plainly held a glamour to which, I was certain, no clinical revelation of the facts could possibly compare.

'Wicked Uncle Vincent,' I said. 'It sounds like a fairy tale. Penelope Snow and the Wicked Uncle. Did you ever meet him?'

'He came to the house sometimes, just for a little while. Before Daddy went away.' She added, disappointed but fair: 'He didn't look very wicked. I don't think he likes children – mostly, he just ignored us – but it was a long time ago and we were very young then. Jo asked him if there were still real Red Indians in America, and if he had ever met one, but he just said: "Not in the property business." He said there were plenty of cowboys, though.' I smiled. 'He didn't mean cowboys in Westerns, did he?' Penny went on. 'I know that. Nowadays, "cowboys" just means crooks. Is Uncle Vincent a cowboy?'

'A very stylish one,' I said. 'A sort of Gucci *gauchero*.'

'What's a *gauchero*?'

'A Spanish word for a cowboy.'

'Uncle Vincent's half Italian, not Spanish.' Penny was a stickler for precision. I noted she did not have to ask what Gucci was. No doubt she had learned that from Crystal. 'Anyway, at least he didn't ruffle my hair. I hate it when people do that. Brendan does – that's why I wear my ponytail right on top of my head: I thought it might stop him. Jo can't do that – he has to put up with it. He tried to bite Brendan once.'

'Your father ruffles your hair occasionally,' I pointed out. 'You don't mind that, do you?'

'Of *course* not. He's Daddy. It's different. I just don't like it when it's a stranger.'

'I know,' I said. 'It's the kind of thing people do when they pretend to like children: they've seen parents do it so they think it's an appropriate gesture. It must be maddening.' Hirsute harassment, I thought frivolously.

'About your birthday,' I resumed. 'Would you mind it being just the four of us? We could have a joint celebration. I had a birthday, too. Last week.' My thirty-third, a long way from twelve and hardly a main event; at work, we had been in the Pub for an hour before Alun enquired what the party was in aid of.

'I'm on the – on the *cusp* of Virgo and Libra,' Penny pronounced solemnly. 'Which are you?'

'Virgo,' I said. 'The critical perfectionist. At least, I was.'

In the event, the tea party went well. Disregarding various rococo confections overladen with frills and furbelows I had settled for a basic chocolate cake, on the principle that chocolate cake is something all children will eat, whatever their other likes and dislikes. The principle held good. 'We don't get it very often,' Jo explained on his third slice. 'Mummy says it makes you fat.' He had inherited Richard's stocky build, which must be giving image-conscious Crystal cause for intolerance. I sighed. Whatever my opinion of her, I had neither the right nor the desire to contravene maternal dictates.

'It's a special occasion,' I maintained. 'Special occasion: special treat. No, you can't have a fourth. That's overdoing it.'

Afterwards, we all watched Penny's present – an unauthorised video of out-takes from children's television, too embarrassing to make the collections of Denis Norden and his ilk. I had obtained it via black market contacts among the technical staff. Penny lost her habitual gravity in peals of laughter and Jo subsequently complained of stomach-ache. 'I do trust they didn't follow all the humour,' Richard said in an aside.

'My God, so do I,' I assented fervently. 'I'm dreadfully sorry. I didn't realise it would be quite so—'

'Doesn't matter.' Unexpectedly, Richard kissed my cheek. 'Censorship does more harm than a few blue jokes. I must take the brats home. You do like them, don't you?'

'Yes,' I said. 'But . . . I'm not going to go all broody over them, if that's what you— Look, they don't need a mother substitute. They're Crystal's brats. Always.'

The conversation was becoming tangled, as conversation with Richard sometimes did. 'Don't leap to conclusions,' he retorted unforgivably. 'It's too soon.'

They departed on a wave of thanks, leaving me smouldering and hot in the face.

Later, over a bottle of wine from my emergency stock – 'Not the Vinho Verde!' – Richard returned to the subject. By then, I was feeling mellow enough to deal with any recurrence of *gêne*. We were sitting side by side on the sofa, too comfortable to go out, too lazy to cook, soaking up the alcohol with the last of the chocolate cake. 'You should've told me it was your birthday beforehand,' Richard said. 'I would have bought you a present. Nothing expensive – you needn't get excited. I've no disposable cash till I get a job. Just something small, cheap, and extremely original.'

'It's the thought that counts,' I said. 'What do you think you'd have given me?'

'A cordless shower. A cuddly Saddam Hussein glove puppet. A teabag.' He grinned; I laughed. 'Thirty-three is a serious age. So – seriously – what are your plans for the future? Have you any? Does your career leave room for – relationships, children of your own, anything?' He flicked a teetering column of videos with one finger. 'The world of TV journalism seems to have taken you over. Even your home is infested with it. Where has Micky got to?'

'This is Micky,' I said sombrely, indicating my surroundings.

'Only this?'

'Maybe. I don't know. I don't know. Is your enquiry general or personal?'

'Both.'

He was asking questions he had no right to ask, bulldozing into the china shop and offering to pay for breakages while admitting, in the same breath, that he had come out without his credit cards. Caveat vendor. I should have told him to go to hell. I didn't.

'Crystal often said work dominated my whole existence,' he continued by way of explanation, 'in particular during the admittedly short period when I was my own boss. She said I was unfair to her and unfair to the children: perhaps that was one reason why she found it so easy to turn to Vincent. It's pointless wasting time on conjecture but I know one thing for sure: I'm not going to make the same mistakes again. Different mistakes, yes – but not the same ones. When I have to, I'll compromise. I don't want my own company any more: it's too much responsibility, it takes over. I don't want my life to be all work and no play, no family, no love. I need to know—' He broke off, rueful but unembarrassed, revising his demands. 'All right, it's unreasonable, I am aware. You've never said you like me and I don't suppose I've said much about liking you. But I need to – check out the terrain before I move in, pinpoint the hazards—'

'Back off if it's too chancy?' I said. 'Fair enough. Back off. It's chancy. My career comes first: I can't change that for anybody. It would make me a bad investment as a girlfriend. I am the Cat That Walks By Itself, and all places are alike to me. You want a domestic pussy.'

There was a lifted eyebrow for my ambiguous terminology, but Richard did not appear to be noticeably deterred. 'You don't know your Kipling,' he said. 'I've read Jo the *Just So Stories* only recently. The Cat That Walks By Itself agreed to spend half its time at the hearthside, playing with Baby for a saucer of milk. Or something like that. You could fit in a little domesticity.'

'I don't like milk. What else is on offer? Of course: a cordless shower – what a concept for an engineer! – a megalomaniac glove puppet, and a teabag. Yes, well, I can live without those too.'

'We might fall in love,' Richard suggested. 'Given time, you know.'

'Might we?' I said, deadpan.

He reached towards me and kissed me. It was undeniably pleasant. No crude passion, no sexual power games, but the warmth of contact, tentative intimacy, the beginnings of sensual communication. More potential than actuality.

'You took your time getting around to that,' I remarked when he had finished.

'Two people fall straight into bed only when they're going to fall straight out again,' Richard said. 'If it's important, you take it slowly. You see the problems coming and try to find some way round them. In any case, all relationships thrive on a little anticipation. Vincent . . . now Vincent was always falling straight into bed with some girl or other. He probably still does. And he never could work out why his love-life had no staying power.'

I know, I thought. I had a sudden insane urge to tell Richard the whole story, to watch him turn away from me, shocked or disgusted or merely disappointed, to yell at him with furious bitterness: 'It's my job. I did it brilliantly. If I hadn't done it, the programme wouldn't have been made and you'd still be wallowing in self-pity on Martyr's Island.' Needless to say, I resisted the compulsion. Phyl used to say that a love affair needs a pinch of dishonesty on top of the froth the way a cappuccino needs a dusting of cinnamon. But I couldn't be dishonest with Richard: his own honesty made that impossible. I couldn't lie to him, I couldn't tell him the truth, I shouldn't get involved. I was drifting where fools rush in, floating on the tide of my emotions, drowning in wishful thinking. Richard was right: I could fit in part-time commitment, part-time motherhood. If I wanted. If I cheated. If the tapes – and the past – stayed locked in a bank vault for good.

We kissed again, starting to explore each other physically, but in the end I drew away. Mind won over matter: the native hue of lust was sicklied o'er with the pale cast of thought. I could not abandon myself to rapture with Richard as I had once done with his cousin; my own unfrankness inhibited me. This was not playtime in paradise, this was for real. Richard didn't ask me what was wrong. He sat with his arms round me while I tried to think of something to say.

'I'm sorry,' I essayed at last. 'I can't give you everything and I don't want to short-change you. I'm a career girl. That's it.'

'That used to be a favourite line of Crystal's,' Richard observed. 'She tried it on Vincent, I believe; also on me, once or twice. An excuse for saying no. I know you're a career girl: so what? Don't you read the blockbusters? Nowadays, you can have it all. Provided you can afford the nanny.'

'Don't be so cynical,' I said. 'I'm the journalist: that's my prerogative. Talking of what you can afford, has your wealthy godfather by any chance decided to adopt you as his heir? I mean, if there was a major legacy on the table – who knows? – you might be able to undermine my resistance.'

'Gold-digger,' Richard mocked. 'In that case, we're both out of luck. Piers doesn't say much but I know he thinks family money should stay in the family. He didn't earn: he inherited. Anyhow, there are some cousins in Outer Mongolia or somewhere like that. He might leave me a couple of silk ties. He says I have no taste in clothes.'

'Are you fond of him?' There was a pause while Richard appeared to consider. 'Is he fond of you? He must have known what Vincent had done but he let things ride for some time.' I had no intention of alluding to my belief that it was Piers who had set the dogs on Vincent's track to begin with.

'He doesn't like to interfere,' Richard said, frowning. 'I've never really understood him. We're not that close. I'm grateful rather than fond, and he – I'm not sure. He might have acted from some sort of . . . sense of duty. I daresay my mother cried on his shoulder while I was away. He and my uncle were great friends: perhaps he feels helping me is something he owes Uncle John. He's been very kind to me but aloof. As soon as I've got a job I'm moving out. I mean to repay him, too, whatever he says.' After a moment, he added: 'He wants to meet you, by the way.'

'Does he?' I said drily. 'I want to meet him.'

'You'll have to come to dinner – preferably before the party. Piers always says you can't get to know anyone at a party.'

'What party?' I enquired blankly.

'Didn't I tell you? My mother's idea. Ritual slaughter of fatted calf to welcome the prodigal home. She's getting sentimental in her old age. God knows who'll be there. A lot of people I haven't seen for years and won't ever see again, probably. She's got a list of old friends of mine from Crystal – which meant *she* had to be invited as well. My mother got into that one and couldn't get out of it: poor love, she assumed Crys would have the tact to decline. She doesn't allow for modern manners. Anyhow, what with my ex-wife, my ex-friends, any chums from my mother's debutante days who might be still alive, and a few arty-farty colleagues of Piers', it's not surprising I'm desperate for moral support. You will come, won't you? Look at it this way: you made the pro-gramme, you brought me back to England, it's all your fault. The least you can do is come to the party.'

'I've gone off big parties,' I said. 'The last one I went to was struck by a hurricane.'

There was a flat little silence, but Richard didn't hear it.

'What an exotic social life you lead,' he grinned. 'Don't worry: there hasn't been a hurricane in Surrey for—'

'Three years,' I supplied. 'In Hertford, Hereford, and Hampshire, hurricanes hardly ever happen. It says nothing about Surrey.'

'Well . . . we're only in September. The monsoons arrive shortly, but hurricanes hold off another month. Live danger-ously, Micky.' He drew a finger down my temple, teasing the short tendrils of hair away from my ear. 'I'd like your company. I need someone intelligent to dance with.'

'My God, do I have to dance too?' I judiciously ignored the progress of his finger.

'Not if your rheumatism's very bad,' Richard said kindly. 'We'll find you a chair in a quiet corner and I'll come and pat your hand from time to time.'

'I can't say I'm tempted. It depends on work. I'm still tinker-ing around with various editions of the current series and we're starting on an international fraudster for the next, so—'

'Come on, Micky. You can take an evening off. Promise me.' He added with a certain deliberation: 'After all, I know you keep your promises.'

I glanced at him, temporarily unnerved. Penny had never referred to the subject with me and I assumed she had forgotten it: adult promises obviously did not carry much weight in her world.

Wrong again.

'Tell me,' he pursued, 'in Barbados, why didn't you make use of it? "I gave my word to your daughter" – it would have been an effective line. Sob stuff. You could have played on my feelings like Nigel Kennedy with a warped violin. No father could resist a spiel like that.'

'Emotional blackmail,' I said succinctly. He would have resisted it, I thought. The obstinacy of the Savages would have carried the day, even at his daughter's expense. 'Besides, it was between Penny and me.'

'You keep your secrets too, don't you?'

Too many secrets.

'About the party.'

'Yes?'

'I'll consider it.'

I should have said no, and I knew it. I was inching further down the road to a relationship I could not have, merely faltering when I should have turned and fled. The way to hell is paved with hesitations.

We went to dinner with Piers Percival a week later. I told myself that I was going, not to see Richard, but to meet Piers, Alun's informant, Jan Horrocks' manipulator, the man who, I was convinced, had dislodged the pebble that started the avalanche. The house, tucked into a fold of countryside a short distance off the M23, was an elegant example of Georgiana, the dignity of its old age only slightly marred by the burglar alarms which adorned its façade like contemporary gargoyles, warding off evil spirits. We had drinks in an ornamental garden which bore signs of illegal sprinkler activity – deep pile lawn, thriving flowerbeds, explosions of blossom sagging with bumblebees or dancing with butterflies. Water gushed from what looked like a stone croissant held in the arms of a youthful Pan, while in the pool below fish glided like golden shadows beneath the lily-pads. Piers gave all the credit to his gardener. 'I know nothing about flowers,' he insisted. 'I am interested in the creations of Man, not the accidents of Nature. All I required was a setting for a few pieces of statuary.' Indoors, the September sun flooded through long windows, no doubt to the detriment of the Oriental carpets. Beautiful food arrived on beautiful china. I encouraged Piers to talk about his possessions, feeling restricted by Richard's presence. 'I am not a true collector,' Piers averred. 'I do not have an obsession with any particular era or artistic school: I am a dabbler in all ages, a jack-of-all-decades. Of course, I have certain preferences – Renaissance pictures, Regency furniture – but I would not call myself a connoisseur, merely a casual acquisitor. I enjoy being surrounded by beautiful things but I am not manic about them. I have come across those who would sell their grandmothers – or their lovers, or their dearest friends – for a twiddle by da Vinci or a piece of Cellini bric-a-brac. Also those who would steal them. We have had three attempted burglaries in the past two years. My manservant sleeps in a different room in the house every night: it is an idiosyncrasy of his. He carries a shotgun – for rats. As I told the police, we have a problem with rats, especially in the main gallery.'

After dinner, I was taken on a species of guided tour, to see what Piers described as his 'favourite treasures'. Richard accompanied us. However, it was little more than a brief reconnaissance: Piers seemed determined to underwhelm me, responding courteously to my equally courteous interest, his comments informative but never effusive, his attitude, for the most part, that of a person whose mind was elsewhere. Possibly it was. He was a tall man, only slightly stooped despite the unspecified war wound which, Richard had told me, kept him in constant pain. Something internal, Elizabeth had said. His thinness was skeletal, his face a skull to which the skin adhered like ill-applied papier mâché, bunched and crumpled round the awkward bits. His hands were beautiful, the hands of an El Greco painting, long-fingered, visibly sensitive, punctuating his rare gestures with the instinctive grace of a dancer. I remember watching him handle an antique duelling pistol, one of a pair displayed on the wall, reputedly the former property of Lord Castlereagh. 'I keep it loaded,' he said, 'since the last burglary. I like to feel there is a weapon available, should I find myself confronting a house-breaker. Richard – dear boy – assures me it is illegal.' He raised the gun as if to fire, wasted limbs stiffening, a new sternness transfixing his features. It was as if the man drew strength and potency from his weapon: together, they became actively dangerous, almost frightening. 'It would be off-putting, don't you think? A crazed old man waving an ancient pistol. Ludicrous, maybe, but off-putting. And it suits me better than one of those new-fangled scatterguns that pulverise everything in sight.'

'Shooting a burglar,' Richard sighed, 'is a serious offence. With a shotgun or a pearl-inlaid antique.'

'Being shot by one is even more serious,' Piers said gently. 'These days, they generally seem to come armed, if not with guns then with knives, axes, clubs. We live in an ugly world. I daresay we always did, if the truth were told, but for many years we were able to isolate ourselves in little pockets of civilisation, thrusting violence and ugliness to the periphery, beyond the walls of our privileged enclave. Now, they have tunnelled their way back in. They have to be tamed, or so the sociologists claim, but not by me. I'm too old for lost causes. I will defend myself, in my own feeble fashion; your generation can worry about the rest. There are few advantages to old age but one of them is that erratic behaviour becomes permissible. Should I find myself in the dock, I will plead senility. I do not really imagine they will put me in jail.'

I smiled; Richard frowned. Piers was showing me a rapier, needle-sharp and as slim as a reed, when Richard was summoned to the telephone. 'His mother,' Piers deduced. 'Dear Lizzy – did he tell you? She has talked me into giving a party for him. I abominate parties. I have always favoured the old communist dictum that gatherings of more than three people constitute a social menace.' ('I don't think that was quite it,' I murmured.) 'The things one does for old friends. And I used to be a believer in never doing anything for anybody – indeed, I still am. The lamentable gap between theory and practice! Elizabeth will keep Richard on the line for hours. Come into my study.'

The study, surprisingly, was not dark and leatherbound as I would have expected but light and bright with cream-coloured walls and bookshelves where the vivid spines of modern tomes jostled for position with more antiquated volumes. There was a small television positioned discreetly in an alcove and a personal computer on the veteran desktop. In a wire tray marked 'Out' there were a couple of letters whose unusual appearance caught my eye: the addresses were printed in dark brown italics on envelopes coloured a pale coffee. I had seen both the stationery and the print before – if I needed further confirmation of my suspicions. In Alun Craig's mail.

There was no point in preambling around the subject. I tapped the corner of one envelope and remarked: 'Your post is rather distinctive. I seem to have noticed it – elsewhere.'

'Of course.' Piers looked mildly astonished. 'Dear me, should I have written to your producer under plain cover, signing off with a codeword? Surely that would have been a tad melodramatic. I had no idea journalism was quite so cloak-and-dagger.'

He thinks I was told, I realised. He thinks Alun put his cards on the table instead of keeping them stuffed up his sleeve. I suppressed a smile.

'Won't you sit down?' Piers motioned me to a chair in front of the desk and seated himself behind it, making me feel rather as if I had been invited for an interview.

'You didn't tell Richard,' I said.

'Nor did you,' retorted Piers. 'Or so I infer. Let us not waste time fencing with one another. Richard can be very trying. He has a certain antagonism to what he sees as my charitable endeavours: there was no point in giving him further cause for obduracy. It's nonsense, anyway. I am not a charitable man. Richard is my godson and thus, to a limited extent, my responsibility, as Elizabeth has so rightly – and so frequently! – reminded me. It was John's idea, of course. He thought it would do me good to exert myself. He would have enjoyed watching my recent exertions on Richard's behalf. Should there be any form of life after death, which I doubt, it would give me great pleasure to walk straight up to him in Elysium and hit him.'

I wanted to laugh, but there was too much pain in the twist of his smile.

'Take my advice, my dear,' he concluded. 'Do not covet long life. There are few things more wretched than outlasting one's friends.'

'Yet you don't want to be shot by a burglar,' I said softly.

'That,' said Piers, 'is a matter of principle.'

He opened a silver box which proved to contain Russian cigarettes; I declined.

'Once I had so many vices,' he repined. 'Now I have so few. Soon, in the inevitable course of nature, I shall have none. Richard, I fear, has no vices already, or none worth mentioning. It is hardly my business, but I gather he likes you. Do you – like him?'

'Yes,' I said. 'But it needn't worry you. I don't intend to – I don't want—'

'Good Heavens, why should I be worried? You seem to me a most eligible young woman. You are, it is plain, highly intelligent, perfectly presentable, and apparently in good health. Even were I given to worrying about Richard, which I am not, I see no cause for anxiety where you are concerned. I was merely curious. Elizabeth spoke of you with approval. How she will feel about Richard's approval is another matter. She is sometimes . . . a trifle over-maternal about her son.'

'Do *you* like him?' I asked abruptly.

'Richard is a delightful boy. Delightful. I cannot wait for him to move out. Please don't be shocked. I am told he is very charming, but charm is something to which I have always been impervious. I do not dislike him – it is not that – but his company grates. He is so friendly, so tolerant, so extrovert, so candid. He brings a spark of action, a zest for life, into my chronically inactive and somewhat lifeless existence. I do not want them there. Forgive me. You are young: you appreciate such things.'

'You would like me to make allowances for the whims of an old man?' I ventured with muted irony.

'Precisely.'

'I only wondered,' I explained, 'because you took your time before – exerting yourself.'

'I am a Hamlet by temperament,' said Piers. There was a pause while he drew on his cigarette, sucking his already sunken cheeks into sharply indented hollows under the bone.

'When Richard got into difficulties, I was neither involved nor informed. He had left the country before I knew anything about it and although Elizabeth had certain lines of communication he apparently wished to remain untraced. Initially, I respected that wish. But Elizabeth was persistent – she always is – and eventually I began to make enquiries. I won't weary you with the details. What I found was a disaster, if not precisely a tragedy, which I should have foreseen – which I had foreseen, I suppose, long before when I watched the two boys growing up together. I could not absolve myself of negligence. I dislike action, but when it becomes necessary, I do what I must. However, impetuosity is a quality more suited to youth. Age is cautious and dilatory. As you say, I took my time.'

'I see,' I said politely, though I was not at all sure how much I saw.

'I brought you to this room,' he continued, 'because I thought you might be interested in that picture.' He indicated the wall behind him. I had noticed the picture; I had not studied it. I looked obediently. '*Achilles and Patroclus*. By an artist who called himself, intriguingly, Sodoma. A quixotic choice of *nom de pinceau*, don't you think? His real name was Giovanni Antonio Bazzi; he worked in Siena in the early sixteenth century. You will detect the influence of Leonardo, of course.'

'Of course,' I agreed politely.

'I have often thought . . . but look for yourself. There is rather too much drapery and napery around, and Sodoma was not strong on historical accuracy – one feels his characters dressed out of an old theatrical wardrobe – however, all that is merely carping. It is a picture for which I cherish a special affection. I acquired it . . . but never mind all that. How does it strike you?'

'Vincent and Richard,' I said, 'I presume?'

Achilles was shown sulking in his tent, long black hair straying across a face whose brooding dark beauty faintly echoed Vincent's. A scarlet tunic slipped in artistic folds off one muscular shoulder and left most of his torso exposed, while over the other shoulder dangled a wolf-skin complete with claws and teeth. At his side, Patroclus leaned forward, obviously pleading with him, fair-haired and earnest in even more artistic folds of vermilion and green. In the background hung the famous armour, suitably golden but bearing little resemblance to the battlewear of Ancient Greece. Patroclus, I recalled, had worn it to lead the Myrmidons into combat in his friend's stead, before being tragically slain, probably by Hector.

'I always saw them like that,' Piers said. 'Richard, I felt, had the capacity for impetuous self-sacrifice; Vincent, the arrogance to drive him to it. As it developed, I was wrong, but maybe not as wrong as all that. Elizabeth alleges Richard trusted too rashly. That I can believe.'

'How did you feel about Vincent?' I enquired.

'Did you meet him?'

'Briefly.' Three days might be called brief.

'What did you make of him?'

'I asked you.'

Piers stubbed out his cigarette in a heavy glass ashtray, watching the thin twist of smoke unravelling upwards. 'In the war,' he said at length, 'I was in Italy. I knew a leader of the Resistance there – a bandit, I understood, who fought the Germans not out of political conviction but from sheer bloody-mindedness, because he did not like taking their orders or saluting any man. Anti-Hitler, anti-Mussolini, anti anyone with power and a jackboot. He was educated, for a bandit: he called himself Luigi Vampa.'

'Dumas,' I said. 'I'm educated too – for a journalist.'

Piers did not smile. 'The Germans caught him in the end, of course. He was tortured, and then shot. Or possibly he died under torture: I am not certain. Anyway, he would not betray his friends nor reveal his identity. He lived and died as Luigi Vampa. I myself never knew his real name.'

Sodoma? I speculated; but I did not say it.

'Vincent reminded me of him, a little. He might so easily have been a hero; he turned out a villain. An Achilles who sacrificed Patroclus himself, one of nature's *banditti* . . . Perhaps that is another reason why I delayed in going to Richard's rescue. I have always had a weakness for Vincent. Not a soft spot; I would not call it that. But a weakness, yes. Of course, I would not have cared to have had him in the house, either – or not for long. He appeared to me to radiate a kind of dark vitality: it would have been most disturbing. There are some things of which I do not wish to be reminded at such close range. Let us leave the subject. Suffice to say that I have – how can I phrase it? – a certain feeling for both the boys, in very different ways. However, on a long-term basis I am afraid I prefer the painting to the reality. The artist captured an ideal; real life must invariably fall short. I am too much of a coward to cope with all that. Now you, you are a practical child. Perhaps you can manage better.'

'I doubt it,' I said. 'I also seem to spend my time chasing after a phantom ideal. But I never catch up.' To divert us both, I switched my attention to a paler rectangle on the side wall. 'By the way, what used to hang there? And – er – what happened to it? Was it stolen?'

'Oh no. That was the Veronese. I have not yet decided with

what I wish to replace it. The modern school, presumably, would consider that blanched patch of plaster a work of art in itself. A memorial to a small sacrifice of my own. Their arguments do have occasional merit.'

'Sacrifice?' I repeated. Some instinct warned me to make the prompt gentle and my tone bland.

'Would you not call it that?' An element of world-weariness had crept into his voice. 'Perhaps you are right. It was, after all, only a sketch. A figure study for the Marriage at Cana. There must be thousands of them. Nonetheless, I was sorry to lose it.'

'Was it valuable?' I probed cautiously. Piers clearly thought I knew what he was talking about. It would be fatal to betray ignorance.

'Undoubtedly. I could not have put an exact price on it – the market fluctuates, in art as in everything else – but I would estimate . . . however, that was not important. I would not measure my loss in terms of monetary value. Nor, to give the Devil her due, would Madame LeSueur so measure her gain. She is a true collector, obsessive, unscrupulous, a dragon gloating over hoarded gold. I saw her on your show: her face was that of a woman but she had a dragon's eyes. Still, at least she can hang the Veronese where it will be seen. Unlike the Palma Vecchio . . .'

Richmond LeSueur. A line of the conversation at dinner came back to me: 'There are those who would sell their grandmothers or their lovers, or their dearest friends . . .' And she had sold Vincent. At a price. So that was why she had been prepared to talk to Alun. Not his silver-tongued persuasion but the bribe which Piers considered a legitimate outlay in the cause of his godson's reinstatement. A small sacrifice.

And he thought I knew.

What else, I wondered, did he imagine I must know?

I said with chill placidity: 'Alun was not stingy with your money, was he?'

'You get what you pay for, my dear,' Piers responded. 'I realised that when I selected him. His reputation was known to me; I had seen *Quest* three or four times. The Prosser affair, for example – very instructive. Craig, I was told, had neither conscience nor probity: he would use any means at his disposal to get

what he wanted. Given the funds, I inferred, he would employ
bribery: it therefore followed that he could also be bribed. It
was clear he was the only man for the job. I dangled the
Walmsley Village incident as bait: he nibbled but did not bite. It
became necessary to proffer more detailed information. He told
me, I recall, that an individual based in the States would not be
of interest to the British viewing public, besides making the
investigative process rather expensive. I added a sweetener. Fifty
thousand, I felt, was not extortionate. Petty cash, we called it.
For extra costs.'

'I didn't know it was fifty thousand,' I said colourlessly.

My brain was numb and my innards had turned to ice, but it
hardly mattered as long as my vocal cords continued to function.
Richard was taking forever on the telephone. Thank God.

'I cannot imagine you saw very much of it,' Piers opined.
'You are, if I may say so, of a different mettle from your nominal
superior. I can believe you might have done it for nothing.'

'I did,' I said.

For nothing.

Piers studied me with sudden acuity, the cobwebbed lines
around his eyes and mouth deepening to clefts. With an effort
that seemed to drain my last resources of energy, I got to my feet.

'Thank you,' I said with mechanical courtesy, 'for filling me
in. Shall we go downstairs?'

I spent most of Saturday and Sunday feeling bloody. I knew
what I had to do – there were no grounds for appeal, no chance
of a reprieve – but that didn't make it any easier. I had been with
Quest for more than four years. I loved my job. I liked my colleagues. I even had an insidious affection for Alun Craig, the
Welsh Macchiavelli with the generosity of a Scotsman. All the
more reason to quit, before it was too late. Touch pitch, my
mother had said. Damn her. For all her shallowness of spirit and
lightness of mind, she was always right.

But it was already too late. The story of my life. I had touched
pitch. All the perfumes of Arabia would not cleanse the forensic
evidence from my contaminated hands.

On Monday morning I went into the office, cleared my desk,
and gave in my notice. On the spot.

'What the hell is the matter with you?' Alun shrilled, his voice climbing the scale as his wrath increased. 'Of all the stupid—'

Jeff, Ranjit and Fizzy, thrust unceremoniously out of the room, were almost certainly listening at the door.

I didn't care.

'Fifty thousand pounds,' I said levelly, 'and a Veronese drawing.'

'Is *that* all?' He actually looked relieved. 'So you talked to Piers Percival: I might have guessed. Look, if he gave another collector a pretty little doodle by some Old Master what has it to do with us? LeSueur came across: that's the bottom line. I don't care why; you don't care why. I wouldn't use a phoney, you know that; but she was one hundred per cent genuine. You don't send the dishwasher back to the factory if it works. Come down from the clouds, Micky. I play dirty – I always did – but I don't fake the evidence. Anyway, you're in no position to quibble. I didn't ask where *you* got the gen, did I? Well, did I? I trusted you and I expected you to trust me. You look bloody silly getting on your high horse when you're as naked as Godiva and your hair's far too short to cover your tits. Don't be so fucking inconsistent.'

'So I look silly,' I said doggedly. 'I don't give a shit. I do what I please but I'm not for hire. You sold us out – you *let me be used* in a private vendetta. I wouldn't expect you to understand – who am I to overtax your intelligence? – but I won't have that. Nobody uses me.'

'You used yourself,' Alun said brutally. 'Give it up, Micky. The result is all that matters. Every single word in that exposé on Savage was true. No faction: all fact. He's a crooked bastard who hits below the belt and we had to go for the balls to pin him down. All's fair in love and television. You know, you're one of the best – you really are – as long as you don't get your conscience in a twist. We make a great team. I'll back you to the hilt.'

'All for one and one for all?' I laughed with real amusement, the first I had felt since Friday night. Charged with hypocrisy, treachery, chicanery – charged with the Watergate robbery or the assassination of President Kennedy – Alun would always remain the same single-minded, double-tongued, irrepressible piece of shit. It was enough to warm your heart. 'No, Alun. I am not about to swallow that. There's the little matter of your initial payoff—'

'If someone wants to give me fifty thousand quid,' Alun said indignantly, 'who am I to stop him? If you want a cut, all right: you can have ten. Most of it went on your bloody air fares anyway. And that lunch at Poon's. You and your principles.'

'Never mind,' I said. 'You won't be bothered by them again.' I picked up my things, hooked my bag on to my shoulder.

Alun stared at me in stunned disbelief. What little colour he possessed drained from his face, leaving it as pallid as cheese. 'Micky!'

'Forever and forever farewell, Cassius,' I said.

I walked out. It was the hardest thing I had had to do since I left Patrick.

4

The party was on the following Saturday. I had a week in which to start job-hunting, avoid Richard and think up a credible explanation, for his benefit, of why I had decided to leave *Quest*. I enjoyed only moderate success in all three projects. On the job front, everybody was encouraging, nobody was definite. It is a curious but irrefutable fact that when in work you are always in demand, from other programmes, rival networks, news teams, investigators, but as soon as you actually become available much of this enthusiasm melts away. Murphy's law, I decided: Micky Murphy's law. Higher authorities had to be consulted, interviews arranged, CVs supplied. The problem, I was informed with weary monotony, was that the entire news-gathering media had departed for the Gulf and showed no immediate signs of coming back. Lured by comparisons with the Foreign Legion, I said I would be happy to depart in their wake; but this, it appeared, was not so simple. Did I speak Iraqi? Kurdish? Iranian? Did I have a degree in Islamic studies? Could I drive a tank? And incidentally, why exactly *had* I ditched Alun Craig? My one firm offer was from Annabel Purdey, who persuaded the features editor on her magazine to commission me for an in-depth article. My mother was thrilled: she had always wanted me to work on glossy magazines. What was the piece? she enquired – Filipino brides, neurotic nannies, the revival of the hat for everyday wear? 'It's serious research,' I said with a hint of derision, mostly for myself. 'An analysis of high-class prostitution. Right up my street.'

   With the object of avoiding Richard I let my answering
machine take all calls, at least until I knew who the caller might
be. This worked till Thursday, when he bypassed the telephone
by ringing the doorbell and announcing he had come to kidnap
me for lunch.

   'Why *did* you quit?' he demanded, over salads in a neighbouring wine bar.

   'I discovered my producer had done something unethical,' I
explained with diligent understatement.

   'Such as?'

   'Can we leave it?'

   'Look, from what you've told me your producer is always
doing something unethical: it seems to be a habit of his. It must
be pretty drastic for you to resign so melodramatically. Did it
have anything to do with Vincent and me?'

   'No,' I lied. 'It was another investigation. I found out he'd
taken a payoff *not* to mention a senior diplomat mixed up in – in
selling arms to Iraq. I can't tell you any more: it's all frightfully
confidential. I can't prove it so I mustn't broadcast it: that sort of
thing. Let's talk about something else.'

   We duly talked about something else – in this case, the snarl-
up of various pre-party arrangements, leading to last-minute
alterations in which, I suspected, Richard was aiming to impli-
cate me. Crystal, in an unusual lapse of temper, had sacked the
resident au pair. 'I expect the silly girl said something to the
kids about Mummy's relations with Wicked Uncle Vincent,'
Richard elucidated. 'It can't have been much – they still seem to
be in the dark about what really happened – but Crys does tend
to overreact to things just lately. You know, I think this whole
business has upset her more than any of us. Poor sweet: she's
just not used to going public with her emotions. The dreaded
agent Brendan is egging her on to tell her story to some scandal-
sheet – *Hullo 'Ullo* or whatever the mag is called – but she still
seems to be hesitating. All this soul-baring isn't really her style.
I saw her yesterday: it isn't my business to give her advice any
more but I told her to think very carefully before spilling her guts
out in print. If she goes too far I know she'll hate herself afterwards.'

   I was silent. In my considered opinion, Crystal might hesitate for one of two reasons: there was not enough money on the table, or the saga of her life could not be adapted to show her in a sufficiently flattering light. However, I am never fair to Crystal.

'Anyway,' Richard said, 'to return to the immediate problem, next Saturday we're left without a babysitter. Crys and I will both be at the party and the Farrows are on holiday. The obvious solution is for the children to spend the night in Surrey. I'll bring them down in the afternoon, they can have supper early, go to their room, play Snakes and Ladders, whatever, and I'm there if they want me. Crys'll be going home, of course, but too late to take them with her. My mother is visiting a friend in Wimbledon whom she hasn't seen for twenty years, so I rather hoped – well, it would be very nice if you stayed with us. You can't possibly wish to drive back to London in the small hours and a taxi would cost the earth. Besides, I need someone to come between Jo and my hangover at breakfast.'

'I don't know,' I said. 'I'm beginning to feel like a fixture in your life. I told you, I'm not ready for that.'

'Don't panic. I shan't come creeping down the corridors like someone in a Blackpool farce, sneaking into the wrong bedroom. Even if we did manage to locate each other, one of the children would be bound to gatecrash just as we were getting warmed up, announcing they wanted to get into bed with us. Jo in particular gets restless in strange houses.'

I laughed. 'I wasn't worrying about any of that,' I said.

'Then you'll stay?'

'I suppose so.' He was right: I didn't want to drive back.

'Piers will be pleased,' Richard said unexpectedly. 'I think he rather took to you – although he looked a bit strange when I told him you'd dumped your boss.'

'He must be delighted to have so many visitors,' I remarked drily. 'Especially the children.'

'Not exactly.' Richard grinned. 'He tells me he's determined to adopt a stoic attitude, but an Englishman's house is his castle and it's a pity he didn't provide himself with an oubliette. Still, it's only for one night, and if we're both there I daresay we can insulate him from juvenile disruption.'

'You want me to spell you?' I concluded.

'Something like that.'

I let him talk me into it.

I suppose I felt, with Richard and Penny and Jo, that I was being offered a brief, tantalising taste of the lifestyle I might have had, if I had remarried, 'settled down', done the things that women are still expected to do, for all our proud talk of equality and liberation. The careerist heroine of the airport novel and TV movie, having reached the pinnacle of worldly success, invariably rejects the trophies of her hard-won triumph for marriage and babies and the Man She Loves. A career, we are assured, cannot fulfil your biological needs or nourish your spirit. And they are right, the scribblers of trash and spinners of cliché: that is the worst of it. We cannot wipe out centuries of wife-and-mother-hood in a single generation. Long ago we were left by the camp fire breast-feeding an infant or two and roasting a haunch of mammoth while Man the Hunter went off into the wild. When the bear and the sabre-toothed tiger ranged in search of newborn meat, we picked up a blazing branch or flint-tipped spear and defended our young against the predators. The task was never meant to be a sinecure. But the cave became a safe place, our spears were beaten into distaffs and our swords into crochet-hooks, and man-made walls went up around us, fencing danger out, fencing us in – into the safe place, the women's quarters, the seraglio, the prison. Now, we want to take up the spear again and go back to the wild. But we are weakened by long incarceration, our limbs shake, our nerves twitch, the heady air of the wide-open spaces makes us giddy. We take the Pill and carry condoms but we cannot forget that sex means commitment and femininity, procreation. You cannot sever yourself from your own history: you must learn from it and grow out of it, into a different future. In the meantime we are caught in a hiatus between escape from the past and the much-vaunted salvation to come, struggling with our half-baked freedoms, rejecting in one breath the social status we reclaim an instant later. It is no wonder that our erstwhile senior partner, Man the Hunter – Man the Stockbroker, Man the Miner, Man the Home-owner, Man the Unemployed – is in a state of shock. For aeons he competed only against his fellows while his womenfolk looked on in mute admiration; now, he does not know whether to fight us or cherish us. Society is in the melting pot and no one yet knows in what shape it will be reforged. The walls are down so we build new ones, makeshift barriers, hurdles to overleap, afraid of a change in the view.

I am typical of my kind. Sex lures me into intimacy, children stir me to nostalgia. My dreams betrayed me with Richard but my body yearned for Vincent, catching me off guard in the watches of a lingering night. I had not worked late in the evening and I would not have to rise early in the morning. There was nothing to tire me out. A hundred years of thought could be fitted in between a doze and a doze. I loved the idea of Richard as one loves a mirage, knowing that if you try to lay hold of it, it will dissolve into nothingness. His grey eyes and fixed principles recalled my father, whose fading image I had not sought to revive for some while. I looked for him then, wanting the advice of a familiar ghost, but he had gone. I recited his poetry but I could not hear his voice or see his scars: the thinning pipe smoke was empty. I was alone. Into the void came the hurricane, fanning a flame in the darkness, filling me with remembered fire. For a moment I was all feeling, all hunger. I wondered if my neglected loins would ever forget the power games I had played with Vincent, surrender, possession, conflict, the passion that I would not dignify with the name of love. In that instant I thought no idealistic sentiment could ever run so deep or take me so high. But it was all nonsense. Sex with Vincent and family life with Richard were not choices which lay before me but closed doors, untenable visions, forbidden fruit. If Richard learned the truth he would certainly no longer want me. As for Vincent, I had pictured him watching the programme often enough, the idea filling me with a strange satisfactory pain. He would hate me, I knew, with pitiless constancy and unabated venom – more than Crystal, more than Richard, more than anyone he had ever hated before. It was a tribute almost as great as love.

I got up, made myself tea, sat for half an hour omitting to remove the sachet from the mug. I have measured out my life in shrivelled teabags. Dawn insinuated itself between the curtains, pale with weariness. October had crept up on me; the longest summer I could remember was drawing to an end; leaves withered swiftly in the persistent drought. I had changed and the world had changed and nothing would ever be the same again.

War waited in the wings. My little affairs were dwarfed by the looming shadow of imminent cataclysm. And suddenly I was conscious of it, the shadow, there in the room with me; not the distant horror of events in the Middle East but something close and tangible, only a footstep ahead of me, a darkness on the edge of my mind which the morning could not disperse. The premonition was so strong – if premonition it was – that I grew cold and an uncontrollable shiver ran through me, an inexplicable quailing of the spirit. I could not imagine what it might betoken, if anything: my life might be in a state of flux but there were no indications of impending doom. Eventually, my thoughts became centred on the party. After all it lay, as required, a little ahead, a focal point on which all threads might possibly decide to converge. On the other hand, it was not a Major Social Event. No superstars would attend; no hurricane was forecast. Vincent Scarpia Savage had not received an invitation. It was ludicrous to endure the agonies of Cassandra when the only gloomy prospect was an evening where the talk would be small and the company large, and I would in all probability have to watch Richard dancing with Crystal. Dull, but not deadly. Little cause for lions to whelp in the streets. But the shadow stayed with me, a penumbra on the borders of my consciousness.

Two cups of tea later I had a shower, washed my face, put on a few items of clothing remarkable for comfort not style. My faithful machine took a call from Jeff Salter, the third that week, and I postponed responding yet again. The next voice to disturb my solitude was Gerry Hibbert. I listened with a sinking stomach. He did not have my home number and must have gone to considerable trouble to get it. Ergo he wanted something. A favour returned.

Reluctantly, I picked up the receiver, cutting into the tape.

'Gerry? It's me.'

'Micky, old girl,' he said. 'Heard you walked out on that sod Craig at last. Lovers' tiff?'

'Actually,' I said frigidly, 'he's sleeping with his computer. It keeps all his secrets and doesn't expect to have an orgasm more than twice a year. Unfortunately, it's the only Amstrad I know with a sexually transmitted virus.'

My humour was on the subtle side for Gerry, but he laughed.

'So how's tricks?' he asked, ruthlessly cordial. 'Got anything lined up yet?'

'Yes – the electricity bill.' I decided it was time to cut the cackle. 'What do you want?'

What he wanted, to my unwelcome surprise, was an invitation to Saturday's party. 'Sounds like quite a bash,' he said. 'De luxe country mansion with wall-to-wall art treasures, guest list of the high and mighty . . .'

Bugger Beggar. He was obviously suffering from delirium tremens and I said so. 'You're seeing pink elephants in a field full of white rabbits,' I declared colourfully, if not very lucidly. 'From what I hear, it's going to be about as glamorous as the Worthing Octogenarians' Annual Reunion. Decrepit county types who once knew Richard's mother, yuppie couples who once knew Richard – oh, and the producer of a very interesting programme on antique coins which Channel Four showed when no one was watching. He's a friend of Piers Percival. Anyway, it's hardly fodder for the gossip columns, is it?'

'You're going, then,' Gerry deduced.

'I couldn't refuse: it would have given offence. I've worked closely with these people.'

'So I hear,' said Gerry with emphasis. And: 'I gather Garoghan's ex is going to be there. Crystal Winter, the mini-model with the sleek bodywork and the pussycat eyes. I can't wait to meet her.'

'If you're hoping for a scene,' I snapped, 'you can forget it. They're on very good terms with each other.'

'What about you?' said Gerry. 'Are you and the fair Crystal on very good terms?'

I didn't bother to deny anything: it would have been wasted effort. Gerry was pursuing his goal with the lowered snout and blinkered vision of a journalist on the trail of a hunch. If he was determined to squander time and energy, who was I to discourage him?

'You owe me one, Micky,' he reminded me. 'You're in with these people: you can fix me up with an invite, no probs. A favour for a favour. Anyhow, we're old pals. You trust me, don't you?'

'I may owe you a favour,' I said, 'but I don't have to trust you

as well. Still, if you really want to go to this dreary little soirée' –
I infused as much boredom into my voice as I could – 'I daresay
I can arrange it. I'll get back to you.'

I called Richard, who had just received two job offers and
would happily have enjoined the whole of Wapping to celebrate
with him. 'That's one of us off the dole,' he said – I could hear
the grin. 'Sure, any friend of yours is all right – as long as he's
not too close a friend.'

'He's not a friend at all,' I said frankly. 'He's an unmitigated
creep. I know too many of them. But I doubt if he'll cause any
trouble. He seems to have got the wrong idea about this party:
thinks he's going to some superstar binge with a scandal behind
every bush. I couldn't bring myself to disillusion him. Anyway,
the journalist who comes through the front door with an official
entrée is never as chancy as the one who sneaks in unasked
round the back.' Not true. A rat is a rat, however he gains
ingress to your house. I was glossing over the facts, but I had a
debt to pay and this appeared to be a fairly undemanding way of
doing it.

'Cinders,' I told Gerry, 'you're in.'

Cinders . . . I shouldn't have said that. Once I had been
Cinderella, off to the ball in my silver dress to try my charms on
a particularly dubious prince. Never mind the fairy tale: I had got
the scoop. I didn't like the precedent. If my premonition was
accurate, I did not want doom to impend in front of Gerry
Hibbert.

But I didn't really believe in extra-sensory perception.

It was nearly lunch time. I burned myself some toast, poured
out a long cold drink. Mineral water. I had little on which to concentrate but the umpteenth rewrite of my curriculum vitae and
my mind strayed wantonly to the contents of my wardrobe. This
time, it would have to be the Roland Klein. After all, I had only
worn it twice. It would do. A dowdy dress for a dowdy party. I
had enough to preoccupy me without worrying about something
as trivial as clothing. Until I got another job, I must be careful
with my finances – besides, spending serious money on frivolous
evening wear was against my principles. I had a principle for
every occasion, I reflected sarcastically: I dragged one out whenever I needed an excuse for not doing something I didn't want to

do, and abandoned them without hesitation if expediency demanded. I had cozened Vincent with scarcely a qualm but I could take a strong moral stand on the issue of a dress. I was lost in admiration of my own rectitude. To hell with everything. My funds were limited and a soothsayer in my head was warning me to beware the ides of October. I recollected a favourite saying of Phyl's: when the going gets tough, the tough go shopping. I needed a tonic, a dose of decadence, a change of plumage. In ethical terms, I was going downhill fast, and – once again – I didn't care.

I went to Harrods and bought a dress. A long slim Montana with even more gaps than the Roland Klein, exposing my back almost to the cleavage in my bottom. Circumstances dictated black, and anyhow, as I told Phyl in absentia, we were no longer in the throes of summer. In the double mirror, I saw neither a Cinderella nor a silver eel but a spider-thin silhouette topped off with a compact haircut, the last of my suntan fading from my shoulder-blades, my small face marked with haggard shadows. A Black Widow. It seemed appropriate. I required blusher, complimentary lighting, and sleep, not necessarily in that order.

That night, worn out by the *nuit blanche* which had preceded it, I slept.

Richard collected me the next day and drove me down to Surrey with the children. After supervising a premature supper he sequestered them in a large bedroom with assorted books, a box of biscuits – Crystal would never approve – Penny's homework, and the television set, moved especially for their benefit. I went to my allotted bedchamber to get ready. Morpheus had done his part, the lighting was pleasantly mellow, and a discerning application of blusher smoothed away the last of the rough edges. My face would pass. Downstairs, Elizabeth Savage had arrived with her friend from Wimbledon, a *grande dame* with a Sitwell nose and several strands of pearls, unquestionably genuine, girdling her desiccated throat. She raised her eyebrows when I came in; I half expected her to peer at me through a lorgnette. 'The journalist,' said Elizabeth in a stage whisper which nobody missed. 'But it's all right: she's really *very nice*.' Piers Percival wore a dinner jacket; incredibly, so did Richard, though it didn't take him long to part company with his black tie. We went up the main staircase to what had once been a ballroom, currently denuded of obstructive furniture and restored to something resembling its original function. Background music spilled unobtrusively from background technology. At one end, the caterers had laid out a superior buffet with poached salmon, terrines of that, galantines of this, and not a quiche in sight; at the other, waitresses were poised to circulate with trayloads of champagne. Bollinger, I noted: the guests might be past their prime but the booze was of the best. We all sipped thankfully and made polite small talk. There are few things worse than arriving for a party before it actually begins. I thought wistfully of joining the children.

An hour later the evening was well underway. People came in trickles; then in a flood. Those inscrutable currents which circulate round all parties duly began to ebb and flow. I saw Gerry Hibbert swept willy-nilly into conversation with a bishop: it served him right. The hapless cleric might, of course, choose to reveal that he had a mistress in Swiss Cottage and a love-child whom he had repudiated at birth, but it seemed unlikely. Gerry's face wore the expression of a big game hunter who took a wrong turning somewhere near Africa and found himself in the Antipodes amid a troop of kangaroos. Presently, in order to rub a little salt into the wound, I introduced him to a director of the Tate Gallery, who assumed he was on the arts pages and pounced on him accordingly. The party was proving more entertaining than I had anticipated. Piers had retired to the sidelines, and stood smoking with an elegance that clearly required an ivory cigarette-holder. Elizabeth was acting as hostess, hovering in the vicinity of the stairs and greeting all comers whether she knew them or not. I suspected Piers must be grateful for this: it saved him the chore. Further down the room Richard was talking to a pleasant-looking couple, possibly in the 'old friend' category, whom he appeared openly pleased to re-encounter. Crystal was late, presumably for effect. I got a refill of Bollinger and conversed with Elizabeth's friend on the subject of her choice, which happened to be rose-growing.

Crystal arrived shortly afterwards. She was not quite tall enough to make a spectacular entrance without the aid of a

descending staircase so she had chosen to go straight to the loo,
one flight up, and then come down into the ballroom. Her dress,
I thought, was a little too good to be true: a symphony in modest simplicity, made of some creaseless supercrêpe as blue as her
eyes; the effect was much as if Bruce Oldfield had been commissioned to design for the Virgin Mary. The only portions of her
anatomy left bare were her arms; a faint dusting of spangles
glimmered at neck and hemline, like the moisture of an early
dewfall; her co-ordinating handbag was also lightly spangled.
Her long hair had been crimped into a cloud of pre-Raphaelite
waves and hung loose down her back. She looked so beautiful I
could hear clocks stopping all round the room. Elizabeth, however, appeared unenthused, though she shook hands with
remorseless courtesy and introduced her former daughter-in-law
to whoever fell in her way. It occurred to me that so much
beauty and glamour was rather wasted on the present social gathering: apart from the few yuppie couples (yupples?) who had
bothered to drive the necessary distance the guests were predominantly relics of past privilege and custodians of past talent,
almost all of them on the shady side of middle age. Many of the
men, I feared, were too old to have their clocks stopped without
risking fatal consequences. Some of the same thoughts may have
struck Crystal: when the tide of the party brought us together
she seemed positively pleased to see me, no doubt because I was
both familiar and contemporary. Richard joined us, and I wondered whether Gerry was watching, and what he would make of
it. The hero, his ex-wife, and his journalist ally and possibly
girlfriend, all in a civilised huddle, any dark passions kept well
under wraps.

In fact, I noticed none. Our chit-chat was innocuous in the
extreme. Crystal said who *were* all these people; Richard said he
hadn't a clue. I said never mind, the food was wonderful, and
asked how she was getting on with her acting. The query was
intended as a politeness but it sounded two-edged and Crystal
eyed me, I thought, a shade warily. However, she ignored my
ambiguity and began to tell me about a possible offer to co-
present a television show on make-up and fashions (not another
one!); also a film role which was absolutely definite if the producer could raise the money. There was no hint of desperation in

either voice or manner but I remember I felt a sudden sympathy for her, a glimmer of kinship. We were not so very different, after all. I too had reached a crisis in my life, a turning point with nowhere to turn, a Rubicon without bridge or ford. My career was on hold and my emotions in overdrive. Crystal had once said she wanted excitement and stimulation while I had had more than enough of both, but at least we had made our own cock-ups, dug our own pitfalls, and now had to struggle unaided through the recovery process. Equally, we had entangled ourselves with the same two men, twentieth-century Savages, forceful, macho, post-feminist, ante-social. I could not like Crystal but in that moment I wanted to understand her, to make some gesture of solidarity.

'You might go up to see the kids,' Richard was saying. 'They won't go to sleep for hours. They should really have been allowed to come but Piers didn't suggest it so . . . well, I didn't want to push. He's been so kind to me, poor man; I feel he's suffered enough. This sort of thing simply isn't his scene.'

'It isn't mine, either,' said Crystal. 'I met a producer just now: I thought he might be useful but it turned out he's into antique coins.' She spoke without a flicker of amusement. 'I'll go up shortly.'

'Good girl,' Richard said.

He moved away, squeezing my arm in passing. I was roused to a violent and irrational irritation: it was my arm, he had no right to squeeze it, he had no rights of any kind. Crystal turned to me, her face more than ordinarily blank, her tone colourless. 'I gather,' she said, 'that you and Richard are becoming quite – friendly.'

Any expression of comradeship died on my lips. I did not know if she was afflicted with a broken heart or lacerated vanity but I sensed, behind the mask, a fragmenting of all she thought secure, a hidden disintegration of the self. This was not the time for sisterly overtures.

'Quite.' I shrugged. I wanted to appear bored, uninvolved, noncommittal. I managed to sound completely unnatural.

'Richard says it's none of my business.' Her gaze roamed the room, missing mine. 'I expect he's right. But I should like to *know* . . .'

'There's a reporter here,' I observed in warning. 'Probably watching us, right now.'

'I see.' She picked her words with her customary diligence. 'I'll be . . . careful.'

'We're just friendly,' I said. I had no obligation to answer her, but I felt she needed reassurance. A sop to her ego. 'Nothing more. There won't be anything more, whatever happens. I promise.' And I keep my promises. *Quod erat demonstrandum.*

'*I don't care.*' The sharpness in her voice startled us both. 'Richard and I are yesterday's news,' she continued more mildly. 'I left him. I must have hurt him terribly. I hope very much that someone else will try to – to make it up to him. He admires you a great deal.'

'He doesn't know me,' I said unhappily.

Crystal stared at me for a minute. Then she turned her shoulder and walked away. Sure enough, Gerry Hibbert was watching. But the hubbub of the party must have covered most of our exchange and in this instance, I trusted my face was as unreadable as Crystal's. I smiled beatifically at Gerry and when I looked round for her, she had gone.

What happened next was never clearly established. Part of the problem was that children do not always stay where they are put, and although Penny was old enough to be well behaved and also a little awed by both Piers Percival and her surroundings, Jo had a natural resistance to childish awe. Tired of books, biscuits, and poor reception on the television, he had gone on an exploratory ramble, ostensibly to the bathroom, leaving his sister with her geography essay. Inevitably, he fetched up in front of the duelling pistols. A horrified Crystal found him standing on a chair to reach them, flourishing the one he had removed with unqualified glee. She later claimed she took it away from him and hustled him off to bed immediately, thrusting the gun in her handbag since she had been unable to replace it correctly in its display position on the wall. Her bag, though not as capacious as one of mine, was sufficiently roomy to take the make-up kit, condom case and hatstand essential to the party-going female. The pistol fitted in awkwardly, with the butt protruding. She said after the initial shock she realised that the weapon could not possibly be loaded: in her view, it was merely a decorative antique which Jo, with a small boy's proclivity for vandalism, might damage beyond repair. It all sounded perfectly feasible. She tucked the children up in bed, read to them from the latest Roald Dahl, and came back to the ballroom with the pistol still in her bag.

Her timing was fatal.

He must have arrived around ten, well after I lost sight of Crystal. The proverbial skeleton leaping out of the cupboard just in time to rattle its bones at the feast. I should have been expecting him, but I wasn't. I had been so obsessed with my various dilemmas and the upheaval in my everyday life that I had forgotten or disregarded his propensity for drastic action. Even in my most extravagant imaginings I had not dared to think that he would come looking for me. How he had heard about the party I couldn't guess: anything from general gossip to inside information. Unlike Crystal, he did not try to make an entrance. He merely walked in uninvited, a daunting figure in his stoniest expression and most formal DJ. He was taller than many of those around him and I saw him almost at once, moving forward into the room, pausing briefly to lock stares with Elizabeth, who stood in the midst of movement and chatter like a petrified tree. As the other guests became aware of him there was a reshuffling of the crowd, a withdrawing from the danger zone, a foregathering into muttering cabals, a murmuring of inquisitive tongues. Normal conversation in his vicinity began to run down, subsiding into whispers, nudges, mumbles. Those who did not recognise him asked who he was; those who did fell silent. Disapproval emanated from all and sundry in a tangible wave.

Somewhere behind me, Piers Percival said: 'Good God. Well, well. The leper at the fair.'

He had seen me now. He came towards me and the fair moved out of his way, avoiding contamination. The aura that surrounded him – hate, hurt, suppressed violence – was plainly unsuitable for a party: they shrank from it as from a miasma. He barely noticed. Perhaps he had grown used to such shrinkage in his social circle. He halted a short distance from me, like a duellist giving himself room to manoeuvre; but I knew there would be no polite preliminaries. I thought: 'He doesn't know what to do. He hasn't dreamed this or planned it. He's riding on emotion.' Behind his stony gaze I glimpsed an intensity of feeling that shocked me, a blackness of pain translated into a blackness of rage. Thus the tiger, wounded almost to death, poised to lash out in the madness of its last fury. And I was far too close for comfort.

I loved him. The truth dawned on me like a great light, an illumination of the heart, hopelessly mistimed, inappropriate, pointless. I had wanted to love Richard – Richard who had lived up to so many of my ideals, who could fulfil so many fantasies – but all that had been little more than a meddling daydream, a game on the side. Sentimental moonlighting. It was Vincent, not Richard, with whom I had danced in the dark. He stood before me in unswerving enmity and I experienced a sense of recognition, as if, in a faceless multitude, I had come across a face I knew, a technicolour figure in a world that was uniformly grey. I had loved him and betrayed him, and given the same chances and the same choices no doubt I would do it again. My soul flamed in triumph.

I said, in a small, cool voice: 'Hello Vincent.'

Not a brilliant opening line.

'Hello. I'm sorry I'm so late. You must have been afraid I wouldn't make it.' He was breathing hard, like a runner. His sarcasm was ragged. But at least he had the vestiges of self-control.

'Don't mention it,' I responded smoothly. 'Your flying dragons held up in fog over Heathrow?'

I was slipping back into the old familiar banter with unexpected ease. Visibly, Vincent's mood changed gear: the stone cracked, anger stalled on surprise.

'Something . . . like . . . that.' His tension had relaxed a notch in spite of himself. 'By the way, you – er – omitted to send me an invitation. An oversight, I'm sure. After all, this little celebration is for me – isn't it?'

'Of course,' I said. 'But you know how it is. There are traditions to be observed. The wicked wizard *never* gets asked to parties. That way he can turn up uninvited, in a huff, trailing bats and spiders – don't overdo the spiders: I'm not very fond of them – and put a curse on the princess. Would you like to curse me now, or do you want a drink first?'

'I don't see any princess,' Vincent retorted. 'It seems to me you're the one in the pointed hat. If you pricked your finger I'd get medical help for the spindle.'

I laughed. Provoking the tiger. In his eyes, for all his fury, I saw a flicker of acknowledgement, a gleam of recognition that echoed my own.

A waitress, oblivious to atmosphere, proffered a tray. I passed Vincent a glass of champagne.

He threw it at me.

It was not a good moment for Richard to materialise, rushing protectively to my side. I didn't need protection.

'Micky—'

'I'm all right.' The liquid had splashed over my chest, soaking through the thin black material on to my unsupported breasts, chilling my nipples into rigidity. I felt like Lady Caroline Lamb in a damped muslin.

'*Brut* from a brute?' I quipped, but the attempt at lightness went unregarded.

Vincent switched a sombre gaze from my nipples to his cousin. 'Congratulations,' he said. 'You seem to have come through every vicissitude with luck on your side and a grin on your face. As usual. You don't even have to right your own wrongs, do you? A rat-pack of crooked journalists dish the dirt to clean up your reputation; a benevolent godfather recalls your existence just in time to pay your debts. Fortune smiles on Richard Garoghan once again. I would drink your health if I hadn't emptied my glass down the nearest sewer.'

'Leave Micky out of this!' Richard made an abrupt movement which I checked. 'Your quarrel is with me – if you still insist on maintaining this stupid feud. As far as I'm concerned, it's over. You did your worst, I did my best, and now we're quits. But if you really want to start another round, start it with *me*. Lay off Micky.'

'Lay off,' said Vincent. 'What a very apposite choice of phrase. Or didn't she tell you? Of course she didn't. She came to your rescue packing a nasty little tape recorder with her sword of truth and shield of integrity and you didn't ask any awkward questions. We live in the days of role reversal. She saved your bacon and you fell for her. A beautiful story with a happy ending. Pity you missed the middle. How did you imagine she got all that shit on me? Did she tell you I talked to the trees and she just *happened* to be listening?'

'Old interviews . . .' Richard was frowning.

'I don't give interviews,' Vincent said. 'I never have.' He looked at me for a long minute, cold-eyed, the muscles tightening around his mouth. I knew what was coming. I could not stop him and it would have been foolhardy to try. All I could do was stiffen my sinews and arm myself for defiance.

'I met her at a party in the Caribbean,' he said, still keeping his eyes on my face. 'She picked me up. I took her home with me and we went to bed. We spent three days together in the aftermath of that damned hurricane. Three days – fate really does have it in for me. If I believed in God I'd be a Satanist. We talked till the candles guttered – there wasn't any electricity – and we fucked and fucked and fucked. She must have taped everything I said – the story of my life, you, Crystal, the lot. She was better than a shrink. I purged my soul and she simply recorded the vomit. What a way to earn a living.'

'*Bullshit*.' Richard was determinedly scornful. 'You know, if you weren't quite so successful you'd be pathetic. You simply have to reduce everyone else to your own nadir, don't you? Micky isn't like that. Do you think I don't know her?'

'Not as well as I do.' Vincent's glance reverted to his cousin. 'Unless – have you screwed her yet? You haven't, have you? Always such a gentleman. Patience is a virtue but it's rather wasted on a whore.'

'You learned everything at school but good manners.'

'I learned everything but insincerity. I'm afraid you're stuck with my leavings yet again. Still, she's better than Crystal – anyone's better than Crystal. She does a nice line in fellatio.'

Inevitably, Richard hit him. I should have been prepared for it but I was bracing myself, not to deny the charges but to admit them, to brazen it out, to maintain my dignity against all odds, to give the best imitation of Joan of Arc ever achieved in such unlikely circumstances. Instead, I clutched in vain at Richard's arm while Vincent sprawled on the floor, red knuckle-marks standing out on his cheek. Already minus his tie, Richard wrenched off his jacket. Vincent scrambled to his feet and did the same, hurling his excess garments to the ground. 'Richard,' I cried, dignity abandoned, 'there's nothing to fight about! It's the truth, you idiot! I slept with him – *I slept with him* – and I don't give a shit!' But Richard didn't hear me. He and Vincent had reverted to the schoolroom, the rugger pitch, the nursery. They came together like the clashing of Titans, like stags in rut, like lager-louts in the football season. They skidded on the parquet and cannoned into the crowd. People backed away, picking up their skirts, dropping their jaws, doing nothing. In those conditions, no one ever does anything. They become frozen in a state of wilful inactivity, spectators at a blood sport which they claim to deplore, too stunned or too scared to get involved. I saw Elizabeth's anguished mien, the motion of her lips: '*Do something!*' Those around her continued to do nothing. Vincent and Richard fell over a chair, scrunched up a rug. They grunted like Sumo wrestlers, waltzed like heavyweight boxers, reeled, stumbled, tried to punch. As a fight, it was long on sound-effects and short on points. Richard appeared to be getting the worst of it. 'Get me a soda siphon!' I demanded of the nearest waitress, she who had proffered the tray and could no longer ignore the atmosphere. 'An ice bucket. *Something!*' A barman passed over a champagne bottle, unopened. I untwisted the wire, angled the neck towards the ceiling, and shook it recklessly. The cork exploded upwards and a jet of liquor doused both combatants.

'Clever girl,' said Piers Percival.

'. . . *che cazzo!*' said Vincent.

It was at that moment that Crystal came back.

She had seen the fight from the stairs and she came running through the assembled guests, scattering them from her path. Her face was effectively pale and her dark hair trailed behind her like smoke. In marked contrast to my wet T-shirt display the blue dress clung gracefully to her slender anatomy, even at speed; only her handbag, overweighted, bounced awkwardly on her hip. I remember speculating briefly as to what she was carrying which made it so heavy.

'*Vincent!*' she exclaimed. 'What on earth are you doing here? Richard! For God's sake, both of you!'

'Crys, darling . . .' Richard was on his feet, attempting to move her away from the battleground.

'Fuck off, Crystal.' Vincent was not playing cricket. He took advantage of his cousin's distraction to catch him off guard with a blow to the head which sent him rocking backwards.

'Stop it!' Crystal and I chorused in unison, she in horror, I in exasperation.

'Morons!' I elaborated. 'Neanderthal phallocrats! Thick-skulled, pea-brained, half-witted—' The waitress tendered another bottle of champagne with a deprecating grimace. More good Bollinger down the drain.

It was Piers who deflected me, his voice sharpened to an edge I had not heard before. 'What in the name of Satan . . .?'

Crystal had produced the gun. She cocked it inexpertly, aimed with slightly querulous deliberation. Her pout was resolute, her sapphire orbs aglitter. 'Stop!' she repeated. 'Stop it, or I'll – I'll shoot! You mustn't do this. I'm not worth it.' The ultimate banality.

Vincent thrust Richard out of his way and rounded on her, not in anger but in annoyance. 'Of course you're not worth it, you silly bitch. We wouldn't waste our energies fighting over *you*. Micky may be a whore but at least she's good at it. You were never good at anything except wearing the right lipstick. Now you can't even do that any more. Put that fancy gun down: it isn't loaded. It's just part of the décor. You look bloody ridiculous playing Sarah Bernhardt when you have about as much talent as a chorus girl at Butlins.' He turned his back on her, resuming the fray, not even troubling to note her reaction.

I saw her face – no longer inscrutable – I saw her raise the gun. Her hand shook but her expression was fixed, burned into her features like the imprint of a brand. In that split-second before disaster I saw everything. But I moved too slow, warned too late, changed nothing, saved no one.

'It *is* loaded!' I screamed. 'For God's sake—'

Crystal fired.

Vincent's body jerked, thrown forward into his cousin's arms. 'Shit,' he said. 'Shit . . .' I thought in passing that if those were his last words they weren't very memorable. To the point, but not memorable. It is extraordinary the stupid things you think of in moments of crisis. Richard said: 'Crys . . .'; Piers said: 'Dear God.' I saw the expression wiped neatly from Crystal's face and I was sure, then and always, that when she pulled the trigger she must have known what she was doing. In the background, the other guests disappeared into a blur of consternation and panic. Then Richard lowered Vincent on to the floor and I was kneeling beside him, yelling for cloths, napkins, anything to staunch the wound, and there was blood on my hands, on my dress, on the gleaming parquet. A fan of scarlet spreading across the whiteness of his shirt. The bullet seemed to have entered just below the right shoulder-blade; I could not see any exit wound. I said: 'Ambulance' but Richard had already gone to telephone. Piers handed me a napkin and I crumpled it into what I hoped was a solid ball and jammed it against the injury. 'Fold them,' I ordered. 'Fold them into pads. Lots of them.' I had no idea what I was doing. Vincent was having difficulty breathing, panting fast and hard, gasping, starting to cough. A spatter of red came from his mouth. 'He must be hit in the lung,' I said to Piers. He was lying on his left side and I had a feeling he should be on his right; at least in that position he would have one lung clear and be less likely to drown in his own blood. Or so I calculated, with what little coolness and logic I could muster. With Piers' help I turned him over, cautiously, supporting him against me. The waitress, having got the hang of what was required, was folding napkins at a desperate rate and passing them over. I slid my hand under the angle of his back, pressing the makeshift padding against the wound. There was wet stuff trickling down my face. Not champagne. Tears. I had not known I was crying: the tears seemed to have nothing to do with me. One fell on Vincent's cheek.

'He's trying to say something,' Piers said, leaning forward. 'It sounds like . . . *Armageddon*?'

'Cretin,' I said, to Vincent, not Piers. 'Don't talk. Breathe.'

Something pink leaned over me: it was the bishop. 'They're on their way,' he confirmed, meaning the ambulance. 'Can he manage a brandy?'

'No,' said Piers, 'but I can.'

Richard did not return: I gathered later that he had been taking care of Crystal. She was said to be 'in shock'. No doubt.

'This is my fault,' Piers averred, in the taut voice of restrained self-blame. 'I should never have left a loaded gun in such a damned accessible place. Although what possessed the girl to take it . . .'

Vincent's respiration was getting worse. Every breath sucked at his ribs as if he were trying to inhale in a vacuum. His breast heaved like a broken bellows. I didn't think he was going to die. I didn't think of it once. The blood soaked persistently through the wedge of napkins: my fingers were slippery with it. I glanced round the room and saw that except for Elizabeth, Elizabeth's friend, and the bishop, the party seemed to have dematerialised. I wondered vaguely where it had gone. It felt like an hour or more since Vincent had been shot; in reality it must have been only ten or fifteen minutes. The ambulance arrived and trained hands took over from my incompetent ones: Vincent was transferred on to a stretcher and carried out. I followed.

'Are you his girlfriend?' a paramedic enquired.

'No,' I said. 'His worst enemy.'

The paramedic assumed I was being satirical.

I have no clear recollection of the journey. At the hospital, Vincent was hustled into surgery. I was left in what was presumably a waiting room: magazines, pot plants, vending machine. I did the things people are supposed to do at such times, sat down, stood up, paced the floor, watched the clock. I had washed my hands in the Ladies but the blood on my dress had dried in stiff discoloured patches; I doubted if it would ever come out. My few excursions into designer clothing seemed to be doomed: no sooner had I donned a new dress than it was ripped to shreds in a car crash or smeared with blood in a shooting. There was obviously a moral there if I could be bothered to dig for it. In future, I would stick to jeans – or my old Roland Klein. Not that it mattered. I couldn't think of the future any more. I had not asked about Vincent's chances and no one had deigned to tell me. I watched the clock, paced the floor, sat down, stood up. The vending machine advertised coffee but when I inserted my money and pressed the requisite buttons all it would do was hiss and splutter and puff out a little steam. Far too much time went past far too slowly.

I had no notion where I was. I asked a nurse and she told me Guildford: I must have looked bewildered because she said was I feeling well? Piers Percival . . . Surrey . . . Guildford. Of course. I said I felt quite all right. I knew there were people I ought to telephone on Vincent's behalf: he shouldn't be lying in hospital fighting for his life with no one in attendance but his least favourite journalist. I should get in touch with Jolanda, Hannibal Barker, possibly Judas Carson. But I did not have the numbers and anyhow, they were all too far away to rush to Vincent's bedside with significant celerity. I would call them in the morning. Meanwhile, Vincent would have to make do with me. He was in no condition to object.

The seconds ticked into minutes, the minutes dragged into hours. I stood on the floor, watched the seat, paced the clock.

Eventually, a doctor came to find me. He looked young and dark and very grave. But perhaps he had a natural air of gravity.

'This is a serious business,' he said. 'A duelling pistol, I understand, that went off by accident. Very dangerous, these antique guns. You don't get a clean shot. The bullet ploughed through his lungs like a dumdum and lodged itself under his ribs. Messy. Could have been fatal.'

Could have been . . .

'You can see him now,' the doctor said.

Vincent lay in state, surrounded by the paraphernalia of modern medicine. His torso was encased in enough bandages for a mummy, tubes and wires festooned him like variegated spaghetti, a transparent plastic bladder dripped its contents into his veins. Beside him, two small screens showed videos of his cardiac and respiratory activity, glowing lines zigging and zagging with reassuring monotony. Lifelines. Wiggle bump, wiggle bump, went his heart. Heave-ho, heave-ho, went what was left of his lungs. Neither screen registered any disruption on my entry. Against the spotless pillows his face had a grubby pallor, the off-white hue of someone who has recently mislaid several pints of blood. Patchy bruising from the fight did little to improve his appearance. He needed a shave. I looked down at him and he looked up at me and for quite a while neither of us said anything. I noticed that there was a grey streak at his left temple and his eyes were the dark green of empty wine bottles. I realised that I, too, must be looking fairly seedy: I had done my best to scrub off last night's make-up in the loo but there was certain to be some left-over mascara blearing my eyelids and a residual trace of lipstick rimming my mouth. It didn't seem to be very important.

'They told me my girlfriend was here,' he said at last. His voice was faint but steady. 'I knew it must be you.'

'Of course.'

Pause.

'Why did you come?'

I said lightly: 'To gloat over your deathbed.'

'Disappointed?'

'I'll survive.'

I pulled up a chair and sat down.

'So much for the final battle,' Vincent murmured. 'Good triumphs: Evil lies bleeding. But I never thought it would be Crystal with the Kalashnikov.'

'It's always the stupid people who need the big guns,' I said.

'Yes. The trouble was, no one told me there was a war on. You had Excalibur; I had – my cock. It wasn't much of a contest.'

'The penis,' I said, 'is mightier than the sword.'

'Not right now,' retorted Vincent.

I laughed.

Presently, he asked for same water. I half lifted him, helped him to drink.

'I can think of some lovely names to call you,' he remarked. 'Mostly in Italian. *Cagna. Puttana. Troia.*'

'Hard words,' I said, 'fritter no bananas. Sex is a legitimate move in the game. You've used it often enough. What about Jan Horrocks of the Walmesley Village Environmental Action Group – or whatever they called themselves?'

'How did you know about that?'

'It was the first little scam of yours I happened to look into.'

'So you decided that to catch the shark you would have to sharpen your teeth?'

'N-no,' I said. 'I didn't plan anything. The Langelaans' party was an outside chance. It gave me the opportunity to take a look at you. I didn't really expect any more. When the hurricane struck – when we got off together – I was acting on impulse. It wasn't some cold-blooded scheme. I did it – because I wanted to.' I added candidly: 'Anyway, I was pissed out of my mind.'

'That Walkman you never used,' said Vincent, 'I presume it wasn't a Walkman?'

'No.'

'You switched on your tape recorder whenever we—'

'Whenever we talked.'

'An unusual example of hot-blooded behaviour,' Vincent said with flagging irony. 'Your feelings really ran away with you, didn't they? You're all heart.'

'I told you,' I said, 'I couldn't adore you uncritically. We're in the nineteen-nineties. Women aren't required to be deaf and blind any more. What's that quotation from Byron? "Man's love is of Man's life a thing apart; 'Tis Woman's whole existence." For thousands of years that was true: we had no option. Husband, children, petty domestic power, that was the most we could ever hope for. We had to dream of a hero because we weren't allowed to dream of a heroine. Now, all that is changing. We shape our own lives, we order our own dreams. I don't want a little tin god to worship, closing my eyes to his ingrowing rust. I want—'

'Fuck me,' said Vincent. 'I was a sacrifice on the altar of sexual equality. Heil Germaine. What *do* you want?'

'Never to compromise.' The words came slowly, reluctantly, as if I were reading my own life sentence. 'To be true to myself.'

'"And it must follow, as the night the day, Thou canst not then be false to any man"?'

'Yes,' I said. 'I suppose . . . that's what I believe. I don't expect you'll understand. I betrayed you. But it would have been a deeper betrayal, to love you and lie to you.'

'Instead,' said Vincent, 'you were dazzlingly honest. Right from the start. I was so dazzled I missed the honesty.'

'So I made a mess of things,' I said, resuming a lighter tone. 'What of it? Making a mess of things is intrinsic to human nature. It's bloody difficult to be consistent. Particularly when . . .'

When your emotions are out of line.

'When?'

'It doesn't matter.'

'Once I get out of here,' Vincent said conversationally, 'I'm going to destroy you. You know that, don't you? Your career will be finished, you'll be a social and professional outcast—'

'Anything you say,' I said pacifically. 'I daresay it helps you to feel better, having something to plan.'

Vincent eyed me balefully for several minutes.

'You and Richard are history.'

'Yes.'

'So much for romance. Picking up my discards. He won't make the same mistake twice.'

'I discarded *you*,' I pointed out.

'Give me another drink.'

I complied. When I laid him back on the pillows, his free hand closed on one of mine. The grip crushed my fingers so that I winced with pain.

'Does that hurt?'

I nodded.

'Good.'

After a moment he released me. I pushed the lank hair back from his forehead although it hadn't fallen forward in the first place. 'I ought to go,' I said. 'I'll send you some flowers.'

'A spray or a wreath?'

'Oh, a wreath, I think. One shouldn't be stingy at a time like this. I was wondering . . .'

'What?'

'Would you like me to make some calls for you? Your mother, America – anyone who ought to be told?'

'Bugger it. I'd infinitely rather tell no one. However . . .'

'I'll do it,' I said.

He reeled off codes, numbers and comprehensive instructions.

'Get better,' I adjured on my way out.

'What for?' said Vincent. 'So you can make a sequel?'

In the doorway I paused, looking back at him. Once again, we left everything unsaid. Even goodbye.

I was permitted to telephone from the doctor's office after I assured him Vincent would pay for the calls. In LA, it was still the previous night. Hannibal Barker received my news with increasing agitation and, as predicted, had to be vehemently discouraged from leaping on a London-bound aeroplane within the hour. 'You're that bird, aren't you?' he said accusingly. 'That blonde he's been boring on about. You've got a bleeding posh up-the-crust voice: I haven't heard nothing like it since I quit the bleeding UK. I'll bet you're her.'

In Italy, as instructed, I asked for Sebastiano Dandolini, and spent some time explaining that Vincent was in no danger and Jolanda did not need to come. (She came anyway.) By the time I was through it was nearly eight o'clock. Did I want to see the press, the doctor enquired, because there were some of them already bivouacked outside the front entrance.

'I *am* the press,' I said indignantly.

In addition, the police were due any minute. Routine in cases of shooting. They would need a statement from me.

I couldn't face any of them.

The doctor, though still grave, allowed himself to be sympathetic. He prescribed a long day's sleep and assured me my civic duties could wait. With the connivance of a helpful porter I was smuggled out of a side door into a taxi. At a news-stand, I stopped to check the morning papers. I might as well know the worst. Several had evidently caught the story too late for inclusion, but there was still a number of headlines to choose from. 'Savage Shooting', said one, unable to resist the pun. 'Shooting in Surrey', declared another: a hint of crime among the rich and cosy. 'Savage Shot By Ex-Model'; 'Vincent Savage: Condition Critical'; 'Party Punch-Up Ends in Bullets'. Doubtless due to the confused accounts of party guests befuddled with Bollinger, most of them seemed to believe the fight had concerned Crystal too.

But there was one guest who had managed to keep a clear head. 'Exclusive!' shrieked the Daily Bombast in triumph. 'Our reporter was there! SAVAGE SHOT AT CELEBRITY PARTY. Bishop Latimer: He Expired at My Feet.' And, along the bottom of the sheet in glaring black letters: 'TV Hackette who Bonked for a Scoop: Page 2.'

I stared at the paper, temporarily incapable of speech or thought. My head swam in time with the motion of the car so that for a minute I felt actual nausea. But I wasn't sick; my stomach was too empty. I had been so caught up in events that the hovering presence of Gerry Hibbert had slipped my mind. More fool me.

When I could think again, it occurred to me that Vincent would not need to put himself out for revenge.

I was finished already.

PART VI

THE PENIS
AND THE SWORD

1

The mess that followed the party took a long, long time to clear up. I went back to Piers Percival's house to change and collect my gear; I would have to catch a train up to London. Richard had already left with the children; Crystal, who had spent the night dosed with sedatives in what should have been my room, had gone with him. 'Perhaps they'll get back together after all,' I said, over a much-needed cup of strong black coffee. 'Richard's always had a complex about damsels in distress.'

'I doubt it,' Piers opined. 'He is chivalrous but not a fool. There is also the little matter of his feelings for you.'

'Feelings can be set aside. In any case, that was – a rose that never opened, a wine that didn't travel. He must have realised by now that Vincent was speaking the truth. With Richard, that'll be the end of it. His moral fibre is not the flexible kind.'

'There is nothing wrong with having high standards,' sighed Piers, 'as long as you don't try to live up to them. But I'm not sure you are entirely right. Richard can be very forgiving.'

'He might forgive; he won't forget,' I said. 'Anyway, I don't want to be forgiven.'

'I see,' said Piers. Possibly he did.

I had declined breakfast but his manservant entered with an irresistible aroma of hot buttered toast and I ate thankfully. The previous evening I had been too busy to do more than exchange a nod with the poached salmon and my stomach was so empty it had probably begun to digest itself. Piers topped up my coffee.

'The police phoned us at an uncivilised hour,' he related.

'Crystal, not surprisingly, wished to consult a lawyer before making a statement. She and Richard were going to leave the children with Elizabeth before calling at the police station. I am to be visited here, later today. I imagine they will want to talk to you as well.'

'I expect so,' I said. 'Do you think they'll charge her?' I could not really believe that someone as naturally chilly as Crystal could find herself in so much hot water.

'Undoubtedly. The question is with what. Apparently, she took the gun from Jonas, who had removed it from the wall and was playing with it. A horrifying thought: I am afraid this house was never designed to be child-proof. Crystal says she tried to replace it but couldn't so she put it in her handbag for safe-keeping. She didn't know it was loaded. When she produced it so sensationally during the fight it was intended to have a purely visual impact. She cocked it for effect, having learned how to do so with a stage weapon on a recent drama course. She is an actress; she was acting. It strains credibility somewhat but it may very well be true. I must admit, my estimation of her thespian abilities has been considerably augmented.'

'Stanislavsky would have been proud of her,' I said.

'However,' Piers went on, 'the police have a low opinion of actresses who shoot their ex-lovers, accidentally or otherwise. They also have a low opinion of guns, even a veteran Wogden once fired by Lord Castlereagh. I am very much to blame and they will probably tell me so, at great length. I find the thought of being lectured on my responsibilities by some oafish pillar of the local constabulary extremely distasteful, particularly when he is in the right.'

'Hell,' I said. 'You can't possibly tell them you kept the damn thing loaded so you could shoot burglars with it.'

Piers shrugged. 'I may not need to. My socially conscientious godson might have already done so.'

'Nonsense,' I said. 'He doesn't like telling lies but he wouldn't deliberately land you in the – in the soup. He'll just say he didn't know anything about it. Being economical with the truth. He wouldn't baulk at that in an emergency.'

'I hope so, indeed,' said Piers. 'Nonetheless . . .'

'We could say you loaded it to show me last week,' I suggested.

'Richard wouldn't have known about it; he'd gone to the telephone. You loaded it to show me, we were distracted, you forgot to unload it again. That looks careless but not wanton. Anyhow, it's an improvement on the facts.'

'Would I have forgotten something that important?' Piers speculated.

'Senility,' I reminded him. 'You forget a lot of things these days. It's one of the penalties of old age.'

'Oh, very good.' Piers allowed himself a slight smile. 'Thank you, Micky. You are a thoughtful child. Audacious, unscrupulous, and calamitously modern, but thoughtful. If I may say so, it has been a pleasure knowing you.'

When I left he kissed me goodbye.

I caught the train home, thinking of my bed. I had nothing else left to think of. At the flat, the police rang to say they were sending someone to see me. Alun Craig called, seething with territorial ire like a rat challenged in its own sewer, to tell me I did not stand alone, we were a team, all for one and one for all, and he personally would see to it that those vermin at the Daily Bombast were forced to eat their own four-inch headlines. By the way, when was I coming back to work? I was easily able to refrain from being touched by his loyalty. I crawled back to bed and buried my head under the duvet. In the early afternoon, the first trickle of reporters had begun doorstepping the flat. The bell shrilled, the knocker thumped, the letterbox flapped. Later on, if not promptly and forcibly discouraged, they would move in with siege towers and battering-rams. And I was already low on milk.

My mother rang around four.

'It isn't true, darling; I know that. I told Charles, you've always had such strong principles. I only wish—'

'It *is* true,' I said baldly. 'Of course it's bloody true. Why not? You're always telling me I ought to have more affairs.'

For several seconds my mother said nothing at all. Then: 'Is that your doorbell I can hear?'

'No,' I said. 'I mean yes, but I'm not answering. It's only the gutter press clamouring for my entrails. There's nothing the tabloids like better than discrediting their rivals in television. They can't wait to tear me apart.'

'You must come down here,' my mother said with decision.

'Don't argue, darling. You must come *immediately*. I'll send – I'll
send Charles to fetch you. You'll be safer here. We can borrow
the Kendalls' Rottweiler – well, actually, it's not a Rottweiler, it's
a boxer, and really terribly friendly, but I'm sure it'll be just as
good as a Rottweiler. Boxers always look so manly and butch,
and anyway, I don't suppose those hack journalists know anything about dogs. I can answer the door and if they try to get in
Pompey will growl and Barraclough can brandish that rake from
the garden that nobody uses any more. I know it hasn't been
thrown out; I saw it in the shed only six months ago.'

'Mummy,' I said faintly, 'whatever you do, *don't* send Charles.
The last thing I need is a vicar.'

'All right, darling, if you say so – but you *will* come?'

'I can't leave London yet,' I said. 'I have to talk to the police.'

'Can they help?'

'About the shooting.'

My mother achieved a moan. 'I never wanted you to be
a journalist,' she remarked. 'I always knew it would lead to
trouble.'

'I was born to trouble,' I said, 'as the sparks fly upward.'

'That particular saying,' my mother stated, 'applies to men.'

'I *am* a man,' I retorted. 'That's what we mean by women's liberation.'

The police arrived shortly afterwards and I made my statement, hoping I was contradicting Richard and taking care not to
cause problems for Piers. Asked for my view of what had happened, I said mendaciously that I was convinced it had been
sheer accident. Crystal, I implied, was temperamental, 'actressy',
inclined to melodramatics. Plausible if inaccurate. I had no desire
to incriminate her, whatever my private opinion of her actions.
The catastrophe was, after all, partly my fault, the spin-off from
my exercise in televisual pseudo-justice. Putting Crystal in the
dock would amend nothing.

Whether Vincent would see it that way was another matter.

The next few days slipped by in a haze, like a sequence of uncon-
nected events in some bizarre dream. An unholy alliance between
Alun Craig and the ex-SCUM supporter in the legal department
forced the Daily Bombast to recant: the only evidence they had

for my sexual antics was Gerry Hibbert's unsupported word, since all the other witnesses to the showdown were found to be too discreet, too confused, or too untruthful to back him up. He subsequently wrote me a note explaining that it was all in the day's work and he bore me no malice; I wrote back to say that was sweet of him. Several job possibilities melted quietly away but I still refused to rejoin *Quest*. On the television, the cameras caught Jolanda as she hastened to her son's sickbed. Flattered by a degree of attention which she had not received in years, she paused to talk to reporters, a spectacular shipwreck of a woman with huge eyes and lop-sided lipstick on a blinding smile, sporting an erratic assortment of jewellery and an enormous hat resembling the one worn by Sophia Loren when she cast herself into the Thames in *The Millionairess*. From its battered condition, it might even have been the original. 'My son needs me,' she told the microphones, grasping the nearest reporter by the arm. 'Always I come, when Vincente needs me. He is the best son in the world – he give me a beautiful house, diamonds, champagne, anything I want. These things they say about him on television, they are not true – it is the English who do not understand him, they are so cold, so *insensibili*, they do not comprehend *il fuoco nell' anima nostra*. He want to be millionaire only so he can take care of his mamma. In England, you have the stiff upper lip, you play the cricket, you do not love your mothers. First you insult Vincente, then you shoot him. It is wicked – like Mafia, like Cosa Nostra – and you, you pretend to be so respectable, so stuffy, so well bred. English *ipocriti*! I call your famous Scotland Yard, then they will arrest these television producers and *giornalisti* who try to *assassinare* my Vincente! You are a nice boy,' she turned to the owner of the arm with bewildering warmth, 'you do not know how many evil men there are in the world. You are Irish, no? You cannot be English, you are too *simpatico*, your eyes are too blue. The Irish are like the Italians, passionate, *impetuosi* . . .'

In the background, I noticed a man of fifty-odd with thinning hair and a petulant mouth too youthful for his other features. Sebastiano, I learned later, the resident toyboy. Somehow, from the way Vincent talked, I had expected him to be thirty-five at most, a handsome parasite, not this tired, middle-aged, anxious-looking creature. Vincent, it was clear, saw him through the eyes of filial jealousy, a Peter Pan who did not change with the years. Typical, I thought, with the fag end of a smile.

When the news was over I rang the florist and ordered Vincent a wreath. Red roses and a black-edged card labelled 'In Memoriam'. I hoped he would appreciate it.

On Wednesday I went down to Grey Gables.

My mother had marshalled Charles the vicar, Pompey the boxer, the decrepit Barraclough, and several of her elderly admirers to act as my protectors. The rake, a vicious weapon whose rust-stained prongs must have been crawling with tetanus bacteria, had been unearthed from the murky depths of the garden shed. I was obliged, regretfully, to spoil their fun, explaining that since we had squashed the sex angle the ardour of the tabloids had started to cool: they might phone but they would not invade. My mother's team of stalwarts departed with fallen crest and frustrated visage. Pompey belied his macho reputation by licking my hand without an introduction and I rumpled his ears and cried into a cup of tea, more or less simultaneously. They were all so idiotically kind, so unquestioningly partisan, so heart-breakingly gallant, so hopelessly incompetent. My mother succumbed to an outbreak of tact and held her curiosity in check. 'Michelle, darling,' she said, stroking my arm; and that was all.

That evening, they announced on the news that Crystal had been charged with grievous bodily harm. Whatever Vincent had or had not said, the police were clearly not satisfied.

It was nearly a year before the case came to court.

In the process of dissipating my savings I went to New York to see Phyl, told her everything, and cried all over again, this time into a cocktail. Farzad walked in to tell me I had come by my just desserts: I was a nice girl who should have got married long ago instead of crusading around minding other people's business. Happily for tranquillity in the home, he flew to Riyadh the following morning, where he was supporting the Allied war effort in some unspecified fashion. Whatever happened to Iraq – or the Allies – I was certain that at the end of it Farzad would emerge substantially richer. 'He's a dear, dear man,' said Phyl, 'but he doesn't understand you. I'm beginning to be afraid he doesn't understand me either.' Warning bells sounded. When Phyl calls her husbands 'dear' and bewails their lack of understanding, they are heading for the 'Out' tray. Farzad might yet have a genuine cause for complaint against me.

In his absence Win took us to Elaine's, where we sat at a favoured table and nodded carelessly to the stars. At least, Win nodded. Phyl said: 'Woody, darling – Warren, darling' with mechanical enthusiasm, and I toyed with my food, drained my wine, and insisted I was enjoying myself.

'No you're not,' said Phyl. 'You're frightfully unhappy. I haven't seen you so unhappy since you left Patrick.'

'I'm not unhappy,' I said. 'I'm just miserable.'

'Why did you make the programme if you'd fallen for him?' Phyl demanded. 'Couldn't you have shredded it or chucked it in the bin?'

'I didn't know I'd fallen for him. Even if I had, it wouldn't have made any difference. Two people can't build a relationship on mutual self-deceit. Yes, I know *you* can, you always do, but I can't. I needed – I needed to defeat him more than to love him. I loathe much of what he is and most of what he does – I can't turn my back on two-thirds of his personality for the sake of a well-developed penis and some entertaining repartee. I suppose I thought, if I could effectively ruin him, it would somehow clear his debts – to Richard, to his chance victims – balance the books, square the circle, enable him to start afresh with a slightly cleaner sheet. That's ridiculous, isn't it?'

'Yes,' said Win. 'He'll still blot the ink no matter how clean the sheet. He isn't likely to reform.'

'I know. My brain wasn't functioning properly. I wouldn't let myself love him, so . . . I gave what I could. Not a gift he'll appreciate but whatever he feels for me – grudging respect, undying hate, anger, contempt – it'll be part of him forever. He's no good at love; he'll be more at ease with the negative emotions. He should be grateful to me: I haven't required of him anything he would find it hard to sustain.'

'Do you regret what you did?' asked Win.

'No,' I said. 'I don't regret any of it. I just wish it didn't hurt so much.'

Back in the UK I took a job with a news agency who promptly

sent me abroad. Not Baghdad, Brussels. While my fellow journalists were dolled up in gas-masks and camouflage jackets, dodging a Scud missile or waving to a passing cruise, I was in the front line of Eurocracy, watching French farmers demonstrating on behalf of unpasteurised cheese. They had brought with them what looked like a gigantic camembert, knitted entirely by their faithful wives and stuffed to the brim with old socks, presumably to furnish the correct bouquet. Riot police turned pale at their approach and I found myself thinking the gas-masks might have been of more use here in Belgium. However, the Foreign Legion it was not. Only the *Sun* equated Jacques Delors with Saddam Hussein. Scandals were wrapped in the EEC flag and beribboned with red tape, and although the unwrapping process was both valuable and interesting I could not help feeling a long way from the action. Besides, my chances of dying heroically in Brussels thus causing Vincent a fleeting pang, were virtually zero. I knew it was idiotic but now and then, well down the second bottle, I decided, like Richard in Barbados, that dying heroically was an attractive option.

Saddam Hussein came to a temporary halt in the Mother of All Battles but the Eurocrats marched on. It was late summer when I returned to England, on special leave for the court case. On the plane, I pictured a worst-nightmare scenario where my mother, Jolanda Scarpia, Elizabeth Savage and the unknown Mona Winter all came together in a pre-trial clash – the Battle of All Mothers – but fortunately, this did not materialise. I had sublet the flat while I was away, and although the tenant had moved out it looked bare and unhomelike, with clothes, tapes, files and PC boxed away at Grey Gables. I rushed out and purchased Vinho Verde and Pouilly Fuissé to liven up the living room and did what I could with a scattering of books on chair and table, a dismembered *Independent*, a mug of cold coffee, and dripping underwear in the kitchen and bathroom. Then I telephoned everyone I could think of.

'Your successor hates you,' Jeff Salter informed me. 'Alun's turned you into a kind of icon, a shining example of the journalist who will do *anything* for a story. She simply can't compete. He's always telling her she'll never be as good as Micky Murphy.'

'Shit,' I said, with feeling.

'Come and have a drink,' he suggested. 'Tease him a little. He won't like you half so much in the flesh, but he still wants you back. He never really understood why you ditched him.'

'They never do,' I said.

Annabel Purdey filled me in on Crystal.

'She's in danger of becoming a heroine of the feminist lobby. Like whatshername who cut all the sleeves out of her husband's suits after he was unfaithful to her. It's called Fighting Back. Capital letters. It's all the rage right now.' Annabel always knew what was all the rage. 'I gather she says she thought the gun was unloaded, but no one bothers about that. They could get a mistrial before they've even started. The case may be sub judice but the papers are warming up already – background stories, Crystal's career rehashed, Vincent's career retrashed, that sort of thing. She even knocked Princess Caroline off the cover of *Hello!* Whether she's found guilty or not, this could make her a star. For a month or two. She's already got a bigger and better agent.'

'And all by half killing her ex-lover,' I reflected. 'The ex factor. Isn't that what you said she needed?'

'What about you?' said Annabel. 'Are you going to stay out of the spotlight this time?'

'Definitely,' I said.

Nobody thought to ask if I was nervous, not even my mother. Vincent had never seriously alarmed me except when driving a car in a hurricane but I feared, on this occasion, that the sight of him, across a crowded courtroom, would reduce me to a state of teenage hypertension, nerves taut, knees weak, pulse turbocharged, all the symptoms I should have left behind long ago. When the day arrived I made up with exceptional care despite selecting a casual garb – jeans, flying jacket, RAF cap. I had forgotten that my uniform was sufficiently well known, especially in the trade. Flashbulbs winked as I went in and voices hailed me by name, whether they knew me or not. The court was packed, inside and out. I waited with other witnesses, including Piers Percival, who kissed my hand, and Richard, who squeezed it. Everyone refrained from alluding to anything remotely embarrassing, which resulted in several long, uncomfortable silences. Vincent wasn't there.

British justice got underway in its usual ponderous fashion, taking a whole morning to progress beyond first base. I had been a participant in too many courtroom dramas to find it other than routine. Crystal had wisely chosen this moment to exhibit some theatrical talent: her hair was scooped into a demure knot high on her head, her black suit was a masterpiece of couture understatement, her complexion was shaded to a hitherto unattainable pallor and her pout was left *au naturel*. She wore fragility like a perfume and the judge, who was venerable even by the standards of the Bench, softened from avuncular to paternal the more he addressed her. In contrast the prosecuting counsel, no matter how reasoned his arguments, could not avoid sounding like Basil Rathbone in one of his more villainous roles. Outside, demonstrators from the Shere Hite Supporters' Club, the Campaign for Every Conceivable Kind of Equality, and, inexplicably, Women Against Rape, prepared to cheer her every entrance and exit. Inside, the likes of Lynda Lee Potter and Anne Robinson scribbled their columns from the press area. I had given my evidence early on the second day, skirting the truth whenever necessary, trusting that God, if He still felt any commitment to the judiciary, would allow me a little leeway on the oath.

Afterwards, in the lunch-time recess, Richard suggested a snack. Unlike the preceding September the weather was far from warm and in the end we settled for pasta, spaghetti carbonara in an American-style Italian restaurant: plenty of spaghetti, not much carbon. We swapped news, updating our respective lifestories, my anecdotes of Brussels for Richard's new job, new flat, new girlfriend. Obviously he was not back with Crystal after all.

'I hope you've checked the terrain carefully,' I said. 'You don't want to stumble across any more unpleasant surprises.'

'It's strictly casual,' Richard responded, adding with a wry grin: 'I'm still checking.'

'Good luck.'

'Thanks. Penny asked after you, by the way. She wants to be a journalist.'

'Discourage her,' I said. 'I have it on my mother's authority that that sort of thing always leads to trouble.'

'Actually,' said Richard, 'she's rather keen. And the school say she's quite good at English . . .'

'That disqualifies her for a start.'

Richard laughed and reverted to his plate, mopping up the last of the carbonara with an apologetic fragment of yesterday's bread. Over coffee, I asked him: 'So what about the case? How do you rate Crystal's chances?'

'Not sure. Her lawyers seem fairly optimistic – but then, you don't pay a lawyer to tell you you're losing. Even if she was found guilty, they seem to think it would only be a suspended sentence. First offence and all that. A good deal depends on Vincent. If he's vindictive the jury will be sorry for her. If he's magnanimous . . .'

'The thought of Vincent being magnanimous,' I said, 'leaves me speechless. The stars would halt in their courses.'

Richard studied me for a couple of minutes without comment, lifted eyebrows crinkling his forehead into his hair.

'Do you think she knew?' I said abruptly, 'I mean, about the gun. Didn't she guess it was loaded?'

'Oh, she knew.' Richard exhaled on a sigh. 'Jo told me. He's pretty well genned up on guns, reads all the wrong comics. He pointed it out to her when she took the pistol away from him. That's why she wouldn't leave it around: she was frightened he'd get hold of it again. She brought it downstairs meaning to give it to Piers. It was just bad luck that she walked in on our lit-tle . . . dispute. Vincent was foul to her – you heard. His reaction was inexcusable. Any opportunity to twist the knife. He doesn't believe in making allowances for weakness of character. She lost her head for a fraction of a second – and that was all it took. She'd fired before she realised what she was doing. The play-acting became a hideous reality. You should have seen her afterwards: she was rigid with shock, following me round like a zombie; she couldn't sleep, couldn't eat, couldn't even piss with-out a prompt. If the psychoanalysts had seen her then . . . Anyhow, we thought it best not to make too many demands on the imagination of the police. She'd pleaded ignorance on a reflex: it seemed sensible to stick by her plea. Besides, I gather the judicial system is notoriously prejudiced against female offenders.'

'That,' I admitted, 'is unfortunately true.'

'The paradox,' Richard went on, 'is that the press think she's wonderful, *because* she shot him. If she'd waved an empty gun they wouldn't have blinked a Nikon. She hates all the furore—'

'Of course she does.'

'—but there's no denying it could help her on this acting lark. I didn't think she was in earnest about it but she's got this new agent – an improvement on the appalling Brendan – and he's found her a part in a TV whodunnit. The murderess, probably. Apparently he says she used to be labelled as a pretty bimbo whom no one would take seriously but this business has given her intellectual credibility. What do you know. She's thrilled to bits. Crys is still a child at heart: dressing up and playing Let's Pretend is what she really enjoys. Model or actress: it's all the same. As it is, everything's going fine for her.'

'Provided she isn't sent to prison,' I concluded. 'That would cause a slight glitch in her golden progress, wouldn't it?'

'Micky, you won't . . .?'

'You know I won't. Who am I to rain on her parade? Vincent is the one to watch. He's not exactly felicitous in his choice of lady-loves, is he? One dissects him on the small screen while the other blows a hole through his lung. Something tells me magnanimity will not be on the menu. But he's no fool: he must know the jury won't go for spite. Particularly after several days' exposure to Crystal's artless anguish.'

'Cut the sneer,' said Richard. 'She's desperately upset.'

So am I, I thought; but I didn't mention it.

Vincent came on the third day. I half expected the court to boo and hiss but he was received in a silence fraught with anticipation, taking his place in the witness box while pencils were poised over notepads and the artist for Channel Four News sketched industriously. He looked well for someone whose right lung was supposed to be held together with bootlace: brisk stride, after-summer tan, the dark vitality to which Piers had once referred emanating from him in controlled vibes. Only the flickering hint of a frown between his brows betrayed tension. His manner achieved a balance between supercilious nonchalance and a species of weary resignation to duty. I was not entirely convinced by it, but I knew my judgement was impaired. At the sight of him a frisson had travelled over my skin, like an almost imperceptible breeze stroking all my fur the wrong way. Normal service, I thought irritably, will be resumed presently. I noted that although Vincent looked at the judge, the jury, the learned counsels and, occasionally, with scant interest, at the accused, he never so much as glanced towards the benches where I sat with other familiar faces in the forefront of an avid public. Yet he must know I was there. He repeated the oath automatically, answered all questions with a brevity that verged on curtness. His posture revealed neither magnanimity nor malice, but only the flagrant *ennui* of a businessman who has been forced to fly three thousand miles out of his way to fulfil his responsibilities as a citizen. The defence case, based mainly on cross-examining witnesses who had testified unenthusiastically for the prosecution, was given an impromptu boost when he divulged that to the best of his knowledge the gun was not kept loaded, he had said as much to Crystal, and nobody had been more disconcerted than he was when a bullet hit him in the back.

'Disconcerted?' echoed the judge, peering at him over gold-rimmed bifocals. 'Isn't that rather a mild word?'

'At the time,' said Vincent, 'I used several stronger ones. But I didn't think you would wish me to repeat them in a court of law.'

'So you were able to speak,' interrupted the defence opportunely. 'In short, the nature of your injury was not such as to render you either unconscious or incapable of articulation?'

'Evidently not,' said Vincent.

'Did you form the impression that when she fired Miss Winter was aiming for any particular portion of your anatomy?'

'I had my back to her,' Vincent reminded him.

'But you saw her point the gun before you turned away?'

'Yes, I did.'

'Did you think that she was aiming, for example, for your heart?'

'I didn't think she was aiming at all,' Vincent said frankly. 'It would have been just like her to get hold of an empty pistol and wave it about in an ineffectual attempt to demonstrate emotional depth. She'd never have had the nerve to fire a loaded gun.'

He believes it, I thought. His boredom might be only skin-deep but his contempt came from the soul. He was plainly unconcerned with vengeance of any kind, legal or personal, wanting only to dispose of the entire situation with the minimum of hassle. It is hardly dignified to be shot in the back by your ex-girlfriend, even if she is lovely enough to cause horological disruption. It struck me that his principal sensation was probably one of embarrassment, something to which he was not at all accustomed. To have a hole in his lung was bad enough, but the dent in his ego must be far more painful.

At the end of the afternoon he left the court, without speaking to me and apparently without seeing me. So much for a tribute greater than love. My ego also seemed to be in need of restoration.

The next day he was back, sitting well to the rear in sunglasses so dark I was reminded of the ones worn by Zaphod Beeblebrox in *Hitch-hiker,* which turned black at the merest glimmering of danger. Vincent's glasses might possibly have possessed the same faculty. The defence produced a bevy of experts to contradict those flaunted by the prosecution, who held forth on matters medical, psychological and antiquarian at wearisome length. I had missed the first batch since their evidence had preceded mine but I could work up little interest in nineteenth-century ballistics or the details of Vincent's acute pneumothorax. Apparently lungs collapse as easily as balloons, and it is perfectly natural for a neurotic female to squeeze the trigger of an empty pistol in the process of exorcising her traumas. Afterwards, determined to bring on the big battalions, counsel summoned the bishop, whom he endowed with profound spiritual insight – the prosecutor did not dare to object – and whose largely meaningless testimony concluded that human nature was fallible, Crystal had been over-wrought, no one had meant anyone any harm. He added, to my amazement, that in his view a tragedy had been averted only by the common sense and quick reactions of the young lady in black. He was sorry: he couldn't remember her name.

'You mean,' said the judge, consulting his notes, 'Miss Michelle Murphy. Is Miss Murphy still in the court?'

'Yes,' I said, feeling suddenly ridiculously shy.

A roomful of people turned to stare at me, never a comfortable experience. I pictured Vincent's glasses turning white with horror, purple with fury, green with malevolence. If I was proved to have saved his life, on top of everything else, it would be the last straw. The camel would never relent.

'The bishop is quite right,' said the judge, weightily. 'I feel I must take this opportunity to commend your behaviour. While the swift response of the emergency services was of course the decisive factor in preventing Mr Savage's death, your actions made a significant contribution. I gather you managed to – er – block the increase of air in the pleural cavity, wherever that may be. Highly commendable. You must have been on one of those do-it-yourself first-aid courses. Myself, I believe they should be obligatory in all our schools.'

Schools? How old did he think I was?

'N-no,' I stammered. 'I just acted on instinct.'

'Instinct. Dear me.' He surveyed me with blatant disapproval. 'We spend years training our doctors and nurses, we provide invaluable first-aid courses, but you save a man's life on *instinct*. Well, well. Where were we?'

Where we were, fortunately, was more or less at the end of the trial. Prosecution and defence made their final perorations, and we were told to come back tomorrow for the judge's summing-up, when the jury would be packed off to consider their verdict. I slipped out, dodging reporters who abandoned the chase only when Crystal appeared. At a distance I saw Vincent diving into a chauffeur-driven car whose windows matched his sunglasses: they had turned black already. At home, I brooded on possible headlines. 'Hack Heroine Saves Man She Ruined'; 'Savage Saved by *Quest* Hackette'; 'I Acted on Instinct to Save the Man I Loathe, Says Murphy'. Gerry Hibbert and his pals would not be deterred by the fact that I had said nothing of the sort.

Absent-mindedly, I opened the Vinho Verde and poured myself a glass. I had picked up my post in passing and I rifled through it with mechanical attention, discarding the rubbish – a holiday brochure for winter breaks, an underwear catalogue, a bill from Visa. I read the remaining letter, put down my glass, read it again, effectively diverted from other problems. It was a job offer. Robert Brink, presenter of the celebrated *Brink Report*, required a new assistant, his old one having left to spend more time with the family. (Sinister.) Brink was rumoured to be quite as tough and probably as unscrupulous as Alun Craig, but the worst allegations were usually discounted in the teeth of his smile. Unlike Alun he employed the personality cult, promoting not only his victims but himself, brandishing charm like a lethal weapon. He had a generous waistline, a voice which rumbled fruitily from the depths of his beard, and small eyes twinkling like those of a robber in a bank vault. After Alun, working for him would merely be an alternative circle of hell. I was seriously tempted.

Back in court the following morning the judge summed up, recapitulating the evidence on both sides with such painstaking thoroughness that nearly everyone nodded off. I came in for moderate praise; Piers, portentous criticism. Crystal, encouraged by the benevolence of the Bench, had tempered her dress to half mourning, pale grey co-ordinates with a single tress of hair escaping from her top-knot and hanging down her back like a black silk tassel. She stood in the dock looking like an aristo in a tumbril: the jury, when they woke up, could hardly fail to be moved by her. When the judge had finished they were discreetly revived and shuffled off to the jury room. In the interim, I avoided Vincent or Vincent avoided me: I was not sure which. His glasses seemed to have grown even darker since the previous day. Richard supported Crystal; Piers, disclaiming any further interest in the case, went home. Reporters composed a headline for every eventuality; columnists, a moral stance. In due course, the court reconvened, the jury returned. Not guilty. A majority verdict. Outside, women's lib activists cheered, although the outcome made nonsense of Crystal's role as a feminist heroine. A thorn-hedge of microphones greeted our egress. As I extricated myself from the crowd and looked in vain for a taxi Vincent's rent-a-Rolls zoomed past me, all but paring my toenails.

He did not stop.

2

Back at my flat, the view had changed. There was no friendly barricade of files to keep the world at a distance: the walls were down, the safe place was safe no longer, my solitary cell was filled with an invasion of emptiness from outside. The Doubts had no need to gatecrash; they had already moved in, becoming absorbed into the shifting pattern of my life. The process of growing up, which lasts from birth until death, is really a gradual acceptance of such uncertainties, a long, slow reconciliation to the utter inexplicability of everything. Maturity is simply the ability to be true to yourself, or to what you know of yourself, in an insecure world. I knew I was growing up because I felt younger, more naked, more defenceless, stronger, braver, and less sure than I had done a year and a half earlier. I sat on the edge of the sofa, one shoe on, one shoe off, remembering the day when Shirley Prosser had cursed me in Sainsbury's. That was when it had all begun. Then, I was self-contained, self-assured, self-reliant: all self. An agent of Pallas, clear-eyed and unflinching, cosily insulated from human turmoil. Now – ah, now I had been swept out of my Self by the winds of earth; I was a fallen angel, reckless and corruptible, as human as Eve. I might fear other things but the lonely depths of the spirit which I had once feared above all had become familiar territory. I could survive love, and hurt, and hopelessness; I could even laugh at them. (I laughed aloud, to prove it.) No one lives happily ever after. You can only dust off your courage, and go on.

The doorbell caught me like that, poised on the sofa's edge one shoe off, one shoe on. I kicked off the shoe that was on and padded to the entryphone preparing my usual response to the importunate press. No comment, no story, I wasn't there, I didn't do it, I know nothing about anything. The voice on the intercom took me off guard. 'It's me.' Vincent.

My heart, that reliable organ which rarely quailed or quickened any more, leaped into my mouth for an unnerving moment and then subsided back into its normal position, battering away at my ribcage.

I said: 'If you're going to strangle me you can't come in.'

'I was contemplating something much more violent than strangulation,' Vincent responded.

If there was a lurking innuendo I ignored it. He rang again while I hesitated, waiting for my pulse to decelerate before going to the door. It didn't.

I let him in anyway.

'Have some Vinho Verde,' I suggested. 'I opened it yesterday, to let it breathe.'

Vincent accepted it without a murmur: his mind was obviously on other things.

'You saved my life,' he said accusingly.

'I'm awfully sorry,' I apologised. 'Anyway, I didn't really. I only made a "significant contribution". Unquote.'

'All judges are superannuated morons,' Vincent remarked abstractedly. 'That morning at the hospital, you might have told me.'

'I didn't *realise* . . .'

'You get a kick out of it, don't you? So sweet and confiding on the surface but underneath you're always hiding some horrifying secret. If World War Three broke out you'd forget to mention it, just so you could enjoy my dumbfounded expression when the first bomb fell on my head.'

'We're getting back to Armageddon,' I said. 'Why is it we converse almost exclusively in military metaphors?'

'Life's a scrum,' said Vincent. 'Time I was back on top.'

Here, the allusion was unmistakable: I could not ignore it.

'You only arrived a minute ago,' I said. 'Whatever happened to the gentle art of conversation?'

'We can leave that till later,' said Vincent. 'After all, we generally did.'

'It's been nearly a year since I've seen you.'

'Too long.'

'Yes,' I conceded. 'Too long.'

A dispassionate adjudication. I took his wineglass to deposit on the table but he was kissing me even before I set it down. Wine splashed on the carpet; the glass rolled away. Away and away. Everything was rolling, time and memory, emotion and sensation, rolling over me like a wave, rolling me on to the sofa, on to the cushions, on to the floor. Love and hate, day and dark, sun and moon, all rolling round and round in the universe, the room rolling – walls and pictures and books and bookshelves – toppling over and over in a futile attempt to keep pace with the force of gravity, the force of passion, which was spinning the room and the earth and the stars on a single pivotal moment. A Catherine wheel, a merry-go-round, a carousel named desire. What did Tennessee Williams know of the mystical link between body and soul, lust and love? All he knew was how to write in a Southern accent. I knew nothing but I felt everything, and the feeling carried me away, away and away, baptised with Vinho Verde, rolling and rolling like a glass on the carpet, like a planet in space. We did it all again, powerplay and foreplay, the shove-and-thrust of intercourse, the urgency of immediate need, the slow build-up to a soaring pleasure. Vincent's penis appeared as a Pillar of Hercules, sustaining heaven: I worshipped it with kisses. He went under me and sucked on my clitoris until the crumpled petal of flesh swelled into a bud and blossomed into ecstasy. I knew that this hour was only a heartbeat in eternity, an instant that would fade and shrink with time, dwindling down the aeons into a microdot of fire; but nonetheless it felt triumphant, imperishable, a supreme act of life. Afterwards we lay on the floor among the fallen cushions and a book or two which had been precipitated in our wake, drank the wine because it was there, talked, touched, turned to light words to cover dark thoughts.

'How's business?' I enquired politely. 'Crooked?'

'I'm coming home,' Vincent said. 'For good. Or as good as it looks. Oh, I'll keep my base in LA, but I want to be back in England. I've bought a house in Chelsea.'

'Why?'

'Why Chelsea?' Vincent was not paying attention.

'Why England?'

'I don't know. The call of the tame. Roots. I'm fed up with sun, sea and beautiful women. I want grey streets, grey faces, rain on Sunday. Perhaps I'm getting old.'

'You've picked your moment,' I observed. 'Society is going grey indeed. John Major totters in the goose-steps of Margaret Thatcher. You could well get rain any day of the week. What's the real reason? If you're thinking of breaking more new ground, there's a recession on. Or hadn't you heard?'

'I know,' said Vincent. 'It's a good time to buy. When prices are low I can almost afford integrity. The market is doing my dirty work for me.' He sat up, refilled his glass, evaded my eye. 'I don't suppose you'd marry me?'

'Imbecile,' I said. 'We'd be in the divorce court in six weeks.'

'Six days, I should think. But at least we'd have given it a try. Someone or other told me recently marriage is a mistake everyone should make at least once.'

'I've been there,' I pointed out. 'Been there, seen it, done it, bought the T-shirt. Are you serious?'

'Yes,' he said. 'No. No and yes. As you say, it wouldn't work. We'd probably murder each other before we ever got around to divorce. Still, I'm afraid I must be in love with you. I think about you when you're not there. I've just spent a year thinking about you: very tedious. Being inside you gives me the most complete physical satisfaction I have ever experienced. Micky . . .'

'Mmm?'

'Are you going back to Brussels?'

'How did you know I was there? You've put those bloody PIs on to me, haven't you?' I was indignant.

'I called here once when I was over,' Vincent explained. 'The guy renting this place filled me in.'

'Nice of him.'

'So *are* you going back?'

'No,' I said. 'As it happens, I've just taken a new job.' My decision was made, then and there, for all the wrong reasons. 'Assistant producer on *The Brink Report*. You may have heard of it. If not, I suggest you check it out in advance. Get Quidnunc to watch it for you. You ought to find out what you're up against. When you move back here, I'll be waiting. If you're a reformed character we'll have dinner. If you're not, we'll still have dinner, but you'd better be careful what you say. Tape recorders are getting smaller all the time.'

'What about the hurricane?' Vincent queried. 'They're in short supply over here.'

I grinned. 'I'll pack my own.'

We dressed in a leisurely fashion, rearranged a couple of cushions, polished off the Vinho and started on the *vin*. I overcooked a double omelette, causing Vincent to withdraw his proposal of marriage.

'You can't withdraw it,' I argued. 'I've already turned you down.'

'By the way,' he said, 'talking of tapes—'

'Were we?'

'No, but we are now. You pinched a couple of Irving's; I can't think why. I should have thought *Quest* would be above that sort of thing – except, of course, for the antics of its employees. Anyhow, could I have them back? Irving's cardiac condition has been deteriorating ever since.'

'Sorry,' I said. 'I used them. I was running out of spare cassettes. Were they important? They were just tucked away at the back of a cupboard, gathering as much dust as the air-conditioning would permit.'

'You *used* them?' Vincent repeated. 'Spare cassettes? *Bloody* hell.'

He went on to detail Irving's concept of a romantic memento. I was still laughing when he got up to go.

'I'll be back in three or four weeks,' he said. 'Don't get your hopes up. I shan't reform.'

'I never thought you would.'

'We may get together. Just for dinner.'

'We may.'

He went without a kiss, leaving my flat no longer empty. Kisses are for hello and goodbye, and we had never said either. I had been all self, all me, and now I was half of two, not a couple but a duel, a duet, an ongoing débâcle. Armageddon, I thought, is continuous and forever, not simply between us all but within us all, a knife-edge struggle of good and evil, truth and lies, neither won nor lost, where, if we try hard, if we never slacken, never weaken, a precarious equilibrium is maintained. I had no false hope but also no unnecessary fear. In conflict, Vincent and I achieved a kind of balance. So be it. The scales might tilt one way or the other, but that was a risk I must take. Nothing worth having is without risk.

There is happiness but no ending. Do not look too far ahead. Death is in the fall of a leaf and rebirth in every spring, and none of it is comprehensible. We may be going somewhere or nowhere: we cannot know for sure and the greatest philosophers can but guess. Only one thing is certain, we were given life to make the most of it. Hold on to the moment. The moment is all.

Little, Brown now offers an exciting range of quality titles by both established and new authors. All of the books in this series are available by faxing, or posting your order to:

Little, Brown and Company (UK) Limited,
Mail order,
P.O. Box 11,
Falmouth,
Cornwall,
TR1O 9EN
Fax: 0326-376423

Payments can be made as follows: Cheque, postal order (payable to Little, Brown Cash Sales) or by credit cards, Visa/Access/Mastercard. Do not send cash or currency. U.K. customers and B.F.P.O.; Allow £1.00 for postage and packing for the first book, plus 50p for the second book, plus 30p for each additional book up to a maximum charge of £3.00 (7 books plus). U.K. orders over £75 free postage and packing.

Overseas customers including Ireland, please allow £2.00 for postage and packing for the first book, plus £1.00 for the second book, plus 50p for each additional book.

NAME (Block Letters) ....

ADDRESS ....

....

....

☐ I enclose my remittance for ....

☐ I wish to pay by Visa/Access/Mastercard

Number ☐☐☐☐☐☐☐☐☐☐☐☐☐☐☐

Card Expiry Date ☐☐☐☐